JOHN STACK

Armada

HARPER

Harper
An imprint of HarperCollins*Publishers*
77–85 Fulham Palace Road,
Hammersmith, London W6 8JB

www.harpercollins.co.uk

This paperback edition 2012
1

First published in Great Britain by
HarperCollins*Publishers* 2012

A catalogue record for this book is
available from the British Library

ISBN: 978-0-00-738989-6

This novel is entirely a work of fiction.
The incidents and some of the characters portrayed in it,
while based on real historical events and figures,
are the work of the author's imagination.

Set in Minion by Palimpsest Book Production Limited,
Falkirk, Stirlingshire

Printed and bound in Great Britain by
Clays Ltd, St Ives plc

MIX
Paper from responsible sources
FSC™ C007454

FSC™ is a non-profit international organisation established to promote
the responsible management of the world's forests. Products carrying the
FSC label are independently certified to assure consumers that they come
from forests that are managed to meet the social, economic and
ecological needs of present and future generations,
and other controlled sources.

Find out more about HarperCollins and the environment at
www.harpercollins.co.uk/green

For Richard John Moran

&

Frances Moran nee Varian

PROLOGUE

18th February 1587. Fotheringhay, England.

Dawn arrived slowly, the dull winter sunlight moving stealthily through the single window into the candle lit chamber, its soulless grey rays drawing all colour from the room. The lady knelt in prayer seemed almost like a statue, her pale skin and white veil stark against a black satin dress. The castle was finally quiet after hours of constant noise and the servants kneeling behind their sovereign listened intently to her murmured words of prayer, catching only snippets of the words spoken in a mix of languages.

Footsteps echoed from the hallway and the servants' eyes darted towards the door. The lady remained motionless, a brief pause in her incantations the only outward sign that she was aware of the outside world. The knock reverberated through the still air.

'It is time,' a voice shouted through the door. 'The lords are waiting.'

'Let them wait,' the lady replied, turning her head slightly, 'I have not yet finished my prayers.'

Her tone was one of command, steadfast and firm, and the voice outside did not protest. The servants looked once more to their charge, drawing courage from her composure. They bowed their heads as she continued her prayers, stifling their tears in a bid to preserve the solemnity of these final moments.

Mary Stuart, Queen of Scots, rose and turned to her faithful retainers. They had been with her for many years, some throughout her nineteen years of captivity. She spoke to each in turn, handing them tokens of her affection, keepsakes and purses that contained all that was left of her meagre wealth, before motioning to her personal groom. It was time.

The groom took down the crucifix from the altar and, holding it aloft before him, escorted his Queen from the room and along the corridor towards the great hall of the castle. The servants followed. As they neared the entrance the Queen turned to them one last time to bid them farewell. Her emissary fell to his knees and wept but she drew him up and embraced him.

'Tell my friends I died a true woman to my religion,' she said and again her retinue took strength from her, her lady-in-waiting adjusting the folds of the Queen's dress one last time on the threshold of the great hall.

The vast room was in silence, save for the spark and crack of a fire in the huge hearth, but the eyes of three hundred spectators were turned to the Queen as she made her entrance. Steps led up to the black-velvet-draped scaffold in the centre. They watched her in awe, her grace and calm preserving the significance of the moment. A slight smile played across her face as she fingered the small crucifix and prayer book in her hands.

She moved to the low stool before the block, her eyes darting to the felling axe lying on the floor. Her expression never changed and she listened in silence as the commission for her execution was read aloud. A Protestant dean stepped forward to pray for her and for the first time the depths of her concealed emotions were revealed.

'I am settled in the ancient Catholic religion,' she said firmly, her tone resolute, 'and mind to spend my blood in defence of it.'

The dean ignored her and fell to his knees to pray out loud for her soul. She turned away and began to pray in Latin, their words intertwining, each voice calling to the same God across a divide that had almost destroyed a realm.

In the silence that followed, the Queen sat on the low stool to disrobe. Her lady-in-waiting stepped forward. With trembling hands the servant removed the two rosaries bound around the Queen's waist before drawing down her black dress. Underneath Mary Stuart wore a dark red bodice and crimson petticoat, the colour of blood. The lady stepped in close, her tear stained lips kissing a white cloth blindfold before tying it in place.

The Queen knelt down and reached out in blindness for the block, her hands tracing over its edges. She leaned forward, adjusting the position of her chin with the tips of her fingers. The executioner bent over and touched her hand, an unspoken sign to withdraw them, and she stretched out her arms, lowering her head to fully expose the back of her neck. The executioner stepped back, the weight of the felling axe light in his calloused hands. He drew up the stroke.

'Into thine hands, O Lord, I commend my spirit,' the Queen cried aloud, 'Into thine hands, O Lord, I commend . . .'

The blade fell, striking her on the back of the head.

'Sweet Jesus,' she whispered and the executioner quickly swung again, this time his axe striking her cleanly on the back of the neck, ending her fate.

The executioner picked up the severed head and held it aloft, turning slowly before the crowd so all could see and bear witness, his loud voice booming across the great hall:

'God save the Queen.'

CHAPTER 1

25th March 1587. Near Plymouth, England.

Robert Varian picked his way across the ancient graveyard, his hands outstretched in the darkness as he wove through the maze of granite and sandstone markers. The noise of the air rushing through the trees filled his ears, and not for the first time, he felt a hollow point of unease at the base of his back. The local yeomanry were sure to be patrolling for deserters and given the lateness of the hour his presence so far from port would be hard to explain.

He looked up at the dark outline of the church spire to his left, tracing its outline with his eyes until he reached its apex. Above it the clouds were racing across the sky, a ghostly white, diffusing the light of the waning moon. He searched for a gap along their line of advance and, seeing one approach, quickly dropped his gaze. An instant later the moon's light shone through a breech, illuminating the ancient stones. He could see it, not ten feet ahead. He was plunged once more into darkness as he stumbled on.

His outstretched hand touched cold sculpted stone and he felt his way slowly up over the curve of an angel's wing, his hand falling to the shoulder of the life-sized statue which was draped over a plinth in lamentation. He followed the arm and paused as his hand reached the angel's. This was his third visit since the full moon, and each one before had brought disappointment. He stretched his fingertips around the angel's hand and smiled in relief as he felt the object loosely clutched within. It was a small wooden crucifix, roughly hewn as if created in haste and Robert glanced over his shoulder instinctively. He could see or hear nothing in the wind-driven darkness and he quickly replaced the crucifix in the angel's hand.

He moved towards the church, his hand outstretched again until he touched the north wall. He turned east and left the bounds of the churchyard to go into the field beyond. His eyes were drawn to a dark mass of high ground ahead, a looming hillock behind which the clouds fled and then reappeared. It was a motte, a man-made earthen mound, and upon it some long-forgotten people had built a rudimentary stone fort, now in ruins. He began to clamber up its slope and the wind clawed at his travelling cloak. He paused as he reached the top. A tumbled down wall was before him and he stepped into its lee. The noise of the wind in his ears abated.

'*Sumus omnes.* We are all,' he said in Latin to the darkness, a language he had been taught in his youth and one known by all educated men.

'*In manu Dei.* In God's hand,' came a reply and Robert smiled, recognizing the deep baritone of the voice.

He stepped forward and was met by the dark outline of a short, stocky man.

'Well met, Father,' he said.

'Robert, is that you?' the priest replied.

'Yes, Father,' Robert said and he reached out and clasped the priest's arm.

'I did not expect . . .'

'I have come from Plymouth,' Robert explained, omitting why he was in that port, knowing the reason would anger the priest.

Robert had known Father Blackthorne for the better part of his thirty years, ever since he had come to live in Brixham when he was twelve years old. It had been a terrifying time for Robert, a new life far from his original home in Durham. From the outset, Father Blackthorne had been his friend, and the young boy had clung to the security of the priest's constancy, using him, like the North Star, as a fixed point in his shattered world.

As Robert grew older the priest had become his confessor. It was a sacrament Robert rarely had the chance to celebrate as a sailor for he spent many months at a time at sea, but he had long ago memorized the sequence of secret meeting places, triggered by the rising of each new moon, and the secret call signs that the priest used. It was that knowledge that had led him to the weeping angel in the graveyard of the Church of Saint Michael, not two miles from Plymouth, and the motte beyond that had become a Mass rock for the Catholic faithful.

'Will you hear my confession, Father?' Robert asked, kneeling down.

The priest nodded and removed a Stole from his pocket, kissing the long narrow strip of cloth before placing it around his neck. He reached out to put his hand on the top of Robert's head as he began the Latin incantation of the sacrament. Robert rose after a few minutes, his conscience calmed.

'Have you seen my parents?' he asked.

'I have,' the priest replied, wondering if the young man really did consider the Varians to be his parents. 'Not two months ago. They are well.'

Robert nodded, glad to hear some news. Brixham was only twenty miles from Plymouth but Robert had not been home for over a year, his own career and now a summons from his patron keeping him away. His adoptive father, his uncle, William Varian, was a local gentleman merchant. A successful man, he kept his business profitable by hiding his Catholic faith and openly conforming to the Protestant religion of the majority. It was a secret fraught with danger for Catholics were associated with so many plots to overthrow the Protestant Queen Elizabeth, their faith was synonymous with treachery and foreign influence.

William Varian remained a loyal recusant, a Catholic who nevertheless firmly supported the Queen. It was a belief he had instilled in Robert ever since he took the young boy into his home. Queen Elizabeth was not of their faith, but she was English, and a staunch defender of England's independence from the foreign powers that lurked across the Channel. For that reason alone, William Varian had taught Robert to be forever loyal to her command.

'It is near midnight,' Father Blackthorne said, 'I must prepare for mass.'

'Will others come?' Robert asked.

'Not many I fear,' the priest replied. 'More and more are turning away from the true faith and following the path of the heretic Queen, may she suffer the hell-fires.'

An instinctive defence of Queen Elizabeth rose to Robert's lips but he remained quiet. He knew that Father Blackthorne did not share his loyalty.

'Tonight, I will pray for the soul of Queen Mary of the Scots,' the priest said sadly.

Robert nodded, feeling the pain of her loss anew. Mary Stuart had been the next in line for the throne after Elizabeth and her coronation had had the potential to change everything in Robert's life.

His decision to remain Catholic went deeper than faith.

For Robert it was the only surviving link to his past, a past he could never relinquish, and one he was forced to hide. That concealment had cost him dearly, for without claim to his true birthright he had been forced to make his way in the world without favour or title.

The noise of approach caused Robert to spin around and his hand fell instantly to the hilt of his rapier.

'*Sumus omnes*,' he heard and he responded with the second half of the passphrase.

Three people emerged from behind the wall, a studious looking man with his wife and young daughter. They were followed minutes later by a second group, then another.

As midnight arrived the mass began. Father Blackthorne preached from behind a large flat-topped rock which served as an altar while his congregation knelt on the stone strewn ground. The wind whistled and gusted around them, whipping away the priest's words but all knew the sermon intimately. As the clouds raced overhead the small group reiterated their faith, speaking outlawed words in the darkness.

The ship's bell tolled six times and Henry Morgan looked east towards the coming dawn. It was minutes away and he used the half-light to survey the ships at anchor around the *Retribution* in Plymouth harbour. There were sixteen ships and seven pinnaces in total, an impressive fleet and Morgan felt his heart swell with pride at the sight, not least because his own command was one of the most powerful ships amongst them. The *Retribution* was a galleon of the new 'race built' class, with her fore and aft castles razed, giving her a sleek, spear-like profile. At 450 tons and with a crew of two hundred and twenty, she carried thirty-two guns, and was a fast and agile purpose built warship.

Morgan looked across at the flagship, the *Elizabeth*

Bonaventure, anchored nearby. It was one of four galleons contributed to the enterprise by the Queen, and the commander, Francis Drake, had taken it as his own. Morgan searched for Drake on the decks, hoping to catch a glimpse of him. He embodied everything that Morgan believed in, his staunch Protestantism and his unswerving loyalty to Queen and country. But the ship was alive with men, both on deck and in the shrouds, and it was impossible to single out one man.

He looked beyond the flagship to the rest of the fleet. All rode easy at their anchors, the gentle pull of the outgoing tide keeping the ships in parallel. Morgan watched as local fishermen sailed their craft between the towering warships, the crews exchanging easy salutes as men near the end of their watch called out to fishermen beginning their day. He felt a presence at his shoulder and turned to find Thomas Seeley, the master's mate, standing beside him.

'Has the Master returned yet?' Morgan asked.

'No, Captain, not yet,' Seeley replied.

Morgan nodded, keeping his irritation hidden behind a neutral expression. The fore-noon watch would begin within the hour and Varian was officer of the watch.

He had known Varian only by reputation until four days before when the royal flotilla arrived in Plymouth from Dover. Varian was one of John Hawkins's men, a recently promoted captain of a merchantman. The son of a minor gentleman he had worked his way up through the ranks on the most arduous of trade routes, the trans-Atlantic triangular; textiles from Europe to Africa, slaves from Africa to America and sugar, tobacco and cotton from America to Europe, and was well known for his sailing skills.

The *Retribution* belonged to John Hawkins, the Treasurer of the navy. He had insisted that Varian be master for the voyage ahead and Morgan had readily acquiesced, conscious that his crew would benefit from Varian's experience. The new master had reported to the *Retribution*, however for the past three nights, Varian had requested permission to go aboard his former ship to ensure that all would remain in order during his absence. On the first two mornings Varian had returned in the middle of the morning watch, at around six a.m. This morning however he was late and Morgan wondered if Varian's tardiness was due to disobedience or merely indifference.

'Longboat approaching off the larboard quarter,' a lookout called, and Morgan looked to the fast-moving boat. Varian was standing in the bow. As he came alongside he called up for permission to come aboard. It was quickly given and he scaled the rope ladder to the main deck just as the sun finally crested the line of the eastern horizon. He made his way towards the quarterdeck. The ship's bell tolled seven times.

'All is well on board the *Spirit*, I trust, Mister Varian,' Morgan said, studying anew the dark weathered features of the master. Varian was a tall slender man, narrow in the shoulders and waist. His eyes had the restlessness of a career sailor, constantly checking and rechecking the ship around him.

'Yes, thank you, Captain,' Robert replied, 'I will not need to attend to her again.'

'Good,' the captain said shortly and turned once more to the flagship. 'I must go aboard the *Elizabeth Bonaventure* for a captains' council with Drake. See to it that the top gallants are replaced during the watch.'

'Yes, Captain,' Robert replied as he moved towards the starboard bulwark. He was joined there by Seeley.

'I was in port last night,' Seeley said offhandedly, 'and came upon the *Spirit* at the southern end of the dock.'

'I didn't realize,' Robert said without turning his head, immediately on guard.

'I asked for you,' Seeley continued, 'but the master there said that you had just gone ashore to see a local trader and would not return until after midnight.'

Robert nodded, silently thanking the quick wits of his friend, Tobias Miller, the master of the *Spirit*. He had worked with the man for over ten years and had requested him as his master when he was given command of the *Spirit* six months before. Robert had not returned to the *Spirit* since being assigned to the *Retribution* and although Miller did not know Robert's secret he knew well enough that if his captain had used the *Spirit* as an excuse to come ashore, he would be best served if Miller supported that lie.

Seeley waited for Varian to explain his absence further but the master continued to stare over the side of the ship in silence. He suspected that Varian had gone ashore to meet a woman, maybe one who was married to another officer in the fleet, or perhaps he was involved in some other wrong-doing, one that necessitated such secrecy. Either way, Seeley disliked the thought that one of the officers of the fleet might be tainted. He believed the upcoming mission, an attack on the Spanish fleet, was a divine one and for them to prevail the heart of every man in the fleet needed to be pure.

Seeley's grandparents had been martyred by the Roman Catholic Queen Mary Tudor, forever known to Protestants as 'Bloody Mary', and she had stripped the family of its title and wealth. Although Elizabeth had restored the Seeley family with its title after she gained the throne, the fortune and estate were gone forever. Now Seeley was determined to avenge the murder of his grandparents by carrying the cause of God and his faith into battle against the hated Roman Catholic Spanish and the antichrist who was their king, Philip II, the former husband of Bloody Mary.

He looked to Varian again. God in his wisdom had placed

him on board the *Retribution* and in the battle to come, when every man in the fleet would be a soldier of the Protestant faith. If the Lord had chosen Robert Varian then, Seeley conceded, he must be wrong about the new master.

The ship's bell tolled eight times and the boatswain, Shaw, called for the changing of the watch.

'Call the men to the main deck, Mister Seeley,' Robert said, eager to begin the day, 'and have the top gallants brought down.'

'Yes, Master,' Seeley replied. His shouted order triggered the sound of bare feet running on the timber decks as all across the fleet the fore-noon watch began.

Robert watched the men take to the shrouds as Seeley directed them from the main deck. The master's mate was a young man, not twenty-two years old but his social rank gave him an innate confidence which was reflected in his easy command of the men. Robert had honed a similar style of command, although his had been forged over years at sea, his experience and skill earning him the respect of any crew he served with. His steadfast time on the triangular trade route had also brought him to the attention of John Hawkins and Robert had finally received his hard-earned captain's commission six months before.

Now he was master once more, albeit on one of the finest ships of the English fleet. He was left to wonder anew at how different his life would be if his true lineage was not tainted and could be revealed. His captaincy would have been attained years earlier, undoubtedly on a galleon rather than a merchantman. For all his skill at sailing and experience of fighting as a privateer he had never commanded in battle. Captain Morgan, on the other hand, although his junior, had sailed with Drake when the English fleet attacked the Spanish Main in the Caribbean two years before. It had been a hard fought campaign and although Robert was aggrieved that he had never been afforded such a chance to prove himself, he respected Morgan's right to command.

Reports that the Spanish were preparing a massive invasion fleet had reached every ear in England and the ships surrounding the *Retribution* had been assembled to sail once more against the enemy, although this time the attack would take place in Spanish home waters. It was a daring gamble. One worthy of Drake, Robert thought, as he looked to the flagship. He immediately saw the longboat bearing the captain returning to the *Retribution.* Even from a distance the agitation on Morgan's face was evident and Robert ran to the gunwale. The longboat came alongside and the captain clambered on board.

'Mister Varian,' he called as he went aft of the main deck, 'report to my cabin.'

Robert walked quickly down the steps from the quarterdeck to the main and doubled back to go aft. He moved swiftly, side stepping the crewmen in the cramped space beneath the quarterdeck, his body slightly stooped in the restricted headroom. The air smelled of boiled meat and unwashed men, while underneath Robert could detect the all pervasive stink of the bilges. Ahead he could see the captain had already entered his cabin at the stern of the ship. He stopped at the door and knocked. A muffled voice commanded him to enter.

The cabin was small but neat, with a cot to one side behind a curtain. Near the stern, under the windows, stood a table and single chair. The captain had cleared the tabletop and was laying out navigation charts, looking at each in turn before pulling another from the rack.

'Lisbon,' he said without looking up, his excitement clearly evident.

'When?' Robert asked, stepping in to view the charts he already knew intimately.

'If the wind holds, we sail with the tide tomorrow,' the captain replied. 'Then we lay off the devil's lair to make sure the squadrons of their fleet do not unite.'

Robert nodded, a multitude of thoughts entering his mind at once, including the myriad tasks which needed to be completed before dawn the next morning. Until four days ago he had been like any other trader in Plymouth, fully aware of the growing threat posed by the greatest empire of the age, but unaffected by it. Now he stood shoulder to shoulder with the men who would stand against Goliath.

CHAPTER 2

8th April 1587. Cadiz, Spain.

The rain fell in steady sheets borne by an onshore breeze that filled the air with the salt smell of the deep sea, smothering the odours of the cramped city on the peninsula a mile away. Evardo Alvarez Morales turned into the wind and breathed in deeply before lowering his head. The rain ran off the brim of his hat and he wiped the wind driven moisture from his face and neatly trimmed beard. The storm was blowing from the south-west and the *Halcón* tugged incessantly at her anchor line, trying to break free, as if to seek shelter from the shattered remnants of the Atlantic rollers that surged past the headland protecting the anchorage at Cadiz.

He looked to the four points of his ship and beyond to the vessels that surrounded him in the upper harbour, many of them belonging to the supply fleet that was hastily being prepared under the protective watch of nine galleys, commanded by Don Pedro de Acuña, anchored in the lee of the city. The *Halcón* was Evardo's first command of a galleon, granted to him at just twenty-six by his patron, the Marquis of Santa Cruz, commander of the Armada gathering in Lisbon harbour. With the planned attack on England only months away, Evardo knew he was on the cusp of writing a new chapter in the illustrious history of his family.

Evardo's grandfather had been a renowned explorer of the Spanish Main, while his father, Alvaro Juarez Morales, fell at the Battle of Lepanto, boldly leading an attack against the galleys of Uluj Ali. For the young Evardo the King's crusade against the heretic English was his chance to make his name and stand shoulder to shoulder with his next eldest brother who, at twenty-eight, was already an aide-de-camp in the Duke of Parma's army fighting the rebels of the United Provinces in the Spanish Netherlands.

Evardo glanced over his shoulder as one of his senior officers, the ship's captain, approached. He nodded curtly to his salute. The ship's captain was in charge of the seventy-five sailors on board while the soldiers, two hundred of them, were under the command of a separate captain. Those men were currently garrisoned in the nearby Puerto Real and would not be embarked until the day before the galleon sailed.

The wind slackened and shifted for a moment and Evardo moved instinctively to the bulwark of the aft deck, looking out over the side as the *Halcón* shifted slightly on her anchor cable. He checked her line to the other ships and to the shore, ensuring that all was well and as he looked up again he saw Abrahan Delgado standing beside him. The older man was staring at him, his gaze intense, as if he was scrutinizing his every action. Evardo smiled.

'All is well, Abrahan,' he said, 'you should return to your cot.'

'While this storm blows my place is on deck, *Comandante*,' Abrahan said gruffly, pulling the collars of his cape tightly around his neck as he looked into the wind, his face twisted in a slight grimace as he eased some ancient pain in his back.

Evardo smiled again, liking the older man. He knew the

real reason Abrahan was on deck was so he could be on hand should Evardo need his advice. After fifteen years the *comandante* suspected there was little else his mentor could teach him on any subject.

Abrahan Delgado was not an officer of the *Halcón.* He was on board as the *comandante*'s personal aid but the senior officers had quickly learned to respect the opinion of the often irascible old sailor. Evardo had witnessed protracted arguments between his mentor and his captains over sailing and military techniques, and many times he had smiled as he saw the officers nodding in assent, conceding to Abrahan's viewpoint.

The wind shifted once more to its previous course and again Evardo looked out over the side. The storm had been blowing for three days, its strength drawn from the deep Atlantic to the west. Evardo's thoughts went to the ships of the *flota*, the treasure fleet from the colonies that were so vital to the cause of Spain and his most glorious majesty, King Philip. In the open ocean the savage power of the storm would be fully unleashed. Evardo whispered a prayer for the safety of any ships that might be en route home.

He remembered his own commission in the treasure fleet at the age of thirteen, a rite of passage for all young aristocrats who wished to serve in the King's navy. The towering fore and aft castles of the *Santa Catalina*, a huge galleon of 900 tons, specially built to take its place in the *Flota de Indias*, the fleet that plied between Spain and the Caribbean. He could still recall his feelings on the day he sailed from La Coruña, his pride mixed with youthful apprehension, his thoughts on his father who had been dead not two years, and how he had looked to his taciturn tutor, Abrahan, standing by his side.

That commission had lasted four years, taking Evardo across the mighty Atlantic many times, from La Coruña to Veracruz via Havana and back. Almost every night he had dined with the officers, and often with the *comandante* of the mighty *Santa Catalina*, learning quickly from these career mariners and soldiers. By the time he had left the *Santa Catalina*, the awkwardness of his first faltering steps at sea had been replaced by the confident stride of an experienced sailor, ready to climb the established aristocratic ladder of command that had eventually led him to the *Halcón*.

The boom of a single cannon from the low lying fort on the seaward promontory of Cadiz interrupted Evardo's thoughts. Noon, the change of the watch. The sky overhead remained iron grey with low cloud, the canopy of a winter evening rather than noontime in spring. The western coastline of Spain was often visited by such tempests, but Evardo was confident that with the change in season only weeks away, the storm was sure to be short-lived.

He looked to the ships of the supply fleet surrounding the galleon, many of which were smaller coastal boats along with caravels and hulks. The men on their decks worked through the rain, spurred on by the end which was clearly in sight. The supply fleet was but two weeks away from being ready. Then it would sail to Lisbon, to stock the mighty Armada. Evardo had decided to sail with them. Although he was not due in Lisbon until the end of the month, he was conscious of the threat posed by English pirates and especially *El Draque*, Drake, the arch-fiend heretic who had wreaked havoc in the Spanish Main not two years before.

Drake's attack was only one of a litany of insults suffered by the Spanish over the previous years. The *flota*, despite sailing in convoy, was under constant threat from English pirates who returned to the bosom of their Queen after every attack, sheltering like cowards under her protestations of innocence and justification. Elizabeth was openly supporting the

Protestant rebels of the United Provinces, in defiance of King Philip's demands that England remained neutral in what Spain believed was an internal conflict.

Now the whole of Spain was rife with the rumour that Elizabeth had murdered her own cousin, Mary Stuart, who in Catholic eyes was the rightful claimant to the throne of England over the bastard queen spawned of an adulterous affair. There could be no higher crime, no greater offence. The English and Elizabeth had gone too far. Although the Armada had been in preparation before Mary's execution, her death had filled Spanish hearts with a religious fervour and a thirst for righteous vengeance that could not be quenched.

Until the English were crushed, the seas around Spain would never be secure. It galled Evardo that his countrymen could not call themselves safe from molestation in their home waters. He reached out to touch the gunwale of the *Halcón*, taking solace from the fact that soon the galleon would be in English waters, repaying tenfold the insults suffered by the Spanish Empire and the divine faith of his forefathers.

The wind howled through the shrouds and rigging, a fearful wail that gave voice to the fury of the storm. Robert leaned against the fall of the quarterdeck, his safety line biting into his waist as the bow of the *Retribution* cut through the crest of a wave. The seawater swept over the bulwark and ran ankle deep across the main deck before fleeing through the scuppers. He looked skyward, searching for the sun he had not seen in days, but the iron-grey clouds filled the heavens, bloated by the unceasing wind.

The *Retribution* was sailing broad reach under bare yards with only storm tops'ls unfurled. The wind had screamed out of the south-west three days before, scattering the English fleet just as it had sighted Cape Finisterre on the north-western corner of Spain. Robert had been on deck ever since, unable to go below and turn his back on a sea that he had long ago discovered rewarded complacency with treachery. He had slept in the lee of the quarterdeck, snatching fitful hours while Seeley took the watch. He had quickly come to trust his younger mate. Seeley's hand and nerve were as steady as his own.

The wind shifted and ebbed slightly and Robert looked again to the line of his ship.

'Steady the helm!' he shouted, his voice carrying through the open hatch to the helmsman, Price, on the main deck beneath him. Price tightened his grip on the whipstaff and braced his powerful legs against the increasing press of the sea against the rudder. The tiller, attached to the other end of the whipstaff two decks below him, remained steady and the bow of the *Retribution* held firm.

Robert smiled despite the gnawing fatigue he could feel permeating his every sense. The galleon was a breed apart from any ship he had ever sailed on before and he marvelled at the genius of her design. Even in such heavy weather her longer, slimmer hull and lower fore and aft castles improved her handling and manoeuvrability beyond measure. He squinted through the driving rain to the sea ahead, searching for other ships of the fleet, but visibility had dropped to less than three miles and the towering grey-backed waves hemmed the *Retribution* in on all sides.

Over the roar of the wind Robert heard, 'Report, Mister Varian,' and he turned to see the captain approach.

'As before, Captain,' Robert shouted, his hand cupped over the side of his mouth, 'wind holding south-west, at least thirty knots. I estimate we are forty-five degrees north, over a hundred miles north-north-east of Cape Finisterre, in the Bay of Biscay.'

Robert could not be sure, for it had been impossible to accurately sight the sun at noon over the previous days to determine their exact latitude, while their longitude could only be determined by dead reckoning, an inaccurate task in such a storm. Captain Morgan nodded regardless, trusting his new master.

'Any other ships in sight?' he asked, wiping the airborne spray from his face.

Robert glanced at the lookout at the top of the main mast. His head was darting from side to side, covering the points of the ship but he showed no signs of having sighted any other sail.

'Nothing,' Robert shouted. 'Not since the *Dreadnought* near dawn. We lost sight of her over three hours ago.'

'And no sign of survivors from the *Deer*?' Morgan asked, his voice betraying his anticipation of the answer even as Robert shook his head.

The *Deer*, a pinnace, had been lost early in the storm, the smaller vessel floundering under the first savage blows as the front overtook the English fleet. Robert, with the rest of the crew of the *Retribution*, had observed her sinking, the ship slipping beneath the waves not four hundred yards off the starboard beam. Many of the men on board the *Retribution* had called out in vain to the few survivors they could see in the water, urging them to make for the galleon or to cling on to whatever debris they could find, to hold fast until the storm abated and the longboat of the *Retribution* could be launched to rescue them. But the wind had never eased, had never backed off, and in desperation they had seen the men disappear one by one, some carried away by the tempest, while others slipped beneath the torrid surface of the sea.

Movement at the top of the main mast caught Robert's eye and he looked up to see the lookout shouting down to the quarterdeck. His cry of alarm was lost in the wind but the direction of his arm pointed out the danger. Robert slipped his safety line and ran up to the poop deck to stare out over the aft gunwale. The approaching wave filled his vision, its wind torn crest standing twice as tall as the waves before it.

'Look out for'ard,' he roared in warning to the crew and he jumped back down to the quarterdeck. The wave crashed over the starboard quarter. A wall of water surged over the ship, engulfing the men on the main deck, carrying one of them over the side. The stern of the *Retribution* swung to port under the force of the wave, bringing her broadside to the storm. The main deck was awash and the crew desperately clawed at the timbers as the sea tried to claim them.

The storm tops'ls lost their shape and the halyard of a brace to the main tops'l yard snapped under the unequal stress of the wind, its block and tackle swinging wildly across the quarter-deck, striking one man on the side of the head, killing him instantly. The yard swung around the mainmast, twisting the sail out of shape and the wind spilled from it, rendering it useless.

'Main tops'l ho!' Robert shouted even as Shaw, the boat-swain, ordered two men, Ellis and Foster, aloft, following closely on their heels as they clambered up the shrouds. 'Helmsman, hard a starboard.'

Price swept the whipstaff to port, the tiller moving in reverse beneath him, coming hard up against the starboard. The bow swung slightly to port but with only the foremast storm tops'l to carry the weight of the entire galley, the *Retribution* could not make headway. She pitched violently as the waves crashed into her broadside.

'Mister Seeley,' Robert shouted over the roar of the wind, 'take men forward and secure the braces to the yards of the foremast. If they fail we're lost.' Seeley nodded and Robert turned his attention to the men ascending the mainmast.

The pitch of the deck was making the climb difficult and more than once the men almost lost their footing on the shrouds as the ship heeled over. They reached the height of the main tops'l yard fifty feet above the main deck and Robert watched as Shaw directed Ellis and Foster to secure a new line for the brace. They worked swiftly, sidestepping out the footrope to the edge of the yard and within minutes Ellis descended with the new line.

'Yeoman of the sheets, make fast!'

The petty officer called the men aft at Robert's command and they secured and hauled in the line, their backs bent against the strength of the wind as they pulled the yard around into position.

Robert looked up at Shaw through the squalling rain and signalled him to come down, their task complete. The boatswain waved before he and Foster sidestepped back across the footrope to reach the head of the shrouds. On deck the crew continued to haul the yard into position. Suddenly the wind filled the main storm tops'l once more. The canvas took shape with a crack and the *Retribution* surged forward as if released from a sea anchor. Her bow swung swiftly around to its original position and the helmsman reacting without command to bring the rudder in line.

The rapid change, magnified by height, swung the head of the mainmast through an enormous arc and Foster lost his grip on the ratlines. His scream for help was cut short as Shaw grabbed one of his hands and the sailor swung out over the gaping drop to the main deck, his only lifeline the iron grip of the boatswain.

Robert heard the cries of alarm and looked up. His brief elation for the recovery of the *Retribution*'s course was immediately forgotten. Shaw clung to the ratlines at the edge of the shrouds with his right hand while Foster hung by his left hand beneath him. The sailor flailing his legs in panic and his free hand clawed at Shaw's wrist as if trying to drag him down. Robert reacted without thought, racing down to the main deck and the base of the shrouds, shouldering past the crewmen who stared in horror at the men above, many of them shouting hopeless counsel. He jumped up onto the bulwark and climbed up the shrouds, his eyes darting between his feet and hands to the men hanging above him.

The wind tore at his body, the rain lashed his face and Robert blinked rapidly to try to clear his vision. Foster's screams came to his ears, desperate cries that even the howling gale could not hide. He could also hear Shaw's entreaties, trying to quell Foster's panic, yelling at him to grab the underside of the shrouds with his free hand. But Foster was oblivious to all help, his fear-ridden instincts controlling him and he clung to Shaw's left hand.

'Shaw!' Robert called as he approached. The boatswain looked to him for the first time. His face was mottled red with exertion, his eyes wild, and Robert could see the muscles of his arm tremble with the effort of holding himself to the ratlines and Foster from his death.

The *Retribution* bucked through the crest of a larger wave, its bow coming up short for a heartbeat before driving through into the trough, the rhythm of the galleon's roll spoiled by a larger wave. All three men were caught unawares and their weight was thrown forward. Robert tightened his grip and held his footing but in that instant Shaw's feet slipped and he swung around the edge of the shrouds. His right hand held firmly on the ratline but Foster was wrenched from his left and the sailor screamed as he fell through the rain to slam into the main deck forty feet below.

Robert scrabbled the last few feet to Shaw, his eyes locked

on the boatswain's precarious grip on the ratlines. Shaw swung out over the deck, his own gaze fixed on the shattered body of Foster below, while the constant waves mercifully washed the deck of blood.

'Hold fast,' Robert shouted and again the boatswain looked to him, this time his eyes betraying his fear.

'I can't . . .' he shouted and Robert reached out desperately as he saw the boatswain's grasp fail.

He grabbed Shaw's hand just as his grip gave way. The weight of the boatswain slammed Robert into the shrouds. A searing pain ripped through his shoulder. Shaw dangled beneath him, re-enacting the last moments of Foster's life. The boatswain reached up with his other hand and grabbed Robert's wrist. His nails tore his flesh, trying to find purchase. Robert held firm, keeping his own body weight centred as the roll of the ship increased the swing of the boatswain's body.

'The ratlines,' Robert hissed through clenched teeth. 'Your other hand, man. Grab the ratlines.'

The boatswain's face was a mask of terror. Robert felt the first weakness of his own grip on the ratlines as the boatswain swung through another pendulum's arc.

'Shaw!' he screamed, the anger in his voice reaching the boatswain. 'Grab the ratlines or you're a dead man.'

Shaw nodded and Robert saw the fear in the boatswain's eyes turn to determination.

'Wait for the pitch,' he shouted. As the *Retribution* crested a wave, the boatswain released his left hand and reached out for the underside of the shrouds. He missed but on the return swing his fingertips caught their outer edge. His hand clasped the rope, clinging to it.

'Pull!' Robert shouted. He used the last of his strength to heave the boatswain up, their hands releasing each other without command as each took their own grip on ropes. The boatswain was now swinging two handed beneath the shrouds and Robert reached out to grab his tunic, pulling him in to allow him to get his feet onto the ratlines. He climbed around to the outside and the two men clung to the ropes side by side, their laboured breaths whipped away by the wind and rain, while the all pervasive roar of the storm smothered the sounds of the cheering crew on the deck below.

Father Blackthorne moved slowly towards the halo of soft light surrounding the single candle framed in the window. He paused, wary as always of a trap, his caution almost second nature after years in hiding. The night was quiet save for the sounds of nature; the scurry of a small animal in the undergrowth, the screech of an owl, but still the priest hesitated, his breathing shallow as he strained for the sounds of some larger predator. His hand slipped inside his cassock and enfolded the crucifix hanging there. He silently mouthed a Latin prayer before stepping forward once more.

He crossed the courtyard and stopped at the door to the kitchen, knocking lightly as he glanced over his shoulder, conscious that he was now standing in the pool of light from the candle-lit window. The door opened a fraction and a man's face appeared, furtive eyes betraying a moment of apprehension before he recognized the priest, smiling as he opened the door wider to allow him to enter. The priest ducked in and the door was closed and locked, the mechanism of the bolt unnaturally loud in the confines of the room.

The draught from the closing door had set the flame of the candle dancing and the kitchen came alive with moving shadows before the light settled once more, its soft glow allowing Father Blackthorne to feel more at ease. He turned to the man beside him and placed his hand on the servant's expectantly bowed head.

'*In nomine Patris, et Filii, et Spiritus Sancti*,' he intoned.

'Amen,' the man replied. He looked up. 'You must be hungry, Father,' he said, ushering the priest to the table in the middle of the room.

Father Blackthorne sat down, his eyes poring ravenously over the table before him. The servant brought the lighted candle from the window sill to the table and the priest moaned involuntarily as he saw the feast in detail. He had not seen food like it in weeks and he reached out to pull the leg off a cold capon as the servant poured him a goblet of wine. He ate quickly, conscious that time was short, ignoring the servant who sat silently across from him.

'I beg your forgiveness, Father,' the servant said tentatively after five minutes, 'but the Duke will be waiting.'

Father Blackthorne made to dismiss the reminder but held his tongue, knowing it would serve no purpose and that the duke's good favour was all important. He stood up and wiped his mouth with the back of his hand, belching softly with regret as he looked over the table of food once more. Its abundance was in stark contrast to the meagre offerings the poorer Catholics would give him in the weeks between now and his next visit to the duke's residence.

The servant picked up the candle and led the priest from the kitchen, taking him along one of the servants' passageways that emerged into the entrance hall of the estate house. All was in darkness. The two men crossed the flagstone floor in an orb of light and the feeble glow from the candle seemed to augment the vastness of the vaulted ceiling above them. Their footfalls echoed in the silence. They came to a door and the servant knocked. His hand was already on the handle as the command to enter was given.

Father Blackthorne entered alone. He felt anxious, as was often the case in the presence of his patron. The room was a small study, its walls lined with shelves holding innumerable books and the priest looked at them admiringly, conscious of their value. The Duke of Clarsdale was standing in front of the remains of a small fire in the hearth. He was surrounded in a thin haze of smoke from the downdraught in the chimney and his back was arched slightly as he outstretched his hands towards the heat. He was a tall man, broad across the shoulders and his iron grey hair gave twenty years to his middle age. He did not move as the priest crossed the room towards him, and Father Blackthorne's eyes were drawn to the two Irish wolfhounds curled up at the edge of the hearth. Their heads turned to track the priest across the room before falling once more onto their extended legs.

'I expected you quite some time ago,' Clarsdale said.

'It is becoming more and more difficult for me to travel,' the priest explained.

Clarsdale murmured a reply and the room became silent once more.

'It is becoming more difficult for us all,' he said after a pause.

'It is through our hardships that we are redeemed,' Father Blackthorne replied, stepping closer to the duke.

Clarsdale did not reply immediately.

'I was thinking of the men who were martyred last September,' he said to the fire, a hard edge to his voice.

'They are already with God,' Father Blackthorne said reassuringly, although he shuddered involuntarily as he thought of their fate.

The Babington plot, so named after the most prominent of the conspirators, had been exposed six months before. Father Blackthorne had only heard rumours of it before its discovery, but he had long suspected that the Duke of Clarsdale had possessed some greater knowledge, even if he had not been directly involved. The conspirators had been sentenced to be hanged, drawn and quartered and such was the brutality and suffering of those first executed, the Queen herself had blanched and ordered the others to be hanged until dead before they were disembowelled.

'They may be with God, Father, for their sacrifice,' Clarsdale cursed, 'but they should be suffering hellfire for their stupidity.'

Father Blackthorne recoiled with shock at the vehemence of the duke's words and crossed himself.

'I have learned that Walsingham knew of their plot months before and was playing them like fools in order to expose Mary Stuart,' Clarsdale continued, turning to the priest for the first time, his face a mask of belligerence. 'So now we have lost our last hope of placing a legitimate Catholic monarch on the throne of England.'

Father Blackthorne nodded. 'Her death is a tragedy,' he said in lament, 'may her soul rest in God's peace. Many of my flock have already lost hope and have cast their mortal souls aside by turning their backs on the true faith.'

'Your flock,' Clarsdale scoffed as he moved to sit down and the wolfhounds became alert once more as their master swept by. 'They are sheep indeed, Father, mere peasants who will follow whoever holds power over the realm.'

'But we need those people,' Father Blackthorne argued. 'We must maintain a wellspring of faith.'

Clarsdale made to retort but he relented, conscious that despite his outward offhand treatment of the priest and his flock, he needed both if he was to retain any chance of fulfilling his solemn vocation of placing a Catholic monarch on the throne. The priest had spoken of his flock as a wellspring of faith, but Clarsdale saw them as a potential wellspring of power, albeit one that was dwindling fast.

Elizabeth's popularity and the constant threats against her

person, supported by foreign powers, were combining to create a kind of nationalism that Clarsdale had never witnessed before. She was weaving a spell over the populace, creating a solidarity and support for her reign that would defeat his cause before it could ever come close to fruition. With Mary Stuart dead, the only alternative was to place a foreign monarch on the throne. It was a sacrifice that Clarsdale was willing to take for his faith, but he was no longer confident the majority would support such a ruler after Elizabeth. Time was of the essence. He indicated for the priest to sit opposite him.

'It is common knowledge that the Spanish plan to invade,' the duke began, lowering his voice instinctively although he was confident of the loyalty of every person within his household. 'When they land they must be met by those who support their cause.'

The priest nodded, his lips mouthing a silent prayer for the coming of that day.

'These men must be trained soldiers, armed men of substance and valour, not peasants bearing scythes and forks.'

Again the priest nodded. 'I know of many amongst those who attend my ceremonies,' he said.

'Good,' the duke replied. 'You must speak to them, ensure they are prepared.'

The duke leaned back in his chair and reached out with his hand to rub the head of one of his dogs, the wolfhound responding with a contented growl.

'There is one other thing, Father,' Clarsdale said. 'The Spanish are assembling a fleet, an Armada, to sail to England, but they desperately lack intelligence on the strength, disposition and readiness of the English royal fleet.'

Father Blackthorne's eyes narrowed. If Clarsdale could command direct access to the Spanish then the duke was considerably closer to the centre of Catholic resistance in England than he had realized.

'The ships that were assembled at Plymouth have already sailed, but I have heard only rumours as to their destination,' the duke continued. 'I need a sailor of rank to keep me informed, in advance, of the fleet's plans.'

Father Blackthorne looked into the middle distance as he called to mind those men he knew at Plymouth. One sprang to mind but he dismissed him straight away, knowing he was merely the captain of a merchantman.

'I will find you such a man,' he said to the duke, unsure of who that man would be, but unwilling to disappoint his patron.

Clarsdale nodded and rose once more. The smoke that had diffused in the air swirled around him as he made his way to the fire. Father Blackthorne looked about the room, noticing for the first time that the invasive cold he had felt over the previous weeks was gone, banished by good food and the luxurious surroundings. It was a far cry from the hovels he would soon find himself in.

'I will say mass at dawn,' he said, rising to stand beside the duke. 'Is her grace, your wife, in residence?'

The mention of his wife brought an immediate slur to Clarsdale's lips but he held his tongue, not wanting to reveal the intimacies of his marriage to the priest.

'She is in London with her family,' he said tersely and looked once more into the fire, ending the conversation. Thoughts of her reminded Clarsdale of how much he had sacrificed for the Catholic cause. However, he was compelled to do no less, for such a sacrifice was in his blood. His family title, the Dukedom, was first granted to an ancestor who had fought in the Crusades. That man had answered the call of his pope and his king and had fought gallantly for the Catholic faith.

It was an act that successive generations had revered and now that the mantle had passed to him Clarsdale was honour bound to fight for his religion.

Father Blackthorne stared at the duke for a moment longer. Men like Clarsdale represented the last bastion of hope for the true faith in England. His lips were verbalizing some indecipherable thought and his face twisted slightly as if grappling with some unspoken demon. For an instant Father Blackthorne was tempted to intervene, wanting to ease whatever pain the duke might be feeling, but he hesitated, intimidated by Clarsdale's demeanour. He left the room without another word.

In darkness the priest walked unerringly to the entrance of his sanctuary on the top floor, a secret panel that led under the eaves of the house where a chapel had been constructed for the duke and his household. In that tiny space he lit a single candle and knelt before it. He prayed, and searched for hope in the entreaties he had spoken since youth, asking God for guidance in the way that many of his flock asked him, conscious all the while that his words were spoken in one of the last remaining footholds of the true faith in a realm that was rapidly embracing a path to perdition.

Robert crashed through the door of his tiny cabin and collapsed on the narrow cot, oblivious to the cockroaches that scurried away from his unexpected presence. He was exhausted and his every muscle cried out for the weightlessness of sleep. The storm had finally abated after five relentless days, and the fleet had rendezvoused once more off of Cape Finisterre. Given its severity, the majority of ships had weathered the tempest well and while many of the older vessels needed running repairs, the only loss had been the pinnace *Deer*.

Now the fleet was once more on course for Lisbon, sailing

on a steady tack. Robert had mechanically seen out an extended watch to allow time for Seeley to rest fully, knowing the younger man was closer to collapse. Only upon his return did Robert finally go below. He was too tired to remove his outer clothing. The seawater that had drenched him through during the storm had long since dried out, leaving a salt residue that rubbed his skin raw at the joints.

The stern cabin was tiny, seven feet by five, but it was private, a singular luxury on a galleon and a far cry from the fo'c'sle and gun deck where the majority of the crew slept. Robert's father had secured him a berth on one of John Hawkins's ships when he was thirteen years old. As a gentleman's son he had been taken on as a cabin boy, a servant to the captain and senior officers. He had quickly learned the harsh lessons of life at sea; the brutal discipline meted out for even the smallest infraction and the need for constant vigilance while off duty against the pederasts on board.

Robert found protection amongst those who themselves had sons serving on other ships. They had made sure he received his fair share of rations – even if the rations were weevil-infested biscuits and foul smelling meat and fish stews – taking only his quota of beer as payment. They had taught him all there was to know about working a ship below and above decks, while the officers informally schooled the eager boy in navigation and sail-craft, quickly marking him as an astute pupil.

The transatlantic voyages of the triangular trade were long and arduous, particularly the slave run of the middle passage, when pestilence stalked the ship, exacerbating the mysterious curse of scurvy that decimated crews too long at sea. Robert had contracted malaria on such a voyage, a disease that had taken him to the edge of death with its first attack, and his body still bore the remnants of that illness, a tinge of yellow in the outer corner of each eye. It had reoccurred too often over the preceding years and Robert constantly feared its coming, conscious of how easily it could end his command in favour of a healthier man.

He rolled over on the cot and stared up at the low ceiling, his hand reaching for the pocket of his breeches. He fumbled with the double fold of material inside, a secure pouch to ensure the items did not accidentally fall out. He glanced at the door and withdrew a silver crucifix and a marble statuette of the Blessed Virgin Mary. The two tiny symbols had once belonged to his father – his real father – and were inscribed with the family name. He rarely took them out, often times forgetting they were even there, and he studied the sacred objects in the dull light of the lantern swinging above him, wondering how his father, if he was alive, would react to his son's commission.

Since receiving the order from John Hawkins to take the position of master on board the *Retribution*, Robert had had little time to think of its import. Drake was taking the fleet to pre-emptively attack the Spanish forces and thereby thwart their plan to invade. Robert strongly believed the Spanish had no right to set foot on the soil of England, but not for the first time he wondered if he, as a Catholic, should somehow support the Spanish King's motives and the blessing given to them by the Pope.

'*Cygnet* coming alongside!'

The call from the lookout interrupted his thoughts and Robert swung his feet off the bed to go on deck.

He stood up and was suddenly lightheaded with fatigue. He reached out instinctively for balance, breathing in deeply until his vision cleared, and was about to open the door when he noticed the crucifix and figurine had fallen on to the floor of the cabin. A breath caught in his throat and he cursed his lapse. On land such an exposure of his true faith would have him condemned as a recusant and his career would be finished. At sea, in a warship sailing towards the enemy, he would be branded as a spy and his life would surely be forfeit. He stuffed them back into his pocket and double checked that they were secure before opening the door to stagger back on deck.

The pinnace *Cygnet* was a hundred yards off the starboard beam and closing. Captain Morgan stood at the gunwale, waiting for his opposite number to come within earshot. Robert walked over to him, his eyes darting to the four points of the *Retribution* as he did, then beyond to the Portuguese coast on the eastern horizon. He recognized the long sweep of the shoreline. Lisbon was but a day away.

'Captain Morgan!' a voice called from the *Cygnet*. All on deck sought out the figure of the *Cygnet*'s captain on the quarterdeck opposite.

'Captain Bell,' Morgan replied, raising his hand.

The *Cygnet* closed to within fifty yards.

'Steady the helm,' Robert shouted instinctively, the close quarter sailing increasing his vigilance.

'New orders from the *Elizabeth Bonaventure*,' Bell called, his hand cupped over his mouth against the wind. 'The *Golden Lion* has captured a small craft and seized papers that speak of a large supply fleet in the Bay of Cadiz.'

Many of the words were whipped away by the wind but the implication of what remained was clear. Morgan's brow creased. Surely Drake was not going to change the priority of the mission.

'You are to come about south-west and bear away from the coast,' Bell continued, 'and strip your masts of any flags that identify you as English.'

'But what of Lisbon? What of our original orders?' Morgan

protested, angry that as a leading officer he had not been consulted.

'They are for naught,' Bell shouted, 'Drake commands and we sail for Cadiz!'

CHAPTER 3

29th April 1587. Cadiz, Spain.

Don Pedro de Acuña paced the aft deck of the *Asuncion*, the command galley of a flotilla of nine anchored in the lee of Cadiz. He walked with his arms folded behind his back and his foot traced a line in the timbers of the deck. He was a short man, with a solid frame and his shoulders swayed in time with the gentle roll of the deck beneath him. De Acuña glanced up at the city as he made his turn at the portside bulwark, his mind drifting back to the meal in the governor's house the evening before and the company thereafter. A smile crept onto his face as he pictured the youthful beauty who had shared his bed.

The wind ebbed for a moment and de Acuña's nose wrinkled at the stench from the galley slaves. There were 144 of them chained to their oars on the open main deck. De Acuña looked upon them with disgust. They sat languidly at their oars, their heads bowed in silence with only the occasional rasping cough emanating from their ranks. They were condemned men, sentenced to serve at the oars of the *Asuncion* at the King's pleasure and de Acuña thought again of how welcome the governor's house would be after the confines of the galley.

The day on board his command ship had been like any other over the previous month; long and tedious, but thankfully it was coming to an end. The sun was already dropping at pace towards the western horizon behind El Puerto de Santa Maria on the far side of the harbour mouth. He looked to the supply fleet anchored a mile further up the harbour, their individual hulls and masts indistinguishable save for the 1,000 ton Genoese merchantman and one of a pair of galleons he knew to be amongst them, its high castles silhouetted against the evening sky.

De Acuña's gaze remained fixed on the distant galleon, a magnificent evolving breed of ship so different to the aged galleys of his command. At Lepanto the galley had reigned supreme but now they were rapidly becoming obsolete in an age where warships were not only measured by the number of men and cannon they could carry, but also how far they could project that power. The sturdy ocean-going galleons had pushed the borders of the Spanish Empire to the four corners of the globe but its success had left ships such as the *Asuncion* languishing in home waters, relegated to guarding merchants and victuallers, a loathsome task for the once noble galley and its *comandante.*

'Ships approaching bearing north-west,' a lookout called and de Acuña spun around to look beyond the harbour mouth and the tip of the headland of Cadiz. A fleet of sail were strung out across the sea lane to the harbour, their number difficult to gauge. De Acuña smiled. Juan Martínez de Recalde's squadron, he thought to himself. Their arrival from the Bay of Biscay was long overdue. He called the galley's captain to his side.

'Signal the *El Gato.* Tell them to come alongside,' he ordered and the captain called to the patache, a small sailing ship attending the galleys.

The *El Gato* tacked swiftly into position and de Acuña transhipped onto the nimble craft, ignoring the salute of its captain as he ordered him to make haste to the edge of the harbour mouth. De Acuña wanted to welcome the commander of the Biscayan squadron personally, knowing how influential and powerful de Recalde was. As the *El Gato* swung away, de Acuña made his way to the foredeck, his eyes searching for de Recalde's flagship, the *Santa Ana*, a magnificent 760 ton galleon that had been launched only the year before.

The oncoming ships bore on, now less than a mile away, and de Acuña's eyes narrowed as he noticed for the first time that none of them had their masthead banners unfurled. He scanned the broad front of the squadron, searching again for the flagship, but the galleon in the van looked unlike any he had seen before. He felt a slight chill of unease but quickly dismissed it, angry at his sudden nervousness. The *Santa Ana* could be sailing at the rear of the squadron, or might even have disengaged at Lisbon.

De Acuña kept his attention on the lead galley. Its decks were frantic with activity and its sails remained unfurled although the harbour mouth was almost upon them. The gap fell to four hundred yards and de Acuña could now make out individual figures on the fo'c'sle. His eyes narrowed against the wind as he tried to focus, unease creeping up his spine once more. They were spaced out along the gunwale and seemed to be. . .muskets! They were carrying muskets!

'Bear away!' de Acuña shouted and he gazed in horror as an eruption of smoke burst forth from the bow chasers of the galleon, followed a heartbeat later by the boom of cannon.

The sea in front of the *El Gato* exploded and water flew up in a torrential spray. The salvo fell mercifully short and the patache heeled over into the turn, its nimble hull, under a full press of canvas, sailing swiftly out of the path of the incoming ships. De Acuña counted the number of enemy ships, his anger at the deviousness of the surprise attack overriding his alarm that such a powerful fleet was arrayed against him. For a moment he wondered who they could be, but he realized quickly there was no other foe who would dare to attack one of the greatest ports in Spain. The galleons were English!

He looked to his galleys. They had already slipped their anchors and the finely balanced vessels were quickly coming up to their attack speed. He called to the captain to steer an intercept course to the *Asuncion*, eager to take command of the flotilla, knowing that every passing minute was one lost to the enemy, and he swiftly made the aft deck of his galley.

'Signal the squadron to form rank and present their bows to the enemy. We must try to hold the line here at the harbour mouth.'

The crew of the *Asuncion* responded with alacrity while all around the other galleys separated to gain sea room, turning to bring their two fore mounted, preloaded, *medio cañónes* to bear.

De Acuña watched his squadron manoeuvre with pride, their movements precise and controlled although they were facing an enemy many times their superior in both number and firepower. The archaic strength of a galley to ram and board could only be used against becalmed galleons, not those with the wind to command. His squadron were following his orders without question, but de Acuña realized that before his ships had fired even a single shot, they were doomed to fight a losing battle.

Evardo heard the cannon's report a mile away. Its sound was muted by distance and he looked to the mouth of the harbour.

A fleet of sailing ships was on the cusp of entering. The welcoming salvo marked them as de Recalde's squadron but Evardo noticed with curiosity that they were sailing under a full press of canvas, a seemingly unwise approach at speed into the confines of the harbour mouth.

'Why such haste?' Abrahan asked, echoing Evardo's thoughts.

'Perhaps he is carrying orders of some import,' he suggested, seeing in Abrahan's expression the same doubt he felt himself. He looked back to the harbour mouth, his gaze sweeping its breadth.

'De Acuña's galleys,' he breathed, noticing their changing aspect, 'they're sallying out to intercept the fleet.'

Evardo hesitated for a moment longer.

'Clear for action,' he roared, walking swiftly to the centre of the quarterdeck. 'Raise the anchor. Hoist top gallants and mizzen.'

The crew of the *Halcón* sprung into action. The men spilled out from below decks to take to the shrouds while below the capstan of the anchor rope began to turn under the strident commands of a deck officer.

Evardo looked to Abrahan and the older man nodded in tacit agreement of the call to arms. Suddenly the air was rent with the distant sound of cannon fire, its intensity ending all doubt. Many of the crew of the *Halcón* froze and looked to the harbour mouth.

'As you were!' Evardo roared, the crew reacting to the whip crack of his command. He looked aloft. 'Masthead, report!'

'At least a dozen warships, galleons,' the lookout called, 'with smaller sail to the rear.'

'What flag?' Evardo shouted.

'I see none, *Comandante.*'

'And de Acuña's galleys?'

'They are fanning out in front of the attackers to close the harbour mouth.'

Evardo looked to the distant fight. '*Que coraje*,' he whispered, his chest filling with pride for de Acuña's forlorn daring.

The *Halcón* pressed forward slightly as the first sails took the light wind, the galleon coming up short against the anchor rope until the flukes gave way. The crew hauled in the remaining line.

'Shall I call for topsails and courses, *Comandante*?' the ship's captain asked as Evardo looked to the waters surrounding the *Halcón*. The supply ships on all sides were already slipping their anchor cables in panic, raising their sails oblivious to the proximity of the other boats around them.

'Hoist no more sail until we clear these other boats,' Evardo replied, cursing his lack of foresight in not placing the *Halcón* in more open water.

The galleon came up to steerage speed and Evardo watched the sea ahead as the captain called out his orders to the helmsman, the two men working together to try to thread the *Halcón* through the heaving labyrinth of ship infested waters. A sudden crash caused Evardo to spin around and he stared in anger at a collision between two merchantmen. The crews were calling across at each other in futile rage, while underneath, Evardo could feel the panic beginning to envelop the hapless supply fleet. He looked ahead once more at the ships cutting loose across the path of the *Halcón*, realizing with dread that they were all but trapped.

'Bring the larboard broadside to bear, Mister Varian.'

'Hard to larboard,' Robert shouted to the captain's command and the *Retribution* turned tightly to starboard, presenting its port broadside to the Spanish galleys. On the gun deck beneath the main, Larkin, the master-gunner, waited patiently for the galleon to settle on its new course. He called out for the gun crews to stand ready. They stood with their linstocks poised. A bead of smoke trailed from each slow match.

Larkin, a bull of a man with hands blackened from his trade, had trained the crews relentlessly. On the gun deck he was in direct command of the most powerful weapons on the *Retribution*, two demi-culverins, eight culverins, and two cannon-pedros chasers both fore and aft that could hurl a 24 pound iron shot. On the main deck above he was ably seconded by the gunner's mate, Peters, who had under his charge a further two demi-culverins, eight lighter sakers and eight man-killing falcons.

The *Retribution* completed the turn and Larkin stared out the foremost gun port to the squadron of Spanish galleys. Their bow mounted guns were firing intermittently, creating a cloud of smoke which compromised Larkin's aim but with an experienced eye he pictured the outlines of his prey beyond the shroud. The outer galleys of the squadron passed before him and still he waited. The galleys surrounding the lead ship were more tightly packed.

'Steady, boys,' he shouted.

The *Retribution* swooped into the trough of a wave, its cutwater slicing up a spray of water. Larkin felt the recovery of the hull in the pit of his stomach, the beginning of the upswing as the galleon began its climb up the next swell. He took a half-breath.

'Fire!'

As one, the linstocks fell on the touchholes of the guns. Larkin's command was followed a heartbeat later by Peters's on the main and the galleon bucked with the force of the double cannonade. The upper decks were engulfed in a blanket of gunpowder smoke and the deafening thunder of the broadside temporarily stunned the gun crews. The *Retribution* reeled but, like a prize fighter recovering from a blow that had winded but not wounded, the galleon quickly steadied.

Larkin was at once roaring at his crews, his throat and eyes burning from the foul smoke that filled the cramped gun deck. The men strained at the ropes to run in the four-wheeled carriages of their weapons and the pulleys squealed in protest as the guns, some of them weighing over 3,000 pounds, rolled across the deck. The crews' discipline made them oblivious to the results of the first wave of fire they had unleashed upon an enemy. Every action counted down the time it would take them to ready their guns to fire again.

Cannon balls tore across the three hundred yards of open water towards the *Asuncion* and the galleys flanking her, striking even as the Spanish crews registered the eruption of smoke from the English galleon. De Acuña straightened his back and tightened his grip on the hilt of his sword, his every instinct screaming at him to take cover, while his rank and honour commanded him to stand tall on the fore deck.

A brace of cannon balls whistled over his head, striking the rigging of the *Asuncion*. Another slammed into the mainmast and the timber disintegrated in a rain of splinters that tore through the ranks of rowers on the open decks, the arrow-like fragments piercing flesh and spirit, spreading blood and panic amongst the defenceless slaves. The heavier cannon-pedro balls struck the hull and oars. The iron shot did not pierce the oak timbers of the bow but the fifteen foot long oars were snapped clean and the recoil of the blow broke the hands and wrists of the slaves still holding their charge.

The *Asuncion* was a maelstrom of noise. The screams of the injured fuelled the chaos of the panicking slaves and they tore the flesh of their ankles as they fought against the shackles holding them fast. De Acuña closed his mind to the noise and fixed his attention on the formation of enemy galleons, watching as the next ship sailed into position to deliver a broadside. Around him the crew worked frantically to reload the *medio cañónes*, their single preloaded 20 pound shot long since expended.

After the opening salvo the leading English galleons had formed into a ragged line and had in turn presented their guns to his squadron of galleys with devastating results. The next galleon swinging into position would be the sixth to make its attack run and de Acuña looked to the galleys on his flanks, his nerve faltering at the sight. The scuppers of each ship ran red, as if the galleys themselves were bleeding from the terrible wounds the enemy cannon balls had inflicted. More than one had been dismasted while the closest galley to the *Asuncion* was listing badly, its crew working desperately to pump out the ceaseless tide of seawater.

De Acuña had known from the start the odds were impossibly stacked against him but he had nevertheless stood firm where others might have fled. Now that resolve was failing. The relentless cannonades of the enemy ships had pierced his courage, forcing him to accept his position was beyond hopeless and bordering on madness. He called the galley captain to his side.

'Take the rowers in hand and signal the other galleys. We sail for El Puerto de Santa Maria.'

The captain nodded and was away. De Acuña turned back to the enemy formation, his gaze falling on the galleon reaching the zenith of its attack run. Its cannons were run out and the baleful black eyes of the muzzles tracked the galleys of his command before disappearing behind an explosion of gun smoke. The boom of cannon was followed by the dreadful whine of round shot tearing through the air. De

Acuña's squadron reeled once more under the hammer blow, unable to respond in kind, and as they turned towards the shelter of El Puerto de Santa Maria, de Acuña could only hope his stand had given the supply fleet time to disperse into the shallows of the upper harbour.

'Hard to starboard! Make way!' Evardo roared with impotent fury, but it was too late and he was thrown to the deck as the *Halcón* collided with the trading carrack that had cut under the bow of the galleon. The momentum of the larger warship bore her on, locking the two vessels together in a tighter embrace. The bowsprit of the *Halcón* snapped off in the rigging of the carrack and the galleon pitched violently as its hull ground along the starboard bow of the smaller ship before coming to rest in a tangle of shattered spars.

'God curse them,' Evardo raved as he stumbled to the gunwale to look out over the carnage.

The *Halcón* had been close to escape when the gunfire from the outer harbour had suddenly ceased. All eyes had turned to see the galleys of de Acuña disperse and the enemy ships advance towards the upper harbour. Many ships of the supply fleet had already fled into the confines of Puerto Real at the head of the upper harbour or were beating up the shallows to take shelter under the guns of the fort of Cadiz. The centre however was still in chaos, and when the enemy ships finally unfurled their banners to reveal themselves as English, the last threads of restraint had unravelled.

From that moment the remaining supply ships reversed their efforts to flee and instead sailed closer to the *Halcón*, seeking protection under her guns, believing perhaps that the English would not attack the formidable warship.

'Take in the sails and make ready to come about,' Evardo shouted. His eyes darted to each point of his galleon and beyond to the approaching English ships. '*Capitán*, send men forward with axes and cut us free.'

'We cannot flee,' a calm voice said. 'You must make ready to defend the ship from boarders.'

Evardo spun around to Abrahan. His angry retort died on his lips as he absorbed the older man's words.

'We have only seventy-five men on board,' he said, speaking aloud his concern and his reason for attempting to flee, ignoring the temptation to lament the absence of his soldiers.

'Then you must find a way to tip the odds more in your favour,' Abrahan replied, his relaxed tone giving Evardo strength and reason for patience. He looked to the men attacking the entangled rigging of the *Halcón* and realized that even if he succeeded in getting underway, the loss of the bowsprit and the sheer numbers of English galleons would make his capture inevitable. He needed time. De Recalde's squadron was overdue and might only be hours away. Or perhaps word was already sweeping inland of the attack and reinforcements could soon be on hand. Either way Abrahan was right; his only option was to make a stand.

He quickly assessed his own position, reversing his role so as to view the fight from the English side. Their galleons would not be able to approach the *Halcón* through such crowded waters, not without risking collision. They were also unlikely to fire upon the *Halcón*, viewing her as a prize, and Evardo's face twisted in contempt as he contemplated such a fate for his ship. He concluded the enemy would therefore advance with boarding parties in smaller boats. The guns of the *Halcón* were preloaded, ready to deliver a single powerful broadside against an enemy galleon, but these guns, ranged over allied ships, would have unpredictable success against small nimble enemy boats. The only guns of value would be the *falconete* swivel guns but there were too few of these.

The English would board, Evardo now accepted that as inevitable, but with Abrahan's help, he could manipulate where that attack would take place. He smiled coldly, now seeing the battle to come from his own side, knowing what he must do to secure his ship. The English would attack, but instead of repelling them he would draw them in. He would allow them a foothold on his deck, let them board in numbers, and then unleash on them a blaze of hellfire to drive them back into the sea. The *Halcón* would not fall without a fight.

Robert leaned into the turn as the *Retribution* came full about, beginning anew a figure-of-eight as it held station at the periphery of the melee. The galleon was flanked by the other larger ships of the English fleet, creating a partial blockade of the upper harbour while the smaller vessels, their crews complemented by additional men from the galleons, wreaked havoc amongst the tightly packed remnants of the Spanish supply fleet. There were over forty ships of every hue, from Spain and all her major allies and dominions, an unprecedented bounty on which the English crews continued to feed. Their appetite was insatiable even after hours of plunder, yet there were ships closer to the centre of the formation that were still untouched.

The evening was foreshortened by a false horizon of clouds to the west behind which the sun had already fallen and the sky was rapidly darkening. Robert took his gaze from the pillage to look to the harbour mouth. The fort of Cadiz was firing its cannon sporadically. It was a futile gesture of defiance, a hollow warning against attacking the meagre flotilla of supply ships that had sought refuge there. Across the mouth, the Spanish galleys that had been driven off earlier had re-emerged from the refuge of shallow water but seemed unwilling to advance once more into the fray.

Robert turned his attention to the chaotic scene of the supply fleet once more. He smiled. The prize from such an attack would be substantial and as the master of a galleon his share could well be in excess of a year's pay on board his own ship, the *Spirit.* Drake's unorthodox change in the established plan had been inspirational, for without supplies the Spanish war fleet in Lisbon were hamstrung and Robert whispered a prayer of thanks. England would surely be spared the threat of invasion for another season.

'*The wages of sin is death sayeth the Lord,*' Robert heard and he turned to see Seeley approach, his face twisted in a malicious grin. 'Today, with His guiding hand, we have shown the papists that they are not safe from our wrath anywhere, on the Main, in the Atlantic and now in their own home waters.'

Robert nodded, sharing that joy, although he felt a thread of unease as he looked at the younger man's manic face, conscious that, to Seeley, the triumph of England took second place to the triumph of his faith.

'Where is the *Spy*?' the master's mate asked.

'Two hundred yards off the larboard beam,' Robert replied, pointing to the English pinnace drawing away from a merchantman many times its size.

Captain Morgan had taken a hundred crewmen of the *Retribution* on board the *Spy* at the outset of the attack on the upper harbour and had thereafter ravaged at least a half-dozen vessels, boarding each with impunity, the watching guns of the galleons making the Spanish mindful only of their lives and not of their possessions. The pinnace turned towards the *Retribution* and Robert saw the captain signal to him from the fore deck of the *Spy*. The two ships drew alongside.

'Mister Varian, man the longboat with twenty armed men and make haste to follow me to that galleon,' Morgan shouted with elation, pointing to the Spanish warship amidst the remaining untouched merchantmen, 'I mean to take her and I want you to command the prize crew.'

'Aye, Captain,' Robert replied with gusto. 'Coxswain to the main! Launch the boat!'

Robert looked to the Spanish galleon. There were men on the quarter- and poop decks. They were motionless and Robert paused, his brow creasing in puzzlement. The Spanish crew's attitude was completely at odds with the pandemonium on board the surrounding Spanish ships. He quickly dismissed his hesitation. The only other Spanish galleon in the upper harbour had fallen in the opening minutes of the battle without a shot fired and Robert could only assume the Spaniards he could see were merely resigned to that same fate, knowing there was no escape.

The longboat was launched and Robert followed the last of twenty men down the rope ladder, taking station at the stern.

'Lay on, boys,' the coxswain shouted and the boat drew away under oars.

The *Spy* was already weaving its way towards the Spanish galleon but Robert ordered the coxswain not to follow. The smaller size of his boat allowed them to take a more direct route and they kept pace with the approach of the faster pinnace. The Spanish galleon towered over them as the long-boat drew closer. Robert kept his gaze locked on the Spaniards he could see and the muzzles of the cannons on the gun and main decks. The coxswain deftly altered the course of the boat to spoil any aim as the cover from the surrounding boats fell away. Robert felt uneasy, not only because they were exposed under enemy guns, but again because the Spanish crew, although they had no weapons in hand, seemed strangely unperturbed by the approach of the longboat and pinnace.

The longboat was twenty yards from the galleon when the

Spy swept in across its course. Morgan brought the starboard of the pinnace up against the hull of the galleon below the main deck and ordered the crew to lash on before leading them aboard. Robert brought the longboat up against the larboard of the *Spy*. He and his men boarded and crossed the deck of the pinnace. They drew their swords as they did so while others nursed the flames on the slow match of their arquebuses.

Robert glanced at the aft decks of the galleon and noticed that the Spaniards there had disappeared. Ahead of him Morgan and more than twenty men were already on the main deck, with more clambering up to join them, their infectious enthusiasm for such an easy prize spurring them on. The men of the longboat joined the back of the push, each man eager to get aboard and find some part of the plunder they could claim as their own. Robert's misgivings were lost in the rush and he led his men in their calls to those in front to hasten their step while all the while the Spanish guns remained quiet.

Evardo tried to quell the blood lust in his veins as he held his men in check. Their hunger for the order to charge was a palpable force in the confines of the enclosed main deck under the quarter. He looked out through a chink in the door. The English were fanning out across the main deck. Thirty men, now forty, their weapons drawn but loosely held. The enemy were still thrilled by the ease of their boarding but Evardo knew it would not last. Their wits were sure to return and they would soon question the deserted decks. He looked to the man leading the English, studying his expression.

Evardo drew up his hand and the two gunners stepped forward, smouldering linstocks in their hands. When the English began their attack on the outer edges of the fleet hours before Evardo had begun his own preparations for the defence of the *Halcón*. The crew had hauled two *medio cañónes* from their positions at the stern end of the main deck and brought them forward to behind the doors leading to the open main deck, lashing them to new mountings in the bulkhead. They were loaded with grapeshot and the crew now stood poised behind them, their weapons drawn, their eyes locked on their captain.

Evardo looked at Abrahan and the older man nodded. They were ready. He set his gaze on the English captain one last time and then backed away from the door to stand between the cannons. The grapeshot would splinter the door into a thousand pieces, adding to the carnage. He glanced at the two gunners and then slowly drew his own sword. The blade rasped against the mouth of the scabbard. He drew in a breath, summoning up the depths of his will to banish the English from his deck and let fly his command with a roar that gave vent to the fury of his soul.

'*¡Fuego!*'

The firestorm consumed the Englishmen closest to the door in a hail of iron and timber. The grapeshot ripped through their flesh to fly onwards to the men behind and the air was whipped by the passing of a thousand missiles as the thunderous roar of the cannons and billowing smoke overwhelmed the main deck. The cannonade slaughtered twenty men, obliterating them at a stroke, while twice that number fell with shattered limbs and torn flesh, and the deafening blast was echoed by the screams of dying men.

Robert was blown to the deck, the men around him falling like sheaves under the sickle as the shock wave blasted over them. The air was rent from Robert's lungs and a cry of pain caught in his throat as a shard of bone pierced his left arm.

He stumbled up and reached out for the bulwark he had cleared only moments before at the head of his men. He was surrounded by turmoil. The uninjured stood dazed while underfoot the injured screamed on the blood-soaked deck.

The smoke began to clear and Robert looked for the captain, seeing for the first time the massacre that was once the front ranks. Morgan was gone and in the sight of such callous butchery Robert felt a rage unleash within him that he had never before experienced. He felt the hilt of his sword in his hand, a part of his mind wondering how he had held onto it. He tightened his grip.

A sudden visceral war cry cut through the air and Robert turned to see the Spanish rush from the gaping wounds in the bulkhead behind which the cannons still smouldered. They surged forward, a second storm of fire, and Robert saw the men around him take a step back, the wounded calling for their comrades to gather them up as panic began to engulf the English. He stepped forward. The deck upon which he stood had already been paid for with English blood. It was theirs. He raised his sword above his head.

'Stand fast, *Retribution*!' he roared and charged forward towards the Spanish.

The uninjured men to his flanks and those yet to board were temporarily stunned by the sudden call. For a moment their flight was checked. Shaw, the boatswain, was first to react, seeing the man who had saved him rush towards the enemy. He followed without hesitation.

'On, *Retribution*!' he shouted and the cheer was taken up by a dozen men, then twenty more as flight became fury and fury begat fight. They followed the master into the fray, every man on board the *Spy* taking to the gunwales to seize the prize they had come to claim.

* * *

Evardo ran out through the splintered doorframe at the head of his men, their war cries filling his heart as he beheld the ruin of the English ranks. He watched one of the enemy turn his back, then another, their hesitation turning to panic and rout in the span of a breath. He shouted anew, urging his crew on, knowing the *Halcón* was his.

A sudden cry from amidst the English ranks caught his attention and in disbelief he saw one of the enemy running towards his men, his sword raised, his face twisted in a grotesque mask of fury. The Englishman's valour rippled across the enemy ranks, gathering men up, and like a seventh wave overcoming a receding tide the shattered English attack began to coalesce, drawn together by a single man.

Evardo reacted without thought, his anger at such a reversal guiding his sword and he turned to charge directly towards the English leader. Suddenly an enemy sailor spun around in front of him, launching into an attack and Evardo was forced to defend himself, dropping his blade to parry the first strike. His sword spun in a tight arc and slashed low, beginning a sequence of strikes that Abrahan had taught him years before. Within seconds his blade sliced into the English sailor's stomach. Evardo twisted the blade savagely, hot blood and viscera gushing over his hand. He wrenched the sword back from the sucking flesh and the sailor fell with an agonized scream.

Evardo stepped back, his sword charged once more. The lines of attack were now completely merged and anarchy reigned. The Spanish charge had been blunted and absorbed. The fight was descending into a brawl and Evardo threw his sword up once more as another Englishman rushed at him. Order was lost and the desperate sounds of combat filled the air; the furious war cries and screams of men and the crack of arquebuses as bullets were fired at point blank range.

Evardo fought on, his sword guided by a desperate anger. The vision of a charging Englishman flashed through his mind. With a terrible dread, he took his first step backwards, the fury of the English attack already reaching a crescendo, spurred on by a demonic leader. The enemy sailor before him fell, but out of the corner of his eye he saw men of his own crew fall. His previous confidence fled. The odds were no longer in his favour and already beyond his control, and as he shouted for his men to take heart, he could hear the hollow ring in his own words, the desperation that spoke of a hopeless defence of a galleon already lost. Only one option remained, one chance: to strike off the head of the hydra and he sought out the English leader once more. A savage vow passed his lips as he spotted him and he charged his sword to fight across the blood soaked deck.

Robert's vision began to clear slowly and his mind registered the numbing pain in his sword arm as he hacked his blade down again and again on the upturned sword of a Spanish sailor, the defender calling out with a pleading voice that Robert could not hear or understand. He whipped his sword around, the razor edge slicing through flesh until it struck bone, and the Spaniard's cries cut short as he fell to the deck.

Robert stepped over him and sensed for the first time the men on all sides who moved forward with him. He had attacked alone, oblivious to all save the need to take the ship for the fallen but now he realized the entire crew was to his back and he pushed deeper into the fight. A bullet whipped past his head and another struck through a fold in his sleeve but still he pressed on, sensing that the pendulum of battle was poised to swing in his favour.

From the edge of his vision he saw a Spaniard rush towards

him and he spun around, throwing his sword up instinctively as the parried Spanish blade swept within a hair's breadth of his head. The Spaniard did not hesitate but came on again and Robert took his first step back as he desperately tried to defend himself against the blur of steel. He locked his gaze on his attacker, knowing the eyes betrayed the sword and suddenly realized he was fighting the Spanish commander, recognizing him as the man who led the initial enemy charge, the man who had wrought such slaughter amongst his countrymen for the fate of a galleon already sealed. He swung his blade to parry a strike before twisting it sharply. The steel edges of the two swords cut along each other, drawing the two men closer together, locking them chest to chest.

'You,' Evardo cursed in Latin, 'damn you and your God-cursed crew to hell.'

Robert's eyes darkened at the invective. 'Murderous son-of-a-whore,' he spat, 'you will rot there first.'

Robert could smell the Spaniard's breath and his face, twisted with exertion, filled his vision. Robert leaned into the attack and tightened his grip through the blood and sweat on the hilt of his sword, seeking to dominate the contest of strength. He bent his knees slightly, coiling the power of his lower body and pushed forward with all his might, breaking the bond between the two swords. The point of his blade darted under the Spaniard's sword but his opponent reacted with incredible reflexes, blocking the killing strike.

Robert reversed his attack, trying to push the Spaniard off balance, but again he recovered and the Spaniard spun his sword around, putting the momentum of his entire body into the blow, the strike of the blades numbing the fingers of Robert's hand. Evardo lunged forward, striking low, and Robert recoiled as the Spaniard's blade sliced across his exposed thigh, cutting the flesh deeply. He stepped back, his balance thrown by the leg wound, and the Spaniard came on, his attack unceasing.

Robert felt his breath catch in his constricted throat. His mouth was dry and tasted foul. He was losing and his defence became ever more frantic as he felt the serpent of fear uncoil in his stomach. The sensation angered him and he stood firm, unwilling to give another inch of ground. He slapped the next strike down with the flat of his blade, breaking the sequence of the Spaniard's attack and gritted his teeth against the pain in his leg as he centred his balance.

He jabbed his sword downwards, looking for the killing strike against the groin. Evardo blocked and made to counter strike but again Robert struck low, forcing the commander to defend. Without warning Robert slashed his sword upward and Evardo tilted back to avoid the point of the sword, hooking his own blade around. Robert followed through. The blades rasped against each other, forcing the Spaniard ever backwards and Evardo lost his footing as he pitched over the inert body of a fallen crewman.

Robert was immediately upon him, his sword darting for the Spaniard's chest. In that instant he caught sight of something that made him stop and his arm trembled as he held the point of his sword an inch from the captain's flesh.

'Yield,' he said, the muscles of his arm and shoulder calling on him to drive home the strike, his eyes locked on the crucifix hanging around the commander's neck, the reason he hesitated to deliver the fatal blow.

Evardo looked up at the mottled face of his enemy. He felt the grip of his sword and knew with certainty that if he moved to knock away the Englishman's blade he was a dead man. A curse rose to his lips but he held back, the instinct to survive surfacing through his anger. The sounds of battle swept over him and he heard the tone of desperation in the Spanish cries.

The *Halcón* was lost. What chance his crew had had been lost from the moment the English counter attacked. He looked with hatred upon the man who had precipitated that reverse.

'I yield,' he spat and he stood up slowly, his arms outstretched.

Robert kept his sword charged, wary of the Spaniard, knowing that the initial relief of salvation could rapidly twist into shame and an overriding urge to fight on.

The last of the Spanish defence collapsed quickly. Many saw their captain capitulate and they threw up their arms to plead for quarter. Others fought on, but they were hopelessly outnumbered and easily overwhelmed. As the last blow was struck, Evardo looked about the ruin that was his main deck. He drew his sword across and, taking the blade in his hand, presented the hilt to Robert.

'I am *Comandante* Evardo Alvarez Morales of the *Halcón*,' he said evenly, with only his eyes betraying the depth of his anguish and bitterness.

'Robert Varian, Master of the *Retribution*.'

Evardo nodded, noting the name. 'The ship is yours, *señor*,' he said and the words tore the fabric of his soul as he lowered his gaze to his empty sword hand. He glanced up, studying the face of his enemy. There would be another time, another battle, God would see to that, and Evardo vowed he would make the Englishman pay a heavy coin for taking the *Halcón*.

Robert stepped back through the ranks of his own men, a sword hanging loosely from each hand. He limped heavily. His breeches were already soaked through with blood and the forgotten injury to his left arm began to throb. A surge of bile rose to the back of his throat and he swallowed hard. He sheathed his own sword and reached out for the gunwale, grateful for the support. Through the remnants of battle smoke on the main deck of the *Halcón*, he looked out over the scene fading in the last light of the day.

On all sides the pillage of the Spanish supply fleet continued unabated. It was as if the slaughter onboard the galleon had never taken place and Robert sought out the *Retribution*, taking a strange comfort from the sight although he had not long known the ship. He felt a hand on his shoulder and turned. It was Shaw.

'Drink,' he said and handed Robert a flask.

Robert opened his parched lips and drank deeply. It was Madeira wine, and the liquid burned his throat. He spluttered but brought the flask back to his mouth, eager to rid himself of the foul taste of battle. He nodded to the boatswain and handed him back the flask. For a moment the wine checked the slip of his flagging strength.

'Secure the ship,' he said, 'make sure none of those poxed Spaniards are skulking below decks, and start sending the injured back to the *Retribution*.'

'Aye, Master,' Shaw replied and shouted to the men around him, organizing them quickly.

Robert felt light headed. He glanced at his injured leg. The pain had turned to a dull ache. The enemy captain's sword in his left hand felt heavy and he looked to it, pausing for the first time to examine why he had spared the Spaniard. An uncontrollable fury had driven him to charge when all around him faltered and when he had recognized the captain for who he was, that fury had only intensified. Yet he had stayed his blade from delivering the fatal strike because of the simple crucifix he had seen hanging around the Spaniard's neck.

The man was his enemy, as were all who threatened the sovereignty of Elizabeth and the sacred soil of England. But Robert shared a bond with these Spaniards, a union of faith that stopped him from striking home the point of his sword past a crucifix. His mind flooded with questions about the depths of his own loyalties but he savagely repressed them, recalling instead the blind fury of his charge, the anger he had felt at the butchery of his countrymen and captain. England commanded his loyalty first, not his faith. He repeated these words to himself as darkness began to encroach from the periphery of his vision. It quickly enveloped him and as he slipped into unconsciousness the mantra faded from his lips, replaced by a creeping doubt that his words held any meaning.

CHAPTER 4

18th May 1587. Lisbon, Portugal.

Nathaniel Young, the Duke of Greyfarne, descended from his carriage and looked out over the harbour of Lisbon. It was a magnificent sight and Young stepped forward to the edge of the dock, glancing left and right to the myriad smaller supply and ordnance ships. Further out the mighty galleons of the fledgling Spanish Armada pulled gently on their anchor lines beneath a canopy of masts and rigging. He held his breath, thinking of the day when the harbour would be filled with such ships.

'They are impressive, no?'

Young spun around and smiled as he recognized Don Rodrigo de Torres, one of King Philip's closest advisors. He was dressed in austere clothes, a black embroidered doublet and gown and a high necked jerkin that accentuated his height. It was a style made popular by the King and Young wondered if any man in Spain now dared to dress differently.

'They are indeed a blessed sight before God,' he replied, his Spanish still heavily accented even after nearly twenty years. Young was shorter than de Torres and at fifty he was older by some ten years, but he looked younger, his constant travels throughout the dominions of Europe keeping him fit and trim.

'Come, your grace,' de Torres said. He led Young from the dockside into the civic building, taking him to his office on the second floor.

The shutters of the room were open and from the height of the balcony, Young was afforded an even greater view of Lisbon's immense natural harbour. Beyond the anchored warships and merchantmen, the harbour mouth was protected by formidable forts and gun emplacements. Between the headlands Young could just make out the darker blue of the boundless Atlantic. He turned around to his host.

'You are smiling, Don de Torres,' he said. 'Is there good news?'

De Torres nodded. 'The arch-fiend *El Draque* has been driven from the walls of Lagos with heavy losses,' he said expansively. He walked behind his desk to sit down. He stretched out his hand, indicating for Young to be seated.

'That is good news,' Young replied, taking consolation from the report. The past few months had been the most anguished of his life. The death of Mary Stuart had dashed so many of his hopes. He had found peace through prayer and an almost constant vigil on the assembling Armada. Its gathering strength had reaffirmed his belief that his long exile would soon be over and his country would be brought once more into the bosom of its true mother church. Then Drake had attacked Cadiz.

'It is a significant victory, your grace,' de Torres continued, 'and one which will show Drake for the inconsequential pirate he is.'

De Torres's words caused Young to glance once more out the open window to the few ships already gathered for the Armada. Drake's raid on Cadiz had taken place over a week before and a pall of uncertainty now hung over the entire enterprise. The loss of supplies was catastrophic and with Drake now commanding the sea lanes to Lisbon, the squadrons from Seville, Biscay and Italy were indefinitely delayed. Drake, he concluded, was anything but inconsequential.

Young's innards burned with bitter frustration. Elizabeth had the devil's own luck. How many attempts on her life had she escaped? How many uprisings, in England and Ireland, had withered and died on the vine after showing such promise? Her reign was now entering its thirtieth year whereas Mary Tudor, her Catholic predecessor, had ruled for only five years, not nearly enough time to reverse the tide of reformation. Now one of her minions, Drake, was in a position to unravel the delicate plans to assemble an Armada to sail against the heretic Queen.

'What do you believe he will do next?' de Torres asked, twisting one end of his moustache with the tips of his fingers, his gaze level and penetrating.

Young considered the question, amused as always how many Spaniards thought he naturally held some insight into the workings of every English mind simply because he was English himself. He had not set foot in his native country for a shade over eighteen years. He kept an exact tally of the months and days, and the ever so brief thoughts of his exile set the door to his bitterness ajar. He slammed it shut, focusing his mind on the problem at hand.

'His defeat at Lagos is a setback, but Drake is tenacious. He will not retreat.'

De Torres nodded sagely, although he knew little of military tactics. He was a master of statecraft and the chief liaison between the Spanish court and men like Nathaniel Young.

'I would counsel caution,' Young continued. 'The garrisons in the area should remain on alert.'

'Thank you, your grace,' de Torres said. 'I will ensure your advice is passed on to the relevant commanders.'

He stood up and walked to the window, clasping his hands behind his back.

'Drake's surprise attack on Cadiz has cost us dearly,' he said after a pause.

Young noted the implicit censure in de Torres's words.

'I sent your request to the Duke of Clarsdale over a month ago,' he replied in his own defence. 'He is a trusted and capable man and, in future, I am sure we will know of the English fleet's plans in advance of any attack.'

In future, de Torres thought scornfully, although he could not openly criticize the duke. He needed the Englishman's access to the elaborate network of contacts and couriers that existed between the remaining Catholics in England and their supporters on the continent. In recent years, however, with the escalation of hostilities between Spain and England, de Torres was finding it increasingly difficult to separate his hatred for the English pirates and their Queen. Men like Young, whose faltering command of Spanish and insistence that he be addressed by his meaningless title only exacerbated de Torres's animosity.

When Young and his fellow exiled English noblemen first arrived in Spain after their failed rebellion against Elizabeth in 1569 they had been openly welcomed as victims of the heretical Queen's oppression. Patronage and support had flooded in from many of the noble families of Spain, allowing the exiles to live in a fashion befitting their titles. But now that support had all but dried up as the rising national enmity towards England stemmed the flow.

De Torres returned to his seat and looked across his desk at this English duke who remained so important to Spain's invasion plans. When Parma's army landed in England, it was vital that men such as Young be amongst the vanguard, Englishmen who could be trusted implicitly to act as guides and negotiators. So de Torres hid his aversion behind a benign expression and the courteous words of diplomacy. With God's grace there was still a chance the Armada might yet sail this season and when it did, it was de Torres's task to ensure that Young and his fellow English noblemen sailed with it.

Robert leaned back in his chair and adjusted his right leg, massaging his thigh above the wound. It hurt appallingly, but it was clean and he thanked the Lord, all too aware of the dread fate of infection. He shuddered as he vividly remembered waking after the battle in the surgeon's room on board the *Retribution.*

It was a hellish place, an enclosed compartment on the orlop deck where the air was saturated with panic and echoed with the cries of the wounded and dying, a nightmarish cacophony that still haunted Robert's dreams. He had been lying on the crude treatment table, a series of planks atop some upended water barrels, the timbers already soaked through with the blood of others. His breeches had been cut away and Powell, the surgeon, had been standing over his leg, his bloodied hands deftly probing the wound. The surgeon had worked fast, a testament to his skill, but his every touch was like the lash of a whip, a searing pain that drenched his body in acrid sweat.

Robert's vision had swirled before him, the headiness of blood loss and the heaving lantern light robbing him of the ability to focus. There were too many injured, there hadn't been time to dull each patient's senses with alcohol, and as Powell prepared to close the wound an unseen crewman behind where his head lay on the table had forced a bit between Robert's teeth.

Through the mists of pain he had seen the white-orange glow of the cauterizing iron, his eyes staring wildly in terrified anticipation. He had bit down with all his might, stifling his screams as the searing metal touched his skin while strong hands held him fast. His nostrils had filled with the smell of his own burning flesh, a sickening stench that engulfed his senses before unconsciousness mercifully claimed him once more.

Afterwards he had awoken in the cabin where he now sat and although more than a week had passed since then, he still felt ill at ease in the room. He took a drink from a goblet of wine, spoils from the Spanish supply fleet, and looked around. His eyes were drawn to the rack of sea charts on the wall and the unopened chest beneath them: Morgan's belongings.

The story of Robert's charge on the *Halcón* had spread rapidly throughout the English fleet and that action, coupled with his natural selection as second-in-command, had secured him a field promotion to captain. Drake himself had come from his flagship to confer the honour, bringing with him his chaplain, and the commander of the fleet had ordered a double ration of grog for the entire crew in recognition of their fight, prompting a cheer from the bloodied men of the *Retribution.*

There was a knock on the cabin door and Seeley entered.

'Well?' Robert asked, sitting up straighter.

'Six dead and nine wounded,' Seeley replied, 'and I fear two of those will not see tomorrow's dawn.'

'Who are they?'

Seeley listed the names and Robert repeated them silently to himself.

After Cadiz the fleet had sailed south to the Algarve coast and the fortified town of Lagos. The English had anchored five miles from the town and Drake had quickly assembled a landing party of a thousand men, taking one hundred from the *Retribution*. Owing to Robert's injury Seeley had taken charge of the *Retribution*'s levy and Robert had watched them march away, only to see the badly mauled ranks return a day later.

'A pox on the Spaniards,' Seeley spat, pacing the cabin, 'they led us all the way to the walls of Lagos before revealing their true strength.'

'We were lucky to escape so lightly,' Robert remarked, conscious that the fleet had been badly exposed while waiting at the landing point.

'It was God's will, Captain, not luck,' Seeley corrected, 'and He has opened our eyes to the perfidiousness of the enemy. We will not be so easily deceived again.'

'We will soon have cause to test that wisdom,' Robert said, leaning forward to offer Seeley a drink. The new master of the *Retribution* sat down, his expression questioning.

'The order arrived while you were below decks,' Robert explained. 'We are sailing to Sagres and Drake means to take the town.'

Seeley smiled and picked up the goblet from the table, swirling the wine within.

'*Rejoice not over me, O my enemy*,' he recited, '*when I fall, I shall rise; when I sit in darkness, the Lord will be a light to me*.'

Robert nodded, recognizing the quotation from the bible.

'It is a small port, but strategically important.' He put his goblet down to lean in over the table, wincing slightly as he shifted his leg. He pulled an opened chart across and Seeley stood up to study it. It was a detailed map of the south-western coastline of Portugal. Together they pored over the annotations regarding Sagres and its approaches.

A hurried knock on the door interrupted them and the

ship's surgeon entered without awaiting permission. His face was agitated and he advanced with his hand outstretched before him.

'What is it, Mister Powell?' Robert asked, consciously suppressing the unwanted memories resurfaced by the unexpected arrival of the surgeon.

Powell was one of the oldest members of the crew. He was a tall man but his back was curved from a lifetime of treating wounded men. He wore a heavy leather blood-stained apron and his arms were stained pink to the elbows.

'I found these in the surgery.' Powell opened his hand to reveal a silver crucifix and marble statuette of the Blessed Virgin Mary.

Seeley shot out of his chair. For the briefest moment his and Powell's full attention was on the artefacts alone. Robert knew his face betrayed the depths of his distress at the sudden revelation. He gathered his wits as Powell advanced further and looked down at the blood stained pieces the surgeon slammed onto the table.

'Papist icons,' Seeley breathed. He rounded on Powell. 'Where exactly did you find them?'

'Under my table. They were hidden under a pile of bloodied rags.'

'Who dropped them?' Seeley took a step towards the surgeon, his hand falling to the hilt of his sword.

'I don't know.' Powell glanced at the master's sword hand but remained unperturbed. A lifetime of serving aboard ship had made him immune to young men like Seeley. 'Dozens of men have been in and out of my surgery over the past twenty-four hours, both the injured and those who carried them. Where I found those,' he looked to the icons, 'hidden away like that, well, they could have been there since Cadiz.'

'A traitor,' Seeley said vehemently, turning to Robert, 'a

Roman Catholic spy, Captain, on board the *Retribution.*'

Robert held out his hand to quieten Seeley. He focused on keeping it steady. He looked again at his father's icons, furious with himself for not thinking of them earlier. Perhaps it was the pain of his wound or the pace of events since Cadiz, but whenever he had recalled his time in the surgery, he had failed to register the significance of his breeches being cut away and discarded.

He glanced at Seeley and Powell.

'Who else knows of this?'

'Only you and Mister Seeley here, Captain. I came straight to your cabin when I found them.'

Robert nodded. His best chance of suppressing any hunt was now, before it began.

'Then we will keep it that way,' he said.

'What? Why?' Seeley's eyes narrowed.

'Because, Mister Seeley,' Robert replied authoritatively, 'I do not wish to have my ship rife with suspicion until we are clear on the facts. Indeed, there may be a simpler explanation as to why Mister Powell found these icons on board. They may have been taken as plunder from a Spaniard.'

Seeley made to speak but the surgeon interjected. 'I thought that too, Captain, but then I discovered that both of these icons are inscribed with an English name.'

'Why didn't you say before, you fool!' Seeley rounded on the surgeon angrily. 'You mean to say that the traitor's name is on the icons?'

'No, Mister Seeley,' Powell said. 'For the name inscribed is not of any man on board. See here.'

He picked up the crucifix and, turning it over, rubbed his thumb along its length to remove the film of blood.

'There is the name: *Young.*'

* * *

Evardo kicked out in the darkness at the creature. The scurrying sound stopped. The rat was close, maybe inches away, and he kicked out again. The rat screeched and scuttled away. Evardo sat up. His mind was dull with fatigue but still he was unable to sleep. His skin crawled as he felt the cockroaches scurry beneath and around him. He rubbed his hand over his face, massaging his forefinger and thumb into his eyes. When he opened them again he focused on the thin shafts of light that penetrated through the cracks in the door of the cell.

He was not alone. There were four other men held captive with him in the forward section of the orlop deck of the English flagship. He listened intently as one murmured incoherently, trapped in some horrible nightmare that would not be relieved by waking. Evardo licked his lips. His mouth was dry and scummy and he reached out for the pail of water, his hand swinging through a slow arc in the darkness until he touched its rim. He picked it up and scooped his hand in, bringing the foul brackish liquid up to his mouth. It did little to quench his thirst. For a moment he was tempted to toss the pail away in anger before thinking better of it, knowing how severely the precious liquid was rationed.

When he had first been brought to the *Elizabeth Bonaventure* he had been formally welcomed by the captain of the English flagship. *El Draque*, disappointingly, had not been on deck, and Evardo had listened bitterly as the captain explained in halting Spanish the terms of his capture. He was to be brought back to England where he would be held until a ransom was paid for his release. It was an ignominious fate, one that would be shared by the four other men of noble birth who shared his quarters in the ship's bowels.

Evardo kept his gaze locked on the shafts of light. They swung slowly with the roll of the ship, sweeping across the near pitch darkness of the cell. He held out his right hand, his sword hand, to allow the feeble light to catch it. He vividly recalled that moment on the *Halcón* after he had handed over his weapon to the Englishman, Varian. Since then, and with a deep sense of shame, he had asked himself if he should not have fought on and accepted the price of death for his honour.

After Varian had walked away from him, he had been jostled, along with the rest of his crew, into the fo'c'sle. His first reaction had been to look for Abrahan. When he saw the older man push through the throng to approach him, he had begun to smile, glad to see his old friend safe. That smile had died on his lips when he beheld the murderous look on Abrahan's face.

'You cursed *cobarde*,' he had hissed, and Evardo had recoiled from the accusation of cowardice.

'I was bested, there was nothing I could do, the fight . . .'

'You surrendered your ship like some Portuguese *hijo de puta* and betrayed your command and your crew!'

'Betrayed?' Evardo had hissed back, dropping his hand to clasp the sword that was no longer by his side. 'After the English counter-attacked, there was nothing we could do, you know that.'

'Then you should have paid for the loss of the *Halcón* with your blood, not your sword.'

Evardo had made to reply, but Abrahan had turned his back on him, pushing through the surrounding crewmen who had heard every word of the exchange. Evardo had looked at them, and while many had averted their gaze, others had stared back with accusing eyes, persuaded by Abrahan's words that their captain had indeed betrayed the *Halcón* and its crew.

In the quiet of the cell Evardo pictured his mentor in his mind's eye. The image brought a flash of anger to his heart but then he thought of the years of comradeship and support that Abrahan had given him. Under his tutelage he had crossed the world, making the leap from boy to man. In many ways Evardo had come to consider Abrahan as the father he had lost to war. As a *comandante* he was accustomed to a solitary existence but for the first time he felt very alone. The feeling sickened him.

In the darkness he closed his hand into a tight fist. The shame of his defeat threatened to overwhelm him, to unman him in that black space, but with savage determination he crushed his regret. Evardo gave his mind over to the boom of the waves striking the hull and the creak of timbers. The journey ahead would be long, but eventually he would return to Spain, and he focused his thoughts on that day. Using the powerful influence of his family he would seek another galleon command. His honour demanded nothing less. Only then would he be able to take the first step in fulfilling the vow that had now become the centre of his being: revenge.

Above the swirling mists of gun smoke surrounding the English fleet in the waters off Sagres, a lookout on the *Elizabeth Bonaventure* spotted the raising of a white flag. He shouted it down to the quarterdeck and across the fleet the order was given to cease fire. In the quiet that followed, Robert looked out across the untroubled waters to the town's castle. The bombardment had lasted a mere two hours, a savage cannonade that had pierced the battlements in several places and silenced the garrison's return of fire. Black smoke was rising from within, billowing past the crude flag of surrender, and on the gentle breeze Robert could hear the desperate cries of a cornered populace.

'Ho quarterdeck, *Cygnet* approaching on the starboard beam.'

'Ahoy, Captain Varian.'

'Ahoy, Captain Bell,' Robert shouted back, raising his arm.

'Orders from the *Elizabeth Bonaventure*, Captain,' Bell called. 'You are to tranship eighty men to the *Cygnet* to join the shore party. Commander Drake has already gone ashore to accept the surrender of the Spanish garrison.'

Robert acknowledged the command and ordered the boatswain to the quarterdeck.

'Mister Shaw, call out and arm the men of the dog watch. Have them assemble on the main deck.'

Seeley approached as Shaw's voice rang out across the *Retribution*.

'With your permission, Captain,' the master said, 'I'd like to join the shore party.'

Robert considered the request. He had already decided, despite his injury, that he would be going ashore. The *Spy* and two other pinnaces were patrolling five miles further out to sea, providing a screen for the landings. Any approach by hostile ships would be spotted well in advance. He looked to Seeley, seeing the justifiable eagerness on his face given the drubbing he received at Lagos. He smiled.

'Permission granted, Mister Seeley. Inform Mister Shaw that he will have command of the *Retribution* while we are ashore.'

'Thank you, Captain,' Seeley replied with a roguish grin. He hurried after the boatswain, adding his voice to the call for order on the main deck.

Moments later the *Cygnet* pulled away from the galleon and turned sharply around its stern. Across the sweep of the fleet, a flotilla of pinnaces was sailing in towards the small port, their decks crammed with men. Robert stood on the bow of the *Cygnet*, his balance shifting with the fall of the deck. Behind him were the chosen men of his crew, their silence a thin veneer that scarcely concealed their expectation.

They were heavily armed but few men were identically

equipped. Robert wore a breastplate of armour, as did over a dozen of his crew. Many of these were cast-offs from previous battles while others wore morions, the ubiquitous helmet of European soldiers. Each man had a sword and at least one dagger and while the primary weapon of the majority was an arquebus gun, the more hidebound veterans were armed with halberds, bills and crossbows. Only two men carried longbows, weapons they had known since childhood and could never be relinquished for another.

Robert bore one other unique firearm, a wheellock pistol, an expensive weapon that he had found amongst Morgan's belongings and he unconsciously fingered the elaborate mechanism as he thought of the man who had previously led the crew behind him into battle.

He looked ahead to the surf-worn beach that skirted the edge of the town. A lone boat was beached there: Drake's launch. Beyond it Robert spotted the fleet commander appear from the town with an escort of heavily armed soldiers. Walking with him was a Spaniard, evidentially the garrison commander.

The longboats rode in through the surf and disgorged their men onto the beach before returning to the pinnaces to gather more. Robert went in with the first of his crew and jumped out into the crashing waves as the boat touched bottom. The cold water helped to ease the throbbing in his leg and he waded ashore.

Within twenty minutes seven hundred English landed, gathering in motley ranks behind their commanders. All the while Drake stood immovable at the head of the beach, his head turning slowly as his gaze ranged over the men. Robert could see he was talking to the Spanish commander out of the corner of his mouth, his expression solemn and imperious. Drake was not physically striking, and his dark curly hair and fairer beard made his age hard to determine. He projected a definite air of authority that belied his humble beginnings, and his gaze was penetrating and direct.

A sense of awe never failed to affect Robert when he was in Drake's presence. He was the first Englishman to circumnavigate the world, an explorer and privateer who commanded the Queen's deepest affections and God's own luck. That four out of five ships had been lost during his circumnavigation and Drake had executed his friend for mutiny mattered little. The *Golden Hind* had returned brimming with gold, silver, spices, and precious stones that netted a near fifty-fold profit for the crown and a knighthood for Drake. To sail with Drake was to benefit from his uncanny ability to survive and profit and the men behind Robert fell into expectant silence as their commander stepped forward.

'Men!' he shouted, his hand sweeping out over Sagres. 'The town is yours. Take it.'

The men erupted in a savage cheer, surging forward like a pack of baying wolves. They attacked, streaming up the beach and between the outlying buildings, jostling angrily at the choke-points as all sought to be the first to savour the plunder of the town.

Robert went with them, his slower pace making him the victim of shouldered charges as men ran around him. One struck him heavily and he was about to fall when a hand grabbed his upper arm to steady him. It was Seeley. Robert smiled amidst the cheers as the last of the crew of the *Retribution* passed them. They reached the whitewashed houses that marked the edge of the town and Robert became aware of the new sound beneath the cheering Englishmen – the tortured screams of the population. Shots rang out from all sides as sailors and soldiers began to kill all who stood in their way.

Robert drew his wheellock pistol from his belt. He held it loosely in his hand and looked left and right down the narrow side streets. The door of every house and hovel was open. The raiders were everywhere, streaming from one place to another, many with booty already in hand. Others stood drinking and carousing, laughing wildly as they upended any bottle they could find. The shrieks of women could be heard above everything and Robert saw one attempt to flee from a house only to be chased and run down by a sailor who dragged her back inside.

He looked at Seeley walking beside him. The youth's face was pale, his eyes darting everywhere at once, and his mouth was whispering unintelligible words. Robert had witnessed the aftermath of a sacking many years before on the Spanish Main, and his time spent on the slave trade had long since hardened him to the cruelties of men. From Seeley's expression, he could only devise that this was the young man's first experience of the fate that awaited every civilian at the hands of an army let loose.

Cheering could no longer be heard. Instead the air was filled with terrible sounds that seemed to emanate from the pit of Hades, the cries and wailing of a people given over to the base desires of men toughened in the forge of battle. The infrequent crack of an arquebus mixed with the angry shouts of Englishmen, fuelled by wine and avarice, fighting over the meagre offerings of the small town. The dead lay everywhere, the men shot or run through with steel while the women had been raped, beaten and discarded. The terror of their final moments was still etched on their faces.

Robert and Thomas reached the main square. On one side the western face of a small church stood tall above the buildings flanking it. A group of men were at the doors, trying to force them open. Without hesitation Robert rushed forward.

He switched his pistol to his left hand and drew his sword. Seeley followed, surprised by the sudden haste. The square was in chaos with men running in all directions, but Robert kept his course firmly fixed on the church door, his face twisting in anger, the pain in his leg forgotten.

'Hold,' he shouted, charging his sword before him.

The sailors turned and brought their own weapons quickly to bear.

'Piss off, sailor,' one of them snarled, ''less you want your blood spilled. This here's our place.'

Seeley came up. Once he had seen the captain's destination he had understood immediately and the anger he saw on Robert's face confirmed it. He felt his own religious fervour rise within him.

'Captain Varian, maybe there's another way in,' he suggested.

'Captain Varian . . .' one of the men repeated and the others lowered their weapons, mindful of the tale they had heard of the captain's charge on the Spanish galleon. Their expressions remained belligerent, suspicious that the officers had intervened so they could claim whatever plunder was inside for themselves.

Robert's mind was in turmoil. He had rushed to the church door to defend it without thinking. Then he realized he could not, for how would he explain his actions? He felt the weight of the sword and pistol in his hands. This was a Catholic church. He should defend it. But he was the commander of a Protestant crew. He could not justifiably stop them, not without coming close to revealing his faith.

'Who's inside, men?' Seeley asked, stepping forward.

'Some shit stinkin' priest,' one of the sailors replied. 'We saw him close the door as we came into the square.'

'We want into that strong box that papists have in their churches,' another said, referring to the tabernacle, and the others voiced their agreement, one of them taking up the shout again for the priest inside to open the doors.

Seeley took charge, ordering two men to find something to ram the door. They returned moments later with a stout wooden bench. The men attacked the door with unbridled aggression and the boom of the battering ram brought more men from around the square. The timbers of the door gave way under the onslaught and the sailors cheered as they pushed their way through. Robert tried to shoulder his way in with the leading edge of the charge, anxious to protect the priest inside, believing that he could somehow excuse his mercy later.

The sailors spilled into the church, the original group in the lead. Their anger and haste were heightened by the dozens of men at their rear, knowing the spoils they sought were under threat. Robert stumbled in. His eyes searched frantically in the gloom of the interior for the priest. The Spaniard was running up the centre aisle, sailors on his heels. Robert watched in horror as one of them raised his arquebus. He swung up his own pistol, bringing it to bear on the sailor's back. He hesitated and the pistol shook in his hand. A second later a blast rang out. The sailor had shot the priest at near point-blank range. His head snapped forward under the hammer blow of the lead ball before he fell to the floor.

'You men,' Seeley roared near at hand. 'Tear down those statues.'

Robert spun around, his rage threatening to slip its bonds. The men quickly desecrated the church, pulling down the ornate statues and smashing them underfoot, while the air resounded with the clang of metal as the sailors attacked the tabernacle doors with their weapons.

'Blasphemous idolaters,' Seeley cursed.

Robert was possessed by the urge to run the man through

but he turned and walked out, unable to trust himself in the face of such destruction. He stood with his back to the church and looked out over the square. Suddenly he became conscious of the pistol in his hand and he stuck it back in his belt. He had thought nothing of the destruction of the town and the massacre of the population; the Spanish were enemies. But the threat against the church and the priest had driven him to the brink of drawing English blood.

He had not, but the shame of witnessing such an attack and doing nothing to prevent it began to consume him. He walked away, anxious to get back to the *Retribution* and find solitude to calm the rancorous voice of his conscience. In his heart he was already convinced it was a hopeless cause.

Seeley watched the captain leave from inside the church doors. He was breathing heavily and his heart raced from the righteousness that had taken hold of him. He was cleansing the church for God, ridding it of its idols and graven images. Although he knew many of his men sought only plunder, others had responded instantly to his order to tear down the statues, answering the call of their faith.

The captain too had answered that call and Seeley remembered the haste he had witnessed when they first encountered the church, the aggressive way Varian had pushed through when the door had been breeched and how he had raised his pistol to shoot the priest. But then the captain had hesitated. His furious expression had been a sight to behold, an outward sign of his religious ardour yet, Seeley marked, he had not taken command of the men, nor stayed to watch the faithful propagation of God's will. Seeley had also heard the accounts of the captain's fearless charge on the *Halcón*, but again of how he had spared the Spanish captain. While he had no doubt that his captain was committed to the cause of defeating Spain, Seeley could not help wondering if Varian's religious convictions matched the depth of his nationalist loyalties.

It was a deficiency Seeley had witnessed in others, an imbalance that placed the Queen above God and put the needs of England ahead of those of the Divine. Varian's actions bore witness to the tenets of his Protestant beliefs which triggered his impulse to attack the idolaters' church and shoot the priest, but for Seeley such religious instincts ran deeper.

When Seeley had first entered the town he had been sickened by the depravity he had witnessed in the streets and it had taken all his will not to vomit up the bile that had risen in his throat. But then he had remembered the defeat at Lagos. The Spaniards deserved no mercy. In the fight against the scourge of Roman Catholic heresy there could be no hesitation, no half-measures. He turned once more to look upon the ruin of the church interior and realized it was his duty to instil in every man he could influence the will to wage unconditional holy war against the papist foe.

CHAPTER 5

6th July 1587. Plymouth, England.

The crew cheered as the anchor splashed down and the *Retribution* came to rest, her hull swinging around gently with the pull of the incoming tide. The last of the sails were hauled in and with all able hands on deck the galleon was quickly made secure, the men using their last reserves of strength with an alacrity born of hunger and impatience. Robert was on the quarterdeck and as he looked out over the port he smiled. 'Home,' he whispered, drinking in the sight of Plymouth docks

The town looked inviting in the warm July sun. The long sweep of the teeming wharfs was crowned by columns of wood smoke from the cooking fires of the houses beyond, while further back the tower of Saint Andrew's church gazed over all. The babble of daily activity was borne on the light wind, its timbre and pitch unchanged despite the arrival home of the fleet. Robert glanced at the eight other ships surrounding the *Retribution*, the remnants of the original fleet that had sailed from this port ten weeks before.

After the sack of Sagres, Drake had ordered the fleet to take station off Cape Saint Vincent. They had intercepted dozens of supply ships bearing all manner of materials for the Armada at Lisbon; timbers for ship-building, oars for galleys and galleasses, and hoops and barrel staves for provisioning the enemy fleet. It had been fruitful labour but as the weeks dragged on an enemy more deadly than the Spanish had begun to attack the fleet; pestilence.

The morale of the fleet had died with the first fatality and as more and more fell ill, Robert, like every other captain, had found it increasingly difficult to keep his crew in check. A sudden violent storm precipitated the first flights towards home, with the smaller ships, under the pretence of necessity, turning for England while they still had sufficient crew to sail them. Even the news of a rich prize approaching the Azores, a trading carrack bound for Lisbon from Genoa, could not stem the tide. Men who had rushed fearlessly into battle cowered before the dreaded ship-fever. The crew of the *Golden Lion*, with the fleet's second officer, Borough, on board had turned her bow northwards despite the entreaties of their captain.

Where lesser men might have succumbed, Drake had rallied, persuading the remaining crews to sail west to San Miguel. His resolve had been rewarded and a dawn attack by the last nine ships had yielded an enormous prize – the *Sao Phelipe*, a Portuguese carrack that was one of the Spanish King's own vessels. After this enormous coup, Drake had been content to end the expedition and the *Elizabeth Bonaventure* had finally led the bedraggled fleet home.

Of Robert's command, seven men had been lost to sickness while another thirty were isolated below decks, the men shivering in their hammocks, crying out in delirium, their bodies racked by fever. Some would survive, God would choose who, and Robert murmured a prayer for all. He wondered, like all sailors, what cursed element triggered the dread disease.

'The ship is secure, Captain,' Seeley said, coming up to the quarterdeck. His frame was lean and drawn from the rigours of the previous weeks.

'Very well,' Robert replied. 'Have the men stand down. Mister Powell will need to see each of them before any can disembark to make sure none of them have ship-fever.'

The master nodded. He ordered the ship's surgeon to the main deck, then called the boatswain to come aft.

'Captain,' Seeley began, as Shaw arrived, 'I would like to question the men one last time before they disembark.'

Robert tried to hide his irritation, but he saw the master's expression change to a frown of annoyance and knew his own face had betrayed him.

Since the discovery of the idols, Seeley's search for the Catholic on board had been relentless. Every crewman had been subjected many times to Seeley's questions while Shaw had assisted his efforts, watching the crew in their unguarded moments below decks when off watch. Many of the crew had reacted with fury when they had first heard of the traitor amongst them. They had vowed to help the master hunt him down but Seeley had refused to trust anyone on board. His obstinate suspicion had eventually put the entire crew on edge, exacerbating the fleet-wide scourges of disease and short supplies.

Robert had been on the cusp of ending the hunt many times, but on each occasion he had hesitated, unsure if his motivation was to guard the dwindling morale of his crew or his own safety. The responsibilities of his rank had continually decided the issue, but at the cost of his patience at Seeley's ever increasing obsession to cleanse the *Retribution* of treachery. This final request to question the exhausted crew could not be countenanced.

'This is our last chance,' Seeley said. 'Once the traitor goes ashore he is bound to disappear.'

'We might still catch him, Captain,' Shaw added, his own enthusiasm for the hunt fuelled by frustration.

'No,' Robert said, 'there will be no further questioning.'

Seeley was about to protest but Robert held up his hand.

'You are dismissed, Mister Shaw,' he said to the boatswain. 'Inform the men of the morning and fore-noon watches that they may go ashore.'

Shaw hesitated for a second before nodding his assent and leaving the quarterdeck.

Robert drew Seeley over to the bulwark. 'You have done enough, Thomas,' he said soothingly, taking a different tack, 'and God has brought us home safe. Be content with that.'

'But a traitor still walks amongst us,' Seeley replied vehemently, glancing unconsciously over his shoulder to the assembled men on the main deck.

'The man you seek might have fallen at Lagos, or may have been one of those who succumbed to fever and was buried at sea.'

Seeley shook his head. 'I searched all the belongings of every man who died and found nothing, no further evidence.'

He paused for a moment, searching the captain's face. 'Don't you want to catch the traitor?' he asked accusingly.

Robert felt his temper flare up but he held it in check. 'Of course I do, Thomas,' he said, endeavouring to sound sincere, a hard edge to his voice. 'But I also have a duty to the crew. They have endured much and deserve to be stood down.'

Seeley could not understand the captain's priorities. How could he allow for even the slightest possibility that the traitor might escape. The captain was Protestant. Did he not feel the fury that burned in Seeley's chest at the thought of a Roman Catholic spy amongst them?

Seeley understood the hardships the crew had endured. He had felt them too, but such mortal suffering was nothing to the torments that would befall those who did not tirelessly prosecute the heretic. No one could ignore the warning in Revelations; that those who were neither cold nor hot, but lukewarm in their actions, would be spat out by God.

'*Do not be slothful in zeal, be fervent in spirit, serve the Lord,*' he quoted, desperate to persuade the captain to grant him permission. 'I tell you, Captain, the Roman Catholic fiend is still alive and even now his breath befouls us all. I must be given one last chance.'

'They are to be given shore leave in watches,' Robert said coldly, his patience at an end, knowing that Seeley would not relent. 'I forbid you from questioning them again. Is that understood?'

The corner of Seeley's mouth twitched in anger and for a moment he stared into Robert's eyes. 'Yes, Captain,' he growled and strode from the quarterdeck.

Robert watched him go below, his own anger burning the back of his throat. He looked out over Plymouth again, trying to recapture the consolation he had felt only minutes before. It was gone. The veneer had been shattered by Seeley and now the thoughts that had haunted him since the attack on Sagres came back once more. 'God has brought us home safe. Be content with that,' he had said to Seeley, but the words were as hollow to him as they had been to the master. Home was not Plymouth. Home was twenty miles east, in Brixham. Robert decided that he would travel there the moment he was relieved of his duty.

The enormous estate house stood nestled on the slope of a vale deep in the heart of Devon. Woodland flanked it on both sides while to the front an ornate garden ran down to the small river that flowed along the valley floor. It was a magnificent house with soaring windows that spoke of the wealth of its owner. The surrounding woodlands hid the myriad buildings attached to the estate save for the spire of a family chapel that reached above even the tallest trees.

On the crest of the opposing slope a copse overlooked the valley floor. It was heavily overgrown with bramble bushes and ferns. Just inside its boundary a man stood motionless. He was John Cross, an agent of the Crown who reported directly to one of the Queen's closest advisors, Sir Francis Walsingham.

With a steady gaze Cross looked across the breadth of the estate buildings and he smiled contemptuously at the overt display of faith that was the family chapel, vowing silently that one day he would visit the chapel and thank God for the demise of its owner.

A loud snort echoed from the trees behind him and Cross spun around. His horse was tethered some twenty yards away. Cross picked up the sounds of approach a moment later and his hand fell to the pistol in his belt. He crouched slightly, his every sense on alert as he tried to read the sound. He saw a flash of dark clothing, and another, and a figure emerged from the dense undergrowth. Cross straightened up slightly, recognizing the man, but he remained wary, his eyes darting around to ensure he was approaching alone.

'You're late,' he cursed.

'Beg you pardon, sir,' the man replied penitently. 'But I couldn't get here faster. The good weather has every gardener and gamekeeper abroad.'

Cross grunted angrily. He had been waiting for nearly an hour, a reckless amount of time. His discovery could have disastrous consequences. He stared stonily at the older man as he covered the remaining yards. 'Well?'

'The priest was last here nearly two months ago. I let him in myself through the kitchen door. He met with the duke in his private study.'

'Tell me everything you heard,' Cross said distractedly, expecting to hear little of any import. The duke was a minor threat, a peripheral player. Cross's surveillance was merely routine.

The man's name was Nichols, and his family had been in the service of the Duke of Clarsdale for three generations. Nichols was the duke's butler, while his wife and three sons were also in the employ of the estate, although Cross had never met them, nor knew if they were aware of Nichols's clandestine activities. The butler relayed the entire conversation between the duke and the priest with remarkable attention to detail. As he spoke, Cross stepped forward instinctively, the substance of the report was more important than he had imagined.

'This was their only private meeting?'

'Yes, the priest stayed only one night. The entire household, including the duke, attended mass shortly after dawn the next day. The priest left immediately after.'

Cross noticed how sneeringly Nichols said mass. His hatred for the ceremony was obvious, made more acute by the fact that he had to masquerade as a faithful Roman Catholic. Cross admired the butler. The risks he himself took were significant but in serving the Crown Nichols had placed his entire family in harm's way.

Cross asked Nichols to repeat the latter half of the conversation, stopping him at points to question him further. The answers were disturbing. Clarsdale's plan to build a private army to meet a Spanish invasion was troublesome but not critical. Such a force had been part of nearly every plot that involved a foreign power. A pre-emptive gathering of men would be difficult to conceal however, and could be neutralized long before a Spaniard appeared on the horizon. The duke's request for an informer in the English fleet was a more alarming prospect. This one man had the potential to be more damaging than a thousand men-at-arms. The composition, deployment and strength of the fleet had to remain secret from the Spanish.

Clarsdale's request also meant he was in more direct contact with the Spanish than Cross had believed. But through which route? There were a number of prominent English traitors working with the Spanish hierarchy in Spain. Any one of them could be Clarsdale's handler.

'The priest hasn't returned since?' he asked Nichols.

'No.'

'When is he due next?'

'A week after the new moon, perhaps ten days from now.'

Cross nodded. There was a little time.

'Listen,' he said, leaning in closer to Nichols. 'The last of the fleet arrived back in Plymouth three days ago. It is possible the priest will be able to secure his man before he meets with the duke. He will have other news, numbers, maybe even names of the men he has acquired as soldiers. Ignore this information. Concentrate only on finding out the name of the informer.'

Nichols nodded.

'Now go. I will be here every day at noon for one hour on the week after the priest is due.'

The butler moved away through the undergrowth. Within a minute Cross was left with only the sounds of nature. He looked to the estate house again. Clarsdale was cleverer than he had believed, and far more connected than he had ever suspected. That the duke was secretly a Roman Catholic had been known for some time and when Nichols had quietly made it known to the local Protestant dean that he was willing to spy on Clarsdale, Cross had received the news with only minor interest. He had set up the initial meetings, wary at first of the butler because his information was unsolicited. He had searched for signs of subterfuge at each meeting. He had found none however, and confident of his judgement and experience, he had come to trust the butler, although his information to date had only confirmed what Cross had long held: that the duke was merely a sympathizer and not an active conspirator.

Now all was changed. Walsingham would need to be informed immediately. Cross walked quickly to his horse and mounted her in one fluid sweep, walking her through to the other side of the copse before spurring her to a full gallop out into the open field beyond.

Father Blackthorne stretched out his arms and gazed up at the east facing window. His voice rose above the murmur of his congregation and his words soon dominated the tiny enclosed room. He narrowed his eyes against the white glare of the morning sun streaming through the plain opaque glass. In his imagination, he pictured a beautiful stained glass image depicting the crucifixion of Christ. It was the window in Saint Anne's, the little church where he had celebrated his first mass as an ordained priest some thirty-five years before. The image was forever close to his heart, a reminder of the times when he had been able to observe his faith in public.

'*Ite missa est*,' he intoned, ending the mass. As the congregation responded, he led them in the last Gospel, striving as always to draw strength from the verses of Saint John, seeking the courage and hope to go on.

Why? To what end? He immediately tried to suppress the thought, angry at himself for questioning his lot. Father Blackthorne was shamed by the unexpected lapse in devotion, the moment of weakness, and yet the voice refused to quieten. *For the true faith.* But the answer could no longer stifle the gnawing protests from his body and mind at the hardships he was forced to endure; the hunger and deprivation, the constant fear of capture that whittled away his nerve.

Again he tried to recapture the ardour and confidence he had felt in the first years after Elizabeth's coronation, when he secretly returned to England to fight the reformation of the church. However that was almost three decades ago. He was a young man then, but that strength was gone forever. Now only hope remained. He pushed his doubts to the recesses of his mind as the final words of the service were spoken.

Father Blackthorne blessed himself and, rising slowly, turned to the four people knelt behind him. He nodded to them with a smile and they rose up, coming to him in turn for an individual blessing – Catherine and William Varian first, then their two servants.

The servants immediately took their leave and Father Blackthorne invited the couple to sit once more.

'That was a beautiful service,' Catherine said. The tone of her words suggested to Father Blackthorne that she somehow understood, and perhaps shared, his inner fears. He took comfort from the belief.

'Thank you, Catherine,' he replied, taking her hand in his, feeling less alone. He saw William glance towards the door. He was a tall man with a full beard and balding pate. When he looked back to the priest, and noticed that his glance had been observed, he coloured slightly. Father Blackthorne smiled.

'There's still time, William,' he said kindly.

'Forgive me, Father, my mind should not wander to such things in this place.'

'It's all right. You must protect your family.'

William nodded and Father Blackthorne reached out with his other hand, placing it on William's forearm.

The daily Protestant service would begin at 7 a.m. in Brixham town church and William would be expected to attend, as were all the prominent men of the town. It was a duality that Father Blackthorne knew he should condemn but in his heart he could not. William Varian was entirely faithful to the Catholic creed and Father Blackthorne understood that his survival, and the welfare of his family, depended on his outwardly cherishing the Protestant faith.

Catherine was the guardian of his spiritual integrity, maintaining a vigil in the tiny room the family used as a secret chapel while her husband attended Protestant services. There she offered prayers for his soul, begging forgiveness and understanding from God for the weakness of wishing to survive.

As William rose to leave the room, Father Blackthorne stood with him.

'*In nomine Patris, et Filii, et Spiritus Sancti*,' he whispered over William's bowed head.

'Thank you, Father,' William said, straightening up his shoulders.

'Go with God, my son. I will be here when you return to hear your confession.'

William left and Father Blackthorne knelt with Catherine before the table that served as an altar. When in Brixham, he would always pray with her while William risked his soul in the Protestant church, comforting her when tears of guilt overwhelmed her, reminding her that God forgave the penitent. Upon the table stood a crucifix and a simple cup that the family used as a chalice. They were flanked by two candles. Father Blackthorne bowed his head and began to recite the joyful mysteries of the Rosary.

He thought of how each time he returned to a town or village, he found that his flock had diminished further. Not a half-mile away, a congregation was being led by the local vicar with readings from the Common Book of Prayer, and soon their voices would be raised in song, in a church that was once Catholic. Many of the congregation had never known a time when Elizabeth was not on the throne, and for them Protestantism was the natural faith of the realm. The conversion of the older people encompassed myriad reasons – many were unable to withstand the pressure to conform, while others believed they had found a more faithful path to God.

For Father Blackthorne the threat of discovery grew with each willing or unwilling victim of the heresy. He could only hope that none had yet spoken out because of some sense of previously held loyalty. But more and more often, call signs went unanswered and doors that had once been open to him were now firmly shut. Some of the occupants pleaded with him to leave as they feared exposure, while others damned him with the righteous zeal of neophytes. He knew his precarious freedom could not last and he shuddered slightly when he thought of the fate that awaited him should he fall into the hands of the Protestant authorities.

He looked sideways at Catherine. She was the fountainhead of faith for her family, her courage and conviction matched only by that of her husband and children.

He found the courage to go on – 'For them,' he said silently, answering his previous question with the certainty of realization. He listened intently to Catherine's responses to his prayers, hearing anew the sincerity with which she spoke and seeing the utter rapture on her face as she gazed upon the crucifix.

As he turned to the window he saw the stained glass image clearer in his mind's eye than ever before. Where there was faith, there was hope, and in this room, this tiny chapel, the faith of Catherine Varian was all encompassing.

* * *

Thomas Seeley stopped for a moment at the wooden gate. His hand played over the weather worn timber as he looked up the gentle slope of the path to the two storey house. Its walls were covered in verdant ivy and the stillness of the scene was one of the visions he had treasured in his memory during the months he had been away. He pushed open the gate, the hinges protesting with a loud creak that drowned out the drone of insects, and he walked up the path, stopping once more before reaching the door.

Seeley looked over his shoulder and took in the familiar view. As so many times before, his eye was drawn to the western edge of the horizon and the large manor house some four miles distant. It was the home of his mother's cousin, the Marquess of Wenborough. Palatial in size, it was a home befitting the title and wealth of the family and Seeley's eyes narrowed, his deep seated animosity rising unbidden at the view he had beheld his entire life. The house behind him, his own family home, was an estate cottage, a one-time hunting lodge that his mother's cousin had granted the Seeley family when their title had been returned by Queen Elizabeth.

That act of charity was an open wound in Seeley's honour that would not heal. Its pain was sharpened by the knowledge that the Wenborough family had survived the reign of Mary Tudor unscathed by adhering to the changing religion of the monarchy. Their faith swung with the prevailing wind and, under Elizabeth, they were now staunchly Protestant.

But Seeley's own paternal grandparents had been burned at the stake for their faith ten years before he was born. As a child he had read, with terrified fascination, John Foxe's *Book of Martyrs*, poring over it secretly in his bed at night. The woodcut prints depicting the executions ordered by Bloody Mary were forever burned into his memory. Even now, in his maturity, they haunted his nightmares, reducing him to effeminate tears of terror each time.

Seeley turned his back on the distant horizon and walked the remaining steps to the front door of his home. It was open and as he stepped inside he met Barker, the senior servant of three, rounding a corner. The older man was momentarily surprised before an unaffected smile transformed his face.

'Master Thomas. You're home.'

Seeley smiled. 'I am, Barker, and it is good to see you well.'

The older man's smile deepened. He liked the youngest son of the family and was glad to see him safe.

'Are my parents home?'

'Your mother is in the garden,' Barker replied, spinning on his heel to lead Seeley through the house. 'Your father is in London and is due back in a fortnight.'

Seeley nodded, disappointed that his father was not home, although he had been prepared for such news.

Despite his title his father was obliged to work as a merchant in order to support the family. It was contrary to his birthright but if the family's fortune was to be rebuilt the offence would have to be borne. Seeley's two older brothers had taken up the mantle of responsibility on reaching maturity. They, like Seeley, were rarely at home. As Seeley walked through the hallway, he found himself glancing in every direction, taking in the familiar, gathering strength from it.

Seeley's mother was sitting under the shade of a sprawling oak tree in the back garden and her son was almost upon her before she looked up. She rushed to her youngest son, embracing him fiercely.

'I prayed for you,' she whispered through tears.

'I'm home.' He held her embrace for a long time before leading her back into the shade.

'Your father is away,' she said.

'Barker said. And my sisters?'

'They are out walking, but will be returning soon. Oh, it is good to see you, Thomas.'

He reached out and placed a hand on her forearm, reassuring her once more, and they began to talk of inconsequential things with Seeley asking after each member of his family in turn. His mother responded to each question gaily but Seeley sensed her happiness was only a brittle façade and she soon lapsed into silence.

'I feared for you,' she said, holding his gaze steadily.

'I was in God's care.'

'We are all in God's hand,' she quoted and Seeley nodded solemnly.

'Was the enterprise successful?'

'More than we could have hoped,' Seeley replied proudly. 'My share of the purse should be significant, enough perhaps for us to increase our holdings. The heretic Spanish have been badly bloodied. Drake is confident that their Armada will not sail this season.'

'*And in your steadfast love you will cut off my enemies, and you will destroy all the adversaries of my soul, for I am your servant*,' his mother recited.

'Amen,' Seeley replied but noticed that his mother was crying again.

'I'm sorry. I should not ask about such things, but . . .'

She covered her face with her hands and sobbed, her shoulders shuddering with each breath she tried to draw. 'They took everything. That antichrist Philip, and Mary, I pray her soul burns forever in hellfire. They left your father with nothing . . . and now we . . . we live . . .' Tears overwhelmed her.

Seeley tightened his grip on her forearm, trying to reach her through her grief. He knew he could not. It was a scene he had witnessed too many times, from his youngest days, and the dormant anger within him reared its head once more.

He had never known the life his mother remembered, the life she had enjoyed in her youth and for the brief years after she married Seeley's father. That social status and wealth had been seared from their grasp by the flames of execution. They had emerged from hiding with the death of Mary Tudor and the ascension of Elizabeth but the lives they had known before were lost forever. Privilege had become strife and over the years their pride was slowly consumed by supplication and labour.

Now his mother was a broken spirit, a shell of a woman, forced to watch her family scatter to the four winds in order to survive. Her loneliness and despair were palpable and Seeley fed off them, using them to fuel the fire of his hatred for the Roman Catholic foe. His thoughts went to the faceless traitor on board the *Retribution* and how he had slipped through his fingers. It was a bitter failure, one he could not dismiss. Despite Captain Varian's suggestion that the traitor might be dead, Seeley was more convinced than ever that he was not.

Seeley had stood squarely with his countrymen and taken the fight to the Spaniards. They had destroyed the fleet at Cadiz, sacked the town of Sagres and cleansed its church, and taken dozens of supply ships, severely wounding the Armada. But it was not enough, not while even one Roman Catholic breathed English air. He would cleanse the realm of their heresy. He would do it for his faith, for his Queen, and finally, his other hand reaching forth to draw his mother into an embrace, for his family.

Robert stood in the middle of the street and slowly rubbed his leg. It was throbbing again after the horseback ride from Plymouth over sun-baked roads and he tentatively scratched the tingling skin above and below the wound. He straightened up to look down the length of the hill to the enclosed harbour of Brixham. All manner of fishing craft were moored there, many of them beached in the low tide. Robert tried to pick out his father's boat from among the larger ones. He could not but he smiled as he thought of the craft in which he had first learned to sail.

Robert had never seen the sea before he came to Brixham when he was twelve. He could still remember the moment when he crested the hill on which the town was built and looked down over the expanse of water. It was a sight he had found both fascinating and fearsome. He vividly recalled the terror he had felt when his adopted father had first taken him to sea to learn his trade. Since that day Robert had come to know and appreciate every facet of the sea, its treachery and power, its beauty and endless opportunity. He had long since come to respect it – although he would never love it as he knew William Varian did.

Robert crossed the street and knocked on the door of the town house. It was one of the larger houses in the town, built in the more affluent area near the top of the hill. Robert looked over the roofs of the smaller houses and hovels beyond. The on-shore breeze carried the stench of habitation and Robert tracked the line of the open sewer running down the centre of the street to the sea. The houses of the poor were miserable hovels but the people were fortunate in their trade. As many as one summer in five could be bad in England, causing widespread crop failure and famine. For the people of Brixham an early winter might curb the fishing season, but it was rare they felt the full wrath of starvation.

The door opened and Robert was greeted by one of the servants who immediately turned on his heel and ran to tell the family that Robert was home. Robert moved into the parlour and smiled as he heard the raised voices of his parents. They rushed into the room together and after Robert managed to disengage himself from his mother's embrace he heartily shook his father's hand. His gaze lingered on William for a moment, wondering as always whether his real mother had looked anything like her brother William. She had died in childbirth delivering her firstborn and Robert had never known her.

They sat and Robert asked perfunctorily after the well being of his two older and two younger cousins, three of whom were living nearby. He had never been close to them, and he felt they had always treated him as an outsider. He quickly moved to ask his father about his business. Like most men in Brixham, William Varian was a fisherman. But unlike most he was not the owner of only one boat. He had been left a small inheritance by his father and he had used it to start a business. That initial investment was followed by decades of hard work over which he had amassed a sizable fleet of leased and purchased boats. He now drew a comfortable living trading the catch of his small fleet to the larger inland towns.

After some time, Catherine sensed a change in the direction of the conversation. She left the room to supervise dinner as William began to question Robert on the recent attack on the Spanish mainland. They had heard from Tobias Miller, Robert's master from the *Spirit*, that Robert had sailed with Drake after the fleet had departed and William knew only that John Hawkins had ordered the transfer.

William had felt a profound sense of pride when he had heard the news. Spain was England's greatest threat and to have his son, albeit adopted, in the vanguard against such a foe brought great honour to the family. It was also a testament to his success in imbuing Robert with his beliefs, a task William had begun from the moment he had taken in his sister's twelve year old only son.

Unswerving loyalty to faith, crown and country were at the core of William's being. He had been taught such principles by his father, as had his father before him, and whereas William had ensured his own children grew up strong in such beliefs, his tuition of Robert had always been hindered by the fact that the boy's first twelve years had been spent under the influence of a father who had rebelled against the monarchy.

To subvert the Crown was to place the entire country in jeopardy and William had abhorred this treason. In the time of William's great-grandfather the nobility had been torn apart by civil war, and out of the maelstrom the House of Tudor had emerged, uniting the factions. It was England's unity, under a strong monarch, that kept her free. Internal divisions would render her easy prey for the expanding dominant powers on the continent.

Robert outlined the events of the previous ten weeks, drawing William's concern for his injury when he spoke of Cadiz, and his admiration at Robert's elevation to the rank of Captain. Robert spoke only briefly on the sack of Sagres, not wanting to be drawn into a conversation that would reignite his guilt. The weeks of skirmishing off Cape Saint Vincent prompted many questions from William and Robert smiled as he savoured the answers.

'Then it is believed that Spain is thwarted?' William asked as Robert concluded.

'At least for this season, maybe even the next. The supplies we captured or destroyed will not easily be replaced.'

'Where is Drake now?'

'I believe he travelled to London. The *Sao Phelipe* was an enormous prize and I warrant Drake wants to present the Queen's share to her in person.'

William nodded and for a moment was silent.

'God protect Drake,' he said solemnly. 'Despite the error of his beliefs he is one of our greatest hopes of keeping the Spanish horde at bay.'

Robert murmured an agreement. He was glad the Spanish had been defeated, yet for a brief moment, when his father had spoken of Drake's misguided beliefs, Robert had pictured the crucifix on the chest of the Spanish commander of the *Halcón*.

'They share our faith,' he said simply, looking to his father, hoping for guidance.

'They do, Robert,' William replied, 'but the return of England to the true faith will not be accomplished through Spanish ambition. I trust you know that.'

Robert nodded imperceptibly.

'Philip may trumpet the Catholic cause but I suspect his pride commands an equal share of his motives,' William continued. 'He will not invade England to place a Catholic monarch on the throne and then simply withdraw his army.'

'But with the death of Mary Stuart surely all hope is gone that an English Catholic monarch will succeed to the throne and we will witness a day when we are free to practise our faith, when I can reclaim . . .'

Robert stopped short, suddenly realizing that he had unconsciously linked a successful Spanish invasion with the return of his title and family honour.

William sat forward, an angry rebuke rushing to his lips, but he held his tongue. From experience he knew that the balance of loyalties between faith, crown and country was difficult to maintain, particularly at time of national crisis. William had known two such occasions when adherence to one or more tenets of his beliefs had threatened another, almost pushing the balance to the tipping point of collapse.

When the Catholic Mary Tudor had been on the throne she had married Philip of Spain. Her decision had threatened to rob England of its independence by making it part of the Hapsburg Empire, pitting William's loyalty to faith and crown against his country. Similarly the excommunication of Elizabeth by Pope Pius V had set his faith in opposition to his loyalty to his monarch. On each occasion however William had stuck doggedly to his principles, allowing him to forge a resolution that satisfied both his conscience and his honour.

Now his adopted son was facing a similar challenge in the guise of Spain's threat to invade. The loyalties that William had taught him were being set in opposition. However, William considered steadfast adherence to one's beliefs as a mark of courage and fortitude, and he was confident that Robert would eventually find his own resolution.

'God will bring England back into the Catholic fold in His own good time,' William said tolerantly. 'Believe in that, Robert, and until that day give Elizabeth every ounce of your loyalty.'

'I will,' Robert replied, troubled by the fact that for a moment he had seen no other way for his family name to be restored than with a successful Spanish conquest.

Without his name he would always be another man's son. While William Varian had cared for him like one of his own, Robert could still remember the shame he had felt when William had let it be known to the townsfolk of Brixham that Robert's father had died of the plague. William had refused to reveal Robert's title and lineage, and at twelve years old Robert had believed this secrecy was motivated by jealousy of his brother-in-law's superior ancestry. He had hated him for it. Only as he grew older did he understand that the subterfuge was for his own safety, learning by degrees of his father's part in the Northern Rebellion and his subsequent self-exile into obscurity and death.

It was a past that Robert had always struggled to accept and he desperately regretted the fact that he had never been given an opportunity to confront his father. Robert knew much about the Northern Rebellion and how the nobles had planned to depose Elizabeth in favour of Mary Stuart, but he had always wanted to know why his father had personally taken part, why he had risked everything, his name, his title and the birthright of his only son on a venture that was, at its heart, an act of treason.

'There is much weighing on your mind,' William said, reading Robert's expression. 'You should speak with Father Blackthorne.'

'He is here?'

'Yes,' William said with a smile. 'In the chapel. Go and see him before we eat.'

Robert rose and left the room. As he climbed the stairs his pace quickened at the prospect of seeing his old friend. He reached the landing and walked down the corridor leading to the back of the house. To his right were two widely spaced doors and Robert paused between them. The entrance to the chapel was invisible in the wood panelling that ran the length of the wall and Robert took a moment to trace his hand over the joints, searching for the small but distinctive knot that marked the hidden doorway. He found it, but did not enter immediately, suddenly remembering why he had been anxious all these weeks to see the priest. The full measure of his guilt swiftly returned to him. He took a deep breath and pushed firmly on the knot. The lock released with an audible click and the panel hinged inwards. Robert ducked his head to enter.

The chapel had been constructed between two existing

rooms, using floor space from both. It was cramped, barely eight feet by ten. Father Blackthorne was kneeling before the altar and he spun around at the sound of the door. He smiled at the sight of Robert and rose to greet him.

'It is good to see you safely returned from Spain.'

'My parents told you,' Robert surmised and Father Blackthorne nodded.

'Why did you not tell me yourself when we last met at the motte beside Saint Michael's?'

'I feared it would anger you,' Robert replied. 'I know how you feel about Drake and his kind, and this attack was planned to strike at the heart of Spain.'

'Your father believes an invasion by Spain will destroy England. But I tell you, Robert, this is God's plan. Spain may be our worldly enemy but they are our spiritual ally and Philip has the power to restore England to the true faith.'

Robert nodded conciliatorily, not wishing to be drawn into an argument. Father Blackthorne had expressed his beliefs many times before and Robert knew they were unshakable.

'I am glad to find you here, Father, for I had planned to seek you out. I need absolution.'

'I understand, Robert. Your participation in the attack on Spain is deeply troubling to me,' Father Blackthorne replied, misconstruing Robert's remorse. He indicated for them both to kneel.

'Drake ordered an attack on a town named Sagres,' Robert began. He told Father Blackthorne of the desecration of the church and murder of the Spanish priest, sparing no detail in an effort to expunge the guilt from his soul.

Father Blackthorne was deeply shocked and he came off his knees to sit down once more.

'These are terrible deeds,' he said, almost to himself, his fingers kneading the cross around his neck. 'Truly God has turned his back on this country if it has spawned such men. And you, Robert,' he said, his eyes flashing with anger and shame, 'what have you become?'

'I tried to stop them, Father,' Robert protested. 'But I could not, not without giving myself away and forfeiting my own life.'

'Jesus Christ laid down his life for us,' Father Blackthorne said piously. 'And we ought to lay down our lives for our brothers.'

'Forgive me, Father,' Robert said, bowing his head low before his confessor.

Father Blackthorne looked down on Robert, his mind in turmoil. Robert's remorse was clearly evident but Father Blackthorne could not see beyond his own anger. How could Robert have stood by while a minister of God was murdered, while His house was defiled by heretics? Suddenly Father Blackthorne thought of the daily life he led himself, of his clandestine existence and his constant fear of discovery. He remembered the story in Saint John's gospel, when the Pharisees brought an adulterous woman before Jesus. 'Let he who is without sin cast the first stone,' said the Lord. Was he not guilty of the same sin as Robert? The sanctity of the nearby town church was corrupted daily by the services of a heretical congregation and he never once thought to confront them and openly condemn their faith. He was too fearful of the consequences.

He reached out his hand to place it on Robert's head, ready to absolve him, when another thought stuck him, an undertaking he had made many weeks before. He hesitated, his hand poised in mid-air, his mind racing. William Varian had mentioned that Robert had sailed as a master on one of the galleons, a senior position, one that was surely privy to a great deal of information. Would Robert be willing to share that information? Would he betray the loyalty Father Blackthorne knew William Varian had instilled in him? Robert was clearly anguished by the actions of his compatriots in Sagres. Perhaps now he could be persuaded to fully commit to the cause of placing a Catholic monarch on the throne, if for no other reason than to atone for his lack of action before. The obvious depth of his guilt certainly made him more susceptible to the idea. A sliver of guilt crept into Father Blackthorne's own mind at the thought of manipulating Robert, but he ignored it, knowing the greater cause needed to be served.

'I cannot give you absolution,' he said.

Robert looked up in shock.

'Not until you have atoned for your sin,' Father Blackthorne continued. 'You must make penance before the Lord.'

'What must I do?'

'I cannot decide now,' Father Blackthorne replied, 'I must pray for an answer. Until then you should return to Plymouth. Look for me in two weeks at the motte beside Saint Michael's. Are you to stay with this new ship as its master?'

'I'm Captain now,' Robert explained, 'although John Hawkins has yet to confirm that command.'

Father Blackthorne's pulse quickened. He had not expected this good fortune. A captain of the fleet; the Duke of Clarsdale would be impressed. The panel door behind them clicked open as a servant entered.

'Master Robert,' he said, 'dinner is served. Father, if it pleases you, I shall bring your meal directly to your room.'

They rose and walked towards the door. Father Blackthorne caught a glance at Robert's pained expression and felt a pang of guilt once more.

'Do not worry, Robert,' he said, placing a hand on his shoulder. 'The Lord will show us a way.'

Robert nodded but took little solace from his confessor's

words. He remained haunted by his sin and his conscience refused to relent. He would return to Plymouth as Father Blackthorne suggested. There he would command the very crewmen and colleagues who had perpetrated the heinous crime that had destroyed his peace. It was an odious task but one which his duty demanded of him. With a heavy heart he left the chapel, his guilt greater than ever.

CHAPTER 6

14th July 1587. El Escorial, Spain.

Nathaniel Young mopped his brow with his handkerchief. The heat in the expansive Patio de los Reyes was oppressive and despite the elevated site of the Escorial Palace no breeze could penetrate beyond the solid wall of five storey buildings that marked the boundaries of the courtyard. He waited in a shaded corner and paced a wide circle, glancing at the edifice of the basilica which was adorned with statues of the kings from whence the courtyard drew its name.

The summons had come unexpectedly and Young cursed his unpreparedness. Upon arriving in Madrid, he had been told to continue on the additional twenty-eight miles to the magnificent palace where Philip now spent most of his time and from where he ruled the vastness of his empire. That the King had requested a personal audience was auspicious. Young had never met Philip, despite the longevity of his exile in Spain and his almost constant contact with one or other of the King's personal advisors.

The sudden change made Young nervous, not least because he was about to meet one of the most powerful men in the world. He was also being presented with an incredible opportunity to advance. Drake's attack on Cadiz and his piracy off the coast of Portugal had raised the tempo of the conflict. Why else therefore would Philip have summoned him here, if not to consult with him directly and garner his advice on Drake and other matters of national interest relating to England? For the first time Young was about to penetrate the possessive circle of advisors and speak directly to the monarch and as he paced the courtyard he steeled his determination to make a good first impression.

Movement caught his eye and he saw Don Rodrigo de Torres beckon to him from the entrance of the basilica. He hurried across the courtyard, closing his eyes slightly against the glare of sunlight that reflected off every surface.

'We must hurry, your grace,' de Torres said as he led Young inside.

The narthex of the basilica was cool and dark, but beyond the interior opened out into a huge space dominated by a dome above the crossing. Light poured in through the windows of the cupola, illuminating the magnificent frescoes and intricate reredos and emphasizing the incredible height of the building. Mass had just ended and Young could see Philip standing at the top of the church speaking with a priest.

In the moment he had taken to look about the interior in awe de Torres had walked on ahead and Young was forced to quicken his step to catch him. They came to a stop some ten yards short of the King and waited. Young took the chance to study the man who reigned over one of the largest empires in the world. Although his physique was slight, he was a handsome man. Young started involuntarily as Philip glanced at him over his shoulder, his gaze penetrating. The King nodded at de Torres and the two men stepped forward, bowing courteously.

Philip dismissed his priest. 'Don Rodrigo. We are pleased to see you.'

'Your majesty is most gracious,' de Torres replied, turning slightly to Young. 'May I introduce to you, the Duke of Greyfarne, Nathaniel Young.'

'Ah yes, our English ally,' Philip said. 'We have heard much of you.'

Young bowed his head in gratitude.

'Thank you, your majesty. I am honoured to hear my humble service has come to your attention.'

'Yes,' Philip said, drawing out the word, his mouth twisting slightly, 'it has indeed been noted. As has your lack of service.'

Young blanched at the softly spoken censure.

'We remain disappointed that the fleet of the Jezebel, Elizabeth, approached our lands unannounced.'

'I assure you, your majesty, I am doing all I can to secure good intelligence from Plymouth and Dover.'

'Your assurance will not redeem our ship, the *Sao Phelipe*, and its valuable cargo,' Philip said coldly. 'Or undo the injury to us.'

'I will redouble my efforts, your majesty,' Young stammered, unable to avert his gaze from the King's withering look.

'See that you do,' Philip replied, his eyes darting to de Torres before returning to Young. 'We have little use for those who enjoy the benefits of our protection while contributing nothing in return.'

The King turned on his heel and walked away, his retinue following discreetly behind him. De Torres and Young bowed deeply to his back and as they rose de Torres set off towards the exit once more. Young followed. He was stunned by the brevity of the meeting and deeply shocked by the King's abrupt, caustic tone.

'My God, de Torres. I never expected . . . What must I do?'

'Not here,' de Torres hissed. 'Sound travels too easily in this place.'

They came out into the courtyard and de Torres led Young to the centre. When he rounded on Young, his expression was furious.

'Curse you, Englishman. Your failure will ruin us both.'

'I cannot be held responsible for the lack of response from my contacts in England,' Young countered defensively.

'You don't understand,' de Torres continued, his voice trembling with rage. 'I knew the King was angry over the losses caused by Drake but I didn't realize he held you partly responsible, and therefore me by association.'

'Then what do you suggest?' Young replied, angrily. 'I have told his majesty I will redouble my efforts.'

'His majesty rarely meets with anyone. He communicates and commands through correspondence or sends his advisors. For him to have asked you here in person shows how important he considers this information. You witnessed his reaction. There can be no more delays, no more excuses.'

'I will communicate with my contacts immediately through our network of couriers. Tell them that this request is of the highest priority.'

'That is not enough. If the English strike again without warning we will both be ruined. You must take command; see that this agent is put in place without delay.'

'But that is precisely what I am doing. My communiqué will leave today.'

'No. You cannot take charge from here. This is too important. You must do more. You must return to England.'

Young was made speechless by de Torres's demand and he took an involuntary step backwards as if the Spaniard had physically struck him.

'I will arrange safe passage to the south coast of England,' de Torres continued, conscious of the gravity of his order but less concerned for Young's life than fulfilling the King's orders. 'From there you must make contact with your people directly.'

'But I cannot,' Young stammered. 'If I am captured my life will be forfeit.'

'If you do not go, your life as you know it here will be forfeit, as will mine,' de Torres replied icily. 'The house you live in, your carriage, the food you eat, the clothes on your back – all are given to you by Spain. You heard his majesty, if you cease to be of use to Spain, then you will no longer enjoy her protection and nothing will shield you from the King's wrath should you fail him again.'

Young was appalled. The Spaniard had never spoken to him in such a way. Living for so long by another's leave, he had come to take it for granted. But having witnessed the King's displeasure in person, he realized for the first time the precariousness of his situation. He was indeed an ally of the Spanish for now, but only for as long as he served a purpose. His previous years of loyal service counted for naught.

The fickle loyalty of de Torres and his King made Young furious but his expression betrayed none of his feelings. There was nothing to be gained from arguing further. He had no choice but to travel to England. He smiled genially and agreed to de Torres's request. The Spaniard smiled in return and, leading Young from the courtyard, began to talk casually about the arrangements for the journey. It was as if the threats spoken in anger only moments before had never been uttered, but for Young they would not be easily forgotten.

He was bound by faith to the Spanish, that much remained, but he knew now with utter certainty that he was not one of them. The self-deluding veil of patriotism that had clouded his judgement for so long was gone. What should have made his bond to the Spanish unbreakable, his meeting with King Philip, had instead emphasized his status as a foreigner and a refugee. As if from a distance he heard de Torres speaking. He would be sailing to England within the week.

The view from the study window of Clarsdale's house in the early morning light took in the full width of the elaborate gardens. The trees and shrubs seemed almost haphazard in their placement but upon closer observation Father Blackthorne could see that their arrangement was such that they both concealed and exposed the more delicate plants around them, as well as the line of the stream at the bottom of the garden. The effect was subtle, tempting the visitor to step outside and explore the wonders in each hidden fold of ground.

Father Blackthorne raised his head and looked beyond the garden to the opposite slope of the valley. Save for a number of small copses the ground had been cleared to the horizon line on the crest of the hill. For a moment Father Blackthorne imagined what it would be like to ride on horseback across such unbroken pasture. It was a passion he had not enjoyed for many years; the freedom to race a horse across open countryside in broad daylight.

As a fugitive from the Crown he was forced to travel only at night and often stayed clear of the roads. He slept wherever the dawn found him, sometimes in a dry ditch but more often in the homes or outhouses of his scattered congregants. Travelling by horseback therefore was impractical, for he had no way to hide such a beast if he needed to go to ground quickly and a tethered horse looked incongruous outside the homes of the more impoverished members of his flock.

As the second son of a nobleman, his path into the priesthood had been decided soon after his birth. It was a decision in which he had taken no part but in all his years he had never questioned it, content in the vocation God and his family had chosen for him. He smiled at a fleeting memory, remembering his first horse and the countryside surrounding his home and he was suddenly filled with the belief that one day he would again have the chance to indulge this simple passion.

The door of the study opened and the Duke of Clarsdale swept into the room followed by Nichols, who held the door.

'Make sure we are not disturbed,' the duke said tersely and the butler withdrew.

Clarsdale's face was flushed and he was breathing deeply. He had ridden hard from the boundary of his land upon hearing of Father Blackthorne's arrival. He indicated for the priest to be seated without courtesy or delay.

'Where have you been?' Clarsdale began angrily. 'I had thought you captured it has been so long.'

'I bring good news, your grace,' Father Blackthorne replied, trying to forestall any argument, conscious that when they had last met he had given the duke the impression that his search for a sailor of rank who could aid their cause would be brief.

'It had better be,' Clarsdale warned. 'In the past two months I have received two messages . . .'

He stopped abruptly and silently cursed his lack of self control. He was revealing too much in telling the priest about any contact with his counterpart in Spain. Both messages had been from Nathaniel Young concerning his lack of progress in securing a naval agent, the second even more abrupt than the first. The criticism of his ability was deeply offensive to Clarsdale, particularly as it came from a penniless, exiled duke. He held Father Blackthorne solely responsible for their failure thus far and was sorely tempted to share the offensive communiqués with him.

'What is this news?' he asked curtly.

'I have secured many men who are willing to support a

Spanish landing on the south coast,' Father Blackthorne began enthusiastically. 'Most of them possess their own weapons and at least a quarter of them have access to a horse.'

'But what of my request for an agent in the fleet?'

Father Blackthorne smiled and sat forward. 'I believe I have found you such a man.'

Clarsdale mirrored the priest's movements and leaned in, his face expectant. 'Who is he?'

'His real name is Robert Young. His father was the Duke of Greyfarne, who took part in the Northern Rebellion in 1569. I believe he subsequently died in exile but before he fled England he placed his son in the care of another family. The boy adopted their surname and to this day his real identity remains a secret.'

The breath caught in Clarsdale's throat at the mention of the Duke of Greyfarne. With an enormous effort of will Clarsdale kept his natural reaction in check and remained outwardly composed, while inside he rejoiced at his good fortune. He noticed the priest was staring at him and realized he had allowed a silence to draw out. He quickly gathered his thoughts.

'This family he lives with. You know them?'

'Yes, and they might pose a problem. They are loyal recusants and Robert is heavily influenced by his adoptive father.'

'Loyal recusants,' Clarsdale spat. The name was an abomination, a contradiction in terms. Clarsdale considered such people to be fools.

'So you have not yet approached this man?'

'No, but I believe I have the means to secure what we need. I am withholding absolution for a grave sin he has committed.'

Clarsdale was surprised by the priest's unscrupulous approach. The act itself did not shock him, but he had not believed the priest would stoop to such levels. The revelation gave him new confidence in Father Blackthorne and a sense that perhaps he could be trusted to a greater degree.

He considered the priest's approach. It had merit, but Clarsdale was unconvinced it was enough and his natural caution made him wary. The priest would need a more persuasive lure than this. Clarsdale weighed up the risk involved in revealing the truth to him against the prize of securing Nathaniel Young's lost son as an agent. He decided in an instant.

'You will only have one chance to approach Robert Young,' he began. 'If his misguided loyalty to Elizabeth runs too deep he could reject your proposal, regardless of his remorse for his actions, and immediately turn you over to the authorities.'

'Never!' Father Blackthorne protested.

'You cannot be sure, despite what you think.'

'Then what do you suggest?'

Clarsdale stood up and walked over to the window. 'In sharing this information with you, Father, I am risking a great deal. But I assure you it will be enough to secure Robert Young's cooperation and loyalty.'

Father Blackthorne stood up, perplexed.

Clarsdale turned to face him. 'Robert Young's father did not die in exile as many believe. He is alive and currently living in Spain.'

'But how . . . how do you know this?' Father Blackthorne stammered, deeply shocked by the news. His thoughts went to the twelve-year-old boy he had first met all those years ago in Brixham, and the years of anguish he knew Robert had suffered for the loss of his father, his family and his name.

'My contact in Spain,' Clarsdale went on. 'The man who seeks information on the fleet. It is the Duke of Greyfarne – Nathaniel Young.'

'Merciful God,' Father Blackthorne whispered. 'Robert's father.'

'The very same,' Clarsdale smiled, although it did not reach his eyes. The recruitment of Robert Young would be a considerable achievement, one certainly worthy of great reward. The Spanish would soon invade England. This was inevitable, regardless of any delay Drake's recent attacks might have caused. When they did invade, Clarsdale was determined he would benefit directly from the reign of whatever monarch they placed on the throne. To ensure such favour he needed to increase his value in the eyes of the Spanish. The recruitment of Robert Young would significantly advance that goal. The only obstruction was Nathaniel Young. As the bearer of each report to the Spanish, he would be first to claim any prize.

Clarsdale looked out the window at the land he possessed and all he risked daily for his faith. He was the seventh duke, a lineage that had remained unbroken despite the Tudors's anarchic reign. Sadly, his wife had borne him no children. Upon his death the title he so dearly loved would pass to his younger brother, a man he despised and the father of a prodigious brood.

On two occasions he had asked Rome for an annulment of his marriage so that he could remarry and father an heir with another woman. The first application had been made purely on the grounds of cold practicality while the second, years later, was an impassioned plea that included a pointed reference to his courageous service to the Catholic faith. Both claims had been dismissed. Clarsdale had often thought how much easier it might have been if his marriage had been Church of England and he had had the option to apply directly to the Crown.

He nodded to himself, his gaze sweeping over his land one last time: it was time to claim a measure of material reward, as well as the place in Heaven his actions had assuredly gained him. He had sacrificed much for his faith. Once Robert Young had been recruited he would find a way to bypass Nathaniel Young completely and communicate directly with a senior Spanish courtier, or with luck, one of King Philip's personal advisors. Then the Duke of Greyfarne would no longer hold sway over his destiny, and the reward he sought would be seen as no more than his due. He turned and looked to Father Blackthorne, who was lost in his own thoughts.

'You must go now, Father,' Clarsdale said, startling the priest. 'I will have one of my men escort you to the edge of my lands. Will it take you long to reach Plymouth?'

'Three, maybe four days,' Father Blackthorne replied, gathering his wits. 'I plan to meet Robert at our usual place.'

Clarsdale nodded. 'Then go with God, Father. I will pray for your success.'

'Thank you, your grace,' Father Blackthorne replied, slightly taken aback by the duke's unusually genial farewell. He opened the door and crossed the threshold, then stopped suddenly, his head darting to the right.

'What is it?' Clarsdale asked from inside the room.

Father Blackthorne did not answer for a second and stayed still, listening. 'I . . .'

He paused. 'Nothing . . . it's nothing.'

He closed the door behind him and walked across the hallway. He glanced back over his shoulder to the study door. Had he been mistaken? It was, after all a large house. Perhaps the noise had come from upstairs. He shrugged his shoulders and continued on. He could have sworn that when he opened the study door he had heard someone fleeing in haste from the hallway. The thought that his conversation with the duke might have been overheard was disquieting but before he could dwell on it further his senses were overwhelmed by the aromas of the kitchen. He hastened his step. The journey ahead would be long and devoid of comfort and he expectantly opened the door to the kitchen.

Robert shifted his weight from one foot to the other as he waited nervously on the main deck. His eyes were locked on the approaching longboat, and in particular on the individual sitting in the stern. John Hawkins was an austere looking man with a narrow, sombre face and despite his advanced age he looked formidable and strong. For many English sailors he was the embodiment of success and Robert had come to admire and respect him greatly in the years he had spent in his service.

At one time or another in his life Hawkins had been a merchant, a slave-trader and a privateer, but for the last ten years he had been treasurer of the royal fleet. In this position of power and influence he had slowly transformed the English navy. His ambitious building programme had spawned what many believed to be the finest warships afloat, the new 'race built' galleons. He had also modernized many of the existing capital ships, revolutionizing them by razing their fore and aft castles. Now the English fleet had a fearsome coterie of warships custom built for the coastal waters of England.

The longboat struck the hull of the *Retribution* with a heavy thud and Hawkins climbed deftly up the rope ladder to the main deck. Robert advanced to meet him with his hand outstretched and Hawkins took it with a firm grip.

'Welcome aboard,' Robert said.

'I should be, it's my ship,' Hawkins replied with a smile. 'How is she, Mister Varian? None the worse for my kinsman's foray, I hope.'

'She's fighting fit,' Robert replied proudly, calling Seeley and Shaw forward.

'This is Thomas Seeley, the master, and Johannes Shaw, the boatswain.'

Hawkins reached for Seeley's hand first. 'This man I already know. It's good to see you, Thomas. How is your father?'

'He's good, sir,' Seeley replied.

Hawkins nodded genially and turned to the boatswain.

'Shaw, eh?' he said, his eyes narrowing in thought. 'You look familiar. Are you related to Peter Shaw, the master of the *Hopewell*?'

'He's my uncle,' Shaw replied, pleased that a man of Hawkins's stature should know one of his family.

'A good man,' Hawkins said, nodding slowly. He looked out over the rest of the assembled crew and noticed that many were not looking back at him but at their captain. He turned to Robert.

'Back to their stations then, Mister Varian,' he said tersely, 'and join me if you will.'

Robert nodded to Seeley and the master scattered the crew.

Hawkins led Robert to the poop deck. In the brief seconds it took to ascend to the stern Robert felt his anxiousness rise again. From the day he had been promoted to captain by Drake, he had known that, as a field commission, his promotion would be subject to review once the fleet returned home. He had continually ignored the possibility of fate's reversal, content instead to believe that his captaincy was official. Over the preceding months he had come to consider the *Retribution* as his own.

This illusion of permanence had been easy to maintain off the coast of Spain and on the return journey home. With a defeated enemy in the wake of the English fleet and the *Retribution* one of only nine ships that had stayed the course, Robert believed he had cause to be optimistic, but with each passing day in the calm of Plymouth harbour his confidence had slowly given way to the inevitable. The captaincy of a galleon such as the *Retribution* was not for a merchant's son from Brixham. It was a position for a man of higher social status. The sheer injustice made Robert bristle.

Robert believed that command of the *Retribution* would have afforded him, for the first time in his life, a real chance to make a name for himself beyond his already established reputation as a skilled sailor in Hawkins's merchant fleet. Two years previously, his low social rank had excluded him from Drake's raid on the Spanish Main in the Caribbean, a lengthy campaign where higher-born men like the previous captain, Morgan, had made their names.

On reaching the poop deck, frustration consumed him. If only he could be given more time to prove his worth to his superiors. Despite his converse religious beliefs he truly felt he was the best man to permanently command the *Retribution.* As Hawkins turned to face him, Robert steeled himself to argue his case. It was surely a lost cause, he knew that, but Robert couldn't allow his best chance to restore his family name and honour to slip through his grasp without a fight.

'Mister Varian,' Hawkins began, but then paused. He turned and walked to the gunwale. 'What to do with you?' he said, looking out over the harbour.

'I don't understand, sir,' Robert replied taken aback, his opening argument dying on his lips.

'Your command, lad, your captaincy of the *Retribution.*' Hawkins turned once more and walked back to Robert. 'I know your mettle, Varian, I would not have made you captain of one of my merchantmen, or indeed master of the *Retribution*, if I had not. But then you do a damn fool thing and charge down that Spanish counterattack on the *Halcón.*'

'Sir?'

'You brought yourself to the attention of my kinsman,

Drake. Then he went and did another damn fool thing and promoted you captain of my ship.'

'But sir, I . . .'

Hawkins suddenly smiled and slapped Robert on the shoulder. 'And now I'm going to do a damn fool thing and confirm that command.'

Robert could not take in the words.

'I saw strength in you from the beginning and by God you proved me right at Cadiz. Now that Drake has seen it too, the *Retribution* is yours to command.'

'But how can I, sir?' Robert said, speaking aloud the thoughts that had most haunted him. He did not pause to gather himself, to think that he was arguing against that which he longed for most. 'Surely the captaincy must be awarded to someone of a higher social rank?'

Hawkins smiled ruefully. 'Don't think I'm not aware of that problem, Varian. In fact I still had my doubts when I came on board. But then I saw something that settled the matter. The men look to you, Varian. They respect you. That counts for a great deal in a captain.'

Robert stayed silent this time, not daring to speak again. As the news began to sink in, he smiled slightly. Hawkins noticed the change and frowned.

'Be mindful, Varian,' he warned. 'I freely confirm Drake's decision. Although this ship is mine, the *Retribution* remains in the service of the Queen. I will need to convince the Privy Council of the wisdom of my choice. I have Drake's endorsement, which carries a lot of weight. He too comes from humble origins and commands the entire fleet. You have proved yourself worthy in mine and Drake's eyes, but now you must put our decision beyond all reproach.'

'Yes, sir,' Robert replied solemnly. Did this mean his command remained as precarious as it was before?

Hawkins nodded, satisfied. As he departed the *Retribution*, Robert remained at the gunwale and watched the longboat pull away until it was lost from sight behind another galleon. The captaincy was his, bestowed by Drake and confirmed by Hawkins – but it was still there for the taking by another, until he could fully justify the faith of his commanders.

The crew was his first priority. The *Retribution* was in need of a master's mate, and Robert immediately thought of Tobias Miller of the *Spirit*. He trusted Miller completely and would need him in the months ahead.

In building the *Retribution*, the shipwrights of England had created a warship that finely balanced a fearsome arsenal of cannon with the sailing abilities of a predator. Robert would need to master that balance if he was to retain his command. The *Retribution* was his, and he silently vowed to do whatever it would take to keep her.

Nichols cursed loudly as he fell heavily for the third time on the wet grass. He looked down at his mud covered breeches and for a brief second wondered how he would explain his appearance should he encounter anyone. He clambered to his feet and continued to run up the hill. The copse was dead ahead, only fifty yards away. He prayed he was not too late, knowing the value of the information he held.

Nichols crashed through the rain soaked undergrowth and stopped suddenly. He cocked his head to listen but his own laboured breathing and the sound of his heart filled his ears. He held his breath to still them but the effort caused him to cough violently.

'Over here,' he heard a voice hiss and he pushed towards it. He saw Cross a moment later standing by his horse, seemingly poised to mount. He was looking beyond Nichols into the trees behind him.

'What news?' he asked. 'Has the priest come?'

'Two days ago,' Nichols replied.

'And?'

'The traitor's name is Robert Young.'

Cross slammed a fist into his open palm in triumph. 'Tell me everything.'

Nichols began to speak, recalling the meeting between the duke and Father Blackthorne with his usual attention to detail.

'The son of Nathaniel Young,' Cross breathed, putting his hand up to silence the butler. Nathaniel Young was near the top of almost every list Cross had ever seen of prominent traitors who were believed to be active on the continent. But he had never heard of his son, or even knew one existed.

'You're sure that is what the priest said?' he asked.

'Yes,' Nichols replied tetchily, eager to continue his story. His next words caused Cross to interrupt again. 'Sacred Heart of Jesus. Nathaniel Young is Clarsdale's contact in Spain?'

Nichols made to reply but Cross indicated for him to continue. Cross barely registered the final part. All he could think of was the contact that had been exposed. Tasked with a mission as important as discovering the movements and strategy of the English navy, Nathaniel Young was surely near the centre of power in Spain. Maybe he even had the ear of Philip himself.

'The priest did not say what position this Robert Young holds in the navy?'

'No. And he does not go by that name. Father Blackthorne said he adopted the name of the family who took him in after his father fled into exile.'

'And the priest did not mention their name?'

'No,' Nichols replied irritably. 'If they had I would already have told you.'

Cross made to reprimand Nichols for his insubordinate

tone but he thought better of it. The butler had proved valuable beyond all expectations, and he needed to keep him firmly on side.

Cross turned and walked over to his horse, stroking her mane absentmindedly as he tried to think of the best way forward. Walsingham would have to be informed. That was paramount, but Cross knew his first question would be the one now foremost in his own mind. What was Robert Young's real name? And what was his position in the navy? This Robert Young might not even be in the navy. He could be an official in Plymouth, one who might be privy to the strategic and tactical plans of the fleet. There was one man who knew who Young really was – the priest – but how to get the information from him? He alone was the contact between Robert Young and Clarsdale. Until the two men met, the priest would have to remain untouched. Cross turned back to Nichols.

'You have done well. Now go back to the house. The priest is sure to return soon with Robert Young, and when he does you must try your utmost to discover his name, or at least set eyes on him somehow. I am leaving now but I'll return here in a week. I will be in this copse every second day at noon should you need to find me.'

Nichols nodded and left without another word.

Cross watched him go and waited for the woods to become quiet again before mounting up. Threading his horse through the undergrowth, he stopped on the far side of the copse, his eyes ranging over the mist covered fields beyond. He had set Nichols a task, and prayed for his success, but in the meantime he would try to supplant him. He must travel to Plymouth and try to uncover this traitor's real identity himself.

CHAPTER 7

25th July 1587. Saint Michael's Church near Plymouth.

Robert reached out with his hand as his foot slipped on the scree, pausing for a moment near the top of the motte. He looked over his shoulder. The sun was setting behind Saint Michael's church and the whole building glowed. It was a captivating sight, and Robert's eyes were drawn to the windows of the nave and the filtered light that shone through the diamond shaped panes onto the field separating the church from the motte. He was suddenly conscious of how visible he was on the exposed hillside, and he continued hastily up the slope.

Robert reached the top and ducked in behind one of the crumbling walls. On the faint breeze he smelled a trace of wood smoke and charred meat and he looked about him, wondering where Father Blackthorne might be hiding.

'*Sumus omnes*,' he said, and smiled as the priest looked out from behind a corner.

'In the hand of God, Robert,' he replied, walking forward with his hand outstretched. Robert fell to his knees and Father Blackthorne blessed him.

'It is good to see you, Robert.'

'And you, Father. Tell me, have you been able to decide my penance?'

The priest nodded. 'Come,' he said, leading Robert back to his smouldering fire.

They sat down. Father Blackthorne glanced across at Robert as he gathered his thoughts. The young man looked haggard and his bloodshot eyes spoke of sleepless nights. Father Blackthorne felt a worm of guilt gnaw at his insides for his delay in easing Robert's conscience, but he comforted himself with the knowledge that the incredible news he was about to deliver would surely bring the young man happiness.

'I have prayed for guidance on how you can be absolved of your sin,' Father Blackthorne began, choosing his words carefully, mindful of Clarsdale's warning that he would only have one chance to persuade Robert to betray the English fleet. 'That prayer has led to visions of the suffering that our mother church endures under the yoke of Elizabeth. We must all work to ease that suffering, Robert. Your penance lies in taking up the mantle of that fight.'

Robert shifted uneasily. He had long known that his confessor was sympathetic to the seditious cause of overthrowing Elizabeth but his words suggested that sympathy also extended to deeds.

'God has chosen one man above all to help us in this struggle,' the priest continued. 'One king whose people share our blessed faith. But that king labours in darkness and needs the light of information to allow him to complete God's will.'

'The Spanish,' Robert spat. 'What information . . .?'

He stopped as he realized what Father Blackthorne was asking of him.

'Merciful God, Father, surely you are not asking me to betray . . .'

Father Blackthorne raised his hand to cut Robert short.

'Hear me out, my son,' he said calmly. 'You have come here to be absolved of the sin you committed in Sagres, but I tell you solemnly, that sin is but a mote to the beam that is the greater sin you commit every day by supporting the heretic Queen who rules this land.'

Robert stood up, his fists balled in anger.

'You are wrong, Father,' he hissed. 'My loyalty to Elizabeth is not a sin – it is my duty as an Englishman. She is our sovereign, regardless of her beliefs.'

'But her reign, and the blasphemous faith she imposes, threatens the soul of every man in England.' Father Blackthorne rose and confronted the angry young man.

'Not mine, Father. My soul is secure in my faith, as are the souls of countless others. I believe that God will not forsake this land. He will save England by opening the eyes of Elizabeth or those of the English monarch who will succeed her.'

Father Blackthorne sighed. Clarsdale had been right about the depth of Robert's loyalty to the Crown. He had hoped to persuade Robert to help him, then reveal Nathaniel Young's involvement as a reward. He now knew he would have to use the news about Robert's father as a lure to convince him. Father Blackthorne firmly believed that Robert's soul was in jeopardy, as were all Catholics who supported Elizabeth, and he was sorry he could not persuade him otherwise.

'Sit down, Robert,' he said gently and he waited patiently for him to comply.

'I regret you cannot see the danger to your immortal soul, but if that blindness prevents you from helping our cause, then perhaps what I am about to tell you will change your mind and open your heart.'

Robert did not reply. His anger was making him restless, so the priest pressed on hurriedly.

'I know you have suffered much for your faith by living a lie under an assumed name. God has seen your pain and in his wisdom he has found a way to both ease your misery and offer you a chance to embrace our cause.'

Despite his previous resolve, Robert turned to leave. He could not countenance another treacherous word from his confessor.

Father Blackthorne quickly blustered out the words he had rehearsed so carefully.

'The Spanish require information on the movements of the English fleet,' he said rapidly. 'That information is to be fed to a local nobleman who would then send it on to his contact in Spain.'

'Enough!' Robert began to walk away.

'Wait. That nobleman's contact in Spain is the Duke of Greyfarne.'

Robert froze.

'Your father, Robert. Nathaniel Young. He is alive, in exile in Spain.'

'It cannot be.' Robert turned slowly around to face Father Blackthorne. 'You must be . . . it cannot be. My father?'

'It's true, Robert. I did not know myself until only a few days ago.'

'He's alive,' Robert said, almost to himself. 'All these years.'

'And still fighting to save England.'

Robert stared at the priest, his mind reeling. His father was in league with the Spanish, with the enemy he was fighting against, the enemy of England. Robert knew he should curse his father for the traitor he was and yet he found he could not. Overwhelmed by conflicting emotions, he staggered over to the fire to sit down before his legs gave way.

'Does my father know you have approached me?'

'I do not think he knows anything about you, certainly not

where you are or what you have become. Clarsdale was surprised to learn of you himself.'

'Clarsdale?'

Father Blackthorne cursed his slip but quickly reasoned that Robert would soon learn that name regardless.

'The Duke of Clarsdale. He is your father's colleague here in England.'

Robert dropped his head into his open palms. He was nauseous and he swallowed hard. He felt like he was staring into an abyss. To step forward meant to become mired in treachery and sedition. But there was a chance to send word to his father, to communicate with him for the first time in nearly twenty years.

He looked up at the man who had been his confessor, his confidant from almost the day his father left England. For the first time, Robert sensed he could not be trusted. Behind the compassionate expression of a priest, Robert now saw the man, as capable as any other of ruthlessness and perfidy. He vowed to remain guarded as he committed himself to his next step.

'When can I meet Clarsdale?'

Father Blackthorne smiled. 'Whenever you can release yourself from your ship.'

Robert thought for a moment. 'Two days.'

'You will not regret this, Robert,' Father Blackthorne said, helping him up. 'God works in ways that astound us all. His hand has guided you and your father together so that you can unite to help restore England to the true faith.'

'Perhaps you're right,' Robert lied, allowing himself to be led to the edge of the ruins. He left the priest with a promise to return within two days.

Scrabbling back down the loose stone on the side of the motte, Robert headed towards the darkened outline of Saint

Michael's. He walked blindly, without seeing the path in front of him, his mind totally consumed by his father's sudden and unexpected return into his life. A part of him hoped that Father Blackthorne was mistaken, that his father was not working with the Spanish, but his heart knew it was true. In many ways it seemed inevitable.

At twelve years old, his father's involvement in a violent uprising against Elizabeth and its ultimate failure had changed Robert's life irrevocably. Now Nathaniel Young's seditious involvement with Spain was poised to change his life once more. But Robert was no longer a powerless boy. He was a man, and an Englishman at that. He would meet Clarsdale, but he would be damned if he would reveal any knowledge he possessed about the English fleet.

'Which one of you pox-ridden buggers is Morales?'

Evardo rose slowly, using the cold stone wall behind him for support. He took a half step forward and stopped, looking down at his tattered clothes. His face hardened in disgust. The filthy straw that covered the floor of the prison had clung to him and he brushed it away. He pulled on the cuffs of his doublet and straightened his jerkin. The effort had little effect, but he straightened up and walked purposefully towards the door of the cell.

His fellow Spanish captives, nearly twenty of them in all, were lying listlessly against every wall. Some looked up at him with unseeing eyes as he passed. Nobody gestured nor spoke. They were all dishonoured men and none had sought friendship during the long weeks of captivity. He reached the stout wooden door where at head height a small opening framed the face of a bearded Englishman. He stared at Evardo with open hostility.

'You Morales?' he spat.

'I am *Comandante* Evardo Alvarez Morales.'

'*Comandante*,' the gaoler laughed. 'Of what, Spaniard? This here prison?'

With limited English Evardo did not fully understand the taunt, but he recognized the tone. He refused to be baited, lifting his chin slightly to show his disdain. The Englishman growled menacingly and wrenched back the locking bolt.

'Out,' he barked, pulling open the door.

Evardo ducked his head through the doorway. The gaoler slammed the door shut and relocked it, then hawked and spat at Evardo's feet.

'Follow me, *Comandante*,' he sneered, leading him along a dimly lit corridor to a flight of winding steps. They ascended and came out into a high-ceilinged chamber, where an official was sitting behind a wooden table flanked by two guards. The gaoler indicated for Evardo to step forward. The official looked up.

'State your full name, rank and last command.'

Evardo spoke with as much arrogance as he could muster. He felt nothing but contempt for these verminous commoners and detested being in their power. The official nodded as he tallied the answer spoken by Evardo with the notes he had in front of him.

'You're free to go.'

At first Evardo did not understand. He stared at the Englishman, who noticed his perplexed expression.

'The ransom for your release arrived this morning,' he explained irritably.

'How?' Evardo asked haltingly.

'The man who brought the money is outside,' the official said, indicating a door behind him. 'Now begone with you, before we decide it's safer to burn all you God-cursed papists.'

Evardo stepped back from the table. Alternating waves of

anger and disbelief washed through him and he trembled with the effort of maintaining his self-control. A little over two months had passed since his capture and during that time revenge and hatred for the English had become an unquench-able fire within him. As he stood over this unwary, loathsome Englishman, Evardo was possessed by a powerful urge to throttle him to death. He balled his hands into fists and took a half step forward before reason stopped him. He was free. The plans he had dreamt about over the previous two months and the path he had vowed to take rushed to the front of his mind.

He stepped around the official and in a half-trance walked to the door. The official's final words echoed in his mind and Evardo wondered who it was that brought the money from Spain. Suddenly he knew who it was. It could only be one man. Evardo's heart raced with anticipation and joy.

'Abrahan,' he whispered as he pushed open the door, eager to see his friend and mentor.

The glare of the sun struck him like an open handed cuff and he brought his arm up to shield his eyes. Four pike-men stood on guard immediately outside the door. One turned around to glance indifferently at Evardo, then turned away again. Evardo saw the guards' attention was on a group of women standing nearby. Some were crying and wailing and as Evardo watched, one of them staggered forward to plead with the guards.

Evardo looked beyond the group to the wider courtyard. It was an expansive area bounded by grey walls and beyond he could see the rooftops of the surrounding city of London. There were people milling in every direction across the open space but one solitary man caught his attention. He was standing still, directly ahead of him. Evardo squinted against the sunlight, his spirits lifting as he recognized the clothing of a Spaniard. The man stepped forward and Evardo started walking quickly forward to meet him.

Suddenly he stopped, his heart plummeting. It was not Abrahan, it was a Pedro Moreno, a senior servant from his family's house in Madrid. Moreno was smiling as he ran the last few steps to stand before Evardo.

'It is good to see you, señor. Truly, I thank the Madonna that you are safe.'

'It is good to see you too, Pedro,' Evardo replied reluctantly, before chastising himself for his lack of good grace. He reached out and clasped the servant's shoulder, smiling gratefully. 'Yes. I am glad to see you.'

Pedro thanked him but then his expression grew serious. 'Come, señor,' he said, looking over Evardo's shoulder to the guards. 'We should leave this place.'

Evardo nodded and followed Pedro across the courtyard toward an arched exit in the outer wall.

'Tell me, Pedro. How did you get here so quickly?'

'It was señor Miguel,' Pedro replied with pride. Evardo's eldest brother, the patriarch of the family. 'From the moment he heard of your capture he began making arrangements for your release. Within a month he had secured passage for me on the fastest ship from La Coruña, along with diplomatic passes and the full ransom in gold.'

Pedro then began to tell the story of his journey in detail, from Madrid to La Coruña and onward to Dover and London where he was granted an audience with the Spanish ambassador, all on the strength of a letter he carried from Miguel. Evardo listened in silence while inside he burned with shame. Over the previous months he had yearned to be free but now he was faced with the cost of that freedom. How could he face his eldest brother and his family? How could he repay the influence and money spent securing his release?

The answer was immutable. He must secure the command of a galleon. It was the only way he could regain his honour. He would have to ask Miguel to canvass on his behalf. That his release from prison had been arranged so quickly was testament to the wealth and power of the family, but what Evardo was asking would require an altogether more denigrating approach. A new patron would be difficult to secure and Miguel would have to pay a heavy coin for someone to overlook Evardo's defeat.

Miguel would help him, of that Evardo was sure. He was an honourable man and fiercely protective of the entire family. Therein lay the root of a further humiliation for Evardo. He was wholly willing to descend to the very depths of humility to achieve his goal. It was the price he knew he had to pay if he was to wreak his revenge on the English. But now Miguel too would have to debase himself if Evardo was to succeed. It was a bitter realization. As he followed Pedro out of the prison, Evardo found it impossible to raise his head.

Robert looked out from the porch of the small chapel into the darkness and driving rain. Although he was soaked through the night was warm. He stilled his breathing as he tried to listen for sounds of approach. Father Blackthorne had been gone for nearly ten minutes and Robert was beginning to wonder if he was having difficulty persuading the duke to come out on such a night. He stuck his head out and glanced at the estate house only two hundred yards away. It was in darkness.

The three day journey from Plymouth had been arduous and nerve wracking. It had afforded Robert a glimpse of the life Father Blackthorne was forced to live. They had travelled only at night and Robert had marvelled at the older man's fortitude and guile. The priest had an established network of Catholic families that would give them shelter but from the outset Robert had insisted that there was to be no contact with anyone until they reached Clarsdale's estate. Father Blackthorne had baulked at the idea of hiding and sleeping in hedgerows when more comfortable accommodation was available, arguing that Robert had frequently met other Catholics when he attended mass on the motte, but Robert had been adamant and Father Blackthorne had relented.

Robert's only goal was to make contact with his father. Everything else was a façade for Father Blackthorne's benefit. While he remained loyal to Elizabeth in his heart, his actions had slipped into the realm of sedition. As a practising Catholic, his faith branded him a traitor, but Robert had always reasoned that to congregate with other Catholics for mass was an act of faith alone, a benign rebellion against the established religion and law of the Crown.

Now however he possessed knowledge of a high ranking traitor. As a loyal Englishman his duty was clear. He should expose Clarsdale for who he was. But to do so was to risk losing perhaps the only chance he had of contacting his father. He could not do it, not yet. For the first time in his life Robert realized his personal aspirations could not be reconciled with his loyalty to Elizabeth. He was walking a traitor's path.

He had already decided that after contact was made with his father, he would find some way to distance himself from Clarsdale and Father Blackthorne. To do so it was vital that he limit his exposure to the web of sedition that surely surrounded the duke. Robert had insisted that his journey to the estate should remain as secret as possible. He had also told Father Blackthorne that he only wanted to see Clarsdale when they reached his estate, no other person, neither servant nor confederate, and that he was to be addressed as Robert

Young at all times. The duke was not to be told his adopted name. It was a thin veil of concealment but one Robert was determined to maintain.

Robert glanced up at the estate house. A single candle was now burning in one of the ground floor windows. The rain had become heavier, pounding on the roof of the porch and cascading over the eaves. Father Blackthorne had argued with Robert one last time before venturing up to the house alone, trying to persuade him to go with him, that he was amongst friends, that it was madness to stay abroad on such a night. Robert had obstinately refused, insisting instead that the duke meet him alone in the solitude of the family chapel.

The light of the candle disappeared, then reappeared a moment later as a door was opened. Two men came out of the house carrying a storm lantern, walking quickly towards the chapel. Robert recognized the gait of Father Blackthorne and stepped out into the deluge to meet them. The man beside the priest looked up as he approached.

'Damn you to hell, boy,' he cursed at Robert. 'What kind of fool are you to insist I come out in this weather to meet you?'

Robert bristled and took a menacing step forward.

'We should get inside,' Father Blackthorne exclaimed, eager to forestall any argument between the two men and, brandishing a key he had been given by the butler, he took Robert by the arm and led him to the door of the chapel.

The interior of the chapel resounded with the noise of rain falling on the roof. It was an austere space. The nave was devoid of any furnishing and the walls were bare and unplastered. Robert and Clarsdale followed Father Blackthorne to the altar where he lit the candles from the storm lantern. As the light increased Robert noticed that Clarsdale was staring at him. The duke nodded, as if confirming something.

'Nathaniel Young's son,' he said slowly to himself. 'You have the look of him.'

'You've met my father?'

'Yes. About fifteen years ago, in France. It was then the link between us was first established.'

'What was he . . .?' Robert stopped himself short. Clarsdale had not asked to meet him to arrange a reunion and Robert suddenly felt embarrassed by his open enthusiasm to know more about his father.

Clarsdale's eyes narrowed. His expression remained neutral but inside he smiled maliciously. Robert Young was an open book. His yearning to see his father was wholly evident and Clarsdale felt his confidence rise. The son of Nathaniel Young would be easy to manipulate. Perhaps the father, given the same bait of making contact with his son, would be equally so.

'Now tell me, Young. Why did you insist that we meet here? Why did you not come up to the house?'

'I thought it best if no one else knew I was here.'

'You thought it best,' Clarsdale scoffed. 'Do you not trust me, boy?'

'Of course he does, your grace,' Father Blackthorne interjected. 'Robert is merely being cautious.'

Clarsdale snorted derisively. 'What is your position in the fleet?'

'I am captain of a galleon, the *Retribution*,' Robert replied, explaining how his command had recently been confirmed by his patron, John Hawkins.

Clarsdale glanced at Father Blackthorne and smiled. Robert Young was perfectly placed within the fleet and would be a valuable resource.

'From this day you must let us know of any new orders the fleet receives. Your contact will be Father Blackthorne,'

Clarsdale said. 'To begin I want you to compile a full report on the strength of the fleet in Plymouth. If possible include anything you hear about other ships stationed in Portsmouth and Dover. Write nothing down. Your report will be verbal. Have it ready for the rising of the new moon, two weeks from now.'

Robert nodded. 'It will be done,' he lied.

'Then this meeting is over. Any information you have is to be given to Father Blackthorne. He will see it gets to me.' The duke turned to leave.

'Wait,' Robert exclaimed, caught off guard by the abrupt end to the meeting. 'I want to send a message to my father.'

Clarsdale paused. He looked at Robert then laughed contemptuously.

'I cannot risk exposing the line of communication for some personal message alone. When your report is complete I will send it to Spain, along with any personal note you wish to send to your father.'

Robert forestalled his protest. His mind was racing. His original goal was now encumbered with a definite act of treason but if he wanted to send a message to his father there was no other way.

Clarsdale noticed Robert's restraint and again he smiled to himself. An open book. Blinded by his desire to make contact with his father Robert obviously hadn't realized that they needed him more than he needed them. Clarsdale nodded imperceptibly, satisfied with his earlier decision. It was not the time to tell Robert Young of the news he had only received days before, the news that had initially shaken Clarsdale's confidence and forced him to rethink his plans. If he was to manipulate events to his ultimate advantage he had to maintain the initiative over both Nathaniel and Robert Young. They could not communicate. If they did Robert would learn what

Clarsdale already knew – Nathaniel Young, the Duke of Greyfarne, was coming to England.

Thomas Seeley paced the quarterdeck of the *Retribution*. His brow was twisted into a scowl and he spun on his heel at the bulwark, muttering under his breath. He was alone, and the crew within eyeshot on the other decks moved quickly to avoid the lash of his tongue. The ship's bell rang four times, the middle of the afternoon watch, and Seeley scanned the waters surrounding the *Retribution* before looking to the distant dockside of Plymouth. Tobias Miller was overdue.

The new master's mate was supposed to have arrived an hour before. Seeley stopped pacing to peer out over the gunwale. In the three weeks since returning to the *Retribution*, he had been unable to advance his quest to find the Roman Catholic spy on board. To his relief, Captain Varian had not ordered him to end his search, although he had demanded that Seeley moderate his investigation. The veil of suspicion that Seeley had placed over the entire crew was adversely affecting morale. The restraint was proving tiresome, and when Shaw had reported at the beginning of the watch that he too was making no headway, Seeley's mood had swiftly descended.

'Quarterdeck ho! Longboat approaching off the larboard beam!'

Seeley spun around. A heavyset man with grey, almost white, hair stood in the bow of the longboat. The sea was windblown and choppy but he was balancing easily, with one leg on the gunwale. Tobias Miller, Seeley thought, remembering when he had first seen him months before.

Miller's commission had come as no surprise to Seeley. Varian had a sizeable task ahead of him in making the *Retribution* his own. It was only natural he would want men around him that he knew well and could trust implicitly. Seeley had already assured the captain of his support. It was sincerely meant, for how else could England stand fast against its enemies if the officers of the fleet were not completely loyal to each other? Despite his continued reservations regarding the captain's commitment to wage total war against the Roman Catholic scourge, he had come to fully respect Varian for his seamanship and bravery.

Seeley heard the longboat thud against the hull and a moment later Miller gained the main deck. He was heavier than Seeley remembered and in the full light of day, he looked older. His eyes darted to every point of the ship before coming to rest on Seeley.

'Permission to come aboard, Master Seeley,' he shouted.

'Granted,' Seeley replied with a genial nod, indicating for Miller to come up.

Miller moved with a seamless agility up the steps to the quarterdeck, thrusting out his hand as he approached.

Seeley took it. The grip was firm and calloused.

'Welcome to the *Retribution*, Master's Mate.'

'Glad to be aboard, Master,' Miller replied.

Seeley searched the words for any sign of insolence, suddenly conscious that he was less than half the age of his new subordinate. He could discern none however, and dismissed Miller to go below and stow his kit.

Seeley watched him leave. Once more he thought of the first time, months before, when he had laid eyes on Miller on board the *Spirit* at Plymouth docks. The man had lied without hesitation to protect Varian, concocting some tale about a meeting with a local trader. It was a lie that spoke of an instinctive loyalty that came from years of shared hardship and toil. It would be difficult to penetrate the obvious bond between the two men.

But penetrate it he must, for Miller was his direct subordinate now, his right hand man. Seeley needed to know he commanded his loyalty. Moreover, he needed to get the measure of Miller's faith. With luck he was as committed to eradicating Roman Catholicism as Shaw had proven to be. Seeley whispered a brief prayer that it was so. If he could gain Miller's trust, then perhaps together they could convince the captain to fully accept the divine task that Seeley believed the Almighty had set them.

'Quarterdeck ho! Longboat approaching off the larboard beam!'

Seeley darted around in surprise. A second longboat was approaching and Captain Varian was sitting in the bow. Seeley went to the main deck to greet him as the longboat moved swiftly alongside.

'Welcome back, Captain.' Seeley wondered where the captain had been for the past week. Knowing Varian, he had taken home leave when they first arrived back in Plymouth.

'Anything to report, Mister Seeley?'

Seeley quickly listed off the routine activities of the past week; the arrival of a new culverin to replace an aging one, the completion of some maintenance on the starboard bow strake timbers of the hull and finally that the new master's mate had just arrived.

'Miller,' Robert said with a broad smile. 'Have one of the men seek him out and send him to my cabin.'

'Yes, Captain.'

'Any change in our standing orders?'

'None, Captain. Only that we are to remain at a state of readiness.'

Robert nodded, his brow creasing in thought.

'What can that mean, Captain?' Seeley asked, thinking perhaps that during the previous week the captain had had some contact with one of the senior commanders – maybe Hawkins, his patron, and that he had some insight into the need for continued caution. 'Surely any threat the Armada posed has passed?'

Robert looked to Seeley as if his question had startled him.

'I don't know, Thomas. Drake has his reasons. Trust in that.'

'Yes, Captain,' Seeley replied. He turned to call a crewman to find Miller.

Robert walked towards his cabin, his thoughts fixed on Seeley's question. Why hadn't the standing orders been changed? The smaller ships had been stood down, but the capital ships remained on alert. What did Drake know that had not filtered down to the crews? That Spain planned to invade England had been common knowledge for over a year, but Robert, like everyone else, had believed that plan had been thwarted, at least for the immediate future. Maybe, he thought uneasily, the raid on Cadiz had not bloodied the Spanish as much as they had first supposed. As he reached the door of his cabin the stomp of boots behind him made him turn.

'Miller,' he exclaimed. 'It is good to see you well, old friend.'

'And you, Captain,' Miller replied, taking the proffered hand of his commander.

Robert led Miller through the door.

'Sit down, man.' Robert poured two tankards of grog. 'Tell me, what news of the *Spirit*?'

'She is in fine fettle, Captain,' Miller replied with pride. 'For the past month we have been ferrying supplies along the length of the south coast. From Dover to Portsmouth and here.'

Robert sat straighter in his chair at the mention of Dover and Portsmouth. His initial question had been innocently asked, but he suddenly realized that Miller had first hand knowledge of what capital, and other ships were stationed at each harbour. He hesitated, not wanting to ask the question that had immediately sprung to mind. He needed to contact his father, and Clarsdale's report was the key. He could give the duke false information, but if his deception was discovered his only chance would be forfeit. Every fibre of his loyalty urged him to expose Clarsdale, while his desire to communicate with his father compelled him to do whatever it took to achieve his goal. He drank deep and the grog seared his throat. He put down his tankard and stared at Miller.

'Drake keeps us at a state of readiness here in Plymouth,' he began, the words coming slowly. 'Is it the same at Portsmouth and Dover?'

'I believe so, Captain. Certainly the amount of stores we are supplying to the galleons suggests they could be ready to sail with less than a day's notice.'

Robert nodded. He watched Miller closely for signs that his question had aroused some suspicion but of course there was none. They had been shipmates for too long and Robert knew Miller would never think ill of him. He felt ashamed, but steeled himself. He had made his decision.

'Tell me about these other galleons.'

Miller began to list off the ships he had seen in Dover and Portsmouth, adding incidental comments that his professional eye had noticed about the condition of each one. He spoke casually, believing the captain's interest was merely professional curiosity. Robert refilled Miller's tankard and remained silent as his mind catalogued each piece of information. All the while a part of his consciousness sought to quieten the bitter protest of his loyalty.

Nathaniel Young heard the crash of the surf through the dark. The longboat reared beneath him and accelerated down the swell of a wave. He glanced over his shoulder past the rowers to the running light of the Spanish galleon in the distance. It was faint but visible. Nathaniel looked back to the blackness of the coast. Where was the signal light of his contact? Looking skyward to the darker outline of the two conical hills that marked the rendezvous point, he reassured himself that he was in the right place.

Suddenly a light appeared directly ahead. The longboat reared again and the rowers deftly balanced the hull as the wave carried them forward. They spoke rapidly to each other in Spanish but Nathaniel ignored them, conscious that soon he would hear naught but his mother tongue. He focused on the light ahead. It was a storm lantern and it seemed to be sitting directly on the beach. No one stood within its illumination.

As the boat crashed through the surf, two of the crew jumped out into the waist deep water to guide the boat ashore. The hull touched sand and Nathaniel jumped over the gunwale. His feet touched solid ground and for a moment he stood still, savouring the moment. He strode forward towards the light but stopped short, crouching down and taking up a handful of sand he let it sift through his fingers. He was home.

'*Señor*,' a voice said in the darkness behind him. 'We will leave you now. God speed.'

'No, wait,' Nathaniel commanded. 'Wait until I am safely away.'

The reply was muttered in gutter Spanish. Nathaniel did not understand the words but he knew their portent. If his contact did not show immediately he would either have to leave with the Spaniards or stay alone. He walked quickly to the storm lantern and stood beside it.

'I am Nathaniel Young,' he called into the darkness.

He was answered with silence.

'*Señor*, we go.'

Nathaniel spun around to protest but in the whiter shade of the crashing surf he saw the men were already clambering back into the boat. For a heartbeat he thought to follow but he stood resolute. There could be no going back. He looked around in the darkness and picked up the storm lantern, then began to walk further up the beach, pausing as his legs brushed against the marram grass above the storm line. He could go no further. There was little point, for his next move was supposed to be decided by his contact. Where in blazes was he? Surely he lit the storm lantern and placed it on the beach. Why did he then retreat? He was tempted to shout out again, but held his tongue. There was no way of knowing who was abroad and he did not want to attract unwanted attention.

The thought brought home the reality of his situation. He was home. This was England. But it was no longer his. The heretic Queen who controlled this land had branded him a traitor and made him an outcast. He had been reduced to fearing discovery by his own countrymen.

'Enough!' he shouted and he walked forward again, oblivious of his course.

'Nathaniel Young,' a voice called out. Nathaniel spun around in the direction of the cry.

'Show yourself.' Nathaniel's hand fell to the hilt of his sword.

'Stand easy, Young. It is I, Clarsdale.'

Nathaniel breathed with relief, which was quickly replaced by anger. 'Why did you not show yourself before?'

'I was wary of the boat load of men who brought you ashore,' Clarsdale lied as he stepped into the light. 'I thought for a moment that news of your arrival might have been discovered and those men were here to capture your contact.'

Clarsdale discerned a slight sneer of contempt from Young at his explanation. He ignored it. What did it matter if Young believed he was meek? It was better if Young continued to harbour a low opinion of him. Clarsdale hid his own scorn behind a neutral expression. He had let Young wait alone in the darkness to ensure the Duke of Greyfarne realized that without him he was just that – alone.

Clarsdale had debated coming himself to meet Young at the landing site. It was a significant risk. But if he had sent a servant with orders to escort Young to his estate, there was a chance the exiled duke might countermand those orders and have the servant guide him to another location. For his plan to succeed, Clarsdale had to strictly control Young's movements from the start.

Clarsdale's original plan, when Nathaniel Young was still in Spain, was to blackmail the exiled duke into revealing the identity of his contact in the Spanish hierarchy. He had intended to tell him that the agent he had secured was his son and if Young did not comply with his wishes Clarsdale would withhold communication between the two, or better yet, threaten to kill Robert. While Nathaniel Young had been in Spain he could have done nothing to protect his son and would surely have stepped aside and allowed Clarsdale unfettered access to the future masters of England.

But Young's announcement that he was coming to England had thrown those budding plans into disarray. For all Clarsdale knew, Young was seeking to bypass Clarsdale and set up a direct link with the agent. And as soon as he found out their new ally was his son that idea would surely come of itself.

Then Clarsdale had realized the incredible opportunity that Young's arrival would grant him. That the Duke of Greyfarne had ended his eighteen-year self-imposed exile spoke of the value Spain placed on the information they sought. Clarsdale had to act, swiftly and decisively. Nathaniel Young was still unaware of his son's involvement. Whether he used subtle blackmail or manipulation Clarsdale still needed Young to reveal the name of his handler in Spain. Then he would reunite father and son to ensure Robert Young's commitment to the task.

With the Duke of Greyfarne in England and within his grasp there was no need for Clarsdale to coerce him into stepping aside. There was an easier way now, one that would ensure Clarsdale would become the all important lynchpin for the valuable intelligence. He would simply kill Nathaniel Young.

CHAPTER 8

10th August 1587. Dover, England.

Evardo spat over the aft as the ship pulled away from the quayside. He turned his back on England and looked to the clear horizon ahead, taking solace from the fact that they were finally away. The journey thus far had not been easy. After leaving the prison grounds in London Pedro had revealed that although he had paid the ransom demanded by the English, he had been forced to pay further bribes to the prison guards and administrator to ensure Evardo's prompt release.

Pedro had been left virtually penniless and so Evardo had gone directly to the Spanish ambassador in London to seek aid. The ambassador had refused to see him. Evardo had pressed for an audience, demanding to know why he was being rebuffed, when he noticed the contemptuous looks of the ambassador's staff. No other explanation was needed. He was disgraced, and no senior Spaniard, certainly not an ambassador, wanted to be associated with him.

Evardo had left London and proceeded to Dover, eager to leave England immediately. The journey had taken nearly a week. They had travelled incognito, knowing their nationality made them a target, and had avoided human contact wherever possible. They had hoarded what little money they had. It would be needed to secure passage on a ship. Evardo had little English but he could speak French, and when they needed to buy food they had passed themselves off as French refugees.

Upon reaching Dover they had found the first available French ship sailing for Calais. It was a stinking barque but the French captain had asked few questions of his Spanish passengers, never looking beyond the silver pieces-of-eight that Evardo had given him.

Evardo glanced at the English capital ships as the French barque passed between them. Their lower, sleeker hulls were so different to the towering castles of Spanish galleons. From a distance it was hard to tell what ordnance they carried but it was well known these new ships were heavily armed. Evardo sneered derisively. Such firepower would matter little when they were grappled and boarded. Therein lay their weakness. Evardo looked forward to the day when he would show the English the depth of their folly.

He turned to the horizon as the barque slipped past the outermost ships in Dover harbour. Once in Calais, Evardo planned to make his way to Antwerp, either by boat or overland. There he would find out where the Duke of Parma was encamped with his army and make contact with his brother, Allante, one of the duke's aides-de-camp. Asking for help would be an ignominious task but it was the only way he could get himself, and Pedro, home to Spain.

Dressed as he was, in tattered rags, it would be humiliating to walk into the camp of the Army of Flanders. Tough, professional and experienced, they were the most feared army in the world. Allante, like his eldest brother Miguel, was sure to help him but as with Miguel, Evardo dreaded the encounter.

He glanced over his shoulder at the diminishing outlines of the English warships and beyond to the mammoth white cliffs that flanked the port of Dover. It was an impressive sight but Evardo drew no pleasure from it. He turned his back once more. England would wait, secure in her conceited confidence, until he returned.

Nathaniel Young stared out the window of the study, captivated by the view. His finger traced the outline of the distant horizon on the glass. The Duke of Clarsdale's estate was so green. It was the English countryside he had pictured in his mind so many times over the previous two decades, the lush fertile land that was so different to the arid soil of his home in exile.

The door opened behind him and he turned to see Clarsdale and his butler enter. Nathaniel stared at the servant. The man held his gaze for a second before looking away. The butler, Nichols, unnerved him. Nathaniel needed to keep the number of people who knew he was back in England to a minimum.

The night before, Clarsdale had led him from the beach to a quiet back road. A servant, the duke's groomsman, was waiting there with horses and the three of them had ridden away with as much haste as the darkness allowed. They had arrived at Clarsdale's estate an hour before dawn and Nathaniel had been shown to a bedroom by the butler, where he found food and warm water waiting for him. Nathaniel had tried to relax in the solitude of his room but he could not. Two wearisome hours passed before Nichols arrived back to escort him to Clarsdale's study.

'See that we're not disturbed, Nichols,' Clarsdale said. The butler nodded to his master and left the room, closing the door behind him.

'You trust him?'

Clarsdale glanced at the closed door.

'I trust all my household staff. Need I remind you, Young,

I have survived thirty years of Elizabeth's reign in the midst of her realm.'

Not safely in exile in some godforsaken foreign land, Clarsdale was tempted to add, but he held his tongue. He could not afford to be at odds with Young, not yet. Since deciding to kill Young Clarsdale had been possessed with an impatience to act, to rid himself of the man who obstructed his path to the Spanish hierarchy, but he knew he had to wait until Young had met his son and secured him as an agent. Only then would the duke be expendable.

'In any case,' he added genially. 'For your safety I have ordered my entire household staff to remain in the house for the duration of your stay.'

Nathaniel nodded in gratitude, although Clarsdale's assurances meant little to him. It was Clarsdale's incompetence that had forced his return to England. Nathaniel felt nothing but apprehension when he thought of how much his safety and the success of his mission relied on the duke. Clarsdale bade him sit but he shook his head. Although he felt lightheaded with fatigue he still preferred to stand.

'So, have you managed to secure an ally to our cause in the navy?'

A hint of a smile played across Clarsdale's face before it hardened once more.

'I have,' he replied slowly.

'Who is he? Is he Catholic?'

'He is. His confessor, Father Blackthorne, recruited him.'

'And you trust this priest?'

Again Clarsdale bridled at Young's suspicions but he endeavoured to hide his anger.

'He is also my priest,' he explained, his voice trembling slightly, 'and yes, I trust him.'

Nathaniel nodded and lowered his head in thought.

'I need to meet this man. Can you arrange it?'

Clarsdale rubbed his chin and pretended to think. He glanced at Young. He looked tired. As the silence drew out Clarsdale decided it was time to play his opening gambit. He shook his head slightly.

'It can be arranged,' he said gravely. 'But I have one concern. The meeting place is someway distant from here and the journey will be dangerous. Should anything happen to you, how do I send the agent's information to Spain? Who can I contact there?'

Nathaniel's eyes narrowed slightly at Clarsdale's request. The duke held his gaze. It was a reasonable request, given the danger Nathaniel was in, but despite Clarsdale's logic, and the fact that he had worked with the duke for years, Nathaniel knew it wouldn't be wise to mention Don Rodrigo de Torres's name. The fewer people who knew the entire network the better. Clarsdale might one day be betrayed himself and captured by the Protestant authorities.

'I cannot give you that name,' Nathaniel said. 'And I already have an arrangement with him. My ship will return for me in exactly one month. If I am not there then it is to be assumed that I have been killed or captured. Either way he will presume that this line of communication has been compromised.'

Clarsdale bunched his fists involuntarily. His face darkened in anger and he stalked over to stand beside Nathaniel at the window.

'You don't trust me?'

'It is not a question of trust.'

'But if you are killed . . . This source is too important,' Clarsdale continued. 'The information he can provide us with will be invaluable to Spain and our cause.'

'I don't even know if I can trust this man,' Nathaniel shot back, angry that Clarsdale was questioning his decision. 'You know him only through your priest. How many times have you met this man? Once? Twice? How do you know he is not working for that arch-fiend, Walsingham?'

'Because of who he is,' Clarsdale retorted, his previously determined strategy forgotten in anger. 'Because of who his father is.'

'Who is his father?' Nathaniel asked dismissively.

'You are,' Clarsdale snarled.

Nathaniel blanched and took a step backward.

'You don't mean . . . Robert,' he whispered.

'Yes,' Clarsdale said. 'Robert Young, son of Nathaniel Young, Duke of Greyfarne.'

'But . . . I never thought . . .'

Nathaniel reached for a chair and sat down. His son, Robert. He had never forgotten him, the boy of twelve he had left at his brother-in-law's house, but like every memory of England, the picture had been eroded by eighteen years of exile. Eventually he had come to think of his son as gone, lost forever to another life.

Nathaniel felt his throat constrict and he leaned forward to ease his breathing. So many times he had thought of the things he would reclaim when England was once more governed by a Catholic monarch. His lands, his title, his honour, and his family – his only son, Robert. Recovering these things was the driving force in his life, but they were also the substance of his dreams and he had long since learned to bury them deeply to ease his sense of loss. But now, suddenly, he was being given the chance to reclaim a part of his past.

'I must see him,' he whispered. 'Does he know I am your contact?'

'He knows,' Clarsdale said coldly. 'Although he does not know you have come to England. If you want to see him you must reveal the name of your contact in Spain.'

Nathaniel looked up, confused.

'Now that you know who the agent is,' Clarsdale continued, 'you must realize that there is too much at risk should something happen to you. We will never find as reliable an ally as your son.'

Nathaniel stood up once more. His emotions were in turmoil but he was more wary than ever of Clarsdale's motives.

'How do I know this man is my son?' he asked, knowing somehow in his heart that it was true.

'Are you willing to sacrifice the chance to see him?'

Nathaniel looked past Clarsdale out the window. The sky was darkening under a rolling blanket of grey-black clouds. He looked back at the duke. Perhaps he should tell him of de Torres. As a man he might not trust Clarsdale, but his dedication to the cause was unquestionable. In any case, de Torres could come to no harm simply because Clarsdale knew his name, even if, one day, the duke might be forced to reveal that information to the Protestant authorities.

Nathaniel halted his thoughts, knowing they were leading him the opposite direction to his earlier caution. Clarsdale was blackmailing him, of that there could be no doubt. It was reason enough not to reveal de Torres's name, and yet, surely such an act on Clarsdale's part spoke to his belief that the information Robert could provide was more important than any one of them. De Torres certainly felt that way. Indeed King Philip himself considered securing an agent in the navy to be of the highest priority. Clearly Nathaniel should follow their lead, particularly now that his son was the agent and his intelligence would therefore be beyond suspicion. He nodded to himself, deciding that he was being overly cautious.

'If I should die the man you must seek out in Spain is Don Rodrigo de Torres. He has the ear of the King and will ensure any intelligence finds its way to the right people.'

'Thank you, Young,' Clarsdale said earnestly, worried that his face might betray his inner triumph.

'Now take me to my son,' Nathaniel demanded.

Clarsdale hesitated for a second. It would be dangerous for him to personally take Young to the rendezvous point on the motte. But, it would expedite his plan. Once father and son had met and Robert Young was fully committed, Clarsdale could dispose of the Duke of Greyfarne at his convenience.

'There is a small church outside Plymouth, Saint Michael's,' Clarsdale explained. 'Beside it is a motte. Your son will be there at the rising of the new moon, three days from now.'

'Three days. So we must wait.'

'No, to avoid detection we must go there by a circuitous route. We leave at sunset.'

Nathaniel nodded. He had an uneasy feeling in the pit of his stomach. Clarsdale's conduct in obtaining de Torres's name had unnerved him. It had been forceful, unwavering, and Nathaniel wondered if Clarsdale's motives went beyond his concern for the intelligence Robert could provide for Spain.

The thought of his son made him wonder if he would see the boy he had once known in the man he was soon to meet. That he was to be an ally in the cause to overthrow Elizabeth filled Nathaniel with immense pride. Nathaniel glanced at Clarsdale, his suspicions lost in amazement at how God, in his infinite wisdom, had arranged for him to meet his only son. He smiled, unaware that this very meeting would precipitate his own death.

Nichols stepped away from the door and walked quickly across the hallway, slipping round a corner and leaning heavily against the wall. His heart was racing. He had been standing at the duke's study door far too long for his own safety. At any time he could have been discovered by one of the other servants who would immediately question why he was eavesdropping on the duke's conversations. In a house filled with people who lived in fear of discovery, suspicion and wariness had become second nature to all.

The conversation between the two traitors had been protracted but Nichols was glad that he had waited. He had the rendezvous point. His problem, however, was how to get that information to Cross. At the arrival of Nathaniel Young, the Duke of Clarsdale had taken the unprecedented step of ordering all his staff to remain confined within the house. Nichols knew he had to comply. After one of his previous meetings with Cross, when he came back to the house with mud-stained trousers, he had drawn awkward questions from the footman and head maid. He had concocted a flimsy excuse about falling while running an errand for the Duke, but the story had sounded unconvincing even to his own ears and he was sure they were still suspicious of that absence.

He would have to wait. There was no other option. His thoughts went to his family, his wife and four children who knew nothing of his activities. It was an innocence that would not protect them if he was caught, despite his wife's misplaced devotion to the Roman Catholic faith. His only chance was to contact Cross after the two traitorous dukes had left the house on their journey to Plymouth.

Nichols considered the consequences of his actions. If Cross confronted and captured the entire nest of traitors at Saint Michael's then Clarsdale would finally be exposed and Nichols would have accomplished his task. He would be free, free to practise openly the faith of his Queen, free to show his wife the errors of her faith and save the imperilled souls of his children. It was a glorious prospect, one that he prayed was less than a day away.

* * *

Cross pulled the collar of his travelling cloak tighter as the wind gusted through the trees around him. The end of the day was rapidly closing in and as he spied the smoke rising from the chimneys of Clarsdale's estate house he thought of the warmth of the fire in the distant tavern where he would stay the night. It was nearly time to leave. Cross cursed the long day he had spent in the solitude of the copse waiting for word from Nichols.

A dozen thoughts had occupied his mind during the day, mixing together to reform into new ideas that were examined and dismissed in turn. He was concerned at Nichols's absence. Had he been discovered? If he had then the plan that Cross had decided on would come crashing down in one fell swoop and the traitors he so desperately wanted to capture would disappear to the safety of Spain.

Cross had been furious when Nichols had told him that Robert Young had already been and gone to Clarsdale's house. Worse still, Nichols had been given no opportunity to see the traitorous informer and so he remained elusive. Cross's visit to Plymouth had yielded nothing. There were simply too many people in the fleet and the port town who could be potential spies for the enemy. He had made contact with Walsingham's local agent there, a man named Francis Tanner, informed him of his search and asked him to keep his ears open, but there was little else he could do.

Cross had also set two men the task of finding the priest. However, he too had disappeared and Cross had come to realize that a man who had managed to remain hidden from the authorities for so long would be nigh on impossible to capture while on the move. The only hope lay in capturing all the traitors when they would inevitably meet. Logically, that meeting place must be Clarsdale's house and so Cross had returned to the estate to keep watch on the house and wait for further news from Nichols.

That wait was now in its eighth day. Cross had become familiar with the routines of the house, but for some reason today had been slightly different. There was less activity and Cross had come to suspect that something was amiss. The nature of his task sometimes made him see conspiracies and anomalies that were not truly there, yet he remained wary. None of the servants attending their daily tasks seemed to be household staff. The sun touched the rim of the western horizon.

Suddenly the breath caught in Cross's throat. He remembered a tiny detail, one that he had dismissed at the time, but coupled with the unusual lack of activity might mean something more. Earlier that morning he had seen the outline of a man standing in Clarsdale's study window. He had thought it was the duke but then another man had appeared beside him. From such a distance it was impossible to see who they were, but Cross could have sworn they were arguing. What if that second man was Robert Young? Or Christ forbid, Cross thought, Nathaniel Young? Nichols had informed him he was coming to England. Perhaps he had arrived and was standing in the house at this very moment.

Cross turned and walked a dozen paces towards his horse. The local sheriff was less than five miles away. He could have the militia here by dawn. Then he stopped in his tracks. Even if he was right, even if Robert or Nathaniel Young was in the house, if he swooped now to capture them the other would escape his grasp. Nathaniel Young was certainly the greater prize, but the son was becoming as dangerous as his father. He needed them both. His plan to catch them all at one time had to remain. He cursed loudly, hating the gamble he was being forced to play.

The sun had fallen below the horizon and the last of its light was poised to follow. Frustration consumed him. He was so close to destroying an entire network of Roman Catholic spies but a gaping chasm of uncertainty separated him from success. As he turned to leave, a movement caught his eye. A man was running away from the house towards the stone bridge that crossed the river. He seemed frantic, glancing repeatedly over his shoulder as he ran. When he reached the bottom of the slope leading to Cross, he vanished behind a fold in the ground, reappearing moments later. It was Nichols.

Robert gained the top of the motte and paused for a moment, listening in the darkness. There was no indication that Father Blackthorne was near at hand. He opened his mouth to utter the password, then hesitated. This was his last chance to pull himself back from the brink of treason. He simply had to walk away. The list of ships he had compiled was in the forefront of his mind, as was the simple message he had composed for his father. If only there was some way to deliver one without the other.

'*Sumus omnes*,' he said aloud.

The password was returned by a familiar voice and Robert stepped forward to greet Father Blackthorne, who led him to a shielded fire on the far side of the summit.

'Would you like me to hear your confession, my son?' Father Blackthorne asked.

'No, Father,' Robert replied sharply. 'I would sooner tell you my report and be on my way.'

Father Blackthorne frowned at Robert's abrupt answer.

'I'm sorry, Father,' Robert said quickly, seeing the priest's expression in the firelight. 'It's just that I need to be back at my ship before the start of the morning watch.'

Robert cursed his lapse. It was better for his confessor to believe that he was fully committed to his task.

'Let us sit then, Robert. I trust you have much to tell me.'

'I have, Father. The fleet at Plymouth . . .'

Suddenly Robert shot up.

'What . . .?' Father Blackthorne began but Robert quietened him with his hand.

'Someone's coming. Are you expecting anyone else?'

Father Blackthorne shook his head.

Robert drew his sword. He peered into the darkness and cocked his head slightly in the direction of the noise. He heard it again – the fall of loose stones. Someone was ascending the motte. He sensed Father Blackthorne rise behind but he did not look back, less the glow of the fire rob his night vision. The sky was cloudless but with a new moon the only light came from the blanket of stars that served to frame and highlight any shape that stood against the sky.

'*Sumus omnes.*'

Robert did not reply.

'*In manu Dei,*' Father Blackthorne answered. Before Robert could curse him, the silhouettes of two men appeared.

'Who are you?' Robert demanded.

'Put down your sword, boy.' Robert recognized Clarsdale's voice.

He sheathed his sword and they stepped into the firelight. Robert looked to the man with Clarsdale. For a moment they stared at each other's faces.

'Father?' Robert whispered incredulously.

'It is good to see you again, my son.' Nathaniel extended his hand.

Robert glanced down and took it without thinking.

'You're here.'

Nathaniel nodded with a smile.

Robert let his father's hand go. From behind him he heard Father Blackthorne gasp in amazement and the priest rushed forward to greet Nathaniel. Robert stood frozen, his eyes still locked on his father. He had changed so much. He was older, of course, but he was different somehow.

Over eighteen years, Robert had turned his father into the embodiment of all that he had lost – his title, his heritage, the honour of his real name. When Clarsdale had told him he was still alive Robert had grasped at the chance to contact him. In restoring the link between him and his father, he hoped to move closer to redeeming his past. But now he was unexpectedly filled with doubt. Maybe his father was not the key to his redemption. Maybe he was just a man, one whose past actions had already cost Robert his true fate and whose presence in England now threatened to take from him all that he had worked for.

'I had to come to secure the naval agent we so desperately need,' Nathaniel said, 'but I only learned of your involvement after I landed in England.'

Robert barely heard the words his father spoke. Instead he studied him closely and realized suddenly that for too long he had shied away from the obvious truth of the man before him, of what he was, of what he had always been.

'I was so proud to find out that you were the agent,' Nathaniel concluded, holding his hand out once more to his son.

Robert recoiled. His father was a traitor of the worst kind. He was not standing tall in the front line of battle, he was skulking in the undergrowth, engaging in espionage in a bid to bring down England from within.

'You say you are proud?' he asked coldly.

'Yes, of course.'

'To learn that I'm a traitor?'

'A traitor? A traitor against what?'

'Against the Crown,' Robert spat. 'Against Elizabeth. Against this country.'

'A collaborator!' Clarsdale leapt forward, drawing his sword.

Robert reacted instantly, drawing his own blade. He dropped into a defensive posture.

Clarsdale side stepped warily, swishing his sword through a shallow arc. His mind was racing. He felt panic swell up inside him. Robert Young had deceived them. Was he in league with others? Was he an agent of the Crown? Clarsdale's eyes darted to each side, trying to see into the dark. He had always been so cautious, ensuring that no one outside his trusted staff knew of his religion and his cause. Now he was exposed. He forced himself to remain calm. Maybe Robert Young was alone. Maybe he was simply the loyal recusant the priest claimed he was. Clarsdale clung to that hope, using it to further quell his alarm and he moved slowly to gain a better attack position. Whatever Robert Young was, he had to die.

'I . . . I don't understand,' Nathaniel stammered. 'I thought you were Catholic. I thought . . .'

'I am Catholic,' Robert rejoined, his eyes on Clarsdale, 'but I'm also loyal to my Queen.'

'You can't be both,' Nathaniel retorted, regaining his wits. 'You cannot be true to your faith and to the heretic Queen.' He looked deeply into his son's eyes, trying to see the boy that was once his. He saw only anger, and another emotion, one that affected him deeply – shame.

'Who are you, Robert?' he whispered. 'What have you become?'

'If you don't know me it's because you left when I was just a boy. I am an Englishman and Elizabeth is my Queen. Without your treacherous influence, I have grown up true to my faith, my country and my sovereign.'

'My treacherous influence?' Nathaniel uttered. He reached out to his son but Robert shrugged him off angrily. Clarsdale seized the opportunity and lunged forward.

Robert parried Clarsdale's vicious strike, turning his blade through a column of sparks from the fire. He leapt back and prepared to attack. Father Blackthorne quickly stepped into the shadows but Nathaniel stood motionless as Robert and Clarsdale clashed once more, their blades striking each other in a fury of steel and anger.

Nathaniel gazed at Robert. The brief moment of curiosity and happiness that he had felt when he first saw him was gone. Now there was only turmoil, and worse, a growing anger at what his son had proclaimed. His son's beliefs were an abomination before God. Elizabeth was the devil's spawn. She was the standard bearer for the Protestant faith. She had to be overthrown.

Nathaniel's anger deepened. When he had left Robert with his wife's brother he had thought that William Varian would keep him true to Catholicism. But Varian had twisted his son's faith into something despicable, destroying the foundations that Nathaniel had laid. His son was no longer Catholic, not in the true sense, not if he supported the jezebel who was the Queen of England.

The fight intensified and Robert neatly parried a killing strike to his groin before reversing the attack, leaping forward to come inside Clarsdale's counter strike. The two men came chest to chest, their blades upturned between them. Nathaniel saw the killing urge that possessed them both and with certainty he realized that in the next moments either his ally or his son would die. His sword leapt from its scabbard.

John Cross stepped through the ditch bordering the graveyard. The chink and rattle of weaponry sounded unnaturally loud in his ears and he glanced over his shoulder at the shadowy outlines of the thirty soldiers who followed him, willing them to quieten their approach. Ahead of them was the looming shape of the motte. It was larger than he had imagined and he cursed the necessity of attacking such a dominating place in darkness.

He felt a tap on his shoulder. Francis Tanner was directly behind him. He pointed ahead to the motte and Cross nodded irritably. He was furious with the agent from Plymouth, not because of his unnecessary directions, but because Tanner had told the squad of soldiers before they left Plymouth that their mission tonight was to capture a group of Roman Catholic spies. The news had been like a red rag to a bull. Although Cross had subsequently tried to quell their zeal for the hunt, explaining to them that he needed the traitors captured alive, he knew many of them were baying for blood and would likely ignore his entreaties.

Cross slowed his pace, looking left and right to the extremities of the motte. He estimated it was at least two hundred paces around and more than thirty feet high. He stretched out his arms, indicating to the soldiers to fan out and surround the site, then looked to the summit. The crumbling walls gave it an irregular shape and he felt the dread of indecision in his stomach. If he attacked the ruins, chaos was bound to ensue and some of the traitors might escape. On the other hand, if he waited for them to descend they might not all leave together, or in the same direction. Worse still, if they became aware they were surrounded, they might cause a diversion in one area and escape in another.

Cross drew his sword and allowed the familiar weight to calm him. He reached the base and heard the men shuffle past him as they went to encircle the motte. He looked up the steep slope. The perimeter of the motte at the summit was half that at the base. If his men gained that perimeter then the net would be twice as effective. He nodded to himself and whispered to Tanner. They would advance up the hill. The agent ran off to tell the rest of the men, whispering to each in turn. Cross watched him disappear into the darkness. He tightened his grip on his sword and took to the slope of the motte.

Cross stopped short. There was a clash of steel, and another. It was a faint sound, muffled by distance and the ruins, but it sounded as if men were fighting on the summit. He increased his pace. Had one of the soldiers already reached the summit? Impossible. The fight had to be amongst the men he had come to arrest. But how could that be? Cross was suddenly filled with apprehension. The prize he so desperately wanted was just yards away. He pushed on up the slope, praying that the men he sought would come to no harm.

Robert slashed his blade down, knocking away the point of Clarsdale's sword. He was breathing heavily and his left hand was dripping with blood from a gash in his forearm, but he was possessed with the strength of his battle lust. He stepped forward again, eager to end the fight.

Clarsdale gave ground, tiring fast. His sword arm was numb and he felt the muscles in his shoulder jar as he parried another strike from a keen opponent half his age.

Robert sensed Clarsdale's desperation, saw it in his eyes, and pressed home his attack, sweeping his blade through a series of sequenced strikes that turned his weapon into a flurry of steel. Clarsdale blocked each attack but his sword was slowly forced outward, twisting the wrist of his sword hand, weakening his grip and Robert suddenly struck the flat of Clarsdale's blade with all the momentum of his attack, knocking the sword from his hand. He went in for the kill but his strike was stopped short by another blade. He spun around, his eyes going to his new foe.

'Lower you sword,' Nathaniel commanded.

Robert did not move.

'You cannot kill him,' Nathaniel warned, keeping his sword charged. His son had chosen to oppose them, he was the enemy and Nathaniel moved around to place himself between Robert and Clarsdale.

'He's a traitor,' Robert said, staring at the darkened features of the man standing before him. 'So are you, Father, and in running off to seek exile in the midst of this country's enemies you have revealed yourself to be worse – a coward.'

Nathaniel's temper slipped beyond the bounds of his control and he lunged forward at the insult. Robert leapt back but he swiftly counter attacked, sweeping his blade in low, trying to draw around to his father's flank. Nathaniel countered but he gave ground, his balance faltering as Robert extended his assault, thrusting deeply into Nathaniel's defence, forcing him to react with greater speed.

Robert feigned left and then switched his attack in the last instant. Nathaniel parried and Robert repeated the sequence, feigning left once more. This time Nathaniel was quicker to react, anticipating the ruse and he struck back with a sharp riposte, slicing through the material of Robert's jerkin. Robert stayed on the offensive, shifting his weight to attack to the left. Nathaniel expected another feint but this time Robert followed through, catching him off guard, his reactions too slow, and Nathaniel instinctively twisted his upper body to avoid the strike, splitting his defence wide open in an instant. Robert immediately reversed his blade and the tip of his sword swept up to his father's throat.

'Robert, no!' a voice cried out.

Robert stayed the blow, holding the tip an inch from Nathaniel's throat. Father Blackthorne stepped out of the darkness.

'He's your father, Robert. You cannot kill him. It is a mortal sin.'

'He is not my father,' Robert breathed. 'He's a traitor.'

'And you are not my son,' Nathaniel spat, his eyes blazing with hatred.

Robert nodded. 'Then I am absolved.'

'You men on the summit!' a voice roared from out of the darkness. 'You are surrounded. In the name of the Queen, I command you to drop your weapons and step forward.'

Robert leapt back from his father and swung around, charging his sword in the direction of the challenge.

'You,' Clarsdale cursed at Robert. 'You have betrayed us all.'

'Have a care, Clarsdale,' Robert warned over his shoulder, 'less I spill your blood and save the executioner his coin. I have betrayed no one.'

'Then who has led them here?' Clarsdale asked, his eyes darting in every direction.

Robert couldn't answer. He peered into the darkness, trying to discern if they were indeed surrounded. From all sides he heard signs of approach. For a moment he was tempted to surrender. He was innocent, he had done nothing wrong, but no one would believe such a claim, especially once they found out one of the real traitors was his father. He had no choice. He had to escape.

'There is no place to hide,' the voice called out. 'You are surrounded. I order you to step forward!'

Robert glanced at the others. Clarsdale was on the verge of panic. His father had taken up an attacking stance once more and his blade was charged before him. He too was searching the darkness. He noticed Robert was looking at him and their eyes locked for a moment in unspoken hatred. Robert looked away to Father Blackthorne. The priest's face was a mask of terror.

'Douse the fire,' Robert said to his father. 'Our only chance is to split up and try and slip through the cordon in separate places.'

'It's no use, we're trapped,' Father Blackthorne whimpered, overwhelmed by the fears that had lived with him for so long.

Robert ignored him and stared at his father, waiting for a response. Nathaniel nodded and stepped forward. He kicked dirt over the fire and the feeble light rapidly gave way to near total darkness. In the corner of his eye Robert saw Clarsdale go to ground. He looked back to his father but he too was gone. Near at hand Robert could see the vague outline of Father Blackthorne. He grabbed him by the arm.

'Stay close.' He pulled the priest down into a low crouch as he slipped behind the nearest wall.

'This is your last warning!' the voice called out again. 'Come forward or we will advance!'

Robert crept forward, moving at right angles to the voice. He dragged Father Blackthorne over a wall and raised his head to look about him. A faint light caught his eye and he stared at it for a moment. It was the glow of a slow-burning match, the tiny smouldering flame that was poised to ignite the charge of an arquebus. He looked left and right of it and saw others close by. The cordon was compact and ordered. There was no chance they could simply slip through. Their only chance was to create confusion and hope that a breach would emerge.

'On my order, prepare to advance,' the voice called out. 'Advance!'

Robert drew out his wheellock pistol and took careful aim at the smouldering match. He fired. A man cried out and Robert heard his arquebus fall to the ground.

'I'm hit,' the man screamed. From all sides others began to shout in the darkness.

'The papist bastards have pistols!'

'Let 'em have it!'

The air was rent with the sound of gunshots. Bullets whizzed over Robert's head and ricocheted off the walls around him. Another man screamed out in pain, then another, while others shouted in anger as they charged forward.

'Cease fire!' a voice roared. 'God curse you, cease fire!'

The order was ignored and the firing continued sporadically as men reloaded. Robert saw a figure lumbering towards him and stood up to meet the charge. Another bullet flew past him. The soldier saw him and screamed a curse, bringing his sword up. Robert saw the silhouette of his arm against the sky. He reacted on instinct and sidestepped. Their blades clashed and Robert backed off, quickly absorbing the momentum of the soldier's attack. The ground underfoot was strewn with rubble and the soldier stumbled. Robert whipped his sword around for the killing strike but in the final instant he reversed his thrust and struck his attacker in the face with the pommel of his sword, breaking his nose. The solider cried out and slumped to the ground.

Robert reached out and grabbed Father Blackthorne. The priest staggered to his feet. He called out incoherently, consumed with fear. Robert dragged him forward.

'Move damn you. We need to go, now.'

He pulled the priest over another low wall. A bullet ricocheted overhead, sending splinters of stone flying through the air. The summit was blanketed in gun smoke and for a moment Robert lost his bearings. He heard the clash of steel nearby and the angry shouts of attackers.

Reaching out with his hand he felt his way forward and began to increase his pace, but ran headlong into a solid wall. The blow stunned him and he tasted blood. He angrily felt along the line of the ruins, dragging Father Blackthorne behind. Suddenly he sensed the fall of the ground beneath his feet. They had reached the edge of the summit. A bullet whistled past, then another, but Robert was already descending.

Father Blackthorne grunted behind him and fell forward, crashing into Robert. The two men tumbled down the hill of loose stone and gorse.

Robert swore as he regained his feet. He glanced up at the smoke strewn summit. It was impossible to tell what was happening. One voice was shouting above the others, the voice that had first challenged them. It was calling for an end to the fighting, for order, but chaos had been unleashed and would only end when the last man regained his wits. Robert looked for Father Blackthorne. He was slumped nearby and Robert grabbed him under the shoulder to haul him to his feet. The priest cried out in pain and Robert cursed his screams, fearing they might draw attention. He lost his grip and Father Blackthorne fell backwards onto the grass. Robert made to seize him again but stopped. His hand felt slick and wet. It was covered in blood.

Cross bellowed in rage as the shooting finally ceased. He stepped out from behind the shelter of a wall and called for torches to be lit. A flame appeared in the gun smoke, followed by a dozen more and he stalked over to the nearest one, grabbing it off a soldier before catching him by the collar of his doublet.

'Find Francis Tanner,' he snarled. 'And spread the word. I want a full sweep of the summit. I want those men found.'

The soldier nodded fearfully and moved quickly away. Cross held the torch out and turned slowly. The body of a solider was nearby and he walked over to see he had been shot in the chest.

The skirmish had lasted for five minutes, five long minutes. Cross's every order to cease fire had been ignored and he spat on the body at his feet, knowing that in the confusion the soldier had probably been killed in the crossfire by one of his own comrades.

The gun smoke was clearing slowly and Cross watched the men, silhouetted by torch light, move in every direction amidst the ruins. His ambush had been a disaster. He had thought that by surrounding and surprising the traitors they would submit quickly and quietly. But they had not. Instead they had turned the tables and Cross realized that whatever the outcome now, it would be worse than he had hoped.

'Cross,' he heard and Tanner approached with a group of soldiers.

'Well?' Cross asked.

'The bastards shot dead two of our men and another was slain by a sword. Two more have bullet wounds.'

'And the papists?' Cross asked angrily, caring little for the soldiers. The fools had brought death upon themselves.

'We got one,' Tanner said, indicating over his shoulder.

'Alive?'

Tanner smiled maliciously. 'He's dead.'

Cross brushed past him and walked quickly through the ruins. A group of soldiers was standing in a tight knot around a body.

One, Cross thought furiously. Out of four, and not even that one taken alive.

The soldiers separated as Cross approached, wary of his murderous expression in the torch light. He looked down on the body. The man was lying face down. He had been shot in the back. Cross turned him over with his foot, crouching down to look at the man's face and unseeing eyes in the orange glow of the torch fires. It was the Duke of Clarsdale.

'Sir,' a soldier called and Cross looked up. A soldier staggered towards him, his blood soaked hand covering his nose.

'Two of 'em got past me over there, sir,' he burbled, pointing behind him.

Cross was immediately on his feet.

'Follow me,' he commanded the assembled soldiers and spun the injured man around, ordering him back to the exact spot. The soldier led them to where he was struck down. Cross shoved him aside and kept going to the edge of the summit. He drew his sword and began to descend, holding his torch out far to his side to scan the ground. The gorse was flattened in places, as if someone had tumbled down the slope. He quickened his descent.

Reaching the base he peered into the blackness beyond the light of his torch. He looked down and noticed a large dark patch in the grass at his feet. He played his torch over it and smiled. Blood. It was not over yet. He turned to the soldiers who had followed him down. There were more than a dozen of them.

'Spread out along a line,' he ordered, looking to each man in turn. 'We can still catch them. But I warn you, I want these men taken alive. If any man fires without my command, I'll see him whipped within an inch of his life.'

The soldiers nodded darkly and moved off, fanning out on either side of Cross. They advanced quickly, their torch lights sweeping the ground before them. Ahead of them the solid outline of the church of Saint Michael's stood resolute in the darkness.

'Enough,' Father Blackthorne cried out. 'Please, I can't go on.'

Robert ignored his protests and dragged him the remaining few feet to the wall of the church. He slumped against it and Father Blackthorne cried out again as he dropped to the ground. Robert glanced over his shoulder. A line of torches was advancing towards them from the motte. There was little time. He crouched down, trying to slow his breathing and regain his strength. Father Blackthorne was weakening quickly and was already a dead weight. Robert looked around him frantically. The graveyard was a maze of tombstones but there was no place to hide. He had to go on. He made to haul Father Blackthorne up again but the priest feebly brushed his hand aside.

'No, Robert,' he gasped. 'Leave me here.'

'I can't, Father,' Robert replied, fearing for his confessor, the man who had been his guide for so long. 'You know what those men will do to you if you are captured alive.'

'They cannot hurt me, Robert,' Father Blackthorne smiled and blood trickled from the corner of his mouth. 'I'm already near death. I feel God's hand upon me.'

'There's still a chance,' Robert protested, glancing up at the sound of voices approaching. The torches had nearly reached the edge of the graveyard. He looked down at the priest. His face was barely discernible in the darkness but after so many years Robert knew it intimately. He was suddenly overwhelmed by regret. His plan to contact his father had ended in total failure, at a terrible cost.

'Forgive me,' Robert said, reaching for the priest's hand. 'I used you so I could contact my father. I never thought something like this would happen.'

'Robert,' Father Blackthorne whispered fiercely. 'It is I who should ask for forgiveness.' He coughed violently and Robert held him as his body shuddered. 'I was blinded by my ambition,' he breathed. 'I betrayed my sacred trust and withheld absolution from you when . . .'

Robert quietened him, not wanting to hear any more. The soldiers' voices were growing louder. They were searching the ditch that bordered the edge of the graveyard.

Father Blackthorne drew Robert down.

'I'm so tired.' The pressure of his grip on Robert's hand fell away to nothing. Robert squeezed the lifeless flesh.

'*In nomine Patris, et Filii, et Spiritus Sancti,*' he whispered, making the sign of the cross over the face of his confessor. He stood up and looked to the approaching torches. Half of them had now entered the graveyard. In less than a minute their light would reach the church walls.

Robert stared at the flames and saw the fire that consumed Captain Morgan and his crewmates on the Spanish galleon. Those behind the fire were the enemy and he felt a blind rage build within him. He whipped his sword from his scabbard and took a step forward when suddenly a figure emerged out of the darkness. Before he could react the tip of a blade was at his throat.

'I should kill you,' the man said.

Robert's rage contracted at the sound of the voice. 'And I should have killed you when I had the chance,' he replied venomously, waiting for the death strike.

It did not come. As the outer reaches of torch light briefly illuminated his father's face, Robert saw his expression of uncertainty and anger.

'Go ahead, strike me down,' Robert hissed. 'You took my life from me once. Why do you hesitate now?'

The light disappeared and darkness consumed them once more. Robert felt the weight of his sword in his hand. He could hear the sound of approaching voices and his own heart pumping in his ears. The outline of his father filled his vision and for a second he imagined him with the face of Father Blackthorne, his mind consumed with the loss of his confessor.

He felt the blade fall away from his throat. In the corner of his eye he saw nearby headstones awash with the approaching wall of light. They were seconds from discovery. He stared back at the outline of his father's face. Why did he not strike? Robert remembered the tip of his own blade trembling at the throat of his father.

'You should go.'

'I will. But know this, Robert. One day soon I will return with the armies of Spain at my back. On that day you will regret the folly of your misplaced loyalty.'

'We shall see.' His killing urge was barely in check as he sidestepped warily away from his father, moving deeper into the darkness. Within a moment his father was lost from sight. Robert turned and began to run as the shouts rang out through the night. They had discovered the body of Father Blackthorne.

CHAPTER 9

3rd December 1587. Barcelona, Spain.

Evardo wept as his eyes beheld the verdant slopes of the mountains that stood stark against the cobalt blue sky – the Serra de Collserola. Nestled beneath them the port of Barcelona slowly came into view. Evardo drank in every aspect, every detail, filling his heart and replenishing his spirit. For a moment he was the young boy he once was, returning from his first trade voyage across the vast Atlantic, seeing his homeland again after too long an absence.

The journey from Parma's camp had taken nearly four months. After a month's delay in Antwerp they had travelled overland along the Spanish Road, the trade and military route that led from the battlefields of the Spanish Netherlands through the heart of Europe to northern Italy. Evardo had sought to take the faster route home by sea along the English Channel, but Allante had insisted he take the safer course. Evardo had been obliged to concede, knowing he had little choice. The overland journey had ended in Genoa and from there Evardo and Pedro had embarked on a military galley bound for home.

The galley swept along the sea lane, its sleek hull threading a path through the slower moving trading vessels under sail, the helmsman altering his course to give way to the less manoeuvrable vessels in the age old tradition observed by all at sea. Evardo studied each ship in turn as they sped past. They hailed from every corner of the Mediterranean and beyond to the Atlantic coasts of Portugal and France. United by the common principles of trade, they also shared a faith that was the wellspring of an empire and Evardo was overwhelmed with a sense of belonging.

Warships were conspicuous by their absence amongst the profusion of sea craft and Evardo wondered if the preparations for an Armada were still continuing apace in the distant port of Lisbon. He recalled the many conversations he had had with Allante about the planned invasion of England during his month-long stay in Parma's camp. His brother had spoken of Parma's constant frustration over the lack of secrecy surrounding the enterprise and Evardo had noticed that even the civilian camp followers argued openly about the best way to tranship the Army of Flanders to the English coast. By necessity Parma would have to divide his available forces and leave sufficient men in the Netherlands to defend those cities already conquered. But Allante had whispered that despite this division the planned invasion force would consist of 30,000 men and 500 horse. It was a staggering amount. Evardo had prayed nightly for the deliverance of such a host.

Allante had gone on to tell Evardo in confidence of the latest plans. Initially Parma had wanted to launch his own surprise invasion from the Flemish coast to the English coastline of Kent and had cared little for the alternative strategy of a supporting invasion force launched from Spain using an Armada. His Army of Flanders was the finest in the world and would be in London long before the Marquis of Santa Cruz, or any other noble, could assemble and launch a fleet.

Now however the element of surprise had been lost. Without a following wind Parma's invasion force might take ten to twelve hours to cross the Channel. Even in the best of conditions the crossing would take eight and during that time the flat bottomed transports would be easy prey for English galleons. Correspondence from Spain spoke of diversionary landings in Ireland, of securing a safe anchorage on the Isle of Wight before any invasion could begin, but these tactics were now incidental to the new crux of the strategy. Parma needed the Armada to defend his crossing of the narrow straits of Dover.

Evardo had marvelled at the ingenious combined strategy, but Allante had seemed uncertain, speaking of the doubts that the Duke of Parma had expressed to his aide-de-camp. Such a marriage of forces would require perfect co-ordination and a synchronicity between commanders that would be nigh impossible to achieve. It took four to six weeks to receive an answer to any query sent to Spain. How much more difficult would it be to communicate with a moving fleet of ships?

Over the course of his journey along the Spanish Road, Evardo had given much thought to his brother's revelations. The difficulties facing the invasion were significant but they were far from insurmountable and Evardo suspected that his brother was influenced by the same mistrust of the sea shared by all soldiers. As a sailor Evardo had more confidence in the Armada's task of supporting Parma's crossing. The Marquis of Santa Cruz, the commander of the Armada, was a daring, formidable and highly experienced naval officer. Spanish ships and crews had forged an empire that spanned the globe. In overwhelming force they would surely sweep the English Channel clear of any fleet that might dare to attempt to thwart their plans.

The galley pulled into the inner harbour and Evardo closed his eyes to listen to the cacophony of sound that was a busy

Spanish port. He was home. The long months of enforced absence from the sacred soil of Spain were over. He opened his eyes and looked above the city to the backdrop of mountains, imagining the road that led beyond through the heart of Spain to his family home. The galley slid neatly alongside the dock and Evardo stepped quickly down the gangplank. Ahead lay a bitter and uncertain struggle to regain his loss, but he was eager to begin.

'Ready . . .'

'Hold . . .'

The gunners blew on their slow matches, fanning the smouldering flames.

'Hold . . .'

Larkin, the master gunner, sensed the pitch of the deck, waiting for the perfect moment.

'Fire!'

The linstocks fell. Plumes of smoke hissed from the touchholes. A second passed and then almost as one the starboard cannons of the *Retribution* boomed. The noise was deafening and in the confines of the gun deck the sound seemed to emanate from every fibre of the ship. Smoke flooded through the open gun ports, engulfing the men, searing their throats and burning their eyes.

'Reload!' Larkin roared and Robert stepped further back to give the men room.

In trance-like determination the gun crews unlashed their guns from the hull and hauled on the ropes. The pulleys squealed and the four-wheeled truck carriages rolled inboard. Men rushed forward to sponge out the barrels, extinguishing any lingering sparks from the previous firing. A ladle of gunpowder was inserted and emptied, then wadding was rammed into the barrel.

The men were using only a fraction of the powder required and they simulated the loading of a round shot before ramming the barrel again. The *Retribution* had precious little supplies and Robert could not afford to waste any in training. The men worked in dogged silence, stepping around each other in a routine that Larkin had honed long before Robert had taken command. A gunner cleaned out the touchhole and primed it again.

The crews worked at slightly different rates and individual commands rang out as the prepared guns were hauled back into their firing position and lashed against the bulkhead. There were seven guns on the starboard side of the gun deck, two cannon-pedros, four culverins and a demi-culverin. The cannon-pedros were the last to be made secure, the 3,000 pound dead weight of each testing the strength of the crew. Individually the gunners shouted out that their guns were ready to fire and as the last declaration was heard, Larkin ordered the men to stand down.

'I make it roughly twenty minutes, Captain,' he said tetchily, and Robert hid a smile behind a solemn nod. He had the impression that Larkin wouldn't be happy even if the men loaded their guns in half that time.

In battle the crews would fire the guns in sequence as each side was brought to bear; the heavy bow chasers as the ship approached the enemy, followed by a broadside, then the stern chasers and finally the opposing broadside. Only then would they service the guns for the next attack. Peters, the gunner's mate, would follow the same pattern on the main deck although he had few guns to service, two demi-culverins and eight sakers in total while the entire crew were trained to load and fire the remaining eight swivel-mounted breech-loading falcons, firing a 2 pound man-killing round shot.

Robert leaned his arm against the deck beam overhead.

After five rounds of reloading and firing their cannons the gun crews were breathing heavily but Robert could see they were satisfied with their work. The men took pride in their guns and the taunts of the faster teams during the exercise had spurred the others on to greater speed. Robert was now familiar with every model of gun on board and although he would never have Larkin's knowledge of cannonry, he had earned the master gunner's respect in his quest to devise tactics which would best combine sailing operations and artillery.

There had been precious little time to find his feet after he took command on the Cadiz raid and so Robert had pushed his crew hard over the previous three months in a bid to get the full measure of them. He had participated in nearly every drill to understand the limits of the galleon and each time his respect had grown for the *Retribution*.

'Well done, lads,' he called out to the gun crews. 'Mister Larkin, a double ration of grog for every man.'

The men smiled and Robert turned to go back up to the main deck.

'Right ye motherless offal,' Larkin roared. 'You're not done yet. I want every gun cleaned out and made ready. Haul 'em in.'

On the quarterdeck Seeley watched the captain emerge from below. He looked satisfied and Seeley tried to anticipate what task he would set the deck crew. He glanced at Miller, but the master's mate was deep in conversation with the boatswain. Seeley took a moment to study the man.

Over the autumn months he had formed a solid partnership with Miller, learning quickly to trust the older man's experience. He had submitted to his judgement many times and Seeley could already sense Miller's influence in how he handled ship operations.

He had had less success, however, in breaching the bond

between Varian and Miller. The captain always issued his orders through Seeley but Miller had often second guessed those commands before they were given, knowing intimately how Varian liked to run his ship. Seeley had also learned, to his frustration, that Miller was not a religious man. He was God-fearing, as were all the crew, but he did not hate the Spanish because of their cursed religion. Miller had been a trader for all his life and his enmity towards the Spanish lay in their monopolies and arrogant claims to the new world that were a stranglehold on English commerce.

'Report, Mister Seeley.'

'All's well, Captain. By your order, the sprit mast and sail have been re-rigged.'

Robert nodded and looked forward. In any collision with another ship, the spritsail would invariably be damaged and steering would be badly affected. Robert had wanted to ensure that the men could rig a new spritsail at sea. The sail was unfurled and looked to be correct but Robert decided to take a closer look. He went forward to the fo'c'sle.

The work was flawless. Robert turned to look back along the length of the *Retribution* and beyond to the western horizon. The winter sun was no more than two hours from the end of its day's journey. It would soon be time to head back to Plymouth and a dread feeling of unease crept over Robert at the thought. It was the same feeling that had assailed him every day since the night time skirmish on the motte and his mind was filled once more with anxious questions.

Was Clarsdale still alive? Was his father still in England? Had he returned to Spain or had he been captured by the authorities? If he had, then he would surely reveal Robert's assumed name under torture. Perhaps the authorities were waiting right now in Plymouth for his return. And how had they known of the meeting that night on the motte? Did they also know of Robert's connection to Father Blackthorne? These were questions that Robert couldn't answer and they haunted his thoughts by day and his dreams by night. He was being hunted but he couldn't tell how close his pursuer was.

He had lived with the fear of discovery all his adult life. For weeks, even months, it remained deeply buried within him, but always it was there, rearing its head every time events beyond his control whipped the Protestant population into a frenzy of suspicion and hatred. Seeley was still determined to find the Catholic spy he believed was on board and Robert had heard that the master was questioning barkeepers in the taverns of Plymouth, asking them whether they had ever heard one of their regular customers, in a drunken stupor, refer to themselves as Young.

Seeley's search was worrying but it paled in comparison to that of the authorities. These were obviously resourceful men. Thoughts of that night on the motte brought Father Blackthorne to mind and Robert's apprehension twisted into anger. They had killed him in cold blood, an unarmed man, a priest, a man who had never brought harm to another. It was a callous murder and Robert immediately thought of the killing of the Spanish priest during the sack of Sagres.

How could he fight alongside these countrymen? The men in Sagres acted with a depravity and lawlessness that Robert had witnessed before in other sackings. They had been possessed by the ferocity of the moment, but the authorities who attacked the motte had laid their plans with care. Robert had ignited the chaos that started the skirmish and ultimately led to Father Blackthorne being shot but he knew that if they had been taken alive then they would certainly have been tortured and killed. These men answered directly to the council and the Queen. Robert had also pledged his loyalty to Elizabeth. How could he share a bond with countrymen who sought to destroy him?

A shift in the wind brought Robert's thoughts back to the *Retribution.* His gaze instinctively ranged over the entire ship. During the previous months he had tried to consume his fears and doubts with work on board the galleon. The relentless training had forged deep within him a connection to the ship and his troubled thoughts eased as he felt the nimble hull respond to the change.

The weather was closing in and he looked to the four points of the compass. It was time to make for port. For a moment, Robert wondered if this would be the day when he would be met by armed soldiers on the dockside at Plymouth. There was little he could do in any event. His fate was in the hands of God. He shouted a course change to the quarterdeck to bring them home.

John Cross raised his head and gazed at the lancet window. The air was still inside the tiny Clarsdale family chapel and Cross allowed the solitude and peace to quieten his mind. He walked slowly to the altar and traced his hand along the smooth polished oak, whispering a prayer of thanks to God. Henceforth the chapel would only bear witness to those who were pure of soul. He gazed around one last time and then walked outside, closing the solid door behind him.

The ground was covered in a thick layer of hoar frost and Cross turned his face from the biting wind, walking towards the estate house. He looked across the valley to the hill opposite and the copse that straddled the crest. It looked cold and forbidding and Cross recalled the many days he had spent hiding there. Resentfully, he looked away.

The brittle grass crunched under his feet as he made his way around to the front door of the house. All was quiet and

Cross paused for a moment at the entrance. The door was slightly ajar. He pushed it open and stepped inside. The hallway floor was covered in debris and animal droppings and Cross slowly gazed around the large interior space. Everything of value was gone.

All that Clarsdale had owned, his lands and possessions, had been forfeited to the Crown. His title had been revoked and his extended family had all been taken in for extensive questioning, an interrogation that had already caused the death of two of the older family members. The Crown forces had taken the pick of Clarsdale's possessions but Cross could see numerous signs of vandalism where the local population had come to steal anything that they could. In many places the elaborate wood panelling had been ripped from the wall, no doubt to be used as firewood during the long winter. In such an isolated place there was no chance to defend the house against such marauding. It would only be safe when new owners acquired it from the Crown.

Cross shuffled through the debris and walked into the room that was once Clarsdale's study. The door was gone, as were some of the window panes and the chill wind made the flotsam of paper that was strewn on the floor rustle and dance with every gust. Cross picked up the torn cover of a book; *Christian Thoughts, Volume II.* A sardonic smile lingered on his face for a moment before his mouth twisted in anger. He flung the cover into the lifeless hearth and stormed from the room.

He strode around the expanse of the house, his footfalls echoing off the bare walls and hollow rooms. He had come so close, he thought furiously, and the failure of his ambush burned in the pit of his stomach. Walsingham had been beyond rage when he had heard that Nathaniel Young had escaped his grasp. He had been on the brink of dismissing Cross from his post but Cross had convinced his superior that he still had a chance to capture his son Robert Young. Walsingham had eventually agreed but Cross was left in no doubt that his reputation and position had been damaged beyond repair.

He made his way back to the front door and paused on the threshold to glance once more at the gaping doorway of the study. He cursed. The Duke of Clarsdale would have been an invaluable captive, as would the heretic priest, but death had robbed Cross of even those prizes. He had ordered the two corpses to be buried in an unmarked grave in unconsecrated ground on the summit of the motte. It was the only measure of revenge he could take and it had brought him little comfort.

Cross left the house and made his way towards his horse. Over the previous months he had scoured the ports of the south coast of England and put all the agents stationed there on the alert for Nathaniel Young, less he try to hire or stow away on a ship departing to the continent. The search had been fruitless and Cross had conceded that the Duke of Greyfarne had either gone into hiding in England, in which case he might never be found, or he had by now found some way off the island of England. Cross's only remaining lead was the search for Robert Young.

But what was the God-cursed traitor's real name? And where was he now? If he had gone into hiding with his father then he too might never be found. It was a frustrating thought but at least, Cross accepted, the danger of him acting as an informer would be neutralized. Perhaps he was braver than that, or a fanatic as many of these religious zealots were. He might have returned to Plymouth and taken up his post to continue his mission. Perhaps he had other contacts besides Clarsdale and the priest and was, at this moment, passing messages to his traitorous father in Spain.

The thought made Cross hasten his step and he mounted

his horse and spurred him into a gallop over the hard ground. The ambush would have made Robert Young more wary, that much was certain, but no man could remain invisible whose very mission called for a position of prominence and importance. Cross was confident he would find him eventually and regain his reputation and standing amongst those who stood for loyalty to the Crown and the Protestant faith.

CHAPTER 10

9th April 1588. Lisbon, Portugal.

Evardo paced through the extended shadows in the small courtyard, his hand held loosely on the hilt of his sword. As he turned on his heel, he glanced at the stout wooden door on the east face. It remained firmly closed and Evardo wondered impatiently how much longer he would have to wait. The thought brought a wry smile to his face. After so long, he could suffer a further few minutes.

Passing through the centre of the courtyard he heard a clamour from outside and he looked to the arched entranceway that led to the docks. Men were rushing past the opening, many carrying provisions and arms, while heavily laden carts were being driven along the docks, whip cracks splitting the air. Evardo felt a rush of excitement and he gazed at the fraction of Lisbon harbour that was framed in the archway. It was choked with all manner of ships and Evardo felt his chest swell with pride.

Drake's attack on Cadiz had severely wounded the Armada. His marauding had kept the squadrons apart and distracted the Empire with fears for the treasure fleets. Lesser nations would have lost their resolve in the face of such adversity but

Spain had rallied magnificently. Preparations for the divine crusade had never ceased and now the Armada was once more a vital, living thing.

During his absence the Armada had been poised to sail a number of times, but supply problems and the winter months had forced delays. With shame, Evardo had thanked God for those setbacks, for despite their effects on Spain's plans, the opportunity to fulfil his vow still remained.

Since his return to Spain almost four months before, his brother Miguel had worked tirelessly to secure Evardo a new command. His initial efforts however had been blocked by the Marquis of Santa Cruz, the commander of the Armada and owner of the *Halcón*. Then in February, to Evardo's secret joy, Santa Cruz had died. The King had swiftly ordered another man into the breach, Don Alonso Pérez de Guzmán, the Duke of Medina Sidonia, one of the highest ranked nobles in the land. Unfettered by the marquis's veto, Miguel was finally successful in securing a commission for his brother.

Evardo turned away from the archway and began pacing again. The heat of the day was rising and he moved deeper into the shadows. He glanced again at the closed door. He had been summoned to this place twice over the past week, both times to meet his new patron Diego Flores de Valdés, the commander of the squadron of Castile. On the previous occasion he had met Medina Sidonia.

The duke was an imposing figure and although he was not the warrior that Santa Cruz had been he was a brilliant administrator. At the time of Santa Cruz's death in February the Armada had been languishing in a mire of supply problems and a chaotic schedule that was struggling to combine the diverse ships and ordinance that had been gathered from throughout the Empire. Medina Sidonia had worked tirelessly from his first day in command and under his firm hand the

Armada had made a miraculous leap forward. The number of ships in the fleet had increased from 104 to 130 and the number of troops sailing had doubled to almost 19,000.

Many problems still remained however. De Valdés had shared some of them with Evardo, but he had not yet named the ship he was to command. Evardo had been forced to wait impatiently over the previous days, eager to encounter and solve the problems that surely awaited him on his new ship. The door finally opened and Evardo walked quickly towards it as an orderly came out to call him. After the heat of the courtyard, the interior was cool and Evardo removed his broad-brimmed hat, wiping the sweat from his brow.

The corridors were bustling with activity. Evardo side-stepped his way around tight knots of conversation and frantic runners as he followed the orderly to de Valdés's office. A cursory knock on the door was followed by the command to enter and Evardo went inside alone.

Diego Flores de Valdés was seated in a high backed chair. He was nearly sixty years old but his dense black hair and moustache gave him the air of a younger man. He was an expert on naval tactics and had been personally appointed to the enterprise by the King to act as one of Medina Sidonia's principal staff officers. Evardo nodded to him in welcome and then looked to the other man standing beside de Valdés, recognizing him immediately. He was Juan Martínez de Recalde, commander of the squadron of Biscay and second-in-command of the Armada. He was known as a cantankerous man, especially when plagued by his sciatica, but he was also respected as one of the most experienced naval officers in Spain. Evardo nodded to him in turn. De Recalde did not return the courtesy.

'*Comandante* Morales,' de Valdés began, looking down at the sheaves of paper that covered his desk. 'Thank you for coming so promptly.'

'Morales,' de Recalde repeated with a contemptuous sneer. 'The *comandante* who surrendered his ship at Cadiz?'

Evardo bristled at the remark but held his tongue. It would not benefit him to argue with such a high ranking officer and in any case it was not the first time he had been harangued over his role at Cadiz since returning to Spain. The whole country seemed to be looking for people to blame for that defeat and he had encountered disdainful stares and whispered conversations at every turn. On each occasion however he had striven to ignore them, concentrating instead on his objective. He looked at de Recalde out of the corner of his eye. The commander could have his opinion. Evardo's commission had come at de Valdés's request and had been approved by Medina Sidonia. He did not need de Recalde's good graces.

'I heard you gave up your sword in the midst of battle,' de Recalde taunted, stepping forward from behind the desk. 'I hope you will not repeat that act when we meet the English again.'

'I defended my ship until the fight was lost,' Evardo retorted angrily, his decision to remain silent forgotten. He took a half-step towards de Recalde. 'I demand that you tell me who told you such a lie.'

De Recalde stepped up to Evardo and stared menacingly into the younger man's eyes.

'You can demand nothing of me, Morales. But if you must know, the man who told me of your surrender is the master of my flagship, the *San Juan*, Abrahan Delgado Vargas.'

The colour drained from Evardo's face.

'Abrahan?' he whispered incredulously.

'And I take Vargas at his word,' de Recalde continued. 'I've known the man forty years. We were fighting English pirates when you were still feeding at your mother's *pezón*.'

'Juan Martínez,' de Valdés said abruptly, rising from his

chair, anxious to put an end to the conversation. De Recalde was pushing Morales too hard. The last thing he needed was the irascible commander duelling with one of his *comandantes*. 'Kindly do me the courtesy of allowing me to address my officer.'

De Recalde glanced over his shoulder at de Valdés. He grunted a reply and looked at Evardo one last time before brushing past him to leave the room.

'He is a hard man, Morales,' de Valdés said, indicating the door. 'But you must not let such words affect you. Your brother has explained to me what happened at Cadiz, and in any case I knew your father and admired him greatly. I would trust any son of his in battle and your record before Cadiz was exemplary.'

Evardo nodded in gratitude, although de Valdés's words gave him scant comfort.

'I have decided on a ship for you,' his patron said, picking up a sheet of paper from the desk. 'Given your previous duty in the *Flota de Indias*, I am giving you command of one of the ships of the Indian Guard, the 530 ton galleon, *Santa Clara*. Here is confirmation of your commission.'

Evardo took the proffered paper.

'Thank you, señor,' he said distractedly, his mind still on Abrahan. That others believed him a coward angered him, but Evardo had already decided their disparagement would not distract him from his duty. In any case, they were strangers and he was not responsible for their thoughts.

But Abrahan was different. Evardo had been angry at his mentor for how he had spoken to him after Cadiz, but he had nursed the hope that after so many months Abrahan might have seen the error of his judgment. Evardo had tried to find him upon his return to Spain. He had gone to Cadiz to learn the fate of the *Halcón*'s crew and was told that apart from those held for ransom, the English had released all their Spanish prisoners when they left the port. But Abrahan had not returned home and Evardo's search had stalled.

Now he had found Abrahan, but it was a bitter revelation. His mentor was still ashamed of him. He glanced down at his commission. *Santa Clara.* He repeated the name. A galleon command. It was what he had wished for and he silently recited a brief prayer of thanks before looking back to de Valdés.

'Thank you, señor,' he said again, this time earnestly, and left the room.

Evardo stood outside the door for a moment. The corridor was as busy as before with men rushing in every direction. Evardo walked through them, his pace increasing with every stride. He went along the courtyard and out onto the docks.

The harbour was a confusion of hulls, masts and rigging with pennants of every hue fluttering on the light breeze. The *Santa Clara* was there somewhere, hidden amongst the multitude. Evardo went in search of a skiff to take him to his new command. There was much to do. The fleet would be sailing within weeks and Evardo had but a short time to ready himself for the battle to come. He had to prove himself to his new crew, to the commanders who doubted his courage, and to his mentor. He could not ask for his honour to be restored – he must win it back.

Robert opened the door to the fo'c'sle and stepped inside. The air was rank with the smell of faeces and stale sweat. He covered his mouth and nose with his hand and looked around the near pitch darkness. The portholes had been sealed tight to protect the men inside from further exposure to whatever foul air had infected them. Powell, the ship's surgeon, was crouched over one of the men, bleeding him. Another moaned nearby and Robert heard the liquid rush as the man's bowels voided. He caught the surgeon's eye and motioned for him to come out onto the main deck. Robert slipped out through the door again and went immediately to the bulwark. Only then did he exhale and gulp in the clean salt laden air of Plymouth harbour.

'Yes, Captain?' he heard and turned around.

'Well, Mister Powell?' He had already deduced the answer from what he had seen.

'It's the flux, Captain. Four cases so far but I'll warrant we'll have a dozen more by tomorrow. I've instructed the swabber to clean out all the upper decks and the liar is giving the head another going over.'

Robert nodded, agreeing with the surgeon's orders. He briefly recalled his stint as a liar when he was a ship's boy, a task given to the first crewman caught uttering a lie at the beginning of each week. Seconded to the swabber for seven days he was always given the loathsome task of cleaning the latrine under the beakhead.

Robert cursed. The men had been on board too long, eating rations that, when they came, were never enough. On the cramped decks of the *Retribution* it was only a matter of time before the thin veil between health and pestilence was torn. Worse still, Plymouth and the entire south coast of England was now rife with rumours that the Spanish were poised to put to sea. They had overcome the setbacks of the previous year and had drawn their forces together from every port in the Spanish Empire to gather the largest and most powerful fleet ever assembled. The *Retribution* could not be stood down. There would be no leave for the crew.

'We should lay to, Captain, and fire wet broom in the holds. That would smoke the cursed pestilence out.'

Robert shook his head. 'Just try and keep them alive, Mister

Powell. I'll see to it that they get the best of the rations we have.'

'Yes, Captain.' Powell sighed, wiping his filth stained hands on the folds of his apron, and returned to the fo'c'sle.

Robert walked along the gunwale to one of the swivel mounted falcons. His hand traced around the mounting. It was the one part of his supplies that were not being consumed while the fleet lay in wait; shot and gunpowder, over fifty rounds per gun. The rations for the men, however, were in a diabolical state. To ensure supplies were not pilfered or squandered they were being issued to the fleet on a month to month basis, but their arrival was erratic at best and delays were commonplace. Robert, like every captain, feared that if the Spanish arrived off the English coast near the end of a ration cycle, the *Retribution* would go into battle with little or no food or fresh water.

Robert brought his hand to his chest to recite a prayer of hope. He clenched his hand into a fist and for a moment wished that he had a crucifix within his grip. He had been in Plymouth town the evening before and had witnessed first hand the palpable fear that stalked the populace. Their naked terror had steeled his determination for the fight ahead. Regardless of Spain's quest to restore England to Catholicism, the Spanish were the enemy. Although their success would allow Robert to freely practise his faith and perhaps even regain his family's title, they had no right to threaten the sovereignty of his country. Robert reached out to touch the cold barrel of the falcon.

The Spanish Armada had to be defeated at sea. It was England's only chance. Robert had come to realize that fact, as had many of the commanders in the fleet. He had seen the local militia, the husbandmen and traders who had been conscripted to oppose any landing in Devon. Many of them were armed only with bows and their ranks were continually being depleted as men deserted to tend to their fields. It was a situation that doubtless was repeated along the entire length of the south coast. Robert dreaded to think how these men would fare against trained soldiers. Some six thousand soldiers, around half of England's professional army, were in the Spanish Netherlands fighting the cause of the rebels. Six thousand more had been sent to secure England's border with Scotland to guard against an attack that might be triggered by the Spanish invasion. If the Spanish landed all would be lost. Parma's Army of Flanders could march an incredible ten miles a day and like wildfire on dry scrub they would sweep aside any local militia bands and descend upon London.

'Captain.' Seeley strode up to Robert. 'Shaw has just returned from shore with good news. A Roman Catholic spy has been uncovered in the office of the Clerk of Ships.'

Robert's lips tightened into a thin line. The crew of the *Retribution* were facing innumerable challenges and yet Seeley was still focused on the threat of Catholic spies. He had even widened his coterie of investigators on board to include the boatswain's mate and the surgeon.

'He might have some information as to the true identity of Young,' Seeley continued. 'Permission to go ashore to attend his interrogation.'

Robert tried to think of some reason to refuse Seeley permission but he could not. He nodded curtly and Seeley called for the coxswain to man the longboat.

'Thomas, wait,' Robert called. 'I will accompany you.'

They descended into the longboat and shoved off. Robert sat alone in the bow. His decision to accompany Seeley had been made on impulse. He could think of no reason why someone in the office of the Clerk of Ships would know his secret but he reasoned it was better that he should witness anything that might be said. In any case he would have a better chance, however minute, of escaping on land.

The threat of invasion had whipped the population into a frenzy of anti-Catholicism. Fearing any uprising of English Catholics the Privy Council had already ordered the internment of known leading Catholics in Wisbech Castle in Cambridgeshire, and the populace, in terror of the Spanish Inquisition, were openly calling for their execution. The older people still remembered Bloody Mary. The Catholics had shown little mercy for Protestants when they were in power. Now that the tables were reversed the Catholics could expect little mercy.

The longboat reached the docks and Seeley led the way to the garrison. A guard directed them to the prison block. They crossed the inner courtyard to an iron-studded wooden door. It led into a guard room where two men were seated at a table.

'I am Master Seeley and this is Captain Varian of the *Retribution*. You have a Roman Catholic prisoner here. We need to see him.'

One of the guards stood up slowly. He looked them up and down and then walked over to the inner door. Taking a ring of keys from his belt he unlocked it and motioned them through.

The corridor beyond was windowless and was lit by torches. A series of doors ran along one side. Only the furthest one was open and Robert followed Seeley towards it as the door to the guard room was locked behind them. A terrible scream pierced the still air, turning the blood in Robert's veins to ice. They entered the room. It was a small airless space and was dominated by a single object in the middle of the room.

Three men stood around it, but Robert barely saw them. His eyes were fixed on the man stretched out on the rack. His ankles and wrists were bloodied and torn by the bonds that held him fast to the rollers at both ends. His limbs were grotesquely extended and his skin had been badly burned in numerous places. He had blacked out from the pain. The smell of faeces and sweat and seared flesh was overpowering. Robert looked at the sweat stained face of the prisoner and his stomach lurched. He knew him. He was one of the locals who had attended mass on the motte beside Saint Michael's when Robert had first met Father Blackthorne there, the man who had come with his wife and young daughter. Robert backed away towards the door.

'Who are you?' one of the men spat.

Seeley told him.

'I'm Browne, Sergeant at arms. If you've come for the interrogation you're too late. The local agent, Tanner, and his men have already come and gone.'

'Who is he?' Seeley asked, unable to look away from the rack. He had only ever seen pictures of the device in Foxe's *Book of Martyrs.*

'His name's Bailey. He's a scribe in the Clerk's office.'

'What has he told you?' Robert asked.

'Plenty,' the sergeant replied with a cold smile. 'He's a traitor alright, a stinking papist. He was found in the Ordnance office, somewhere he wasn't supposed to be. They suspect he was looking for the artillery manifests for the fleet. When he was challenged he panicked and tried to flee. They searched him and found he was wearing a crucifix under his doublet. That's when they brought him to us. He claims he's not a spy, the lying bastard, just a recusant. He gave us the names of some other Roman Catholic families in the area, and the name of his papist priest, a Father Blackthorne. Tanner said he already knew that name and that the priest was dead. He's out tracking down the other families now and we already have his wife and daughter locked up.'

'Did he mention the name Young?' Seeley asked

Browne thought for a second and then shook his head.

'Sergeant, I need to know if this man knows another Roman Catholic named Young.'

Browne took a torch down from the wall and brought it over to the rack, twisting it slightly in his hand to ensure the flame was strong. He thrust it into Bailey's side. Bailey surfaced from unconsciousness with an ear-piercing scream. He fought his bonds but he couldn't move and the struggle increased the pain in his tortured joints. He shouted incoherently.

'Shut up, you treacherous whoreson,' Browne shouted. 'This officer wants to ask you a question.'

Bailey continued to speak. He started begging for mercy, his head jerking from side to side.

'Do you know a man named Young?' Seeley shouted.

Bailey seemed not to hear and again Browne stabbed at him with the torch. His screams filled the room.

'Do you know what name Young uses?' Seeley shouted, appalled by what he saw, the torture sickening him. He steeled his nerve. Bailey was a Roman Catholic, a heretic, an abomination before God.

'No,' Bailey cried. 'I don't know, please!'

'Give him another twist,' Browne said and the two men took a grip on the handles.

They put their weight behind the lever. Bailey's screams reached a higher pitch and Seeley watched in grim fascination as the pawl of the ratchet moved along the length of a tooth. There was a loud popping sound as something inside Bailey's arm snapped and as the pawl slotted into place the room went quiet. Bailey had blacked-out again.

'Get a bucket of water to wake him up,' Browne ordered.

'No,' Robert said. 'Enough. He doesn't know the man you're looking for, Thomas.'

Seeley's eyes were on Bailey's face. It was twisted in agony. He felt a twinge of pity and he angrily suppressed his leniency. God and righteousness were on his side. He had to be strong.

'Get the water,' he said to the sergeant.

Robert turned and left the room. He hammered on the guard room door and went out to the courtyard. He could barely breathe. He was sure Bailey knew nothing of his real identity but he felt nauseous with fear. He had witnessed the fate that surely awaited him if he was ever caught, and if he survived the torture, he would be burned at the stake, with men like Seeley igniting the pyre.

Robert walked unsteadily back towards the docks. The Spanish were coming. It was inevitable, but Robert also hoped it would be soon. He had enemies on two fronts. To his rear the authorities were hunting Robert Young while to his fore the Spanish sought to crush him and his countrymen. Only in battle would he attain the clarity of facing a single enemy.

Evardo slowly paced the main deck of the *Santa Clara*, his gaze ceaselessly ranging over the entire ship as he watched the crew at work. She was a fine galleon, not five years old and had been built in Cantabria, the birthplace of over half the fighting ships of the Armada. Designed for transatlantic trade voyages the galleon had a massive hold over which ran a single gun deck high above the water line.

The crew were swarming everywhere and the air was charged with excitement. The expedition's banner had recently been consecrated and it hung from every masthead in the fleet, a flag adorned with the royal arms and depictions of the Virgin Mary and the Crucifixion superimposed on red diagonals. A general fleet muster had been held. Everything was ready. The mighty Armada waited only on a fair breeze to take them out of the mouth of the Tagus.

Evardo stopped pacing and looked to the quarterdeck as the sailing captain, Arnaldo Ramos Mendez, shouted an order to the men working in the rigging of the mainmast. He was a hard taskmaster but Evardo had already come to appreciate his skill and efficiency and the manner in which he commanded the eighty-six sailors on board. Evardo's first impressions of the other three captains on board were equally positive but like all *comandantes*, his main concern was how his four direct subordinates would work together.

Upon assuming command Evardo had immediately determined the social rank of each. All four were near equals, which would foster cooperation, but more importantly Evardo's lineage was superior to them all, thus legitimizing his command, not only for the four captains but for the entire crew.

The two military captains, each commanding a 100-strong company of soldiers, were new to the *Santa Clara*. Francisco Alvarado, the older of the two, was a veteran of the Dutch revolt and the brief war against Portugal. He was lean and wiry, a career soldier who spoke openly of his ambition to lead a command under Parma in the invasion of England. He was brash and flamboyant, but was known to be steadfast in battle.

Hernán de Córdoba, the second military captain, was a heavyset man with a shaven pate. He was deeply religious and had sworn a vow of temperance while in the service of God and his King. For the past three years he had led a company of soldiers on a galley in the waters surrounding Italy, fighting an almost continuous battle against the scourge of Muslim raiders on the trade routes of the Empire. He was obdurate and was an ardent believer in the strict military discipline that was the backbone of every Spanish company.

Two thirds of the soldiers on board the *Santa Clara* were

raw recruits, levied from Spain and Portugal. The remainder were veterans and hailed from every corner of the Empire. They were richly attired, with no two men dressed alike. Their jerkins and breeches were of every hue, bright garish colours with elaborate braiding and embroidery, while almost every hat was festooned with plumes of feathers.

Evardo had impressed upon each of his captains the need for a shared sense of purpose, particularly between sailors and soldiers. Given their calibre he was also concerned about what his men might have heard of his defeat at Cadiz, and from the moment he had stepped on board five weeks before he had constantly been on guard for any remark that might be construed as disrespectful, knowing he had to stamp out any insubordination until he had a chance to prove himself.

He left the main deck and went below. The gun deck was cramped and he stepped over the long trails of the gun carriages as he made his way aft, his eyes looking left and right at each cannon. Because the gun deck was high above the water line, for stability the cannons were of medium calibres. Nevertheless the *Santa Clara* had a considerable arsenal under the command of the gunners' captain, Diego Suárez. Like Mendez, Suárez had been with the *Santa Clara* since she had first been launched. He was a keen advocate of artillery warfare, a fledgling concept in the Spanish fleet, and since the *Santa Clara* had arrived in Lisbon he had successfully lobbied the fleet quartermasters for two additional *media culebrinas*, bringing the total numbers of guns on board to twenty-six.

The biggest of these were the two Italian and six Spanish bronze *media culebrinas* which fired 10 pound iron shots, and four *medio cañón pedreros*, firing a 7 pound stone shot that would shatter on impact, devastating a tightly packed deck. Before battle each gun would be loaded with the assistance of soldiers who would then report back to their posts in the fore and aft castles and the fighting tops. The guns would be lashed to the hull and although the *Santa Clara* carried a considerable store of powder and shot the guns would only be fired once for each attack, just moments before the *Santa Clara* would close on a ship for boarding, thereby causing the maximum of casualties and confusion amongst the enemy.

Gunnery tactics were continually evolving and Evardo, like every other *comandante*, was well aware of the English navy's prowess in this area. If allowed to command the weather gauge they would sweep in, firing their heavy bow chasers, followed by their broadsides and stern guns, before retreating to windward to reload. It would be a fearsome attack, one the *Santa Clara* might have to endure, but in centuries of naval warfare boarding was the proven method of securing an enemy ship in battle, one that the Spanish had perfected over generations.

If the English wished to defeat the Spanish Armada they would have to close and board, thus putting themselves within reach and Evardo smiled involuntarily as he thought of that moment, that brief second after the broadside was fired into an enemy ship, when his entire crew would be poised to follow his command to board. Nearly a third of the soldiers on board were armed with muskets while the remainder carried arquebuses. From the towering castles of the *Santa Clara* they would bring down a rain of hellfire upon the English while others fired the two swivel-mounted *falconetes* and twelve wrought iron breech loading *falcon pedreros*. Ceramic pots filled with gunpowder, spirits and resin, would be set with lighted fuses and cast into any knots of resistance while the dreaded *bombas*, wooden tubes filled with gunpowder and grapeshot, would scatter the enemy and clear them from the gunwales.

Only then would Evardo give the order. The enemy ship would be secured with grappling hooks, sealing the fate of the English crew, and with a war-cry that Evardo could almost hear, the crew of the *Santa Clara* would storm over the gunwales, cutting down any who stood in their way, cleansing the ship of its heretic crew.

Again Evardo smiled, only now it was a cold sneer that did not reach his eyes. In his mind he was leading his men onto the *Retribution* and before him stood the man who had come to symbolize his fight against the English, Robert Varian. He would be the first to fall. But he would not be the last. The battle would not end until the English fleet had been swept from the Channel, until the Army of Flanders had made their crossing and the Armada was sailing up the Thames estuary. Only then would victory be assured, for God and Spain.

'Patache approaching off the starboard beam,' Evardo heard and he went aloft to see the approaching ship. It was small boat, lightly armed with only fifty men on board. It was one of a squadron of such craft that carried dispatches and supplies between the larger vessels. The patache came alongside and Evardo's commander, de Valdés, came on board followed by four men, one of them a priest.

'*Comandante* Morales,' de Valdés said, moving aside to allow the others to step forward. 'I would like to introduce you to some guests of his majesty's Armada who will be sailing with you on the *Santa Clara*.'

Evardo nodded genially and looked to the four men. He had expected this arrival for he had learned from other *comandante*s that such guests were sailing on nearly every ship of the fleet.

'This is Padre Ignacio Garza,' de Valdés began, indicating the priest. 'He will conduct mass for the ship's company once a week and tend to the spiritual needs of your crew.'

'You are most welcome, Padre Garza,' Evardo said sincerely and bowed his head to receive a simple blessing from the priest. He took strength from the Latin words of the benediction and recited in his mind the exhortation, written by a Jesuit in Lisbon, that had been circulated throughout the fleet; '*We are not going on a difficult enterprise, because God our Lord, whose cause and most holy faith we defend, will go ahead, and with such a Captain we have nothing to fear.*'

God supported the Armada's mission to restore Catholic rule to England. King Philip and Medina Sidonia had declared this fact in every communiqué and Pope Sixtus V had issued a special indulgence to all who sailed in the Spanish fleet.

'These two gentlemen,' de Valdés continued, 'are Irish nobles, Maurice Fitzgibbon and Diarmuid McCarthy. They were forced to flee their native land after the defeat of the Earl of Desmond's glorious rebellion.'

Evardo nodded to both men and welcomed them to the *Santa Clara.* They replied in deplorable Spanish and seemed ill at ease on board ship but Evardo could see they possessed the wariness of hardened fighters. They would not be a burden in the battle ahead.

'And finally,' de Valdés said, indicating the last man, 'I would like to introduce his grace, the Duke of Greyfarne, Nathaniel Young.'

Evardo nodded courteously.

'Welcome on board, your grace.'

The duke replied in near flawless Spanish but his accent jarred and Evardo hid his innate dislike for the Englishman behind a genial smile.

'The Duke will act as one of the interpreters and guides for the invasion army,' de Valdés explained, 'and will also assist you in the interrogation of any prisoners you take in battle.'

Again Evardo nodded and he called for Mendez to find suitable accommodation for the four men. De Valdés took his leave and his patache slid away from the hull of the *Santa Clara.* Evardo watched it leave, his thoughts on his new passengers.

The priest was truly welcome. Perhaps too the Irishmen, for they could prove valuable in battle. But the Englishman?

Evardo looked to the companionway leading below decks. He tried to separate the man's nationality from his faith. It was difficult, but Evardo was reminded of the attitude he had tried to impress upon his captains. Everyone on board the *Santa Clara* shared a common purpose, and whatever their individual motives they all sought the defeat of the Crown forces of England. It was enough. Evardo resolved to think of the duke not as an Englishman, but as a fellow Catholic.

Nathaniel took the small rolled blanket from under his arm and cast it on the low cot. He glanced over his shoulder at the two Irishmen who shared the tiny cramped cabin with him. They were speaking together in Gaelic and the lyrical guttural tones of the language set Nathaniel's frustration and anger on edge. He looked down at the blanket. Apart from the clothes he was wearing, and the pieces of eight in the purse hanging from his side, the blanket contained all his worldly possessions – some personal items and a family copy of the Latin bible.

For years Nathaniel had listened to rumours and plans for this great fleet. He had spent many months in Lisbon harbour watching it grow from its infancy into a fledgling power. He had foreseen the day it would take to the seas and had pictured himself on the quarterdeck of the *San Martin*, the flagship of Medina Sidonia, in conference with the duke and his senior officers. Never once had he dreamt that he would hold such a lowly place in its ranks, cast aside to some anonymous galleon. He felt old and defeated. His life's endeavours had come to naught.

That night at the motte had brought him to this point. He thought of Robert and looked to the sword hanging by his side, the sword with which he had almost killed his only son, and he wondered if given the chance again he would strike him down. He could have been the one who betrayed them to the authorities that night, although Nathaniel was also suspicious of Clarsdale. The duke had insisted on knowing de Torres's name. Perhaps he was in league with the Protestants? Nathaniel had not returned to Clarsdale's estate after the attack, so there was no way to know the truth. Not until he returned to England and confronted Clarsdale.

After the ambush Nathaniel had fled back to his prearranged rendezvous point on the coast. Clarsdale knew of the arrangement; the scheduled return of a Spanish galleon after one month. If the duke had been captured or was in league with the authorities, then he would surely lead them to the coast, but Nathaniel could think of no other way to leave the country without being detected and so he had resolved himself to wait. The three weeks had been an eternity of fear and deprivation. Nathaniel had been forced to live like a savage out in the open, stealing what food he could from the local farms, all the while waiting for the authorities to swoop down and capture him. But they had not come and the Spanish galleon had returned as arranged, picking up their sole passenger off the isolated beach in the dead of night.

Upon returning to Spain Nathaniel had been forced to wait endless weeks for a meeting with de Torres. The Spaniard had finally granted him an audience, but only to tell Nathaniel that he was no longer of any use to the Spanish Empire and he was to remove himself from the court at Madrid. Nathaniel had pleaded, no begged, de Torres for a reprieve, requesting only that he be allowed to sail with the Armada. The Spaniard had relented, but Nathaniel had seen the disgust in de Torres's eyes. He was struck by a wave of nausea as he recalled his humiliation.

Nathaniel felt the deck shift beneath him and heard the crew of the Spanish galleon cheer. In the distance a single cannon boomed, a signal for the fleet to form up. The Armada was under sail. Nathaniel went quickly back on deck. The rigging was alive with men. One after another the sails unfurled with a crack as the wind took hold of the ship. The galleon continued to turn under his feet and Nathaniel looked aft to the land behind. The soil of the Spanish Empire. With God's grace, he prayed, he would never see it again.

He could never come back to Spain, there was nothing for him here. His whole world consisted of England. With the help of these strangers he would soon be back in his native land, but he felt no loyalty to the Spaniards he sailed with. Loyalty was based on reciprocity and Spain had turned its back on Nathaniel Young.

His years of faithful service had been forgotten, cast aside, and while in the fight to come he would still give the Spanish every assistance, the alliance would be temporary. His fall from favour had revealed the truth of his position in his adopted country. Even after twenty years he was still an outsider, an Englishman, and for the first time in many years Nathaniel felt a longing for his country that went beyond his quest to see a Catholic monarch on the throne.

When the Spanish seized power from Elizabeth and her cursed Privy Council he would endeavour to have his title restored by the Spanish authorities. But thereafter, he vowed, he would strive to rid England of the invaders. He could do little else, for he was an Englishman, and England was his home.

CHAPTER 11

2nd June 1588. Plymouth, England.

Robert watched from the poop deck of his galleon as the standard of the Lord Admiral, Charles Howard, was raised above the flagship, the *Ark Royal*. A cheer went up around the fleet and Robert looked to Drake's ship, the *Revenge*, moored alongside the flagship. It was flying a vice-admiral's standard and altogether some sixty fighting ships were now moored in Plymouth harbour. With dozens of smaller ships in support the fleet looked formidable. However the outward display of power belied an inner fragility.

Over the previous months Drake had done everything humanly possible to prepare the fleet. Nonetheless one area continued to elude his mastery – supplies. The men were already on reduced rations, and in such a weakened state they were easy quarry for pestilence. Robert could only hope that the arrival of such a senior officer as Howard might improve the situation.

Coupled with this, the fleet still had no reliable intelligence as to the disposition of the Spanish Armada. Rumours continued to flood into Plymouth, preying on the nerves of every man, and Robert, like all his crew, craved the order to make sail. It was widely known that Drake was actively canvassing for a pre-emptive strike similar to his daring raid of a year before. Robert supported the plan, preferring it to the unbearable strain of waiting. Howard had the authority to order such an attack. With reports circulating that the admiral had arranged for a further squadron of forty ships, under Lord Henry Seymour, to guard the Straits of Dover, there was every chance the fleet could put to sea when sufficient supplies were secured.

Robert turned his back on the flagship and went down to the quarterdeck. The summer heat was rising and his shirt was drenched with sweat under his jerkin and doublet. His stomach ached. He ignored the protest and with annoyance he scratched a flea bite on the back of his arm. A latent anger, caused by weeks of tension, suddenly rose within him. Where were the cursed Spanish? Had they sailed from Lisbon? Were they now off Cape Finisterre, or Biscay, or Ushant? Perhaps their plans had changed. Perhaps the reports that had reached Plymouth were false and the Spanish were sailing to Ireland to incite rebellion there.

He looked to the heights above the protective headlands of the harbour. Each one was capped with primed signal fires. Similar beacons had been placed along the length of the south coast. If the Armada was sighted they would be lit and the news would speed to London and beyond to the entire kingdom. But what then? Robert had confidence in the *Retribution* and her crew. His ship was a breed apart, faster and more nimble than any craft the Spanish possessed. But many of the enemy ships were behemoths, built for the rigors of the mid-Atlantic. The *Retribution* and her sister ships would be like terriers nipping at the heels of wolfhounds, and should any English ship fall within grappling range they would be quickly overwhelmed.

Robert tried to suppress his doubts, knowing they were caused by the weeks of anxious waiting and the never ending supply problems. The future was not yet written, it was in the hands of God. Robert strived to impose his personal convictions upon the battle ahead. For his whole adult life he had sought ways to regain his family name and honour. He had lost hope many times, but through prayer and faith he had always recovered his way. The battle ahead was no different. The victory was not assured. All they had was hope, but Robert had to believe that with God's help they would prevail.

'All hands!' Evardo roared, a wave of seawater taking the last of his words. 'All hands on deck!'

The *Santa Clara* shuddered beneath him as she tore over the crest of a wave, her storm tops'ls bearing her onward. Evardo spat the seawater from his mouth and looked to the four points of his ship. The storm was on all sides, enraging the sea with a bitter wind that whipped the surface into a hellish trial for the Armada. Evardo could see distant sails behind him to the south-west, running broad reach before the wind. The stern of the *Santa Clara* shifted a point to starboard, the wind clawing at her towering castles.

'Steady your helm,' Evardo shouted instinctively, his command echoed by the sailing captain, Mendez.

A sailor ran up to the quarterdeck. 'The level of water in the main hold has risen to three feet, *Comandante*.'

Evardo pushed past him and staggered to the forward rail. A wave crashed over the bulwark, swamping the main deck.

'More men to the pumps,' he roared.

Through the rain soaked air he could see Nathaniel Young standing with his arm locked around the distant foremast. The Englishman had been on deck for every waking hour since the Armada had left Lisbon, and had continued his vigil throughout the storm. Such action spoke of some inner fire. In a quiet corner of his mind, Evardo wondered what specifically could fuel such grim determination.

'Land ho,' a voice called and Evardo followed the signal of the masthead lookout.

'The Isles of Scilly,' Mendez shouted, his hand cupped over his mouth.

Evardo wiped the spray from his eyes to focus on the low lying islands. The south-west tip of England, hidden by the storm, was some thirty miles east-north-east from the archipelago. They were so close, but as Evardo scanned the sea around the *Santa Clara* he could see they were all but alone. The storm had scattered the Armada like chaff. He could not go on and worse still his ship might be spotted by the enemy, alerting them to the relative position of the Armada.

'Two points to port,' he shouted and Mendez ordered more men to the rigging.

The *Santa Clara* turned her bow away from the Isles of Scilly towards southern Ireland. Evardo leaned into the turn and lifted his face heavenward to pray for a wind that would allow him to bring his ship back to La Coruña to rendezvous with the flagship, and for a change in the ill-fortune they had already suffered since leaving Lisbon.

The journey up the coast of Portugal had been tortuously slow. From the outset the Armada had been plagued by contrary winds, forcing them to continually tack to stay on course. The *Santa Clara*, and the galleons like her, had taken to the task with ease, but the pace of the fleet was dictated by the slowest moving vessels. The twenty-three massive merchant hulks, the auxiliary ships of the fleet, were unwieldy leviathans with abysmal sailing qualities.

During the two weeks it had taken them to sight Cape

Finisterre, Evardo had been given the chance to study the ships of the rest of the fleet as they sailed about him. Some of the largest of these were the eleven ships of the Levant squadron. Designed for grain and other bulk transport in the Mediterranean, many of them were near and over 1,000 tons. They had been commandeered over the previous year and were now heavily armed and crammed with soldiers. With such overwhelming manpower they would have an incredible advantage in close-quarter fighting and despite their mainly Italian crew, whom Evardo considered inferior to Spanish sailors, he was confident that no English ship would be able to survive a boarding attack from a Levanter.

The squadron of Portugal contained many of the foremost battleships of the Armada and was headed by the *San Martin*, Medina Sidonia's flagship. Some of these vessels had been acquired by Spain when Portugal was annexed but the others had been built on the King's orders to protect Portuguese trading routes. All were heavily armed, with the 1,000 ton *San Martin* alone boasting some 48 guns, the heaviest capable of firing a 30 pound iron shot.

From the Basque ports of Spain, the Armada had requisitioned twenty large and sturdy trading ships which made up the squadrons of Guipúzcoa and Biscay. As with the Levanters, the armament of each ship had been considerably enhanced and soldiers now occupied every available space on board, in many cases tripling the size of the ships' original crew.

The overall deployment of the fleet had been minutely planned, with each ship assigned a place in the designated battle formations. The hulks and support ships were to remain in strict formation, surrounded by the heavily armed merchantmen. Any active defence against the enemy would be carried out by the warships of the fleet, the *Santa Clara* amongst them. However, she would not sail with her sister ships of the squadron of Castile. The squadrons were for administrative purposes only. The warships were to act as independent fighters, holding position in the fleet when they could, but at all times capable of detaching to defend themselves or any vessel under attack.

Such flexibility would allow for maximum protection of the transport ships carrying vital supplies to Parma's invasion force and King Philip, though Medina Sidonia, had consistently impressed upon all commanders that the aim of the Armada was not to attack and defeat the English fleet, but rather to hold them at bay and defend the crossing of the Army of Flanders. Only after Parma had landed on the English coast would the Armada be free to engage.

Only one squadron was expected to fight as a unit, one elite group under Don Hugo de Moncada – the squadron of Neapolitan galleasses. These four hybrid ships had a galley-like hull and galleon-like rigging, combining oar and sail to create a deadly predator that reigned supreme in coastal waters. Heavily armed, they were painted blood red. Their sails depicted a bloody sword and the rowers had each been issued with a red jacket, all to inspire fear amongst the crew of any ship that dared to stand against them.

Evardo now searched the spray torn horizon for any flash of red that might betray the fate of those galleasses. The storm had transformed the seascape into an endless series of towering rollers. Outside the range of a dozen miles, it would be impossible to see the low hulled galleasses and Evardo could only hope they would weather the tempest.

A sudden cold shiver fouled his thoughts and Evardo stepped back into the lee of a bulkhead. He had been on deck for more hours than he could count. He was exhausted, every joint in his body ached and his face stung from the lash of the salt riven wind. He leaned against the bulkhead, weak from hunger, and for a moment imagined the comfort of a warm meal and his cot in the main cabin. He mercilessly suppressed the reverie and ordered himself to step forward to the centre of the quarterdeck. He had to tolerate what the rest of the crew were enduring and he angrily rubbed the fatigue from his eyes. He could not go below. He was duty bound to stay on deck, and no such meal existed on any ship in the Armada.

Within days of leaving Lisbon Evardo began receiving alarming reports from his quartermaster that most of the ration barrels he had opened contained rotten food and fouled water. The barrels were of poor quality, the timber staves too green to form a proper seal. It was a further repercussion of Drake's raid on Cadiz over a year before, for one of his prizes had been a trader carrying seasoned barrel staves to Lisbon. Its loss had forced the suppliers to use inferior stock. In the rush to prepare the Armada for sea, the state of the arriving rations had been overlooked. Evardo had been left with no choice but to dump the fetid rations overboard.

The crisis was repeated on every ship in the Armada and Medina Sidonia had issued a fleet-wide order for reduced rations. The duke then sent word ahead to the provincial governor of Galicia, ordering him to send out supplies when the fleet reached Cape Finisterre. But the rendezvous with the supply ships was never made and after five days of waiting off the cape, while a favourable wind finally arrived to bear the fleet northward to the entrance of the English Channel, Medina Sidonia had been compelled to order the Armada into La Coruña to restock.

It was a bitter and frustrating set-back, one Evardo had felt keenly, but he had taken heart from the fact that the diversion would be just a delay, not realizing that the Spanish fleet was poised for an even greater blow. Before darkness fell, Medina

Sidonia had managed to lead thirty-five ships into the harbour of La Coruña. The remainder of the fleet had been obliged to remain off shore and await the light of dawn before making their approach. It was during that night that the storm had unexpectedly arrived, tearing out of the south-west of the deep Atlantic to scatter the fleet beyond the furthest reaches of the Bay of Biscay.

'Helm answering new course,' Mendez shouted near at hand. 'New heading north-north-west.'

Evardo nodded grimly and glanced over his shoulder at the rain swept outline of the Isles of Scilly as they passed abaft of the *Santa Clara.* With fortune's favour, he would see them again soon, but until then he could do nothing but wait for the storm to relent.

Robert leaned out over the gunwale of the quarterdeck and drank in the cool breeze blowing over the larboard quarter. He filled his lungs, savouring the taste of the open sea air and checked the line of the hull as it cut through the racing waves. The galleons of the English fleet surrounded him on all sides and Robert smiled as he spotted his nearest companion, the *Antelope*, taking advantage of the fair wind by laying on extra sail.

'Mister Seeley,' Robert called. 'Main top gallants, ho!'

'Main top gallants aye, Captain,' the master replied and men were sent dashing to the rigging.

With a critical eye Robert checked the trim of his ship, finding no flaw in the master's work, and his gaze wandered once more to the ships sailing on the flanks of the *Retribution.* The fleet was bearing south with Howard in the van, following his order, and Drake's plan, for a pre-emptive strike against the Armada.

For long days a terrible south-westerly storm had savaged

the waters off Plymouth, reinforcing the supply-induced captivity of the English fleet. In its wake a strong northerly wind had blown up, a fresh and constant breeze that seemed to implore the crews to raise sail and go on the offensive. Hamstrung by short rations, the fleet had continued to wait but then, on the 3rd July, a full month's supply of rations arrived in Plymouth.

The crews had spent that entire night frantically restocking their ships. The following morning Howard had raised his standard and led the fleet out through the protective headlands of Plymouth. The wind had proved fickle. Squalls had threatened the fleet's progress off the Scillies and again north-west of Ushant, but the skies had eventually cleared to a deep blue and the clouds now raced in irregular shreds ahead of the fleet.

'Mister Seeley,' Robert called. 'What's our position?'

'About 120 nautical miles north-north-east of The Groyne, Captain.'

Robert nodded. The *Retribution* was making close to eight knots. Fifteen hours would see them at the door to the Armada's lair.

'All hands, clear the decks for action.'

The crew reacted instantly to Robert's command and the ship came alive with the sound of shouted orders from junior officers.

During the south-westerly storm, reports had been received in Plymouth from the Scillies telling of numerous distant towering sails. There could be little doubt, the Armada was at sea in the Bay of Biscay. The English fleet commanders had devised that the same wind that now hastened the English south had probably blown the Armada back to one of its home ports. In these waters that meant The Groyne, the port the Spanish called La Coruña. With luck they were still there, neatly docked and ripe for the taking.

Robert watched the crew at work. Each man knew his task and they moved without comment or pause. Their bellies were full, their weapons primed and a strong breeze bore them on. The *Retribution* was as ready as Robert could make her. She was a weapon poised for the fight and Robert felt the first stirrings of battle lust in his chest. His doubts were forgotten, banished by action and the future that raced towards him. The reasons his men fought would become his own and his would become theirs, their common bond as Englishmen overcoming all others.

Evardo drummed his fingers impatiently on the gunwale as he watched the supply laden patache approach. She was the last one and Evardo looked to the main deck of the *Santa Clara* where the quartermaster was sorting the fresh supplies that had already been received before ordering them down into the hold.

'Captain Mendez,' Evardo called. 'Inform the quartermaster that he is to speed his progress and clear the main deck for the next load. I will brook no delays.'

'Yes, *Comandante*,' Mendez replied and he hurried from the quarterdeck.

Evardo began pacing the deck. His ship had been one of the last to reach La Coruña. She was therefore not yet fully restocked and Evardo feared that the order to sail might come before he was ready to answer the call.

Not a single vessel or life had been lost in the storm and Medina Sidonia had insisted that God had watched over them all, declaring His intervention to be a miracle. Despite this assertion however, and the fresh supplies that were already banishing the last of any sickness amongst the crews, the morale of the men remained low. The duke had recognized this and ordered the men of each ship to land on the island of San Antón in the harbour to have their confessions heard and receive a blessing. Evardo had believed it to be a clever move, a reaffirmation that the men were carrying out God's will, but the fact that Medina Sidonia had insisted the ceremony take place on an island had not escaped him. If they had been allowed on the mainland some of the men would have undoubtedly tried to desert.

Evardo ran his hand along the sea-worn timber of the gunwale. The *Santa Clara* was a good ship. She had weathered the storm well and protected the lives of her crew. There was little more Evardo could ask of her. In return he would protect her in battle, save her as much as possible from the shot and fire of the enemy before bringing her alongside her prey. The English galleons would not be an easy target but Evardo trusted the mettle of his men. They may be downhearted, but a few days of good fortune would quickly raise their spirits and the sight of the enemy would put fire in their blood.

'Zabra approaching off the starboard beam.'

Evardo rushed to the other side of the quarterdeck. The small dispatch ship was coming up fast. The commander of the squadron of Castile, de Valdés, was in the bow.

Earlier that morning Evardo had watched the senior officers in their pataches sailing to the flagship, the *San Martin.* A council of war had been convened and once again Evardo glanced at the supplies being loaded onto the *Santa Clara.* De Valdés came quickly alongside.

'Ready your ship, *Comandante* Morales,' he shouted from the zabra. 'We sail for England on the next favourable tide!'

The crew on deck cheered at the news and Evardo waved a reply to his commander. He looked to the banners on the masthead of the *Santa Clara.* They were barely stirring in the feeble wind. He had time. Evardo called for the men on the main deck to redouble their efforts. The order had been given. At any time the wind that would bear the Armada to England might arise and Evardo was determined that the *Santa Clara* would be ready for the fight.

Robert cursed loudly and spat over the side onto the still waters surrounding the *Retribution.* The sea mocked his scorn and continued to lap against the hull while the sun reflected off the smooth undulating surface as it shone from a clear blue sky. For three days the wind had blown steadily from the north, bearing the fleet on like an arrow loosed from a bow, but then, not sixty miles from La Coruña, it had suddenly died, leaving the English fleet becalmed.

Robert shaded his eyes from the glare of the sun and gazed about at the fleet, searching to see if any of their sails showed signs of catching an errant breeze. He could hear the undertones of his ship, the steady creak of timbers and the mixture of voices below decks, muffled and absorbed by the hull. The ship's bell rang eight times, marking the beginning of the first dog watch.

Near at hand Seeley called out the order for the change and bare feet thudded across the decks as men went to relieve their crewmates.

'I've ordered more men to the fighting tops to act as lookouts, Captain,' the master said, and Robert nodded his agreement. So close to the Spanish coast, they were liable to be seen by a local trader or fisherman and any surprise they might hope to have over the Armada would be lost. Robert smiled sardonically to himself. If they did see a Spanish vessel in the distance, without a favourable wind, there was little they could do to stop them escaping.

'Sixty miles,' Seeley spat. 'If the wind had held we'd be in The Groyne now.'

'Patience, Thomas,' Robert said, although he keenly felt the frustration of having been denied the chance to take the fight to Spanish waters. 'We still have time.'

A flash of movement caught Robert's eye. One of the masthead banners had rippled open and collapsed once more. The air stirred, caressing his cheek.

'Quarterdeck, ho,' a shout came from the top of the main mast. 'Wind coming up!'

Robert felt it again and this time the masthead banners snapped out with the force of the gust before wilting.

'Mister Seeley,' Robert called. 'Get 'em aloft.'

'All hands of the watch, to the rigging!'

The wind gusted again and the smaller top gallant sails began to take shape.

'We have 'em.' Seeley smiled.

Robert stayed silent. He looked to the sun and checked his bearings. The fleet had been becalmed in the featureless sea for over twenty-four hours and in that time the ships had drifted and spun with the subtle undercurrents of the water. The wind was still to their backs, but their bows were no longer pointing at La Coruña, they were pointing northwards, to England. Robert looked to Seeley. He was no longer smiling and Robert saw the delayed awareness dawn on his face.

'God in His Heaven,' Seeley muttered. 'It's a southerly wind.'

The sails began to fill as the wind stiffened and all around the *Retribution*, the ships of the English fleet began to get underway. The fortune that had carried them south had been exhausted sixty miles from their destination. Now it had been neatly reversed and Robert ordered all hands on deck to lay on every inch of sail.

If it held, the wind would carry them all the way home to Plymouth, but in remaining true it would also swiftly bear the Spanish Armada from port and send them hard on their heels. The plan to fight the Spanish in their home waters was no more. The enemy now held the advantage and the battle to come would be fought in the English Channel, with the men of Elizabeth's navy standing with their backs to the very coastline they were sworn to defend.

CHAPTER 12

30th July 1588. Plymouth, England.

John Cross paused at the door of the tavern and looked up at the sign swinging lazily with the onshore breeze. The paint on the side facing the sea had long since faded but on the reverse Cross could just make out the name, The Bosun. It was all but redundant; the tavern was no different from the dozen or so others on the narrow street and Cross wondered for a moment what had happened to the families who had once occupied these tiny hovels in the oldest part of Plymouth.

It was late afternoon, but the tavern was quiet and Cross glanced through the small smoke stained window to the side of the door. This would be his last stop for the day and he consciously shrugged off the weariness of his search. He had tried every conventional ploy in his hunt for Robert Young, but as he did not know his assumed name he had constantly been frustrated. He could not go back to Walsingham empty handed. He had to go on, and with all other options exhausted he had been reduced to trawling the back streets of Plymouth in a vain search for good fortune.

The gallop of horses at the harbour end of the street caused him to turn and he moved back from the door to gain a better view, carefully stepping over the rivulet of sewage that tricked along a channel in the cobblestones. What he could see of Plymouth harbour was filled with the ships of the English fleet and while the presence of so many vessels would normally herald a busy time for the taverns, the crews had all been denied shore leave. The Armada was coming. No one knew when, but they were at sea with a fair wind and it was only a matter of time before they reached the mouth of the English Channel.

That dread warning had arrived with the English fleet's return over a week before, along with a call from Howard to the town and surrounding countryside for fresh supplies for the fleet. Cross was convinced it was a forlorn hope. The marketplaces had already been stripped bare of their goods and there was little chance the sparse population of the surrounding countryside could provide any more for such a confluence of men. In any case, war was coming to the shores of England and Cross suspected that many people had already taken to hoarding their food.

He went back to the door of the tavern and pushed it open. It closed behind him and he stood for a moment in the gloom. The place smelled of stale beer and vomit while the air drifting in through an open door to the rear carried the faint stench of urine from the latrine outside. A barman stood behind a rough hewn counter of planks supported by upended casks. He was an older man, broad across the chest, and his frame still carried a residue of the strength he had in his youth. He looked Cross up and down.

'There's no one here, constable,' he sneered, and indicated an old man slumped over an empty tankard in the far corner. 'Just me and Black Ned.'

Cross approached the counter. 'I'm looking for someone.'

'And I told you there's no one here,' the barman replied

menacingly. 'Have a look out back in the pisser if you want. You bastards have had 'em all for that fleet.'

'A man by the name of Young,' Cross continued evenly, ignoring the barman's aggressive stare, searching his face for any sign of recognition. He saw one and felt his pulse quicken.

'I don't think you heard me,' the barman said. His hand slipped below the counter and he brought up a cudgel. He placed it on the counter with a heavy thud.

'I'm not a constable,' Cross said, never taking his eyes off the barman's face. 'I'm an agent of the Queen. If you know any man of that name I warn you, you would be best served to tell me.'

'The Queen don't drink here,' the barman said belligerently, although out of the corner of his eye Cross saw the barman's hand move away from the cudgel. To threaten a constable was one thing, but he would be a fool to strike an agent. 'Now why don't you just bugger off?'

Cross remained silent for a moment. The barman had heard the name before, he was sure of it. He had to get him to reveal what he knew.

Cross had encountered such hostility in each tavern. Every able seaman in Plymouth, out of loyalty to the Crown or eager for any plunder that might be had in the impending battle, had volunteered to make up the shortfalls amongst the crews of the Royal ships. The taverns were bereft of customers and the barkeepers had taken to acting out their anger at the loss on any official of the fleet. The vast majority of these volunteers were still at their posts but there had been scattered reports of desertions now that the fleet was once more in port. The constables were trawling the town and surrounding area for the fugitives. With his bearing and dress Cross had been taken for one at every turn.

'Give me a drink,' Cross said. 'Whisky if you have it.'

The barman grunted and took a chipped wooden tankard from the shelf behind him. He poured in a measure and pushed it across the counter. Cross picked it up. The tankard was filthy and the whisky had the raw smell of sour alcohol. He put it to his lips and took a taste. It seared the back of his throat. He reached into his pocket and took out a crown. It was as much as the barkeeper could be expected to make in a day from a dozen thirsty customers and Cross turned the coin over tantalizingly with the tips of his fingers.

'This man I seek, Young. He's a traitor, a Roman Catholic.'

'A papist?' the barman spat. He glanced down at the coin in Cross's hand and then to the old man passed out in the corner. Cross could see the barman's mind at work in his expression. It would be bad for business if he became known as someone who spoke to the authorities, but they were all alone in the tavern. Cross could see that he was wavering.

'There'd be a reward for any information that would lead to his capture,' he said. The barman turned back to Cross and, glancing at the door, leaned across the counter.

'I don't know anyone of that name,' he said. 'But there was someone in here a few weeks ago looking for the same man. Said his name was Seeley.'

'Seeley?' Cross asked perplexed. 'Where was he from?'

'He didn't say, but he was a sailor. He demanded I tell him if any of the men who drink here ever went by that name. He even threatened to draw his sword if I didn't tell him.'

'He didn't say what ship he sailed on?'

'No, but he was definitely an officer. A stuck-up little prick he was, full of piss and wind.'

Cross was shocked by the news that someone else was looking for Robert Young. Who in God's name was Seeley? Perhaps Walsingham had lost trust in him completely and had assigned another agent to the hunt. He asked the barman to recall exactly when Seeley had been in. His reply ruled out that possibility. It was before the night on the motte, before Cross had been disgraced. It couldn't be another agent. So who was he, and why was he after Young? Did he know Young was a Roman Catholic, or had he some other grievance to settle? That Seeley had threatened to draw his sword certainly spoke of his determination to find him. Perhaps he already had. Either way, Cross realized, after too many weeks, he was finally getting closer to his prey.

He tossed the coin to the barman and left the tavern, pausing in the middle of the street to look towards the harbour. On board one of those ships there was an officer named Seeley. Cross had to find him. He would find him. Seeley's information, combined with his own, might provide him with the answer he so desperately needed.

The hunting ground had diminished to the roll call of a hundred ships. As Cross began to walk towards the harbour he became more and more convinced that Seeley was searching for someone amongst his own. Robert Young was a sailor in the fleet. More than likely he was an officer, for any credible spy would need to be in a position of authority to be privy to naval plans.

The thought made Cross quicken his pace. The Armada was poised to attack. The English fleet would soon be engaged, with a cancerous traitor deep within their ranks, one who was sure to betray them at a crucial time in battle. Cross had to get to him before it was too late.

Captain Fleming looked anxiously over his shoulder. The south-westerly wind blew directly into his face, causing his eyes to water. He rubbed them furiously as he tried to focus on the distant horizon. It was clear, but in his mind Fleming beheld the sight he had seen at dawn, the multitude he knew was just below the farthest reaches of his vision.

Fleming had never witnessed such a sight before. Few under God had. Although he was one of a squadron of captains sent by Howard to patrol the approaches to the Channel specifically to warn of the Armada's arrival, he had been deeply shocked and awed by his first sighting. The Spanish fleet was enormous, with scores of ships over 500 tons, sailing under a forest of spars and rigging, their sails and banners emblazoned with the heraldic symbols of an entire empire.

He checked the line of his ship and immediately called for a minor course change, hoping to garner an extra half or even quarter knot of speed from his bark, the *Golden Hind.* He looked to the coastline off his larboard beam. Plymouth was at least another hour away and he searched for any sign of smoke from the signal beacons. The *Golden Hind* had been sailing some ten miles off the Lizard when they sighted the Armada. Visibility had been limited and it was evident that the watchmen on land had yet to sight the enemy. Fleming had to reach Plymouth as swiftly as possible. When lit, the beacon fires would overtake and outrun his ship, but they could only tell the fleet in Plymouth that the Armada had been sighted. Fleming could show them exactly where the enemy was on his chart and give details of their displacement and direction.

The renewed realization caused him to glance over his shoulder again. He ordered their speed to be checked again. Eight knots. The course change had had no effect and he searched his store of local knowledge for some advantage of current or conditions he might have overlooked. There was none. He would have to rely solely on his 50 ton bark. He uttered a silent prayer that the fleet at Plymouth would be ready to sail upon his arrival. The situation there had been critical when he had sailed out days before. The fleet was shackled to the port by the shortages in rations, unable to sally out until sufficient victuals were secured, and in the confines of the inner harbour, they would be easy prey should the Spanish attempt a blockading attack.

The *Golden Hind* sailed on. Over the horizon the Armada pursued in her wake, the south-westerly bearing all towards their fate. On the eve of battle in an undeclared war all uncertainty had now been banished. The Armada, so long in coming, had arrived. The future of one nation and the ambition of another would be decided by the chosen sons of each realm. Faith against faith, ship against ship, man against man, they would fight. Two naval powers set in opposition, their strength distilled and fed into the hearts and souls of men ready to die for their cause. God's will was unfolding, and the day so long prayed both for and against, was at hand.

CHAPTER 13

2 a.m. 31st July 1588. Plymouth, England.

The crewmen of the *Retribution* grunted and strained through the pull, their backs bent against the bars of the capstan, shoulders bunched and muscles trembling as inch by inch, foot by foot, the anchor rope snaked in through the hawse-hole. Seawater streamed from the rope, each drop catching and reflecting the dull lantern light that illuminated the low ceilinged gun deck. The air was musky with the smell of sweat and the bare-chested men cursed and cajoled the dead weight they pulled against as they slowly marched in a fixed circle.

Robert watched them without comment, studying each man, searching for signs of weakness. He indicated one of the men to Shaw and the boatswain tapped the sailor on the shoulder, signalling him to step out from the bar. Another rushed forward from the waiting ranks to take his place, maintaining the strength of the whole. Robert glanced at the relieved man. He was doubled over, breathing heavily and Robert acknowledged his hard work with a curt nod. On all sides the crew continued to shout encouragement to those men at the bars. They laboured on, not to lift the anchor, but to haul the entire weight of the 450 ton *Retribution.*

Like a lighted taper cast into an arsenal, the arrival of the *Golden Hind* in Plymouth harbour the evening before had set the English fleet ablaze with frenetic activity. Every ship had immediately cleared their decks for action but the order to sally out could not be given. The tide had been in full flood, rushing against them through the outer headlands and the English crews had been forced to wait in agonizing dread of a Spanish blockading attack. By God's grace it had never materialized. When the tide finally turned before midnight the crews had cheered the order to make all haste out of the lethal confines of Plymouth harbour.

Without an assisting wind the ships were warping out of the harbour with the ebb tide. It was a laborious and excruciatingly slow process. The ship's anchor was carried forward in the longboat to the full extent of the line before being dropped overboard. Once secured, the line was then hauled in, dragging the ship forward using the strength of the crew. More than half the fleet had already completed the task and were now waiting in the lee of Rame Head.

Robert sensed the *Retribution* shift beneath him and the men at the capstan moved more swiftly as the anchor gave way from the seabed below them. The galleon continued to move slowly with the current of the tide. The anchor cleared the surface and Seeley was immediately on hand with the longboat. Robert looked through the hawsehole. 'Veer away the line!'

The men lowered the anchor slowly into the small boat. The rope slackened and as Seeley urged the rowers to pull away, Robert went aloft to the quarterdeck.

'This should be the last time, Captain,' Miller said in the darkness.

Robert scanned the four points of his ship. 'Keep a firm hand on her, Mister Miller.'

The risks of manoeuvring a ship in the midst of a fleet at night were significant. The older man nodded reassuringly. So far the fleet had come out in good order, without a collision, and Miller would be damned if his charge should suffer such a humiliating fate.

Robert heard the call from Seeley in the black waters ahead and the *Retribution* steadied on her outward course as the men took the strain in the anchor line once more. Dawn was not four hours away and in the near darkness Robert could see the silhouettes of the ships gathered in the cusp of Rame Head. Once a sufficient number were gathered Howard would order them to sea. The wind was blowing west-north-west, abaft the stern castles of the Armada, giving them the weather gauge, the advantage, should any ship attempt to stand before them. The English had to wrestle that advantage back.

Evardo listened in the night to the calls and commands from the ships surrounding the *Santa Clara*. In the glow of running lights men were working feverishly on final preparations. The Armada was now firmly in hostile waters. Earlier that day a fishing boat from Falmouth had been captured and under pain of torture the crew had revealed that the English fleet commanded by Howard and Drake was poised to sail from Plymouth. The enemy were nigh and all suspected that dawn would see the English fleet arrayed in battle formation before them.

Barefooted sailors rushed past Evardo under the whip crack of Mendez's voice. On the poop and fore decks Alvarado and de Córdoba were assigning positions to their musketeers, ensuring that all would be ready when the call to arms was given. The captains were standing apart from their men, commanding them without lending assistance. They were gentlemen and would not engage in physical labour.

Evardo watched his crew with pride. They were strong and eager for the fight, replenished by the supplies loaded at La Coruña and inspired by the righteousness of their cause. Hours before, at dusk, Padre Garza had led the ship's boys in a recital of the Ave Maria on the main deck. All the crew had attended, and many had sought absolution, while afterwards the padre had conducted a private mass for the senior officers and guests on board. On the eve of certain battle, in the *comandante*'s cabin of his own galleon, it was one of the most beautiful services that Evardo had ever attended. Now, standing on the quarterdeck, he felt the power of God's favour.

Evardo prayed for that favour to be extended to the entire fleet. Strong winds had carried the Armada swiftly across the Bay of Biscay, but the fleet had been subjected to the lash of one last storm as it approached the English coast. That tempest had cost the Armada the four Portuguese galleys sailing under the command of Don Diego Medrano. Their shallow draft, which allowed for close inshore support of a landing, secured their place in the fleet, but it was their undoing in heavy seas. Although Medina Sidonia had sent pataches to stand by and assist the galleys during the storm, they had disappeared during the night.

A more mysterious casualty had been the 768 ton carrack, *Santa Ana*, the lead ship in the Biscayan squadron. With 30 guns and more than 400 men, she was one of the most heavily armed fighting ships of the fleet. She was a stout vessel with an experienced crew and her disappearance during the storm had been seen as a bad omen by many of Evardo's crew. He had tried to quell their unease, enlisting the help of Padre Garza, but the unnerving fact remained that before a single shot had been fired in anger, the Armada had lost five valuable fighting ships.

'*Comandante* Morales . . .' Nathaniel Young approached. 'I wanted to thank you for inviting me to mass in your cabin.'

'You are welcome, your grace,' Evardo replied genially.

Over the previous weeks Evardo had remained true to his conviction to see past the English duke's nationality and treat him as a fellow Catholic. Their initial terse conversations had swiftly given way to mutual respect.

'Truly God's hand is upon us this night,' Nathaniel said, gazing at the myriad lights that surrounded the *Santa Clara*.

'But I pray that from hereon the weather will be our ally,' Evardo remarked.

'*On the wicked he will rain fiery coals and burning sulphur; a scorching wind will be their lot*,' Nathaniel quoted from the psalms. 'The heretic Queen's fleet will know a tempest far deadlier than any born of the sea.'

Evardo nodded in agreement and looked along the length of his galleon, checking her position in relation to the surrounding ships.

The fleet was sailing in 'line of march' formation. To the fore was the vanguard of fighting ships under Don Alonso de Levia, including the *Santa Clara*. Medina Sidonia commanded the centre, the main battle group, which consisted largely of the transport and auxiliary vessels, while de Recalde commanded the rearguard.

'We are near Plymouth?' Nathaniel asked, indicating the darkness beyond the larboard flank of the Armada.

'Yes, it is about eight leagues north-west of here,' Evardo replied, and with regret he thought of the missed opportunity to blockade the English fleet. On the day the storm had abated the bulk of the Armada, including most of the fighting ships, had found themselves within striking distance of Plymouth. The *comandantes* of the vanguard, Evardo amongst them, had taken zabras to de Leiva's ship, *La Rata Encoronada*, expecting to receive orders to attack but instead they were told to take in sail and wait for the forty or so stragglers to rejoin the fleet.

Afterwards it was rumoured that both de Leiva and de Recalde had advocated an immediate surprise attack but Medina Sidonia had dismissed their arguments, strictly adhering to King Philip's explicit orders that the Armada's primary mission was to support Parma's crossing, not defeat the English fleet. His general order to take in sail had delayed their advance up the Channel by twenty-four hours.

Nathaniel looked in the direction Evardo had indicated. He had come to appreciate the commander's company on the long voyage from Lisbon. The Spaniard was a driven man, completely obsessed with victory over the English Crown forces. On this common ground alone the two of them had formed a professional alliance. It was as much as Nathaniel was willing to concede and he peered into the darkness, hoping to catch sight of some light on land.

His first glimpse of the storm-lashed Isles of Scilly had left him with a growing desire to gaze upon the mainland of England. He had felt a similar yearning almost a year before when he had first set foot in England after eighteen years, but now so much had changed. Nathaniel still hoped the Spanish would defeat the English forces and dethrone Elizabeth but he no longer acknowledged Spain's right to control England after that victory. He had believed that the bonds of faith outweigh the bonds of nationality. De Torres had taught him that not all Catholics shared this conviction.

When Nathaniel had access to the higher echelons of power in Spain he had dreamed of high office in the newly liberated, Catholic England. Now he realized all he could hope for was the restoration of his lands and his title. With Spain as his ally these were within his grasp. But Spain could not give him back his honour and his family.

As an Englishman his honour would be found in ensuring that after his country was free from the plague of Protestantism it would not be dominated by a foreign power. As a father he did not know how he could bridge the gulf between him and his son. Their loyalties were incompatible, although he was beginning to realize that in many ways he was seeking what Robert had already found.

He looked to the grey light of the pre-dawn on the eastern horizon. There was every chance the coming of day would bring the onslaught of battle. Nathaniel wished it so.

Robert stood on the fo'c'sle as the illusory light of the pre-dawn gave way to the first rays of the rising sun. He had been on the quarterdeck when the call had been given, a frantic shout that spoke of the lookout's disbelief. Robert had immediately rushed forward, wishing to see the sight without obstruction.

What he saw defied his every experience. His mouth opened in silent awe as he gazed upon the host that was the Spanish fleet. The ships were of every hue and province, of the Mediterranean and Atlantic. No sooner was Robert's attention captivated by a single ship than another, greater vessel, caught his eye. His mind echoed stories told to him as a child by his adopted father, of great battles and mighty fleets, of Lepanto and Salamis, of Actium and Cape Ecnomus. Robert knew he was witnessing a sight that would surely be remembered in history.

A shouted command on a nearby ship returned Robert's wits and he spun around to his own crew. 'All hands, battle stations! Tops'ls and top gallants, ho! Lookouts to the tops and sprit!'

The crew of the *Retribution* exploded into frantic activity at Robert's commands. Men spilled out from the lower decks and ran to the rigging. The gun-ports slammed open and on Larkin's command the cannons were run out. Robert went quickly to the quarterdeck where Seeley and Miller were waiting for him. He issued terse orders to both and they moved away to command the crew, giving Robert another opportunity to study the Spanish fleet, this time with a tactical eye. He smiled.

The number of English ships waiting in the lee of Rame Head had reached a tipping point soon after the *Retribution* had joined them, and in the darkness of the small hours Howard had given the command to sally out. The ships at hand had sailed beam-reach on a southerly course, right across the expected approach of the Spanish Armada. The remainder, who had yet to warp out of Plymouth, had taken a different course to act as a diversionary force; tacking along the coastline as far west as dawn would take them.

The *Retribution* had sailed with Howard. Robert had spent the entire time on deck, never daring to go below, constantly expecting to see the running lights of the Armada looming out of the darkness. As the command was given to turn westerly and then northerly he had begun to believe that the incredible feat they had set out to achieve had been met. His first sight of the Spanish Armada had thrust that belief from his mind, but it now returned to him in full force.

Howard had done it; the English fleet were to windward of the Spanish. They had taken the weather gauge, the all important advantage of being able to approach or withdraw from the enemy at will. Robert felt the first stirrings of blood lust within him as his ship came up to battle tempo. They were ready to attack. Robert was waiting only for the order to advance from the flagship, but in those brief moments of pause the sight of the Spanish fleet arrested him once more. The massive formation of ships began to transform right before his eyes.

Evardo's gaze shifted continuously as the *Santa Clara* turned beneath him, his mind at once on the fleet of English ships to windward, on the trailing line of enemy ships to the north along the coastline, and on the dexterous manoeuvres of the ships surrounding his galleon as the Armada redeployed to Medina Sidonia's orders. Above him the rigging was alive with men. The shouted commands of Mendez filled his ears and in the periphery of his vision he checked the identity of the ships closest to the *Santa Clara* with the plan of deployment.

'We are in position, *Comandante*,' Mendez said close at hand. Evardo nodded his approval of the sailing captain's flawless control of the galleon.

The Armada was now in combat formation, a massive crescent with the wings trailing back in the direction of the enemy threat. The larger ships were sailing in tight formation, with the dispatch carrying feluccas and zabras darting between them, feeding communications to every point in the fleet. De Leiva's vanguard had become the left wing with de Recalde's rearguard on the opposing landward wing. Medina Sidonia continued to command the vulnerable centre, allowing him to dictate the direction and speed of the entire fleet, secure in the knowledge that any enemy vessel that attempted to approach the vital transport ships would have to run the gauntlet of the protective wings. The Armada could now defend itself without halting the main battle group.

Evardo brought his captains aft to the poop deck to study the English fleet.

'The masthead lookout estimates close to eighty ships to windward, *Comandante*.'

'We should have bottled them up at Plymouth when we had the chance,' Alvarado growled. 'Now they are loose in their own home waters.'

'His majesty did not give us leave for such actions,' Evardo said, fixing Alvarado with a hard stare. Despite his own reservations he was angered that one of his captains should openly question the orders of his superiors.

'There are at least thirty more sail there,' Mendez pointed to the coastline.

The line of English ships slowly tacking into the wind on the flank of de Recalde's distant rearguard was poised to join the main enemy fleet and Evardo's brow creased as he tried to think what additional threat they posed.

'They are fine sailors,' Mendez remarked grudgingly.

Evardo spun around.

'Then we are well matched,' he replied, a hard edge to his voice. He looked to the faces of his captains, seeing in each the grim expressions of seasoned fighters.

'Ready your men, *mis capitánes.*'

Evardo turned his attention to the line of his ship and its position at the outer end of the vanguard wing. They were ready to receive the enemy and Evardo closed his eyes in prayer. He called on God to keep him strong, to give him the courage to endure until the victory had been won, and to protect his ship and her crew. They were in the service of the Almighty and Evardo's gaze climbed to the Armada's standard trailing out from the head of the mainmast, his lips moving silently as he mouthed the battle cry imprinted there.

'*Arise O Lord and vindicate Thy Cause!*'

Standing beside Seeley at the fore rail of the quarterdeck, Robert watched the Armada transform into a defensive crescent, over two miles wide from wing to wing.

'*Sancta Maria, ora pro nobis*,' he whispered involuntarily.

Seeley's eyes darted to his captain.

'Quarterdeck, ho,' a lookout called. '*Disdain* beginning her run!'

All eyes went to the 80 ton bark and the crew watched in silence as it sailed out alone to approach the Armada. Isolated between the fleets, her small size accentuated the massive crescent formation. Howard had sent the *Disdain* out to issue a challenge, a traditional gesture in the absence of a formal declaration of war. Robert felt his pulse quicken as the tiny bark sailed gallantly on between the wings, closing on the centre before spinning around broadside to the main body of the Spanish fleet. She fired a single cannon, the shot disappearing into the massed ranks of the Armada.

The distant sound brought an enormous cheer from the crew of the *Retribution*, strengthening Robert's resolve to seek battle. The Armada was indeed a sight to behold. Spain had conquered the far reaches of the globe with her navy and with its power King Philip had humbled countries and monarchs. But here, in the English Channel, the men of a single nation would stand in defiance of that authority.

The crew of the *Retribution* hailed from across the southern counties of England, from Cornwall and Devon, Sussex and Kent. They were noblemen and commoners, men of substance and men in search of fortune. They were adventurers and patriots, privateers and merchants. Each man had been drawn to the conflict by different motives but under the banner of Saint George they were all Englishmen.

The *Disdain* came neatly about and began beating its way back towards the fleet. Almost immediately Howard's *Ark Royal* broke ranks and the warships nearest her began to fall in behind in a rough line as she set course for the seaward flank of the Armada.

'Courses and tops'ls, ho. Helmsman, hard a larboard!'

'Yeoman of the jeers, main course, ho!'

The *Retribution* swooped into position under Robert's orders. He checked the sun. It was some three hours after dawn and the wind was steadily rising, stirring up the sea. White horses fled before the bow. The uneven line of warships sailed below the seaward flank of the Armada and then turned sharply to cut across the rear. Robert kept his gaze locked on the windermost Spanish ships, those on the outer edges of the trailing wing, but they stayed firmly on course, seemingly oblivious to the approaching English attack.

The first ripples of cannon thunder fled on the wind as the *Ark Royal* fired her heavy bow chasers and she bore in to within four hundred yards to loose her first broadside into the enemy ranks. She luffed up to go about, allowing her stern guns to come to bear and then turned neatly away, firing her second broadside guns as she tacked upwind to reload. A second English warship repeated the sequence, followed by another and another.

'Two points to starboard,' Robert roared, his voice carrying above the sound of cannon fire from the ships ahead, the outlines of the enemy ships visible through the massive clouds of gun smoke.

Like a warhorse reacting to the touch of a warrior rider the *Retribution* responded to the helmsman's hand on the whipstaff, her cutwater slicing through the chop, her sails filled with the freshening breeze, her deadly cannon coming swiftly to bear. The bow chasers boomed, smoke billowing over the fo'c'sle. Robert called for another subtle touch on the whipstaff to present the *Retribution*'s starboard broadside to the enemy. He held his breath, his gaze locked on the enemy ships amidst the smoke, the white clouds erupting with the muzzle flashes of angry Spanish cannons.

The enemy were swiftly abeam. The *Retribution* soared over the crest of a wave. Robert whispered the command to fire, willing Larkin to respond, his fists balled by his side, consumed by the urge to let fly at the enemy. Through the deck beneath him, he heard the first utterance of the master gunner, but the sound was engulfed within the span of a heartbeat by the deafening roar of the broadside guns firing in sequence and the *Retribution* shuddered in recoil.

'Come about. Hard a starboard!' Robert roared, gun smoke smothering his every sense. He felt the hull turn beneath him, his balance shifting with the fall of the deck.

The wind swept the enveloping smoke from the *Retribution* as the galleon began its turn to larboard. The crew were working without conscious thought, training and duty combining to control their every reaction. Oblivious to the sporadic whistle of passing shot, the acrid smell of gun smoke, and the hellish noise of the cannons' roar, they strove to wield the fearsome weapon that was the *Retribution.*

'Come here and fight, you English *bastardos*!' Evardo roared, his face mottled with rage and frustration, his sword charged in his hand.

From four hundred yards away the English warship fired its cannon. Iron shot tore across the open water. The air whistled with fire, and a rigging line parted with a whip-crack, a crewman screamed as a searing cannon ball obliterated his limb, the individual sound lost in a cacophony of defiant shouts, the Spanish crew baying for English blood, cursing them to engage like men.

The enemy had the weather gauge. They had the advantage of manoeuvrability and while Evardo had expected them to fire some devastating salvos with their heavy bow chasers the English were using a tactic like none that he had ever witnessed in battle, with each warship sailing roughly in the wake of the vessel in front of them, weaving a pattern that allowed each to present all their guns before sailing on. They were intent on attacking but were not closing to board. Did the English really believe they could win the battle with cannon fire alone? The approach defied the logic of Spanish military strategy and Evardo could only surmise it was an act of desperation by the English, the tight formation of the twenty ships of the vanguard wing proving too much for their nerve.

The wind was holding steady at west-north-west and Evardo's hands trembled as he willed it to come about. Every warship in the vanguard had turned towards the attack. The bow of the *Santa Clara* was as close up to the wind as Mendez could bring her. Another half a point and the galleon would be in irons, but still the English would not approach. Evardo was powerless to close as endless waves of gun smoke from the distant cannonades swept over the decks. Near at hand he heard the boom of Spanish cannons from the ships flanking the *Santa Clara.* They were expending their pre-loaded shots in vexation and Evardo struggled to contain the same impulse. Once fired the cannons would be difficult to reload and Evardo had to believe there was still a chance, however slim, that he might be given the opportunity to close and board an enemy ship.

The angry shouts of the crew rose as the next English galleon sailed into position, the black maws of her cannons exposed along her painted hull. Evardo looked to her decks and above to her masthead banners. Suddenly his eyes shot wide in recognition. Within an instant the galleon had disappeared behind an explosive wall of fire and smoke, but its image remained indelible. It was her. It was the *Retribution.* As the shot from her cannon struck the vanguard Evardo ran to the shrouds to climb above the obstructions on the quarterdeck.

Through wind and speed the English galleon cleared the cloud of her own gun smoke. Evardo's eyes watered as he tried to focus on the distant enemy quarterdeck as it swung away. It was crowded with men. There was no way Evardo could confirm if one of them was the man he could see so clearly in his memory, but he was sure that Robert Varian was on board. Smoke erupted from her stern guns, obscuring his view. He jumped back down to the deck.

'*Capitán* Mendez! Fall off. Bring the larboard broadside to bear!'

The sailing captain hesitated for a second, his every instinct telling him it was madness to present the full profile of his ship to the enemy's fire. Evardo strode towards him, his expression unholy, his sword still charged in his hand.

'Helmsman,' Mendez shouted. 'Hard a larboard.'

The *Santa Clara* turned swiftly and heeled over with the force of the wind. Mendez sent every available man to the shrouds, his voice loud as he steadied the helm, his galleon out of sync in the close quarter formation of the vanguard.

Evardo rushed below to the gun deck, roaring to Suárez, the gunners' captain, to come forward. He manhandled him to the nearest gun port on the larboard side, pointing out the *Retribution* through the banks of drifting smoke and the ever-moving galleons of the English attack.

'Target her aft decks.'

'Si, mi *Comandante*.' Suárez hurriedly ordered his men to make ready.

Evardo stepped back and stood behind one of the four *media culebrinas* straddling its trail. He looked down along the length of its eleven foot barrel and across the expanse of water to the enemy fleet. To his left and right, the gunners stood poised beside their guns, with the smaller *medio cañón pedreros* aft of the broadside and the heavy bow chasers to the fore. He left them to go aloft, reaching the quarterdeck as the distant *Retribution* came around for her second broadside. She was two points off the larboard quarter and would sail past the beam on the *Santa Clara* within a minute.

The *Retribution* didn't fire as before. Evardo understood in an instant that the English galleon was waiting to come abeam of the *Santa Clara*, marking her as the only Spanish ship sailing broadside to the attack. He smiled. For the briefest of moments he had feared that the *Retribution* might turn prematurely away from his guns. Now the exchange was inevitable. His savage war-cry echoed the command of the gunners' captain below.

'*¡Apunten!* Make ready!'

'Fire!'

The *Retribution* bucked under the recoil of the broadside and Robert peered through the clearing smoke, anxious to see what carnage his targeted attack had wrought.

A minute before, Larkin had been on the cusp of unleashing the broadside into the massed ranks of the seaward wing of the Armada but Robert had stayed the order, spotting the lone Spanish galleon out of formation with those around her. He had sent word to the master gunner, ordering him to hold fast and target the wayward ship, wanting to maximize the effectiveness of their second broadside. The first had simply disappeared into the midst of the Spanish ships, with no signs of visible damage. Although Robert knew it was impossible to witness the strike of each shot, he had the sense they were simply pricking at the colossus that was the Spanish fleet, scratching its flesh but drawing no blood.

Robert studied the Spanish galleon through the infuriating haze. Her main course was ripped through in two places with shot and parts of her rigging seemed shredded, but her hull looked sound. He could see where his shot had struck. The paint had been seared away, exposing the timbers. They were raw but unbroken. A curse rose to his lips but died as his mind registered the firing of the forward guns of the Spanish galleon.

'Incoming!'

Robert's breathing stopped, waiting for the hammer blow, the whine of inbound shot increasing to a terrible pitch in the blink of an eye. He didn't flinch, his eyes blazing, locked on the Spanish galleon as he saw her mid and then aft guns fire in sequence. At four hundred yards the precise aiming of heavy guns was nigh impossible but it was obvious the Spaniard was targeting the quarterdeck, each gun blasting forth as they came level with the stern of the *Retribution.*

Shots flew overhead, cauterizing the air, punching holes in the canvas of the main mizzen sail. The boom of a strike against the hull reverberated across the deck. A final shot smashed through the larboard bulwark of the poop deck, splintering the weathered timber, scattering fearsome shards that pierced the flesh of half a dozen men, sending them screaming to the deck.

'Hard a larboard,' Robert shouted. 'Mister Shaw, see to the injured. Get them below to the surgeon. Mister Seeley!'

The master came quickly to Robert's side.

'Mark the bastard, Thomas. Mark her well.'

'Aye, Captain.' Seeley ran to the poop deck, looking to the masthead banners of the Spanish galleon that had fired upon them, memorizing their patterns and heraldry.

'Mister Miller, watch our bearing, maintain our position in the attack.'

'Aye, Captain.'

Robert went to join Seeley on the poop deck, stopping for a moment to watch Shaw attend the injured. Only one of them was seriously hurt. A large splinter had pierced his lower leg. He was bleeding heavily and Robert knew the man would take no further part in the battle. With luck he would keep his leg but chances were Powell would have it off before nightfall robbed him of sufficient light. It was not a serious loss but Robert was angry nonetheless. 'Well, Thomas?'

'I'll recognize her if we see her again.'

'*When* we see her again.' Robert looked to the last of the English ships sailing into position to harry the seaward wing. He spun around. Ahead lay the landward wing, still unmolested, although Robert could discern the distant lines of Drake's ships beyond the Spanish formation, descending on the enemy from the outside flank.

A mile off the starboard beam of the *Retribution* was the soft underbelly of the Armada, the transport and auxiliary ships, but Robert knew that no English ship could venture there. Inside the curve of the Spanish crescent an English ship would forfeit the weather gauge to the trailing wings and would be easily cornered. Spanish boarding skills were well known and rightly feared.

The only hope the English had of carrying the battle was to blast the Spaniards out of the water. Any closer contact could only end in defeat. But how to find that balance, Robert wondered, glancing over his shoulder at the seemingly ineffectual attack they had just unleashed on the seaward flank. Too far away and their shot did not have enough power to inflict serious damage, too close and they ran the risk of being grappled and boarded.

The boom of gunfire ahead caught Robert's attention and he went back to the quarterdeck as Howard's *Ark Royal* engaged the landward wing. He glanced over the side. The cannons of the starboard broadside were reappearing, fully loaded and ready to fire again.

'Quarterdeck, ho. Enemy redeploying!'

The ships of the Spanish wing began breaking ranks, turning independently in the face of the English attack.

'They're attempting to close?' Seeley was unable to discern the enemy's intention.

'No,' Robert's pulse quickened. 'They're running. They're retreating to the centre.'

The solid coherent posture of the landward wing disintegrated in the time it took the *Retribution* to cover a dozen ship-lengths. Only one Spanish ship remained on station, one ship that did not run but rather turned her broadside to the enemy. It was a sight to see, a single enemy vessel facing down the extended English attack from two sides, but Robert's command instincts overrode any semblance of admiration. The isolated Spanish ship was vulnerable and for the first time there was a chance to draw real blood.

'*¡Cobardes!*' Evardo cursed in shame, the appalling sight of his countrymen fleeing before the enemy forcing foul-tasting bile to the back of his throat. He spat over the side. The English ships were clouded with gun smoke, the boom of their cannons a continuous roll of thunder across the two miles of open water between the wings. They were holding their attack line, not turning in to pursue the fleeing Spanish ships. Evardo felt his chest constrict as he saw the reason. A single ship was holding them at bay, a massive galleon that was now the eye of the fire storm. Evardo shouted up to the masthead to identify the ship.

'I think it's the *San Juan, Comandante.*'

'Juan Martínez de Recalde's command,' Mendez said close at hand.

'Abrahan's ship,' Evardo whispered in reply.

The lookout called down once more from the masthead,

this time to direct Evardo's attention to the centre of the crescent. De Moncada's four galleasses had left their station and were advancing rapidly against the wind to the aid of the *San Juan.* Two feluccas had also detached and were heading for the vanguard wing. The lead felucca quickly tacked to de Leiva's *La Rata Encoronada,* remaining there for only a moment. As it pulled away from the command ship the *La Rata* came about to sail beam reach across the mouth of the crescent. Evardo watched the other felucca approach the *Santa Clara* with mounting expectation.

'The Duke's compliments, *Comandante,*' the captain of the felucca called as it sailed past. 'You are given leave to break formation and sail to the *San Juan*'s assistance.'

Evardo spun around and began shouting commands before the end of the message was delivered. The *Santa Clara* heeled hard over as the felucca sailed on to deliver Medina Sidonia's order to the other warships of the vanguard.

The *Santa Clara* fell into the wake of de Leiva's massive carrack, quickly closing the initial gap and overtaking her on the lee. A dozen other ships had detached from the vanguard wing and they sailed swiftly with the wind abeam as Moncada's galleasses closed in on the intense fighting around the *San Juan.* Evardo went to the fo'c'sle. Less than a mile away, the *San Juan* was enveloped in gun smoke. The noise of cannon fire was all consuming, making it almost impossible to think. The sound filled Evardo's mind, fuelling his aggression and cutting all threads of restraint and reason. Abrahan was in danger, the *San Juan* was in peril and with a galleon to command Evardo knew that God was giving him his first opportunity to regain his reputation.

He turned to go back to the quarterdeck when a sudden concern made him go below to the gun deck. The English were still firing at the *San Juan* from a distance. Even with their initial overwhelming numbers, they had not closed to board the isolated galleon and it was clear the enemy were hell bent on destroying the *San Juan* with cannon fire alone. Until they gained the advantage of the weather gauge the *Santa Clara* and every other Spanish sailing warship would have to fight using English tactics and return fire with fire.

Evardo's initial concern increased as his eyes adjusted to the gloom of the low ceilinged gun deck. One of the ten-pounder *media culebrinas* was athwart the centre of the deck. It had been unlashed from its gun port and brought inboard. Because of the length of its trail the gunners had been forced to turn it diagonally to give them space to reload it. All eight gunners were working on the single cannon.

'*Capitán*,' Evardo called. 'How many guns have you reloaded?'

'Two, *Comandante*.'

'Where are the soldiers who are assigned to help you?' Evardo asked, a hard edge to his voice.

'They're aloft,' Suárez replied perplexed, surprised by his *comandante*'s question and tone.

Evardo stepped forward angrily when realization struck him like an open cuff. Before the battle Suárez would have enlisted the assistance of thirty or more soldiers, assigning a group to each skilled gunner who would oversee the loading of their cannon. Thereafter these soldiers, who had only a rudimentary knowledge of cannonry, would have returned to their designated place in the fighting tops and castles to make ready for a boarding attack.

In ordering a broadside fired at the *Retribution* Evardo had expended that preloaded shot. The soldiers had never thought to return to the gun deck after the cannons had been fired, for there was no precedent for such a thing. Likewise Suárez would not think to ask for such valuable fighting men to be brought below decks in the midst of battle, so was reloading the cannons using his own meagre crew of gunners.

Evardo urgently explained to Suárez the need to change tactics to match the English, then went back to the quarterdeck, ordering de Córdoba to send men below to assist the gunners.

The *Santa Clara* was now less than a half-mile from the fight. The sea was rising, the galleon crashing through the crest of each wave, and the rhythmic thud transported Evardo back to his captivity in the black hold of an English galleon. He did not shirk from the memory. Instead he let it fill his heart.

Sweat ran in dark rivulets down Larkin's face, washing away the soot stains, giving him a grotesque, demonic visage. His mouth was opened wide, exposing his blackened teeth as he roared his commands, trying to override the deafening din of battle. The gun deck of the *Retribution* had become the crucible of a foundry, a place of unremitting toil and savage heat, of dark shapes and shattering noise, sounds that numbed the senses and stripped the men of every thought but the one to go on; to heave, sponge, load, ram, prime, heave. To stand clear as the touchhole was kissed with fire, the cannon roaring in anger, gun powder exploding within its tempered walls, propelling out the shot.

Above this hellish place, the crew of the *Retribution* toiled in the rigging and on the decks, seemingly oblivious to but constantly aware of the fire of the enemy, their eyes stinging from gun smoke, their throats dried by the wind and their buried fear. They climbed the ratlines and footropes, the *Retribution* responding to their every touch and adjustment as sail and rudder combined to bring the guns of the warship to bear on the cursed enemy.

Robert stood in the centre of the quarterdeck, his eyes

restless. The ragged line of attack had long since disintegrated, the battle descending into a chaotic brawl, with each English ship acting as an independent command, swooping in to fire their guns before sailing away to reload. The lone Spanish galleon was off the starboard bow. She was a massive ship, at least a thousand tons and the *Retribution* had already twice given her the fire of her every cannon.

Spanish reinforcements were beginning to arrive. The first of these had been four galleasses. The sight of their blood red hulls and crowded decks had brought every man on board the *Retribution* to a standstill. Only the rising sea and wind had thwarted these mongrel ships from closing. Robert remained wary of their position, fearing their blunt nosed rams and heavy bow cannons.

'Quarterdeck, ho! Enemy ships approaching off the stern.'

Robert looked aft as the cannons beneath him boomed once more. His vision was spoiled for a moment by smoke and he coughed violently. Larkin was keeping up a tremendous rate of fire; Robert estimated just under three shots-per-gun-per-hour. He glanced at the target of their heavy guns, the lone Spanish galleon that still sailed defiant and unbroken. Her rigging and canvas was lacerated but the galleon showed no signs of mortal injury and her crew seemed far from the brink of surrender as her small calibre deck guns continued to fire sporadically.

Over the stern more than a dozen Spanish warships were descending rapidly on their beleaguered comrade. Robert studied their line of advance. The wind was holding firm. There was little danger the Spanish would be able to outmanoeuvre the English galleons but they were poised to deprive the English of their first prize.

'Hard about,' Robert called over his shoulder, the *Retribution* turning her bow towards the oncoming threat.

Three ship lengths away an English galleon was unleashing bow chasers on the audacious Spanish galleon. Even from four hundred yards, Robert could see Spaniards fall. Parts of the superstructure had shattered under the onslaught. The *Retribution* would be given one last chance to inflict such a blow on the 1000 ton behemoth but Robert already knew it would not be enough to slay the galleon. He prayed that the English fleet might instead take a prize from the smaller ships coming to her aid.

'Two points to starboard.'

Mendez repeated Evardo's order and the helmsman responded with alacrity, the *Santa Clara*'s bow turning slightly to larboard. The *San Juan* was now directly ahead, three hundred yards. Two English galleons had just sailed across her stern, raking her decks with a withering fire, but now they were withdrawing in the face of the *Santa Clara* and the dozen ships behind her, bringing themselves back to windward of this new threat.

Off the larboard side, the sea was alive with English warships. The *Santa Clara* had already taken erratic fire from their long range cannon, but Evardo had not responded, knowing he would need every shot in his arsenal.

'*Capitán* Mendez. Make ready to take in the courses and lay to. Set your helm to take us between the *San Juan* and the English. We must go directly to her aid.'

'But *Comandante* . . .'

'I mean to draw the English fire from the *San Juan* and give her a chance to withdraw.'

Mendez made to argue again but seeing the *comandante*'s expression, he swallowed his retort. With grim resignation he nodded his assent.

The *San Juan* was two hundred yards ahead. The fire

directed at the *Santa Clara* began to concentrate, her ever increasing proximity to the centre of the maelstrom drawing the attention of the more heavily engaged English warships. At one hundred yards the *San Juan* filled Evardo's vision, his mind oblivious to the English jackals and the increasing storm of fire. Fifty yards. Mendez called for a final touch on the whipstaff and the furling of the courses, the *Santa Clara* swooping in like a bird of prey under the larboard beam of the *San Juan.* The squall line of the fire storm swept over the *Santa Clara*, consuming her in a wave of iron. Behind her the other ships of the vanguard wing closed in, determined to bedevil the enemy's attempt to take one of their own. But for now, the *Santa Clara* stood alone.

For the briefest moment Robert hesitated, awed by the display of courage. The landward wing of the Armada had fled before the English guns, giving Robert cause to hope that the Spanish had no stomach for the fight, but any such thoughts were now banished by the sight of a single Spanish galleon standing square before a stricken comrade, becoming a partial shield for the larger ship.

'It's her,' Seeley shouted angrily beside him. 'It's the whoreson who targeted us in the first attack!'

Robert looked to the masthead banners of the Spanish galleon. His eyes narrowed, this unasked-for revenge dual in the midst of a battle filling his thoughts. In the moment of the hull's perfect pitch, the cannons of *Retribution* fired their deadly charge across the chasm that separated the mortal enemies of England and Spain.

Evardo stood tall at the gunwale, his knuckles white from the intensity of his grip on his sword, his face turned towards the enemy barrage, striving to subdue his instinct to take cover.

Some men feared death, but for Evardo it was the somehow more terrible fate of a grievous wound, the loss of a limb, or his sight, or the slow lingering death of a stomach wound. Every passing round shot fed his fear, but he refused to give in. His lips moved almost of their own accord, repeating a benediction to God, asking his divine patron for protection. With feigned indifference he glanced at the crew working around him, willing them strength to endure.

The decks of the *Santa Clara* were alive with a disciplined turmoil that only battle could create. The voices of the captains could be heard at every quarter, overriding the gutter curses of the crew who shouted at the English foe. On the upper castles men were rapidly servicing the breech loading *falcon pedreros*, firing them at the English in an act of defiance, the range too far for an effective kill. The preloaded broadside had long since been fired. Now only the sporadic vibration of single cannon shots could be felt by those on the main deck, the fired rounds too few and too interspersed to spoil any English attack.

Devastation swept over the *Santa Clara* as one English galleon after another sailed in to fire their cannon, cutting men and material down with impunity before turning neatly away from the fray. A voice in Evardo's mind screamed at him to concede his ground, not out of fear, but to stop this slow annihilation of the crew and ship he had sworn to protect. That voice was echoed by the injured and dying, their cries increasing in number with every sweeping attack. Evardo's mouth twisted in anger. Only if the enemy closed for ship-to-ship, hand-to-hand combat would the men of the *Santa Clara* be able to exact an equal measure of butchery.

Evardo looked to the sea on the flanks of the *Santa Clara*. The other ships of the vanguard wing were deploying to leeward of his ship, completing a screen behind which the

San Juan could safely withdraw. The sea was becoming rough, the wind no longer steady but gusting and fewer English ships were coming forward to engage, wary of the sea change and the newly formed wing.

A cannon ball slammed against the fo'c'sle of the *Santa Clara*, while another struck the hull amidships, parting shots from the withdrawing English galleons. Evardo finally sheathed his sword, the clean un-bloodied blade rasping against the scabbard. He had never drawn his sword in anger without using it. The frustration sat like a knot in the pit of his stomach. He turned his back on the English, taking a moment to survey the ravaged deck of his galleon. The *Santa Clara* had taken the heaviest casualties amongst the ships coming to the aid of the *San Juan*. As the firing ceased Evardo looked to the groups of men huddled around their stricken comrades, tending to their wounds as best they could, their cries of pain becoming louder in the absence of cannon thunder.

'*Santa Clara*!'

Evardo spun around at the call. The *San Juan* was beginning to pull away, coming about under the press of the wind to withdraw to the sanctuary of the main battle group. On the quarterdeck stood the imposing figure of de Recalde, his hand cupped to his mouth. Evardo acknowledged the hail. There was a moment's pause. De Recalde raised his hand to his forehead and casually saluted his thanks. Evardo returned the gesture but his eyes were no longer on de Recalde. They had shifted to the man who had come forward to stand beside him – his mentor Abrahan.

The gap between the ships increased, passing fifty yards, but Evardo's gaze never wavered. Just as the *San Juan* was poised to sail behind another galleon Evardo, saw Abrahan nod slightly. It was a small movement, barely discernible across the distance, but it was there. Evardo smiled. After half a lifetime spent under his care Evardo knew it was as much ground as his taciturn mentor would ever give. One act of reckless courage would not erase his failure in Abrahan's eyes. Evardo nodded to himself. The battle had only just begun.

CHAPTER 14

4 p.m. 31st July 1588. The English Channel, two leagues off Plymouth.

Robert paced the width of his cabin, his thoughts consumed by the events of the morning. He held a goblet of Madeira wine loosely in his hand, the last of his stock taken a year before during the Cadiz campaign, and he gulped from it with each turn of his heel. Outside the wind whistled through the rigging. Erratic gusts played merry hell with the sails and Robert could hear Miller sending the men to the running rigging.

Robert finished the goblet and went for the bottle. He poured out the last of its contents and slammed it down on the table. The wine had done nothing to quell his anxiety. He began to go through the sequence of the morning's fight once more, trying to examine each aspect in turn. Larkin had reported after the battle that he and his men had fired off nearly 120 rounds during the four hour fight. It was almost a tenth of the ammunition on board and for all that, and the fire of the other English ships, not one Spanish vessel had been taken.

Despite a moment of panic the Armada's formation

remained intact and was now sailing some four miles ahead of the English fleet. It had never stopped. Even when its trailing wings were under attack, the main body of the fleet had continued under shortened sail, allowing them to make headway and maintain cohesion.

As an inexperienced battle-captain of a ship Robert knew it was not his place to resolve the tactical problems of the English attack, but as a veteran sailor he could do little else. Ahead on the English coast lay the safe anchorages of Weymouth and the Solent. Perhaps the Spaniards were planning on taking one of these havens to support their invasion of England, or perhaps they were intent solely on linking up with Parma in the Low Countries. Whatever their ultimate plan, their formation was an impregnable fortress and as long as it remained so there was nothing the English fleet could do to stop them.

Seeley pored over his charts in his tiny cabin under the poop deck, his finger tracing every inlet and headland of the Devon coastline. There was a knock on his cabin door. Shaw and Powell entered.

'Well?'

'Nothing to report, Mister Seeley,' Shaw replied.

'Curse it,' Seeley spat. He had warned the boatswain, his mate and the surgeon to be extra vigilant now that battle had been joined. Whatever Young's position on the ship he was bound to reveal himself when asked to fight against his own kind. His hesitation would be his undoing.

'This battle has only just begun,' Powell said assuredly. 'We'll find him.'

'Perhaps we should widen our circle of confederates,' Shaw suggested. 'It would increase our chances of catching Young.'

'We can't,' Powell replied, 'not without running the risk of having a papist in our midst. A significant proportion of the population of England is still Roman Catholic. Given the size of the crew it is wise to suspect there are at least a handful of them on board.'

'You believe there are others besides Young?'

Powell nodded.

'But surely we would know of them,' Shaw protested. 'I grant you one is difficult to find amongst over two hundred men. But a group of them?'

'They are well hidden, Mister Shaw, even in battle,' Powell explained. 'They fight like any other Englishman.'

'Against their fellow papists?'

'Many Roman Catholics consider themselves to be loyal recusants. Despite their religion they fight because Spain is the enemy of England.'

'You consider these traitors to be loyal Englishmen?' Seeley asked menacingly.

'I did not say that I did, only that these recusants believe they can be both Roman Catholic and loyal to the Crown.'

'Protestantism is the religion of England and our Queen,' Seeley retorted angrily. 'To believe in another foreign faith is treason in itself. Now, return to your posts.'

Shaw and Powell left the cabin. Seeley returned to his charts but he could not concentrate. *Loyal recusant.* The term was offensive. Roman Catholic Englishmen were traitors by their very existence and to suggest otherwise was an act of complicity. He called to mind Powell's warning that there may be other papists on board beside Young and his thoughts went to the moment the Armada changed formation before battle was joined.

'*Sancta Maria, ora pro nobis*,' he said quietly, enunciating each syllable slowly. '*Holy Mary, pray for us.*'

The words sounded foreign in his ears, not merely because

they were spoken in Latin, but because he had never heard a Protestant say them before. Captain Varian had undoubtedly said them without thinking. The sight of the Armada skilfully redeploying into the crescent formation had struck every man with awe, but this made their utterance all the more baffling.

As a Protestant, Seeley revered Mary, but only because she was the mother of Jesus and therefore deserved veneration. His faith taught him that he could pray *with* Mary, but he should not pray *to* her, that prayer and entreaties should be recited only to God. *Sancta Maria, ora pro nobis.* This was the prayer of a Roman Catholic, a misguided petition based on a fallacy inherent in their corrupt faith. But Captain Varian wasn't one. He couldn't be. Seeley recalled what he had witnessed at the sack of Sagres, how the captain's first instinct when he saw the Roman Catholic church under attack was to rush to join the others at the door, and how he had raised his pistol to shoot the priest, only to be denied by another.

After the morning's action, as the fleet was redeploying to windward of the Armada, Howard had sailed alongside in the *Ark Royal* to pass his compliments to Captain Varian on his handling of his ship during the first engagement. Varian had sailed the *Retribution* into the thickest part of the fight and had remained in the battle long after others had withdrawn. He had stood squarely on the quarterdeck and made sure every shot fired was sorely felt by the Spaniards. These were not the actions of a traitor.

But on the other hand, Varian had never fully supported Seeley's attempt to find Young. He had not hindered the investigation, but he had not assisted in it either. If the *Retribution* had been Seeley's ship he would have taken her apart timber by timber until he found the treasonous rat. Suddenly a thought struck him. Perhaps Varian was trying to protect a fellow Roman Catholic from exposure, or maybe, Seeley thought in horror, Varian was Young. Perhaps it was his real name, changed to conceal his true faith.

Seeley laughed abruptly. There was no logic to this. If Varian was a Roman Catholic traitor, why was he fighting the Spanish? There was no such thing as a loyal recusant. If there were any English papists fighting in this war, it was those who were widely rumoured to be sailing with the enemy fleet, seditious outcasts who had betrayed their countrymen and forfeited their souls for a foreign cause. The captain couldn't be Roman Catholic. His actions in Sagres, his maniacal charge on the *Halcón*, his aggressive tactics in the morning's action; everything spoke of his loyalty to the Crown and England.

Yet Seeley could not ignore the sliver of doubt that remained. He had often thought the captain lacked the religious fervour that he himself possessed in the fight against the Spanish. Perhaps Varian did not think of the war against Spain as a religious matter, and was more ambivalent towards Roman Catholics. Men had different motives for fighting the Spanish. Miller, the master's mate, had often expressed his hatred of the Spanish stranglehold on trade in the New World. Perhaps Varian's only motive was to keep England safe from foreign invasion, regardless of any enemy's faith.

Seeley shook his head to put an end to his deliberations. His lack of success in his search for Young had affected him deeply. Clearly his suspicions were now feeding on themselves, creating enemies where none existed. Their captain was not a traitor. Seeley looked to his charts, his attention returning to the coastline, but all the while his lips moved without conscious thought, mouthing a prayer he could not forget: *Sancta Maria, ora pro nobis.*

In the soft glow of lantern light Evardo stepped over the prone bodies of the wounded, his boots grinding the sand underfoot that had been strewn there to soak up the blood of the maimed. He looked down at each man in turn. Many of them returned his gaze silently, their eyes neither accusing nor accepting. The orlop deck was quiet. The screams of the most grievously injured had ceased, and beyond the pall of light cast by the lanterns Evardo could hear the creak and squeal of the whipstaff and rudder in the dark recesses of the aft section.

Evardo knelt down beside one of his men. The sailor was lying on a filthy blanket, his head propped up on some coiled rigging. His eyes were closed, his head jerking from side to side as if trapped in some horrible nightmare. He was soaked with sweat. Evardo looked down the length of the sailor's body. A wave of nausea swept over him. The man's arm had been blown off below the elbow. The flesh was horribly mangled and the wound had been cauterized to stop the bleeding. Huge bluebottles were already settling to feast on the charred flesh and pools of blood, their incessant buzzing rising angrily as Evardo tried to wave them away.

The combination of smells was overpowering; the stink of burn, like meat left too long on the flame, the tang of fresh blood, the acrid smell of sweat, and the stench of faeces. The sailor had soiled himself, and for a brief moment Evardo wondered if the pain or the sight of the red-hot iron used to seal his wound had caused the sailor to lose control. The thought made Evardo stand up abruptly and he looked away from the injured sailor, quickly turning his focus to the huddled figures at the other side of the deck.

Padre Garza was kneeling beside a dying soldier, solemnly reciting the Last Rites. The man was holding desperately onto the priest's hand, biting down on a leather thong to silence his cries. Blood trickled from the side of his mouth, a visible sign of his terrible internal injuries. Evardo found himself staring into the soldier's eyes. They were wide with pain, and something more terrible. Fear. The soldier's eyes darted from the priest kneeling over him to the two shroud-covered bodies lying near at hand; the fate that would soon be his. Again Evardo looked away, this time to preserve the man's dignity. The consequences of the morning's action had been sharp, but not severe. Two men had been killed instantly during the battle. Padre Garza's charge would be a third. Twelve men had been wounded, two badly so, including the sailor who had lost his arm.

'*Comandante.*' Evardo saw Captain de Córdoba approach. 'I did not realize you had come below.'

'I wished to check on the wounded,' Evardo replied.

De Córdoba nodded appreciatively. He looked beyond Evardo to the shroud-covered bodies and the dying soldier under the padre's care.

'López,' he said quietly. 'He and the other two were manning a *falcon pedrero* on the fo'c'sle when it was hit.'

Evardo nodded and looked back to the young soldier. 'What were the names of the others?'

'De Arroyo and Garrido.'

Evardo memorized the names. It was common for *comandantes* to issue false casualty lists to the paymaster in order to draw 'dead men's pay' but Evardo would record them faithfully. The men deserved nothing less.

'Your company fought well today *Capitán* de Córdoba.'

'Thank you, *Comandante.* They would have fought all the better if the English had closed and we were afforded the chance to board.'

Evardo nodded. He couldn't fathom what the English hoped to achieve with their artillery attack runs. Despite the incredible rate of fire the enemy had maintained in the morning's action the *Santa Clara* had suffered only minimal damage and even this was confined to the superstructure, sails and rigging. The hull, although it had taken over a dozen direct hits from round shot, was still sound. The *Santa Clara* had weathered her first fire storm under Evardo's command. He reached out to touch the hull, his fingertips feeling the tiny vibrations in the timbers caused by the pounding of the waves and the pull of the wind.

'I suspect the English were probing for weaknesses this morning, perhaps to ascertain where the fighting ships lie in our formation.'

'If they plan on stopping our advance they will have to engage in a proper battle,' de Córdoba said. 'They will have to board and fight as we do in the Mediterranean, ship to ship, man to man.'

'I pray to God it will be so.'

Suddenly Evardo felt the deck shudder and the air was filled with a massive explosion, a noise that spoke of some terrible inferno. Evardo started running, keeping his head down in the low-ceiling deck. Aloft the crew were lining the starboard bulwark. He pushed through them. A quarter of a mile away, one of the Armada's bigger ships was engulfed in thick black smoke. An order to bring the men to battle stations rose to Evardo's lips but he stopped himself short. This was no attack. It was something far worse.

'It's the *San Salvador* of the Guipúzcoan squadron,' a crewman shouted. His call was met with a chorus of agreement.

The boom of a single cannon caused Evardo to turn and he saw a puff of white smoke issue from the larboard side of the *San Martín.* It was the signal for the Armada to stop. Evardo shouted the order as he went to the quarterdeck. For a moment he was tempted to come about and go to the aid of the *San Salvador* but he knew he could not. After the morning's action and the retreat of the warships of the rearguard wing, *sargentos mayors* had been dispatched in pataches to every ship in the fleet with a message from Medina Sidonia. Henceforth, no *comandante*, on pain of death by hanging, was to retreat from his designated position in the fleet. For men of honour it was a stinging rebuke and although Evardo knew such an order was not meant for him directly, as a *comandante* he was tainted by association.

A call went out from the masthead, alerting Evardo to the approach of a felucca off the starboard beam. She carried orders for half a dozen ships, the *Santa Clara* amongst them, to break formation and assist the *San Salvador*. Evardo called for the course change and ordered extra lookouts to the fighting tops and bowsprit, wary of the English fleet not four miles away. The *Santa Clara* turned neatly through the chop, her deck heeling over under the press of the wind.

Evardo's concern mounted as they neared the stricken galleon. Cries of alarm and command mixed on the wind with screams of agony and despair. The aft decks and stern castle of the *San Salvador* had been completely annihilated. Her steering and mizzen masts were gone and already the wind and tide were beginning to turn her broadside to the weather. Feluccas and pataches were milling around her towering hull, picking men out of the churning sea, while others took secured tow lines to the attending galleons nearby. The *Santa Clara* sailed past the *San Martín* and Evardo answered the hail of the flagship to bring his galleon astride the stern of the *San Salvador* and hold station there.

Evardo ordered the longboat launched. Despite being from the Basque region, the men of the *San Salvador* were fellow Spaniards and the crew eagerly responded to Evardo's bidding. The longboat descended into the choppy sea. Evardo gave command of the quarterdeck to Mendez and went forward to the fo'c'sle in time to see the longboat reach the outer edge of the halo of debris surrounding the *San Salvador*. They pulled a charred, blackened body from the water, only to throw it overboard again. Evardo focused on the larboard quarter of the galleon thirty yards away.

The entire aft section of the *San Salvador* had been torn open by the explosion, exposing her inner decks and cabins. The dead lay everywhere, many burned beyond recognition, others horribly mutilated by the blast, spared their savage injuries by the merciful hand of death. Smoke billowed from a dozen open wounds in the hull. Pataches were lashing on to the *San Salvador*, their crews clambering up onto the main deck to fight the fires that were still raging.

For every man who climbed on board, others were abandoning ship, many carrying the heavy coin chests of the Armada's paymaster who was sailing on the *San Salvador*. The walking wounded were also being taken off and while Evardo could see that many would be fit to fight again, the galleon herself was perilously close to sinking and was surely beyond salvaging.

The sudden sound of collision caused Evardo to spin around. Not two hundred yards away the flagship of the Andalusia squadron, the *Nuestra Señora del Rosario* had slammed into her sister ship, the *Santa Catalina*. Earlier that morning, as the *Rosario* had sailed to support the *San Juan*, she had accidentally collided with one of the Biscayans and had damaged her bowsprit. This had badly affected her steering and she had been forced to drop out of the fight. Now that compromising damage had caused her even greater misfortune, crippling the *Rosario* further. Her foremast rigging was in complete disarray. Evardo uttered a prayer, watching in horror as the foremast bowed under the press of the wind, threatening to snap at any moment.

He glanced back at the *San Salvador*. The longboat of the

Santa Clara had reached its hull and was helping with the evacuation. It was dangerous work, the pitiless sea foaming, and more than once the men in the longboat were thrown from their feet as rogue waves slammed their small craft against the hull of the galleon. Many of the pataches and feluccas were cutting loose to go to the assistance of the latest casualty, the *Rosario*, and Evardo went back to the quarter-deck, his attention turning once more to the enemy.

The evening was swiftly closing in. The English still commanded the weather gauge. Only the inconsistency of the wind and sea and the Armada's unbroken formation was keeping them at bay. But how long would those protective forces hold? With two badly wounded ships hampering their progress the Armada was significantly exposed. Evardo could only hope that the experienced commanders advising Medina Sidonia would find a way to achieve an effective running defence of the *San Salvador* and the *Rosario*. Like wolves, the English were silently observing their prey.

John Cross pounded on the wooden door and stepped back into the middle of the street. The imposing limestone façade of the four-storey civic building was in darkness. He pounded again.

'In the name of the Queen, open up,' he bellowed.

An angry voice shouted at him from the down the street to be silent but Cross ignored the tirade and hammered on the door once more, the noise sparking further anger from another quarter.

It was nearly thirty-six hours since Cross had begun his search for the officer named Seeley. From the outset he had been beset by delays and frustration. Almost immediately after he left the tavern the town had ignited with the news that the Spanish had been sighted nearing Plymouth Roads. The local population had quickly taken to the streets, many packing up their meagre belongings to flee to the surrounding countryside while others simply milled around in chaotic fear of the foe that was suddenly on their doorstep.

The clogged streets had delayed Cross and by the time he had reached the town's main civic building the port officials had already left to attend the admiral of the fleet. Cross had waited until darkness fell. Then news came that the fleet was warping out of the harbour with the outgoing tide. In bitter anger he strode to the torch-lit docks to witness the departure in person. His quarry was on board one of the departing warships.

Dawn the following morning had brought news of the opening moves by the English fleet, of how Howard had gained the weather gauge and the Armada had sailed past Plymouth, and the population had taken to the streets again, this time to cheer. Cross had shared their joy at Howard's opening success, but his elation had been tempered by news given to him by a clerk that the port officials were shadowing the flagship in a local barque so as to be on hand to offer assistance while Plymouth was in range of the fighting.

That day had passed slowly, with Cross standing on the quayside amongst the local population as small local tenders returned from sailing with the English fleet, each one carrying news of the opening encounter, the short sharp action that had seen the fleet take the fight to the enemy. With the return of night Cross had abandoned his vigil. He had slept fitfully, convinced that the officials must soon return, now that the fleets were moving further east. He had risen in the darkness before dawn to return to the civic building, determined to continue his search.

'Open the cursed door,' he roared again.

Glancing up he saw a light flicker in one of the windows

and intensified his hammering on the door. The light moved away, only to appear moments later as a shaft washed out from underneath the door.

'Stop that banging, damn you,' a muffled voice shouted angrily from inside.

'In the name of the Queen, open up.'

'Who are you? What do you want?'

Cross stated his association with Francis Tanner, Walsingham's local agent. The mere mention of Tanner stilled the voice inside and Cross was rewarded with the sound of a bolt being slammed back. He pushed at the door even as it was being opened, forcing the man inside to step back.

'What do you want?' the official asked again irritably, holding a candle out at arm's length. He was an older man, his face haggard and blackened, and he had clearly been sleeping in his clothes.

'I need to see the crew manifests for the English fleet, immediately.' Cross paid no heed to the open hostility of the official.

'The crew manifests? At this hour? Do you realize where I've been for the past twenty-four hours, you insolent cuss. I should have you in irons for coming here unannounced in the middle of the night.'

'The crew manifests,' Cross repeated, a hard edge to his voice. 'Before I have you flogged for impeding the investigation of one of the Queen's agents.'

'You can't speak to me . . .' the official began but the words died in his throat as Cross took a menacing step forward. He abruptly turned on his heel, muttering half-hearted threats under his breath as he led Cross into his office. Placing the candle on the desk, he went to a large pile of loose pages on a nearby shelf, gathered them up and put them on the desk.

'These are copies of the paymaster's lists,' he spat. 'They are not to leave this room.'

Cross moved around the desk to sit down. The official left with a final huff of annoyance, leaving Cross with the candle as he returned to his bedroom through the dark corridor.

Cross quickly went to work. Each page contained the full muster of a ship. The captain was listed at the top, followed by the crew's names in order of when they joined. Each page had been amended many times, with annotations regarding promotions and transfers cluttering the margins on all sides. It was a tiresome process and an hour passed swiftly, followed by another. Twice Cross came upon the name Seeley, but both times he was disappointed to discover that the man was a mere seaman. The barman at the tavern had been confident Seeley was an officer. Nevertheless, Cross marked the names and put the pages aside, continuing his search as the faint sounds of the coming day began to creep into the room. He began to wonder if the barman had been wrong about Seeley's rank. Maybe there was no such man as Seeley, and the barman had spun Cross a tale to get him out of his tavern.

The black of night was fading to a dull grey. Dawn was not far away. Cross looked down at the page before him, one of only a half-dozen left, his eyes mechanically following his finger down the list of names.

Seeley.

Cross's breath stopped at the sight of the name and he followed the entry across the page. He stood up and leaned in closer to re-read the entry. Thomas Seeley, rank: Master's Mate. The 'Mate' had been crossed out and the pay grade had been amended accordingly. It was him, it had to be. Cross swiftly flicked through the remaining musters to ensure there was no other Seeley listed. He returned to Thomas Seeley and looked at the top of the page for the ship's name. It was written in a larger, more elaborate script, a flourish of artistry on what was once a blank page. He read out the name, enunciating it slowly as the pace of his heart increased. For the first time in days a smile stole onto his face. It was a fitting name for his quest.

'*Retribution*.'

Robert peered through the darkness at the light of the stern lantern ahead. It was moving sedately with the fall and rise of the sea, a regular, almost hypnotic motion. He had to force himself to look away. A memory of the soft glow of the lantern remained in the centre of his vision. He blinked his eyes to clear them and turned his focus to the shadowy bulk of the *Ark Royal* sailing some thirty yards off the starboard bow.

The lantern light was from Drake's *Revenge*. The English fleet was arrayed behind it to ensure that they remained together during the night time passage. The light had moved steadily on an easterly course, save for a time at the beginning of the night when it had disappeared altogether. It had reappeared, dimly at first, and slightly off centre, as if the *Revenge* had made a sudden course change and pulled further ahead but Robert had kept the *Retribution* on the shoulder of the *Ark Royal* and together they had re-established their course on Drake's guiding light.

The wind blew steadily into Robert's face and he drank in the cool cleansing air. If it held through dawn then the morning would certainly bring another order from Howard to attack. At their current speed the Armada would be abreast of Weymouth in less than a day. It was strong anchorage, safe from the prevailing winds and easily defendable, and it was possible the Spanish might attempt to secure it. Only continued harassment would forestall that attempt. Robert had already ordered the men of the mid watch to ready the ship for a dawn assault.

Robert turned again and looked eastward beyond the

light of the *Revenge.* In anticipation of the sun the stars nearest the horizon had already disappeared. True dawn was less than thirty minutes away and for the first time Robert could see the darker outlines of the Spanish ships ahead. His brow crinkled. They seemed very close and Robert wondered whether the sheer size of the enemy fleet, combined with a trick of the light, was giving him a false impression of proximity.

'Mister Seeley.' The master answered the hail by crossing the quarterdeck. Robert indicated the horizon ahead. The Spanish seemed to be stretched out across the full width of the field of vision afforded to them by the gathering dawn light.

'They seem damned close,' Seeley said warily.

Robert nodded, his eyes darting to the *Revenge*'s light and then to Howard's ship. Both were steady, but Robert could not suppress a mounting sense of unease.

'Thomas, get aloft to the masthead. Check our flanks.'

'Aye, Captain.'

In less than a minute the last of the darkness on the horizon turned to grey-blue. The outlines of the Armada became starker, exposing the upper decks of the hulls beneath the multitudinous masts.

'Spaniards dead ahead! Two hundred yards! Enemy off the beams!'

'Sweet Jesus,' Robert whispered to Seeley's call. Each passing second increased the illumination, revealing the folly of their course. They had followed the light of a Spanish ship. They were in the teeth of the enemy, in the centre of the crescent.

'Hard about! All hands on deck. Tops'ls and gallants, ho! Battle stations!'

The *Retribution* heeled hard over through the turn, the deck tilting as the galleon came abeam of the wind. Out of the corner of his eye Robert saw the *Ark Royal* make a similar turn. Another English ship, the *Mary Rose*, was on her opposing flank but beyond that they were alone. The rest of the English fleet was scattered across the breadth of the Channel.

Evardo lifted his eyes to the slowly brightening sky as the words of the Salve Regina, sung in the unbroken voices of the ship's boys, drifted over the decks of the *Santa Clara*. Padre Garza was leading the men in a recital of the sorrowful mysteries of the rosary, their deep murmured responses mingling with the graceful hymn. Nearest the priest de Córdoba was kneeling with a number of his soldiers, while behind them the rest of the men stood with their heads bowed in humility.

Evardo longed for their serenity but his mind refused to quieten and his thoughts dwelt on the previous day. Despite their best efforts, the *San Salvador* and the *Rosario* had been unsalvageable. With twilight rapidly giving way to night Medina Sidonia had ordered every ship back to its position while they still had sufficient light to navigate. Then he had ordered the Armada to proceed as before. The *San Salvador* had been stripped of everything but its stock of ammunition, almost a gross of powder barrels and well over two thousand round shot. It was a significant loss, made all the worse because, with fifty of her most severely injured crew still on board, the *San Salvador* could not be scuttled. She had been simply cast adrift as a bloodless prize for the English.

The *Rosario* too had been left to her own fate. Her foremast had finally snapped and become entangled with the mainmast, a cataclysmic repercussion of the collision from which there could be no recovery. Evardo had watched from the *Santa Clara* as a patache was dispatched by Don Pedro de Valdés, the *comandante* of the *Rosario*, to Medina Sidonia's flagship, no doubt requesting that the duke halt the Armada's progress to allow for the *Rosario* to be repaired. The answer had come in a general order to all ships to retire to their positions.

Evardo suspected that his patron, Diego Flores de Valdés, who sailed on the *San Martín*, had had a hand in the decision to abandon the *Rosario*. His enmity for his cousin Don Pedro was well known, but Evardo also knew that Medina Sidonia was ruthlessly determined to carry out the orders of the King. The Armada's objective could not be delayed. Evardo shuddered as he thought of the fate that awaited any ship that could not keep pace with the fleet.

The pre-dawn light slowly gave way to the rising sun. Evardo checked the line of his galleon with those surrounding him in the vanguard wing. The night had passed without incident. Mendez and the other sailing captains had kept their charges neatly in position and with the defensive crescent still firm Evardo's thoughts went to the enemy. He looked aft, expecting to see the English fleet arrayed in battle formation behind the Armada, still holding doggedly to the weather gauge. The sea however was almost empty. Only in the far distance could he see the outlines of their masts and sails, and even these were scattered across the horizon.

'Quarterdeck! Enemy ships off the larboard beam.'

Evardo spun around in disbelief, expecting subterfuge but instead he was greeted by the sight of three English ships close to the centre of the crescent, turning rapidly to escape. Evardo recognized the masthead standards on the lead ship. It was the English flagship; the *Ark Royal*, Admiral Howard's galleon. The Spanish ships of the centre were not turning to engage, they were allowing the English admiral to escape unhindered. It was an appropriate response, Evardo conceded.

The abandonment of the *San Salvador* and the *Rosario* was an ignominious act brought about by necessity, but Medina

Sidonia, being a Spanish duke and commander of the Armada, was still a man of honour. As such he would never deign to allow an enemy flagship to be overwhelmed in an unfair fight. It was a chivalrous decision. Evardo began to turn his attention away when suddenly he recognized the banners of one of the other ships. The *Retribution*.

He was immediately struck by an overwhelming urge to defy all convention and order his ship to attack. The English galleon was vulnerable. In the trailing vanguard wing the *Santa Clara* was still slightly upwind. Evardo had the weather gauge. There might never be another time.

With an enormous effort of will, Evardo fought his desire for revenge. He could not attack. He was bound both by duty and honour to hold fast, and he balled his hand into a trembling fist as he watched the nimble English galleon sail beyond his reach. It was a bitter concession to gallantry, particularly as the dishonourable nature of the English surprise attack on Cadiz had precipitated his disgrace. Evardo turned his back on the *Retribution*, consoling himself that there would be another time.

Robert called for the sails to be shortened as the *Retribution*, the *Ark Royal* and the *Mary Rose* came in contact with a flotilla of a dozen English warships and a handful of pinnaces. The Armada was over three miles to leeward. The *Ark Royal* turned and took the lead but with such a small number of ships to command there was little Howard could do beyond shadowing the enemy's progress, so he dispatched the pinnaces to round up the rest of the fleet. Robert stood his crew down from battle stations and gave command of the watch over to Seeley.

The westerly wind was holding steady. It was a fair breeze, a perfect foil for the fearsome weapon Robert commanded and he looked in frustration at the enemy sailing unmolested along the coastline of England.

'We were fortunate to escape,' Robert heard, turning to find Seeley standing beside him.

'We were more than fortunate. For Christ's sake, Thomas, we spent the night following a Spanish stern light. Where in God's holy name did the *Revenge* go?'

Seeley ignored the captain's blasphemy and thought back. 'When Drake's light disappeared he must have changed course.'

'And with the fleet scattered all to hell, we haven't a chance of regrouping before the end of the day.'

A pinnace was approaching from the south, turning neatly in the wake of the flotilla before coming alongside the *Ark Royal.* Robert saw the captain hand dispatches to Howard before drawing away to hold station beside the towering warship. Robert called for a slight change in heading bringing the *Retribution* within hailing distance of the pinnace. He recognized the captain and the two men saluted each other.

'What news?' Robert called, his hand cupped over his mouth.

'It's Drake, he's taken a huge Spanish prize, the *Rosario*, and without firing a single shot. The gutless Spaniards simply gave her up.'

The pinnace captain's call was heard by others on nearby ships and questions and cheers rang out, precluding Robert's chances of getting any further information. It was enough however. Drake had doused his light and changed course to claim a Spanish prize. It was a dereliction that staggered Robert and shattered his faith in Drake.

During the Cadiz campaign a year before, when many other captains had returned to England, Robert had stayed the course and followed Drake without question. It was a decision determined not only by loyalty to one who had given him a field promotion, but also by an instinctive fealty to a man who embodied everything that Robert thought an Englishman should be.

Now Robert saw something else in Drake. He was first and foremost a privateer, a self-centred opportunist. Presented with the chance to take a prize he had ignored his responsibility to the fleet. It was a sobering realization. Drake's image was suddenly replaced in Robert's mind by that of his father.

Here too was a man whom Robert had largely come to know through his own thoughts and perceptions. During their many years apart he had built him up to be a man whom he could admire, someone he hoped he could one day openly call his father.

But Robert no longer saw his father as that man. Nathaniel Young was not someone whom Robert could associate with pride, or loyalty, or heritage. He was a traitor. In his determination to resurrect his family name, Robert had ignored it.

Now his father was truly gone, banished forever from England, and from Robert's heart. The thought stopped Robert cold. If his father was gone forever, then so too was his only link to his family's lineage. Young or Varian, he was still the same man; a true Catholic, loyal to his Queen and country. It was his actions that defined him as a man, not his ancestors.

Robert's captaincy of the *Retribution* had been secured through his own merit, not by some favour of birth. He felt a deep sense of pride at his achievement, one far greater than any he had ever felt for his ancestral name. He had raised himself through merit alone. The thought brought him full circle back to Drake, the low-born commander who had become the touchstone for a generation of sailors.

Drake was a powerful, fearless man. His relentless, aggressive pursuit of England's foes had made him an inspiration to his countrymen, but on this day his mercenary instincts had cost the English fleet dearly. The Spanish had held their formation during the night. Because of Drake the English fleet was scattered, and during the long day to come the enemy would remain free to advance towards their unknown objective. Despite the value of Drake's prize, the privateer had handed an even greater one to the Spanish – a day's respite from attack.

CHAPTER 15

5 a.m. 2nd August 1588. The English Channel, off Portland Bill.

Evardo lay in his cot, his head propped up on his enfolded arm, his eyes locked on the single shard of orange light on the cabin wall. It grew with each passing second and Evardo traced it across the cabin to the corner of a window, his focus shifting to the rising sun that was its source. With a deep groan he raised himself from the cot and ran his hands through his dishevelled hair before putting on his wide-brimmed hat. He had slept lightly over the previous hours, a part of his mind remaining alert to every sound on board. But he felt completely refreshed, gathering up his sword belt as he left the cabin to go aloft.

Pausing on the main deck to get his bearings, he quickly took in the horizons off the larboard and starboard sides. He glanced up at the masthead banners and then looked aft. The enemy fleet were arrayed in battle formation over three miles astern. The semblance of order amongst the English ranks was in marked contrast to dawn on the previous day and Evardo smiled sardonically. Such an impressive display. While yesterday such a formation might have given Evardo cause for immediate concern, this morning there was little the English could do to harass the Armada.

During the night the westerly wind had completely fallen away, leaving both fleets becalmed. The result was an eerie standoff. Soon after midnight Evardo had finally persuaded himself that it was safe to go below to his cabin, leaving strict orders with Mendez that he was to be notified of the slightest change in conditions.

'The Isle of Portland,' Mendez indicated as Evardo came up to the quarterdeck.

He turned to look at the rugged low-lying promontory taking shape off the larboard beam. Before sailing from Lisbon every *comandante* had been given a set of maps from the cartographer Ciprián Sánchez. On these Portland was shown to be a land-tied island shaped like an inverted teardrop with its point jutting out into the sea. To the immediate west of it, beyond the return curve of its shoreline, lay the port of Weymouth.

'Ahoy *Santa Clara*, *Comandante* Morales!'

Evardo looked over the side to the patache approaching under oars.

'Compliments of Don Alonso de Leiva, *Comandante.* You are invited to join him on board his ship.'

Evardo called for the longboat to be launched and he was rowed across to *La Rata Encoronada.* He climbed up the towering hull and was directed to the fo'c'sle where a table had been erected under a canvas awning. The *comandante*s of the vanguard were seated around it.

'Ah *Comandante* Morales,' de Leiva called from the head of the table. 'Come and join us for some food.'

Evardo nodded gratefully to de Leiva and sat down. A conversation had already begun about what the next days might bring.

'Medina Sidonia dispatched another patache to Flanders

yesterday evening,' one man said. 'It sailed out just before dusk.'

'And still none has returned,' another remarked.

'So we have yet to have any communication with Parma. We've no idea if the Army of Flanders is ready to embark or even whether Parma knows the Armada has reached the Channel.'

'He must know, surely one of our pataches has got through.'

'There's no way to be sure. To reach Parma a patache has to run the gauntlet of any English ships that might be ahead in the Channel and the Dutch flyboats that we know are blockading the coast of Flanders. It's possible that none of them have reached Flanders.'

A shadow passed over Evardo's thoughts as he listened. He recalled the conversation he had had months before with his brother, Parma's aide-de-camp. Allante had said that Parma doubted the possibility of close coordination between two disparate forces, particularly where one, the Armada, would be constantly in motion. At the time, nearly a year before, Evardo had dismissed those doubts, believing them to be ill-founded, but now in the fluid battlefield of the Channel they could no longer be ignored. The pace of the Armada's advance was strictly dictated by the weather and the intensity of the English attacks. A scheduled rendezvous could only be achieved through constant communication with Parma.

'Don de Leiva,' one of the *comandante*s asked, 'how exactly are we to rendezvous with Parma's invasion fleet? We possess no secure port on the coast of Flanders deep enough to accommodate the capital ships of the Armada. Are we planning to send our smaller ships forward to escort Parma's transports past the Dutch blockade?'

'We cannot,' another *comandante* interjected. 'With the English fleet hard on our heels such a division of forces would be madness.'

'So if the Armada cannot detach ships to run the Dutch blockade and Parma cannot sally out alone in unarmed transports, how and where are we to meet?'

All eyes turned to de Leiva.

'The King has ordered us to "join hands" with Parma, so that is what we shall do,' he said reassuringly. 'How this is achieved will be resolved when we reach Calais.'

'Perhaps his grace, the duke, should order the fleet to a safe anchorage on the English coast,' Evardo suggested. 'Weymouth perhaps. We could wait there until a line of communication has been established.'

Others around the table voiced their agreement.

'The King's orders to the Duke of Medina Sidonia are very clear on this matter,' de Leiva replied, levelling his gaze at Evardo. 'We can only seek to gain a safe anchorage on the English coast *after* we have rendezvoused with Parma. In all these matters we must adhere to the plan outlined by his majesty. His will is guided by God.'

Evardo nodded solemnly, resolving to place his faith in the wisdom of his King.

Evardo registered the gentle kiss of air on the back of his neck. He turned around but it was gone and as he began to believe he had imagined the sensation a tiny gust of wind dried the moisture on his lips. Spinning around he looked aloft to the masthead banners of the *La Rata*, his right index finger pointing north as he orientated himself. The banner stirred in a lacklustre attempt to unfurl. Evardo held his breath. It stirred again, and Evardo smiled as the banner started to dance. The rigging groaned. A ripple ran across the main course and everyone around the table stood up. The wind was rising, but not from the west. It was blowing from the north-east. It was a light breeze, no more than a couple of knots, but it was enough. The Armada had the weather gauge.

Evardo turned to the flagship in the distance. The Armada's primary mission was to secure Parma's crossing, not defeat the English fleet, but surely, Evardo thought, the duke would realize that the easterly wind was a gift granted by the divine. He silently compelled the duke to act. A plume of smoke shot out from the side of the *San Martín* and the boom of single cannon rolled across the Armada. The pace of Evardo's heart quickened, and he didn't dare to believe his eyes. The duke was lowering the topsails of the *San Martín*. It was the signal to engage the enemy.

'All hands, battle stations!'

A dozen voices repeated the command in half as many seconds, shattering the pre-dawn calmness of the *Retribution*. Men ran to the shrouds and rigging, pushing past each other on the narrow decks, their frantic pace hastened by the strident calls of the officers. A deep rumble permeated the air and the decks trembled as the cannons were run out, the gun crews shouting as one as each was made fast and ready.

Robert was on the quarterdeck, his hands on his hips, his eyes narrowed slightly against the wind blowing into his face. The frustration of the previous twenty-four hours was forgotten. Now there was only focus. The enemy had the weather gauge, granted to them by a trick of the wind. They were coming about, the ships of the fighting wings making the turn with a pace that spoke of their eagerness to take advantage of the conditions. Whatever action needed to be taken to counteract the threat had to be taken fast. Robert turned to his sailing masters.

'Options.'

'We should come about north-north-easterly,' Seeley said first. 'Sail close-hauled to the wind and try to outflank them on the landward wing to regain the weather gauge.'

Robert nodded. 'Mister Miller?'

'No signal yet from Howard, Captain. But I agree with the Master. The bastards might take this opportunity to make a play for Weymouth.'

Robert contemplated the course change for a second.

'So ordered, Mister Seeley, lay close. Helm to north-north-east.'

'Aye, Captain.'

Seeley moved to the fore rail of the quarterdeck and shouted a string of commands, the crew responding swiftly as thousands of hours of sail-craft guided them. Robert took a moment to observe Seeley's handling of the manoeuvre. Sailing a square-rigged ship close-hauled was a delicate task, requiring a touch that could not be taught or imitated. It was an intuitive ability, granted only to the best sailing masters and Robert nodded with satisfaction as Seeley quickly struck the perfect balance between wind and sail.

He turned his attention to the gap between the enemy's landward wing and the coastline. At the leading edge of the Isle of Portland was the headland, Portland Bill, but beyond that, some three miles to the south-east and below the surface of the sea was a sandbank known as The Shambles.

'Captain,' Miller called. 'The *Ark Royal* is coming about.'

Robert looked to the distant flagship. Howard had come to the same conclusion and the ships closest to the *Ark Royal* were already falling into her wake as it turned to outflank the enemy. Half a dozen ships closer inshore, including the *Retribution*, had pre-empted Howard's command. The *Triumph* was leading the pack, Martin Frobisher's 1,100 ton galleon, the largest in the English fleet. Robert called for Seeley to bring the *Retribution* up closer to Frobisher's galleon.

Evardo felt his spirits soar as the squall of cannon fire erupted. There would be no escape for the English. Through the gathering clouds of gun smoke half a mile away he tried to see whether any of the English ships had finally been boarded in the close quarter fighting.

Thirty minutes before almost every fighting ship of the Armada had turned simultaneously north-north-west to cut off the enemy's attempt to outflank the Armada to landward. Most of the English ships, and Evardo recognized their flagship amongst them, had quickly gone about to opposite tack, reversing their tactic by trying to force the seaward flank. With the wind to command the galleons and Levanters of de Leiva and de Bertendona had cut across their path and were now heavily engaged with the enemy.

But not every English ship had turned and the *Santa Clara* and a number of other warships had been ordered to hold the landward flank at all costs. Beyond dividing his forces to allow the transport ships to remain a safe distance from the fighting, Medina Sidonia had done little to organize a coherent attack and the skirmishes that were rapidly developing were a confusion of individual duals and ripostes.

'*Comandante*,' Mendez called and indicated off the starboard bow.

Under blood red sails and oars de Moncada's four Neapolitan galleasses were forging a path to the headland. They had the bit between their teeth. A small group of English ships, no more than a half dozen, were trapped on the far side of Portland Bill. They had cut their course to the flank too finely, and close inshore, in the lee of the headland, they were becalmed and completely cut off.

Evardo ordered the *Santa Clara* to pursue the galleasses, eager to share in the spoils. Like the wind, this gift was surely heaven sent. He clasped the crucifix around his neck as the deck tilted beneath him.

The wind was light, but it filled the sails and bore the *Santa*

Clara on. Four other galleons of the Squadron of Castile slipped into her wake and within a dozen ship-lengths they formed into a rough echelon behind her. Evardo gave them only scant attention. His focus was firmly fixed on the fearsome galleasses a quarter-mile ahead and the hapless prey beyond them.

Robert flinched as the muzzles of the galleasses' heavy bow chasers disappeared behind billows of smoke. The air screeched with passing round shot and from fifty yards away he heard a scream of pain from a crewman of the *Golden Lion*.

'Steady boys,' he shouted.

The Spanish galleasses advanced at speed, their blunt-nosed rams surging with every pull of the oars, their decks crammed with heavily armed soldiers.

'Frobisher has led us into a death trap,' Seeley cursed quietly so only Robert could hear.

'Fear not, Thomas. Frobisher is no fool.'

When it became obvious that the Spaniards would cut off the English fleet's attempt to outflank them to landward, and Howard had gone about to the opposite tack, Frobisher had signalled the galleons sailing behind the *Triumph* to stay on course and follow him. Robert had complied, deferring to Frobisher's seniority, quickly figuring out the commander's plan. Along with four other galleons Frobisher had led them into the lee of the headland. The *Retribution* could barely make steerage speed in the flat calm and so close to the coastline Robert had dropped anchor, transforming his nimble, mobile warship into a vulnerable target, ripe for boarding.

Initially their presence had gone unnoticed and Robert had felt the first sliver of uncertainty that Frobisher's plan might not work. That feeling had turned to shame when he watched Howard engage the enemy while his galleon skulked idly out of the enemy's range. A lookout's call had ended those misgivings. They had been spotted, by four galleasses and a troop of galleons. There was nowhere to run. The *Triumph* and her consorts were hamstrung by the breathless air and Robert carefully estimated the range as the galleasses sped onwards.

'Mister Miller,' Robert called. 'Orders to Mister Larkin; tell him to give the Spaniards a taste.'

'Aye, Captain.'

'Mister Seeley. Prepare to weigh anchor and present the larboard broadside.'

'Will I order the men to make ready to repel boarders?'

For a moment Robert did not reply. He looked to the *Triumph.*

'I believe Frobisher would tell you that won't be necessary.'

Seeley hesitated for a moment, puzzled by the captain's response, but the urgency of the moment compelled him to move. He shouted his orders as Larkin let fly with his longer range cannon.

Robert's hand went to the hilt of his sword and he drew the blade an inch from the scabbard. The Spanish galleasses were less than twelve hundred yards away and were still coming on apace. Their course was steady, their hulls slicing through the calm waters with Portland Bill off their starboard beams.

Again Robert estimated the range. The Spaniards had passed The Shambles. The underwater ridge lay a mile behind them in their wakes. The enemy should be in position. They had taken the bait, but Frobisher's plan relied not only on location, but on timing. As the galleasses consumed the distance between them and the English galleons, Robert began to pray that Frobisher had indeed judged the conditions correctly.

Evardo drew his sword and twisted the weapon slowly in his hand, examining the keen edge as the sunlight reflected off the long narrow tapered blade. He glanced up at the galleasses two hundred yards ahead, marvelling at their sleek, spear-like hulls and the hypnotic glide of the oars as they rose and fell in seemingly effortless grace. The stranded English galleons would be helpless against such predators. Evardo became acutely aware of the weight of the sword in his hand, knowing he would soon have a chance to wield it on the deck of an English ship.

Evardo checked the line of his galleon. He nodded, confident that Mendez was garnering every knot of speed he could from the light breeze. The galleasses would certainly reach the English first. Their lead was increasing fractionally with every draw of the oars, but once the galleasses engaged at close quarters the *Santa Clara* and the galleons behind her would be upon the enemy in minutes.

Then Evardo noticed that some of the starboard oars of de Moncada's flagship, the *San Lorenzo*, seemed to be out of sync. The entire bank of oars lost their cohesive tempo. The bow of the *San Lorenzo* skewed violently and almost hit one of her sister ships. The galleasses slowed, their once arrow-straight trajectories falling foul of some unseen force that defied their purpose.

'Rip tide,' Evardo whispered, recognizing the consequences of the dreaded phenomenon.

'Mendez, shorten sail,' he shouted, his command coinciding with the sailing captain's own instinct to slow the pace of the *Santa Clara*.

Within minutes the floundering galleasses had steadied their hulls, but they were no longer advancing. The rip tide was holding them fast. Evardo balled his fist in anger and sheathed his sword, unsure of what he should do next. He could try to go around the galleasses, but he had no idea how far the tidal race extended. With such an insipid wind there was little chance he could forge a path through the rip. The tantalizingly close enemy slowly turned their broadsides to the struggling galleasses.

'Give 'em hellfire,' Robert whispered a heartbeat before Larkin's voice was drowned by the tremendous boom of the broadside cannonade. The *Retribution* shuddered from the recoil, the decks trembling as if in fury, its firepower marking the galleon as a warship born for the maelstrom of battle.

'Hard about, Mister Seeley. Chasers to bear,' Robert called coldly, drawing on his loathing for the mongrel galleasses and their fearful rams.

Seeley called for the change, his focus locked on the calamity that had befallen the Spaniards.

'Portland Race,' Robert explained, seeing Seeley's expression.

'Of course.' He had heard of the tidal race but had never encountered it and knew little of its power. It had never occurred to him that this was Frobisher's stratagem – to use the massive disturbance caused by the tide flowing between The Shambles and the tip of Portland Bill.

At five hundred yards Larkin's guns were having little effect on the structure of the galleass in the *Retribution*'s line of fire, but the round shot had torn bloody swathes across her open decks and the crimson hull could not conceal the devastating effects of the broadside. The *Retribution* continued to turn in an agonizingly slow figure-of-eight, the gun crews poised expectantly behind their charges, while near at hand the broadsides of the other galleons fired off in uncoordinated salvos, the ships firing as they could. As bait they had held their nerve and kept their fire in check. As aggressors they would let fly with all the wrath they could muster.

* * *

'Neapolitan *cobardes*,' Evardo shouted, unable to contain himself. 'Why don't they pull through?'

The galleasses were still arrayed before the *Santa Clara*, unable or unwilling to advance. It appeared that de Moncada had lost his nerve for the fight. Where initially the galleasses had been clapped in the irons of a rip tide they were now paralysed by their indecisive commander. If only the galleasses were commanded by Spaniards. They would not shirk. The Spaniards were warriors, not whore-bred traders like the Neapolitans. While Evardo's own ship was a slave to the wind, the galleasses' oars should allow them to break through and take the first prizes of the campaign. The strength of a ship needed only the courage to wield it. For a moment Evardo was tempted to close and board the nearest galleass and take command of its crew.

The boom of a full broadside washed over the deck, followed an instant later by the whistle of round shot, many of them missing the galleasses to tear holes in the air around the *Santa Clara*. Evardo had ordered his gunnery captain to return fire with the bow chasers if any targets presented themselves but with the galleasses under their sights the guns of the *Santa Clara* had remained quiet, robbing Evardo's crew of the satisfaction of fighting fire with fire.

'*Comandante*,' Mendez called.

'What is it?'

'The wind, *Comandante*,' the captain replied, alarm registering in his voice and expression. 'It's shifting.'

Evardo's gaze shot up to the masthead. The banners were thrashing in the breeze but they were no longer pointing away from the north-east. They had spun around to the call of a new wind, a stiff southerly breeze that mocked Evardo even as he watched it take hold of the sails.

In his heart Evardo knew it was God's punishment. He had

lost patience with the Armada. He had granted them a favourable wind, a divine force to allow them to bring the fight to the enemy, only to see it squandered through uncertainty. Now He had given the weather gauge back to the English.

'So be it,' Evardo said quietly. Before the day was through he would prove that the Spanish were worthy of God's favour.

'Captain Mendez, bring us about.'

'*Si, mi Comandante*,' Mendez replied, seeing in his superior's face the ferocity he had witnessed when he ordered the *Santa Clara* into the breech before the *San Juan*.

Robert wiped the sea spray from his face, his hand lingering over his mouth as he tasted the salt water, his nostrils filled with the smell of the sea-borne breeze. He was standing on the bowsprit, leaning out over the surging bow, his hand tightly gripping a foremast stay. To windward the English fleet was redeploying, taking immediate advantage of the weather gauge, their earlier fighting withdrawal swiftly becoming a vigorous counter attack.

From the moment the wind had changed the flotilla around the *Triumph* had headed away from Portland Bill to link up with the main body of the fleet. Howard had set a convergent course with Frobisher's cohort, but only those galleons closest to the *Ark Royal* had taken their lead from the admiral. Further south Drake, in the gaudily painted *Revenge*, was attacking the Spanish seaward flank with upwards of fifty English ships.

The *Retribution* was sailing close-reach to the southerly wind. Howard's centre was directly ahead but over a dozen enemy warships were beating towards the *Ark Royal* in an obvious effort to oppose Howard's course. Robert quickly assessed the situation. The English had the weather gauge but the Spanish were desperately trying to retain the initiative.

'Let them try,' Robert muttered as he left the bowsprit. He

ordered Seeley to maintain their heading, a course that would take them right into the developing storm of battle in the centre.

'*Sancta Maria, ora pro nobis*,' Evardo whispered in awe as he watched the *San Martín* sail into the maw of the English centre, the deafening roar of enemy cannon shaking the very heavens as the flagship was consumed by a cloud of gun smoke that concealed the terrifying conditions within. The *Santa Clara* was beating against the wind, trying to claw its way back into a battle that had little shape and strategy. Like bare-knuckle prize fighters each side was pummelling away at each other, searching for weaknesses that could be exploited.

To the south-west the seaward flank of the Armada was being hard pressed. Medina Sidonia had engaged the English centre. The duke had evidently decided that the seaward flank was in greater danger and several warships bore away from the *San Martín* to sail in support of the rearguard. Now the duke was alone in his attack. Evardo shouted to Mendez to lay on more sail and speed their approach.

'Bear away!' Robert roared above the thunderous thump of cannon and the concussive sound of musket fire.

The air around the quarterdeck was alive with the sounds of passing shot, an invisible predator that gave no warning to those it took. Robert's eyes were everywhere at once. The *Retribution* was one of a cadre of galleons supporting Howard in his attack on the Spanish flagship, their close formation sailing testing every master's skill as the galleons wove in and out of each other's wakes, laying on their fire in turn upon the Spanish foe, before sailing upwind to reload their guns and returning to the fray.

The enemy flagship was almost invisible in the gun smoke,

the cannons' disgorgement holding sway over the breeze that tried in vain to clear the air. Only the muzzle blasts of heavy Spanish weapons could be seen, fiery sparks spurting out of the gloom as the enemy answered defiantly to every attack run.

'Quart—ho!—off—quarter!'

Robert was unable to comprehend the lookout's call above the din of battle but he followed his outstretched hand and saw a second enemy warship emerge off the bow of the Spanish flagship. She was a behemoth, a towering merchantman, her decks crammed with soldiers. She erupted in smoke, firing off a single broadside that sliced through the rigging of the *Elizabeth Jonas* not thirty yards off the *Retribution*'s bow.

'Mister Miller, orders to the Master Gunner; new target off the flagship's bow. Mister Seeley, steady as she goes. Look to your helm.'

The *Retribution* completed its turn to larboard, her hull cutting cleanly through the swell. Robert felt the tilt of the deck beneath his feet, sensing the movements of his ship; the response of the *Retribution* to the wind in her sails and the bite of her rudder in the blue-green sea. The sensation steeled Robert's every nerve. He was master of a creature that knew no fear, a warship that obeyed his every command and he would match her will ounce for ounce. As his galleon swung into range of the Spanish he roared a command to set loose the wrath of *Retribution.*

'*¡Fuego!*'

The *Santa Clara* shuddered at the ferocity of her broadside cannonade. Evardo called for an immediate course change, turning his galleon in as tight a circle as possible as they came in under the stern of the *San Martín.* At almost twice her tonnage and ordnance the flagship towered over the *Santa*

Clara but they stood shoulder to shoulder, taking the enemy's punishment as they denied them leave to advance.

Evardo checked the line of his ship, ignoring the firestorm that swept his decks. On the far side of the flagship a Guipúzcoan merchantman was holding station. Beyond them Evardo recognized another galleon of the Castilian Squadron, the *San Juan Bautista* or the *San Pedro*, he could not be sure which. For nearly thirty minutes the *San Martín* had been alone, now she had allies and with each arrival the flagship was spared more of the English fire.

On the fo'c'sle Nathaniel stood behind the wall of Spanish musketeers lining the gunwale. He had no weapon to wield against the distant English warships. Alvarado stood close by, yelling orders to his men, urging them on, to increase their rate of musket fire and speed the loading of the *falcon pedreros.*

The fight was hopelessly one sided, with the English warships advancing individually to within three hundred yards before firing their cannons and sailing away again almost unscathed. The Spanish could only reply with side arms and the smaller, more easily serviced guns on the fore and aft castles. Their main guns were silent.

In the midst of battle Nathaniel could not quell his blood lust and he echoed the gutter curses of the Spaniards, cries that fuelled the conflict that raged within him. The Spanish were firing on his countrymen but if Nathaniel was to return to England then the English navy would have to be defeated.

Dice-shot cut a swathe through the ranks close to Nathaniel, striking down the soldiers manning a swivel-mounted 3 pound *falconete.* He rushed to take command of the gun, taking hold of the trailing handle, pointing it at the nearest English ship. He hesitated. For him the Northern Rebellion had been a bloodless uprising. Never before had he wilfully drawn English blood.

A Spanish soldier ran to Nathaniel's side, a lighted taper in his hand. He glanced at Nathaniel, checking to see if his aim was set. For a moment Nathaniel could not move. He nodded. The soldier dropped the taper to the touchhole. The *falconete* bucked in Nathaniel's hand, spewing out a cloud of smoke that engulfed him.

'Reload!'

Men rushed to Nathaniel's command. A war cry rose to his throat, born from the depths of his hatred for the Protestant monarch, but he could not cry out. Were the men on the English warships truly his enemy? For all he knew his son was amongst them and Nathaniel stepped back from the gun before angrily silencing his remorse. His path was set; he had to see it through. Victory for the Spanish was crucial.

Another English ship sailed into position opposite the *Santa Clara*, her bow chasers firing in unison. Shouted warnings of incoming fire were lost to the smash of timber and the cries of the wounded. Alvarado called for a volley of fire, his command followed by the cackle of muskets. Suddenly his strident voice ceased and Nathaniel turned to see Alvarado fall. The rate of fire from the fo'c'sle fell away as more men looked to their stricken captain. In the distance the English warship turned broadside.

'Back to your stations, resume your fire,' Nathaniel shouted. 'Ready the pedreros. Fire as they bear.'

The soldiers reacted to the voice of command.

'You men, get below. We need more power and shot.'

Nathaniel drew his sword. '*¡Apunten, Fuego!*'

The two pound pedreros fired as the English ship let fly with the heavy guns of its first broadside. More men fell around Nathaniel and he began to shout the words of encouragement he had heard Alvarado call.

Off the stern quarter the *San Martín* was withdrawing

towards the centre of the Armada as more Spanish trouble-shooters completed the shield around her. The English rate of fire was falling. Denied their prize many of the enemy warships were disengaging. Only a few were continuing the fight but they remained out of reach, deftly using the advantage of the wind and their faster ships to dictate the pace of the battle.

CHAPTER 16

8 p.m. 3rd August 1588. The English Channel, off the Isle of Wight.

Robert moved slowly back along the cramped gun deck, ducking his head beneath the smoke-stained beams as he stepped over the ordnance arranged behind each cannon. The men were gathered between the guns, chatting aimlessly as they tucked into their first hot meal of the day. The tinny smell of stewed beef overrode the stench of burned gun-powder and the musky odour of men crowded together below decks in the mid-summer heat.

One of the crew had a fife and was playing an ancient sea shanty, a traditional tune that prompted many to hum along. There was laughter but Robert marked its brittle tone and he saw how exhausted his men were, weighted down by the low ebb often experienced after the blood rush of battle. But the hot meal and a double ration of beer were beginning to raise their flagging spirits, and an animated game of dice had begun amidships in the space between two culverins.

Robert reached the aft section and stood silently for a moment as he watched the surgeon make one of the wounded comfortable. He reached out and touched the breech of a cannon. Following the battle the day before off Portland Bill, when the Spanish had been denied Weymouth, there had been further skirmishes earlier that morning and although many hours had passed since then the cannon was still warm. He removed his hand and looked to the crewman under Powell's care. He was no more than a lad, one of the quarter gunner's mates who fetched and carried on the gun deck. His chest was heavily bandaged. Two more crewmen lay supine beyond him.

Powell had brought all of the seriously injured up from his surgery on the orlop deck. At night the smell of blood would draw rats from the depths of the lower hold and, left unattended, the unconscious wounded would be easy prey for the scavengers. Robert caught the surgeon's attention and Powell rose stiffly, arching his back as he stepped forward.

'Well?'

'The lad should be fine, Captain. I've sealed his wounds with boiling elderberry oil and the cauterizing iron. As for the other two, I'm fairly sure I got all the splinters out of Gray's arm. But Ellis? There's little I can do with a head wound like that beyond bleeding him. I fear he won't last the night.'

Robert looked beyond Powell to the injured crewman. Dark viscous blood had soaked through the bandages around his head, attracting a host of flies that buzzed and settled. His flesh was deathly pale and in the lantern light it looked like God had already taken him. *One more for the butcher's bill*, Robert thought grimly.

The rising sun that morning had revealed a Spanish straggler, an armed merchantman, *El Gran Grifón*, trailing behind the seaward flank. Drake had immediately attacked, with those closest, including the *Retribution* following in her wake. They had hammered the broad-beamed, sow-bellied hulk from as close a range as they dared, with broadsides and raking fire to the stern. The *El Gran Grifón* had been heavily armed with at least three dozen light and medium guns and she replied with dice and round shot, killing two of Robert's crew in the opening salvoes before her rate of fire fell away.

A melee had quickly ensued with Spanish reinforcements beating up to support the lone merchantman. The Armada had been abreast of the western approaches to the Solent, the safe anchorage between the Isle of Wight and the mainland. From the outset it had seemed unlikely the enemy would try to breech this more difficult side, but Howard had fed more warships into the fray to put the matter beyond doubt.

By midday the wind had pushed the battle leeward of the western approach and Howard had ordered the fleet to withdraw. The action, although short, had been very sharp with the *Retribution* continually engaged in the shifting heart of the battle, a tenacity that had cost Robert another crewman dead and a dozen injured. The Armada had been badly mauled, particularly *El Gran Grifón*, but as before the Spaniards had continued on, with every ship taking its place in the defensive formation. Despite another massive expenditure of shot, the English fleet had still not managed to cripple or destroy one Spanish ship in action.

Although it was warm below decks Robert's hands were cold and he felt frustration tingle under his skin; an itchy, grating feeling that set his nerves on edge. He thought back to the battle the day before. The *San Martín* had been under near continuous fire for almost thirty minutes as one English ship after another had sailed up to fire its cannon at her. She had been struck hundreds of times and yet she had survived, withdrawing into the centre of the Armada's defences without assistance.

The thought caused Robert to look away from the wounded crewman and turn to the cannon beside him. After the battle, Larkin had called Robert below decks to the shot lockers on the orlop deck. Two-thirds of their ordnance stock was already gone, fired off into the seemingly indestructible black heart of the Armada. Another few days of indecisive skirmishing would see the end of their remaining ammunition and Robert suspected that every ship in the fleet was in a similar position. Later he had heard that there were supplies to be had from the two captured Spanish ships, the crippled *San Salvador* and Drake's prize, the *Nuestra Señora del Rosario*, and had since dispatched Seeley along with the Peters, the gunner's mate, on a pinnace to Weymouth.

Thus far the English attacks had been scrappy and indecisive, with individual ships and small groups taking action where they saw fit. Tomorrow however would see the Armada within striking distance of the eastern, more navigable, approach to the Solent. It was imperative that the enemy be prevented from taking the anchorage and so after the morning's action Howard had deployed his fleet into four squadrons under Drake, Frobisher, Hawkins and the admiral himself, to better coordinate their defence of the Solent. The *Retribution* had been assigned to Hawkins's squadron and was now sailing off the larboard quarter of the commander's 800 ton flagship, the *Victory*.

'Nightingale approaching off the starboard bow!'

Robert went aloft at the call in time to see the pinnace pull alongside the *Retribution*. Seeley was first to board.

'Good news, Captain. We've managed to secure powder and over a hundred shot.'

'What calibre?'

'Mostly culverin but also a score of 24 pounders for the cannon-pedros.'

Robert slapped Seeley on the shoulder, pleased with the haul. He quickly ordered the crew to begin transhipping the supplies.

'There's something else,' Seeley said, following Robert to the quarterdeck. 'The *San Salvador* had been left with over fifty wounded Spaniards on board. I managed to talk to some of them and by describing the masthead banners I was able to uncover the identity of the ship that has continued to target us. She's the *Santa Clara*, Captain, an indies galleon.'

'And her commander?'

'Evardo Morales.'

'Of the *Halcón*?' Robert said incredulously. 'How in Christ's good name is Morales commanding a galleon and not rotting in one of her majesty's prisons?'

'He must have been ransomed,' Seeley replied icily. Robert noted the censorious tone of his voice.

His memories of the brief moments after Morgan's death on the *Halcón* were clouded by the mindless fury he had felt, but he vividly remembered his duel with the Spanish commander. He had spared Morales on impulse at the sight of his crucifix, the sacred symbol of their shared faith. In that moment he had placed his religion above vengeance for his murdered countrymen. Now he felt sickened by his choice.

Seeley's censure had been well placed. Robert had failed his crewmen and England by sparing Morales. And the Spaniard had returned, as determined an enemy as he had ever been, despite Robert's act of mercy. He should have killed the Spaniard when he had the chance, regardless of how much such an act opposed his other loyalties. England was fighting for its sovereignty, its very right to exist as a nation free from oppression. No other loyalty should stand in the way of that cause. For the briefest moment Robert was reminded of his father, of how he was poised to strike him down on the motte. He would not wait for Morales to seek him out. He would look for him, and with the guns of the *Retribution* to command, he would not hesitate at this second chance to strike down the Spanish foe.

Cross slowed his horse to a canter as the sun finally fell below the western horizon. The road was deeply rutted and in the soft afterglow of twilight he feared injuring his mount. Off his right shoulder he could see the tallest houses of Portsmouth and beyond them the distant eastern tip of the Isle of Wight far out on the horizon. The Armada was out there somewhere, still shadowed by the English fleet. Over the past few days Cross had heard all manner of rumours as to how the battle was progressing. One thing was certain however, and on this all accounts were agreed – the Spanish were still advancing up the Channel.

Cross had followed the course of the battle, staying away from the meandering coastline in favour of travelling a more direct route inland. He had covered over 130 miles in the past three days, an exhausting journey that had taken every hour of sunlight in the long summer days. The roads had been busy, slowing his passage, but in many places his journey had been further hampered by the trained bands of militiamen, many of them marching in the opposite direction to the advance of the Armada.

Forewarned by the lighted beacons along the entire length of the southern coastline, the lord lieutenants of each county had gathered their trained bands of militia to oppose any Spanish landing. The Armada had sailed past Cornwall, Devon and now Dorset, and while the militia from each county had been ordered to proceed along the coast to fight in the inevitable battle, many of the laymen had simply decided to return to their homes and farms, knowing they were no longer under any direct threat.

Cross had been appalled by the self-centred attitude of the

militiamen but in reality he knew their actions were to be expected. As an agent of the Crown he had travelled the length and breadth of southern England, but most ordinary people had never been beyond the bounds of their parish. London was as distant to them as any of the major cities on the continent, and their lives were only impacted by the Crown in matters of law and administration.

In any case, the untrained militia would be no match for the soldiers sailing with the Armada. Nine thousand men had been gathered in Southampton to defend the port while the governor of the Isle of Wight had a further three thousand men at his disposal. Their numbers were in no way a reflection of their strength and they would quickly be routed by a Spanish force equal to a fraction of their ranks.

Cross was weary to the bone. Every muscle in his legs ached, but he was finally ahead of the battle. Tomorrow the Spanish might try to take the Solent, but whether they did or not mattered little to Cross. His fight was not with the Spaniards, it was with an Englishman. He needed to secure a boat to take him out to the English fleet and the *Retribution.* His goal had never been closer. Before the battle was over he would have Young in his custody. The only question was whether he would pre-empt Young's act of treachery, or punish him for it.

Nathaniel knocked on the door of the great cabin and waited for the call to enter. He went inside. Commander Morales and Captain de Córdoba were seated at the table eating a meal of rice and charcoaled fish.

'Your grace, please,' Evardo said, indicating the chair opposite him.

Nathaniel sat down and Evardo offered him a goblet of Candia wine. He drank deeply.

'You fought well yesterday, your grace,' Evardo said. 'I have heard many reports of how you took command of the fo'c'sle after *Capitán* Alvarado was killed.'

'Thank you, *Comandante*,' Nathaniel replied, shifting slightly in his chair.

Evardo stood up and walked around to refill Nathaniel's goblet.

'I want you to take temporary command of his men for the remainder of the voyage.'

Nathaniel froze. After yesterday's action, when the fighting had ceased and the blood lust in his veins had cooled, Nathaniel had been assailed by further thoughts of uncertainty. His hatred for Elizabeth and his desire to see her overthrown had been with him for over twenty years. It was the driving force behind everything he did. In the Northern Rebellion he had led his fellow Catholics in defiance of her rule, but they had been his countrymen, they were Englishmen, fighting to save England. Now however he was being asked to lead foreign troops against his own country.

'Alvarado's men followed my orders in the heat of battle, immediately after their captain had been struck down. Now that that moment has passed, surely they will not submit to the commands of an Englishman.'

'They will,' Evardo replied confidently. 'They follow social rank and they follow courage. You have both, your grace.'

Nathaniel nodded with feigned courtesy.

'You will retain command of the fo'c'sle while *Capitán* de Córdoba will hold the aft castle.'

'May I offer one piece of advice, your grace,' de Córdoba said. 'While the English persist in their tactics of laying off you must continue to return fire with the light deck guns and muskets. But make sure your arquebusiers hold their fire. They will need their ammunition for the close quarter fighting to come.'

'You believe the English will eventually close?' Nathaniel asked.

'Yes,' Evardo said, frustration in his tone. 'Their ships might be more nimble, and their cannonry more accomplished but they must know they will never take a Spanish ship without boarding her, and the moment they clap sides, we will have them on our terms.'

Nathaniel nodded, thinking back to the action earlier that day. 'I thought they might have attempted to take *El Gran Grifón* this morning,' he said.

'They would have,' de Córdoba replied. 'Had *El Gran Grifón* been a little further adrift of the main fleet.'

Nathaniel made to reply but Evardo silenced him with his hand, his brow creasing in thought. He turned on his heel and left the cabin without another word, making his way aloft. He called for the nearest zabra to be hailed and boarded her as she came alongside.

'The *San Martín*, quick as you can.'

The zabra spun around and began to weave through the larger capital ships and transports while Evardo anxiously paced the deck, his head bowed in thought.

'The *San Martín, Comandante.*'

Evardo called up for permission to board and went directly to Medina Sidonia's cabin. The duke was inside with many of his senior officers, including de Recalde and de Leiva, standing around a large chart table.

'Your grace,' Evardo said. 'I need to speak with you.'

Medina Sidonia looked up. He was a short, stocky man, and was one of the youngest in the room. He was heavily bearded and though his face was drawn with lines of fatigue his eyes were alert.

'*Comandante* Morales,' he said. 'This is a closed meeting. Might I trust that what you have to say can wait until afterwards?'

'What I have to suggest is of vital import, your grace.'

Medina Sidonia lightly fingered the insignia of the Golden Fleece that hung around his neck. 'Very well, *Comandante*.'

Evardo stepped up to the table. 'This morning, as you all know, *El Gran Grifón* was set upon by a pack of English warships because she was adrift of the fleet. Only the courageous actions of others saved her from capture. But what if the ships that extracted *El Gran Grifón* had not been able to reach her? What if she had been completely isolated?'

'Then the English would have taken her as they did the *San Salvador* and the *Rosario*,' de Recalde said.

'But they could not because the fighting ships of the Armada were within reach,' Evardo said.

'So you believe if *El Gran Grifón* had been out of our reach she would have been boarded by the English?' Medina Sidonia asked.

'Or if the English had perceived she was out of our reach,' Evardo said.

'Bait,' de Recalde said with a smile. '*Comandante* Morales is suggesting that we lure the English into a close quarter action with bait.'

'But the King has said we must not delay our advance with a general engagement,' de Moncada said to Medina Sidonia.

'We only need to bloody their nose, your grace,' de Recalde countered. 'The English are sure to take the bait and try to board the straggler. If we swoop down and capture some of their capital ships they might become less daring in their attacks.'

'Over sixty of my crew on *El Gran Grifón* were killed in this morning's action,' Juan Gómez de Medina cautioned. 'Any ship adrift of the fleet for longer would pay a heavy coin for the prize of capturing some English warships.'

'I believe it is a price worth paying,' Evardo said. 'I volunteer the *Santa Clara* as bait. She is a warship and therefore better suited to the task. Once grappled we could defend her upper decks until reinforcements arrived.'

The senior officers began to discuss the proposal in detail, with those for and against making their arguments to the duke.

After some minutes Medina Sidonia raised his hand for silence. His instructions were to avoid engaging with the English fleet if at all possible. However he had already contravened those instructions when he ordered the fleet to attack off Portland Bill. He had deemed that attack to be tactically necessary and could defend his decision. He considered Morale's plan one last time. It could be argued that tactically an ambush would be to the Armada's ultimate advantage.

'I have heard enough,' he began. 'We rendezvous with Parma within days. That is our primary mission. But I agree that our chances of success will be greatly increased if we can first inflict some casualties on the English fleet and gain some sea-room to windward. Your plan is approved, *Comandante* Morales.'

'Thank you, your grace.'

'Might I make one amendment?' de Leiva asked, forestalling Evardo's departure. 'A single ship might be too easily overwhelmed before reinforcements arrive.'

'We will hold,' Evardo replied.

'I do not doubt your resolution or that of your crew, *Comandante.* But for the plan to succeed, no ship will be able to advance to your aid until after the English have clapped sides. I believe two ships together would stand a better chance.'

Medina Sidonia considered the proposal. With no experience of naval warfare to draw upon he quickly deferred to one of his most trusted advisors.

'Agreed,' he said. 'I will call for a volunteer from my own

squadron of Portugal to act as the second. Don de Leiva, you will be in charge of the reinforcements.'

'Yes, your grace.'

'Then it is settled. *Comandante*, a ship from my squadron will seek you out before dusk. After dark you will both lay to and fall off from the fleet. With luck and God's favour tomorrow will see the Armada claim its first prizes.'

Evardo nodded. He glanced around the room, looking each senior commander in the eye for a moment before withdrawing from the cabin.

CHAPTER 17

5 a.m. 4th August 1588. The English Channel, off Dunnose Point.

'Quarterdeck, ho! Enemy stragglers a mile off the larboard bow!'

'All hands, battle stations,' Robert shouted, running to the fo'c'sle where he was joined by Seeley. Off the larboard bow was the shadowy coastline of the Isle of Wight. The Armada was close to Dunnose Point, the most southerly point on the island and from there the coast swept inward to the eastern entrance to the Solent. The two Spanish galleons were in close support of each other but completely isolated from the Armada's defensive formation. It was a perfect opportunity and Hawkins's squadron was closest to the prize, however just before dawn the westerly breeze had died away.

'Where is the cursed wind?' Seeley spat.

'Coxswain! Launch the longboat,' Robert shouted over his shoulder. He turned to Seeley. 'If we've no wind, Thomas, then we'll just have to use brawn. Cast a line from the bow to the longboat and hail any oared coasters nearby. Tell them we need a tow.'

'Aye, Captain,' Seeley said with a wry smile and left the fo'c'sle.

Robert wondered how the isolated galleons could have got so far out of formation. One or both of them must have encountered some problem. Either way they were a prize worth pursuing. The commander of the *Victory* had come to the same conclusion and had already lowered his ship's boat. The two Spanish galleons would soon be under English guns.

'I count at least a dozen.' Nathaniel was standing amidst the senior officers on the quarterdeck.

Evardo smiled. The English were as predictable as the rising of the sun. They had taken the bait regardless of the conditions. Fifty yards off the starboard beam the *San Luís*, an 830 ton galleon of the Portuguese squadron under *Comandante* Mexía, was readying for action.

In the distance the crescent formation that had carried the Armada thus far was no more. It was widely suspected that the English had a second squadron of warships further along the coast operating out of Dover and so the fleet was now arrayed in a new formation, one that had been devised to allow for a running defence should the Armada be attacked from the front or behind. It was more rounded, with a strong vanguard led by the flagship and a rearguard commanded by de Recalde and de Leiva. The transport and auxiliary ships were in the centre.

'All hands to their posts, *mis capitánes*,' Evardo said. 'Prepare to repel boarders.'

'*Si, mi Comandante*,' the men spoke as one.

The approaching English warships being towed towards them had increased in number. Two ships were in the lead and were closing at a faster speed with the assistance of small oar-powered dispatch boats. One was a galleon that looked similar in size to the *San Luís*. The other was a smaller warship comparable to the *Santa Clara*.

Evardo felt a shiver of doubt run up his spine and angrily shook off the sense of foreboding. The *San Luís* and *Santa Clara* were going to be more heavily outnumbered than he had expected, certainly more than *El Gran Grifón* was the morning before. Evardo could not suppress the tentacles of fear that crept over his resolve. He thought of Abrahan and how, as a boy, his mentor had taught him that without fear there could be no courage. The memory steeled his nerve and he tried to recapture the impulse that had compelled him to volunteer, the desire to prove his mettle to all.

The boom of cannon split the still air and Evardo flinched as the round shot swept past his deck. The two leading English galleons were five hundred yards away. The second one fired her bow chasers. One of the shots struck the *San Luís*, the crack of timber followed an instant later by the scream of an injured sailor. The men of the *Santa Clara* began to shout defiantly at the oncoming English, single voices that quickly grew until the ship was awash with strident calls, an outburst that banished all fears and opened the floodgates of battle lust.

Evardo allowed the noise to feed his soul. He hoped the sound would carry to the ear of every Englishman, compelling them to answer the Spanish taunts and end their cowardly tactics of firing from a distance. The *San Luís* and *Santa Clara* were all alone. This was the enemy's opportunity to close and board.

Robert climbed hand over hand, his grip firm on the ratlines as he ascended the shrouds through the heavy pall of gun smoke. Bullets zipped through the air, the near misses causing him to spin his head around while beneath him he could hear the heavier whoosh of small calibre round shot. With every step the smoke cleared further and he quickly reached the fighting top above the main course.

Two lookouts and musketeers were stationed there and they moved aside to allow their captain to climb atop the head of the main course. Robert took a grip on the main mast and felt a tremor run through it as the heavy guns of his ship were fired on the decks. He steadied his feet and looked to larboard, the clearer air affording him his first view of the Spanish galleons since the *Retribution* had fired its broadside.

The enemy ships were two hundred yards off the beam. With no wind their masthead banners hung limp, frustrating any attempt to identify them from such a distance. The smaller galleon was to the fore while behind her the heavier warship was engaged with the English ships that had attacked from the opposing flank. It was the closest that the *Retribution* had engaged any enemy ship so far and Robert could immediately see the effects the shorter range was having on the Spanish galleons. Their courses were shot through in dozens of places, with rigging and tackles hanging like gallows' ropes from the stays. The upper decks were heavily damaged, with railings and superficial fittings shot away in several places. Robert counted a score of hits in the hull, although it seemed none had penetrated.

As the first ship to engage, along with the *Victory*, the *Retribution* had the most advantageous firing position. Sitting stationary in the water, she was still tethered to the ship's longboat and two coasters, with Seeley and Miller in constant communication with the coxswain, ensuring that no trick of current turned the galleon's hull off true. From the distinctive boom of the heaviest guns, Robert estimated Larkin's men were averaging a rate of just under twenty minutes a shot from the larboard battery.

Despite the range and intensity of this fearsome barrage the gunwales of the Spanish galleons were heavily lined with soldiers. Their swords were drawn, their mouths open in grotesque masks of anger, their taunts and curses lost by language and the almost constant roar of cannon fire. Robert lifted his gaze to the men directly across from him on the fighting tops of the nearest Spanish galleon. Each one was crammed with musketeers, loading and firing as quickly as they could in the confined space of the tops.

Robert saw one of them turn his musket towards him, the sweep of the barrel changing to the black circle of a muzzle as the soldier took aim. The Spaniard fired, disappearing behind a puff of smoke. At two hundred yards he was well beyond effective range. In the continuous whine of passing shot he briefly wondered where the bullet meant for him had struck. The smoke around the Spaniard's head cleared and he lowered his gun to see the result of his shot, his face twisting in fury as he discovered he had missed. He raised his fist and screamed some obscenity, his voice lost in the din of battle.

Robert did not respond, glancing instead at the two musketeers beside him. They too were taking pot shots at the enemy galleons but it was obvious from their frustrated expressions that they were not hitting any targets. Robert looked down at the eerie cloud of gun smoke that enveloped his ship. At two hundred yards his cannon were firing at half the distance they had engaged at on the first day. But it was not close enough. The Spanish crew of the nearest warship was being badly mauled by the larboard broadsides. There were wounded and dying on every open deck, but the galleon itself had suffered no heavy damage. Robert let go of the mainmast and readied himself to climb down. If they were going to destroy the enemy galleon they were going to have to get a lot closer.

The noise on the *Santa Clara* was like the opened gates of hell, a terrible clamour of tormented screams and war cries, of shouted orders amidst the boom and whine of gun fire.

Shot, dice and bullets saturated the air, giving little sanctuary to those on the weather decks. Underfoot the timbers ran with fresh blood. Smoke filled every throat, searing the eyes and flooding the nostrils with a scorched smell that barely masked the odour of torn flesh and rank sweat. Battle lust filled every heart, suppressing the instinct to yield, creating a trance-like courage that kept every man at his post through the endless hail of fire.

Evardo thought his heart would burst. Frustration and anger consumed him. The God-cursed motherless English were not closing to board. The enemy had overwhelming numbers, the *San Luís* and *Santa Clara* were isolated. If the tables were reversed a Spaniard would not hesitate to grapple on and take the prize. Yet the English were persisting with their infernal tactics, firing their cannon at a rate that beggared belief.

Nearly a dozen English ships were targeting the *Santa Clara* alone. The firestorm was all but continuous and Evardo looked in anguish across the decks of his galleon. His crew were paying a terrible price for a failed plan, a trap that could not be sprung because the enemy had not the courage to advance and press for a decisive encounter.

At least a score of his men were dead. The wounded lay where they fell, their cries unheard, their horrific injuries untended. Evardo's jerkin was soaked in blood, much of it his own from a deep gash in his cheek caused by a wooden splinter. More was from a sailor who had taken a round shot to the chest, his torso disintegrating under the hammer blow, his flesh and viscera spraying across the quarterdeck, staining everything it touched.

The sound of English cannon fire reached a deafening crescendo, a crash of unnatural thunder that for a moment stunned every crewman of the *Santa Clara* into fleeting submission. Evardo looked to his own cannon. The crew were rapidly servicing the small man-killing guns on the upper decks but Evardo could pick up no telltale trace of vibrations from the main guns below. Despite his standing order to the gunners' captain to match the English cannonade the heavy cannon of the *Santa Clara* had yet to fire a second round after their opening salvo.

Evardo went forward to go below to the gun deck. Through the smoke he could see Padre Garcia issuing the last rites to a crewman on the main deck, the priest reciting a prayer before God amidst the anarchy of battle. The gun deck was another, but equally chaotic world after the upper decks. The thunder of cannon fire was muted below decks but a more terrifying sound pervaded the cramped low-ceilinged carapace. Round shot pounded off the hull, each percussive strike shuddering the weatherbeaten timbers.

Peering through the suffocating smoke and press of men, Evardo searched for Suárez, his calls unheard over the piercing noise of battle. He moved forward along the deck. Men shouldered past him, rushing in all directions. The nearest gun-port was drenched in blood and Evardo watched as a gunner straddled the barrel and sidled out through the opening to service his muzzle-loading cannon outboard. The upper part of his body was outside the hull, his hand reaching in for each proffered tool and ingredient. It was bravery that touched on madness and Evardo gasped in horror as the gunner suddenly disappeared, struck through by an unseen round. Another crewman immediately rushed to take his place, continuing the suicidal reloading of the cannon. '*Comandante*!'

Evardo spun around. '*Capitán.* How soon before we can return fire?'

'The men are working as fast as they can, *Comandante*. The *media culebrinas* will be ready within the hour.'

'And the pedreros?'

'We have already re-fired one of them, *Comandante*.'

Evardo bristled with frustration, knowing that the slow rate of fire was not the captain's fault but angry nonetheless.

'What of those guns?' He pointed to two of the eight *media culebrinas* which stood idle in the forward section.

'Those Italian spawn,' Suárez cursed. 'None of our Spanish 10 pound round shots will fit them. The *idotias* have cast their *media culebrinas* to a different calibre to ours.'

Evardo could scarcely believe what he was hearing. Two of his heaviest guns were useless. Drawn from a foreign forge, their specification had no bearing on Spanish standards. As a warship, the *Santa Clara* had begun the campaign with its own battery of guns and had only received these additional two Italian *media culebrinas* to complement its artillery. The merchantmen however, some of the largest and heaviest armed ships in the fleet, had been up-gunned with a hotchpotch of cannon from foundries across the Empire. If their gunners were encountering the same problems as Evardo's, with guns silenced by mismatched ammunition, then the English advantage in firepower would be further increased.

'There is one other thing, *Comandante*,' Suárez said. 'You must order the crew on the upper decks to slow their rate of fire, our stock of 2 pound shot is almost gone.'

'For now, those guns are the only practical weapons we possess,' Evardo replied sharply. 'I would rather have that shot fired at the English ranks than languishing in our lockers. We will replenish our supplies when we take our first prize.'

Suárez nodded and Evardo motioned him to return to his duty before taking to the gangway that returned him to the main deck. He glanced at the nearest *falcon pedrero* and the precious mound of 2 pound stone shot at the feet of the soldiers manning the gun. One of the gun crew was badly injured. His leg had been crudely bandaged by a comrade and he lay propped up against the bulwark, his expression betraying how close to collapse he was. He held a 2 pound shot in his hand and was carefully chipping away the remaining irregularities on the stone ball to ensure a more perfect fit with the barrel. When the shot was called for he handed it over before taking another from the pile, his teeth gritted against the pain of his leg.

Evardo went past the wounded soldier to the quarterdeck. The intensity of the English fire had not lessened and he looked across to the *San Luís.* The sight filled Evardo with sorrow. He was looking at a mirror of his own galleon, a once proud but now savaged beast, trapped in a snare of its own making. He could give no further order; all he could do was wait. The English were unwilling to engage in a close quarter attack. The initial plan was for naught, but Evardo prayed Medina Sidonia would still spring the trap. Even without being grappled, the bait had lured the English forward and while the *San Luís* and *Santa Clara* remained the focus of the enemy there was still a chance to draw English blood.

Nathaniel spat out the taste of smoke that clung to the back of his throat. He swallowed hard. Men pushed past him, carrying the injured away from the gunwale as others rushed to take their place in the firing line. Above the clamour of battle he could hear de Córdoba shouting orders to his men on the poop deck. But Nathaniel remained silent. He could not summon the encouraging words he had shouted two days before in the heat of battle. The Spanish soldiers were not his men and the aggression that had possessed him was gone.

As the English ships were approaching Nathaniel had been gripped by a terrible fear, not of combat, but at the thought of leading these foreigners against his own countrymen, of spilling English blood in the defence of a Spanish galleon.

Mercifully the English had not clapped sides and in the face of their continuous cannon fire Nathaniel had felt only relief, and turmoil.

For so many years his path had been clear. Even during the first days of battle, when the sight of England and the English navy had caused him to doubt his ideals, he had doggedly stuck to his objectives and those of Spain. He had believed there was no other way for him, that this was the only path to redemption.

But his son was forging another way. Robert was fighting with the English navy, maybe as an officer, in command of his own countrymen, leading them into a battle to save the sovereignty of England. Nathaniel had thought Robert a fool to believe he could be true to both his faith and the heretic Queen. But for his son Elizabeth was England, they could not be separated.

But what of the souls of his countrymen, Nathaniel thought bitterly. As believers of a false Protestant faith their souls were in mortal peril. Even his son's soul, however true he was to the Catholic creed, was in jeopardy. Elizabeth had been excommunicated. To follow her was to defy the Papal Bull issued by Pope Pius V.

Nathaniel's belief in the righteousness of his faith touched the very core of his convictions, but he could draw no strength from there. Now there was only doubt. In his quest to see a Catholic monarch on the throne of England, he had put the freedom of his own people in danger. He had forsaken them. The men of the English navy were fighting to ensure an English monarch controlled the destiny of England. Nathaniel also wanted England to be her own master. In a battle between nations he realized he had to be firmly on one side or the other.

* * *

'Galleasses approaching off the larboard bow!'

Robert spun around and peered through the gun smoke in the direction called by the lookout. He could barely make out his own bowsprit.

'Mister Seeley, get aloft. I want a full report. Mister Miller, order the master gunner to cease fire and have the coxswain pull us clear of this infernal smoke.'

'Aye, Captain.'

Within seconds the cannon fire ceased, creating an eerie oasis of calm amidst the continued fire of the surrounding English ships. Robert felt the pull of the longboat and coasters and ordered the helm to match their course, streamlining the hull of the *Retribution* with the draw of the oarsmen. The smoke began to dissipate as Seeley returned from the fighting top.

'Three galleasses under oars, Captain,' he said, breathing heavily. 'One of them is towing a massive carrack.'

'How far off?'

'A thousand yards and closing fast, at least four knots.'

Sunlight pierced the remnants of the cloud of gun smoke and Robert shielded his eyes as he finally spied the outlines of the approaching reinforcements. They were on course for the heart of the fray and were poised to split open the becalmed English flotilla. The heavy bow chasers of the galleasses would wreak terrible carnage at close range but Robert was more fearful of the leviathan one of them had in tow. The carrack was undoubtedly crammed with soldiers who would quickly overwhelm any English crew in a boarding attack. Furthermore a ship that size could be carrying cannon serpentines and royals, massive guns firing shots of over 50 pounds that would smash through the timbers of even the strongest hulls.

For the first time since the battle began Robert didn't know what he should do and for precious seconds both his reason and courage floundered. So close to the attack and the advance of the reinforcements, the *Retribution* was best placed to counter the threat, but no single English galleon was a match for a Spanish galleass or a carrack of that size. Only the combined firepower of a score of galleons would divert such a force. Robert was paralysed by doubt. Despite Howard's new squadrons, the English captains were used to fighting as individuals. There was no guarantee that if the *Retribution* stood to face the Spanish reinforcements she would be joined by others in time to form an effective defence. Alone, his ship would be overrun.

Many of the ships in the thick of the fight seemed oblivious to the approaching danger. Others in the flotilla were coming about but with only their own longboats to tow them, their progress was extremely slow. Robert felt his resolve harden. With three boats towing his ship he had the advantage and the imperative. He turned to the enemy. If he hoped to deter the Spaniards from pressing home their attack he knew he had to bring as many guns to bear as possible.

'Mister Miller,' Robert shouted, swallowing the last of his fears. 'Orders to Mister Larkin; tell him to bow the broadside guns. Mister Seeley, order the coxswain to bring the prow about and then strike the tow lines. We make our stand here!'

The *Retribution* quickly completed her turn in the calm waters, her bow coming about to point directly at the oncoming galleasses. The guns of both broadsides had been run out and bowed, their muzzles turned as far forward as possible. Five hundred yards away the Spanish galleasses swept onwards, their blood red oars propelling them across the surface. Robert closed his mind to the fight over his shoulder; the English cannonade that continued to batter the two wretched Spanish galleons. He focused on the oncoming ships and prayed for the strength to endure. His fate and that of his crew were now firmly in the hands of God and the other captains of the English fleet.

The galleasses surged across the surface, their rams furrowing through the swell, creating a bow wave that swept along the length of their hulls. Their massive oars glided through the water, devouring the strength of some nine hundred slaves, their backs straightening through the draw. The gap quickly fell to four hundred yards.

'Steady, boys,' Robert shouted, his call echoed by every officer.

The *Retribution* was a warship built for speed and manoeuvrability, with a massive, complex rig that readily consumed the labour of its sailing crew when the ship was in motion. Becalmed, the majority of the crew were deprived of the frantic duty that would see them through battle and they could do nothing but watch the approaching enemy in silence.

Suddenly Larkin let fly with the bow chasers and the crew roared in response, a release that put courage into the heart of every man. Only Robert remained silent, his gaze locked on the centre galleass. Her six bow chasers were run out, the pitch-black muzzles falling and rising with the swoop of the bow. Robert could almost see the Spaniards behind the long barrels, the smouldering flame on their linstocks poised above the touchholes and as the oars of the galleass propelled her through the upswing the cannons fired in a blaze of fiery smoke.

The volley of iron shot struck a terrifying blow, each ball tearing a bloody path across the decks of the *Retribution.* The timbers of the superstructure exploded, propelling razor sharp splinters in every direction that shredded the courses and riggings. The hull boomed with the strike of a massive round, a 50 pound ball from a *cañón de batir* that ripped across the fo'c'sle, blasting a saker from its mounting, obliterating its gun crew.

On the gun deck Larkin's men worked with a speed that defied their previous best, their bodies drenched in sweat as they prepared the bowed broadside culverins, their laboured breathing made worse by the choking smoke. Desperation crept into their task, their haste spurred by the knowledge that the very life of the ship was in their hands. A piercing cry of pain cut through the smoke as a gunner's foot was crushed beneath the four-wheeled truck of a culverin, the 4,500 pound carriage crushing bone and cartilage as the crew hauled on the rope to run it out. One of the men pulled him clear, the process of reloading never abating as the touchhole was primed and the weapon fired without pause for command.

A second galleass let fly at the *Retribution*, her six chasers wreaking fresh carnage as death and injury consumed the crew. The foremast was split through, the weathered oak spar snapping like a switch. Cries of alarm overrode the cacophony as the stays and rigging crashed onto the fo'c'sle. Robert stood transfixed. The crew within earshot responding to his shouted commands; men dragged the wounded below or secured what rigging they could, and the all consuming clamour of the battle raised every voice to an ear splitting pitch.

Robert watched for the strike of Larkin's shots. He couldn't see them; they were too infrequent, too ineffectual to check the advance of even a single ship. It was only a matter of time before the *Retribution* was overrun. All of a sudden the fore-rail of the nearest galleass seemed to disintegrate under a hail of fire. A moment later the air around her foremast was riven through with shot, her rigging split asunder. Robert saw a dozen Spaniards fall and he spun around to look aft of the *Retribution.* Three English galleons were off his stern, each one firing their bow chasers at the enemy. Another joined even as Robert watched and he looked to the fore to see others take station there, their combined firepower making a mockery of the opposing bow chasers of the galleasses.

The line formed rapidly, a dishevelled confusion of towed galleons, each firing whatever guns they could bring to bear until a solid phalanx had been formed, a defensive formation that quickly negated the enemy's threat to the flotilla's flank. The galleasses slowed their approach, their course no longer clear, and a stalemate quickly developed, an uneven contest of fire as upwards of thirty galleons turned their cannon towards the Spanish reinforcements.

Evardo clutched the crucifix around his neck, the carved figure of Christ pressing painfully into his flesh. The galleasses had remained stoical under enemy fire for nearly an hour, paying a heavy coin in damage and casualties as they returned fire with their bow chasers. They were no longer advancing towards the English, but had bore away to come to the direct assistance of the *San Luís* and *Santa Clara*. One of the galleasses was listing badly although Evardo could not tell if she had been holed below the waterline or whether her internal ballast had shifted. The giant ornate stern lantern of another had been shot away and the third had damage to her ram and prow. Distance and the ever present clouds of gun smoke concealed the extent of the casualties amongst their crews.

The enemy ranks remained firm, although their rate of fire had dramatically decreased with many of the English galleons being towed away to gain sea room. The day's battle was only just beginning and already Evardo could see distant fire and smoke as a further action, driven by localized sea breezes, developed closer to Dunnose Point off the southern coast of the Isle of Wight.

The hope that real English blood would be spilt had yet again been dashed. The galleasses, one of them towing De

Leiva's carrack, *Rata Santa María Encoronada*, were supposed to have sealed the trap and enveloped any enemy ships that grappled the *Santa Clara* and her sister bait. Instead they had been forced to play the English game once more, resulting in yet another protracted impasse.

When the galleasses had first engaged Evardo had hoped they would strike deeply into the English ranks. But the enemy had responded swiftly. A single ship had towed herself towards the oncoming galleasses, bringing them under fire and alerting every English galleon to the threat to their flank. The single ship was soon joined by others and their defence quickly coalesced behind a storm of cannon fire.

'Signal from the *Girona*,' a lookout called, indicating the nearest galleass. 'Ready a tow line and prepare to withdraw.'

Evardo nodded to Mendez and the captain repeated the order. Evardo slumped against the main mizzen mast. The exhilaration he had felt at dawn that morning was gone, leaving him cold and exhausted. Through hooded eyes he surveyed the decks of his ship. The crew were moving quietly about the ship, ignoring the sporadic fire of the English, the solitary whistle of passing shot. They moved with purpose, gathering up the injured and dead. Evardo counted twenty-five shroud-covered corpses laid out in a row on the main deck.

Padre Garza was attending to the dead, his own head heavily bandaged. Evardo spied Nathaniel Young on the fo'c'sle standing alone beside one of the *falcon pedreros*. Evardo closed his eyes and listened to the muted voices of his men, the low tones that spoke of their anger, a bitter rage that Evardo felt in equal measure. Every previous close action had resulted in a similar imbalance between their casualties and those of the English, the artillery tactics of the enemy making a mockery of every Spanish attempt to fight man-to-man.

On this day however the crew had been prepared for heavy casualties. The trap demanded it, but all believed they would have a chance to bloody their swords. Though initially outnumbered, they had believed that their sacrifice would finally allow the fleet to take the fight to the enemy.

A tow line was thrown from the bowsprit of the *Santa Clara* and the deck shuddered beneath Evardo as the *Girona* took the strain. The distant gunfire was increasing in intensity, signalling a definitive shift in the centre of battle, but Evardo ignored the temptation to turn his attention to landward. His eyes instead were on the English flotilla not two hundred yards off his starboard beam. Some of them showed signs of damage from the guns of the galleasses but they were mere scratches, nothing that could be heralded as a victory. As the *Santa Clara* sailed slowly past them Evardo tightened the grip on his crucifix until the Christ-figure punctured his skin. A trickle of blood ran down his wrist. He had sacrificed the safety of his ship and the lives of his crew for nothing.

Robert stepped aside as crewmen carried one of the dead past him. The sailor's face was covered with a bloodied cloth and Robert bade them stop. He lifted the corner of the cloth. The dead man was a yeoman's mate and Robert stared at the unseeing eyes for a moment before indicating to the men to carry on. The stand against the galleasses had cost him four dead, with thrice as many wounded. He looked balefully at the half-breed ships off his larboard beam.

'Ahoy *Retribution*, Captain Varian, ahoy!'

Robert turned to the call. The *Victory* was under tow off his starboard quarter and he acknowledged the wave of her commander, John Hawkins.

'Nicely done, lad,' Hawkins shouted, doffing his hat. 'Nicely done.'

Robert returned the gesture. Hawkins held his gaze, his smile changing to a solemn look of respect as he nodded gravely before turning away.

Robert turned once more to the withdrawing enemy ships. At two hundred yards they were well within range but the guns of the *Retribution* remained silent. From the moment the galleasses had disengaged and turned their bows towards their stricken galleons, and the threat of engagement had passed, Larkin had sent an order to Robert to cease fire. The ammunition stocks were perilously low. Over three-quarters of their shot was gone, including the additional supplies they had garnered from the Spanish prizes.

The tremendous rate of fire, three shots per-gun-per-hour, had pulverized the two galleons and forced the galleasses to withdraw, but as before no prizes had been taken and no enemy ships sunk. Robert studied the closest galleon, the smaller of the two that had found themselves adrift of the Armada formation at dawn. Her upper decks were punctured through in several places. Jeers and stays were hanging loosely from every yard and mast, shredded rigging that told of the countless strikes the galleon had suffered. But in reality it was superficial damage. Only God and the Spaniards knew how many crew had been lost, but whatever the butcher's bill the enemy had never seemed to be on the verge of striking their colours.

A gentle gust of wind swept over the *Retribution.* Robert checked his bearings. A south-westerly. The English fleet had the weather gauge. Seeley's voice rang out and the crew took to the rigging, the topsails unfurling as the breeze steadied.

A mile away Howard and Drake had begun a concerted attack on the seaward wing of the Armada, forcing the Spaniards to tighten their formation, pushing them deeper into the Channel. Frobisher, in the mighty *Triumph*, was off

Dunnose Point, pitting tide and circumstance against the foe, the weather gauge giving him speed and agility that none in the Armada could match. The earlier skirmishes had given way to a fleet-wide battle with the English mounting a full offensive. The Spanish were holding firm, but the wind and waves were against them and as the day progressed a fated reality became apparent. Coveted or not, the Spanish would be denied the Solent.

CHAPTER 18

2 p.m. 5th August 1588. The English Channel, south of Eastbourne.

The air was heavy, a sun-warmed veil that drew sweat from every pore as the men of the *Retribution* worked to repair the battle damage. The ship resounded with the staccato beat of hammers pounding against timber and iron, cut through by the strident voice of the master carpenter as he directed work from the main deck, while aloft the yeomen of the sheets and jeers oversaw the re-rigging of a new mizzen mast.

Robert was in his cabin, lying supine on his cot, his eyes half-focused as he studied the grain on the deck beam above his head. The fleets had been becalmed since dawn and were separated by some three miles, creating a lull in the fighting. Robert had spent the morning on the quarterdeck, determined to occupy his mind with the work demanded of his galleon, but his efforts had proved futile. He had gone below, inviting Seeley to accompany him and over the previous two hours they had discussed the action of the day before, specifically how the Spanish galleons had survived the firepower of ten times their number. Without reaching any conclusions the conversation had eventually fizzled out and both men had lapsed into silence.

There was a knock on the cabin door. It was Larkin. He requested permission to see Robert and was invited in. Seeley poured him some grog.

'It's our ammunition stocks, Captain,' Larkin began. 'Without resupply we'll soon have to withdraw from the battle.'

'Tell me exactly what remains.'

The master gunner gave Robert a full account, including powder. It was enough for two to three days' skirmishing at most. One day in a full engagement. Robert took a swig of grog to stifle his growing anxiety. Not only had the massive amount of shot they had already expended not inflicted any serious damage on the enemy ships, now they were faced with the prospect of having to disengage.

Despite all their efforts the Armada was only days from its objective. The English navy should have secured a score of prizes by now and driven the rest of the Spanish fleet into the depths of the North Sea. Instead they had failed to take any Spanish ships by their own actions and with every encounter their chances of stopping the Armada were diminishing.

'It's not enough,' he said almost to himself.

'Where are the cursed supplies we requested?' Seeley said. 'Every warship in the fleet has the same problem and yet the only significant amount we've received so far has come from a ship the Spanish abandoned.'

'Begging your leave, Captain,' Larkin said. 'But that's why I wanted to see you. What we have *might* be enough, if the conditions were right.'

'How?'

'Well, sir, so far we haven't been able to cripple any of their ships, even with our cannon pedros.'

'And?'

'It's the range, Captain. It's too far.'

'But we're firing well within range, even for the sakers,' Seeley interjected.

'Any one of my culverins can throw a ball over a thousand yards, but their effective range is nearer four hundred and already at that distance they're only good against men and rigging. Even at half that we've seen our shot bounce off the Spanish hulls. If we want to punch through their timbers we need to get a lot closer.'

'How close?' Robert asked.

'Fifty yards.'

'At that distance we'd have precious little distance to manoeuvre,' Seeley warned.

Larkin remained silent. He was convinced his solution would work but it was not his place to tell the master how to con the ship.

Robert stood up and began to pace the cabin. Fifty yards. It was incredibly close. At that distance a sudden trick of the wind could give the Spaniards a chance to close and board. Once grappled any English ship would surely be lost. Also, at fifty yards the weather decks would be within range of the massed ranks of musketeers and arquebusiers on each Spanish ship. It would be a bloody task but if Larkin was right . . . He looked to the master gunner.

'Give my lads a chance, Captain,' Larkin said. 'We'll show those Spanish papists the real power of this galleon.'

Robert saw the determination in Larkin's eyes. He was a master of his craft and no one knew the guns of the *Retribution* better than he. Once the wind picked up the Armada would continue its relentless progress to the coast of Flanders. It had to be stopped, at any cost.

'Thomas, I want you to inform your mate and the yeomen that at the first opportunity I intend to grant Mister Larkin his wish.'

'Aye, sir.'

'Mister Larkin, you will have your fifty yards.'

The master gunner nodded and rose from the table.

'Captain to the quarterdeck!' a call came from above.

Robert left his cabin to go aloft.

'Pinnace approach, Captain,' Shaw said as Robert came up. 'She's flying Hawkins's standard.'

Robert went down to the main deck as the pinnace came alongside.

'Ahoy, Captain Varian,' Hawkins called. 'I bid you come aboard and accompany me to the flagship.'

Robert leapt across to the smaller craft as the hulls kissed and they bore swiftly away under oars. Robert stood beside Hawkins at the bow.

'How's my ship?' Hawkins's eye swept the *Retribution* from bowsprit to the poop deck, pausing to focus on the more obvious damage.

'She's strong.' Robert was slightly irked that Hawkins would refer to her as his. 'But we are low on ammunition, sir. Especially for the cannon pedros.'

'It's the same throughout the fleet, lad,' Hawkins replied. 'Lord Howard has already decided that we won't engage the enemy again until we come up as far as Dover and rendezvous with Seymour's squadron. Maybe then we can push this blasted fight with the Spanish to a conclusion.'

Robert nodded. With Lord Henry Seymour's forty ships the English fleet would outnumber the Spaniards and the Dover squadron still had full shot lockers.

'Is there a chance we will receive more ammunition before that battle?'

'Howard asked the Privy Council for more power and shot before sailing from Plymouth,' Howard replied angrily. 'Instead they sent him a squad of musketeers to assist in close quarter battle and since then he has received a dispatch asking why we have not boarded and taken any Spanish ships.'

'Surely the admiral is not contemplating such an attack?'

'No, lad. Howard knows the value of our ships and the suitability of our tactics. And I for one haven't created a fleet of race built galleons to see them clap sides with Spanish hulks. But I do fear we have overestimated the effectiveness of our heavy guns.'

'My master gunner believes we can inflict serious damage if we can get closer, to within arquebus shot,' Robert said.

'I have heard similar opinions from other masters. But that approach depends upon first breaking up the defensive formation of the Armada. Without achieving that goal, our superior gunnery is for naught.'

Robert nodded and they lapsed into silence. He studied Hawkins's narrow face out of the corner of his eye.

'Why am I needed on the flagship, sir?'

Hawkins turned and smiled.

'You'll see, lad.'

The pinnace continued on over the placid sea, weaving in and out of the towering hulls of the stationary warships, passing through their cold shadows. The oars creaked in the locks and between the passing ships Robert looked out beyond to the distant formation of the Armada.

'Here we are, lad.'

The pinnace came alongside the *Ark Royal* and Hawkins was swiftly up the rope ladder. Robert followed. The main deck was crowded. Soldiers stood in serried ranks fore and aft while in the centre a large group of captains and senior commanders stood around the Lord High Admiral, Sir Charles Howard. Robert paused hesitantly at the gunwale, unsure of what was happening or how he should proceed.

'Ah, Captain Varian, come forward if you will.'

Robert walked across the main deck to stand before the admiral. Howard was twenty years older than Robert. He had a long face with a prominent nose, and a sharp chin under a tightly shaped goatee. A favourite at court and an able statesman and soldier, he was a born commander of men.

'Now, we are all here,' he said affably. 'We shall begin.'

'Begin what, my lord?' Robert was perplexed.

Howard smiled. 'It seems Captain Hawkins has not told young Varian why he has been summoned here,' he said over his shoulder, and the other commanders laughed genially.

'You are here, Captain Varian, along with these other captains and commanders, because I mean to reward those who are deserving, and encourage others who would aspire.' Howard raised his voice so all could hear. 'Your bravery at Cadiz gave you command of the *Retribution*. Your ability confirmed that captaincy, and thus far in this battle you have proved your worth time and again. You are one of England's finest sons. To honour your courage you will be counted amongst those I have deemed worthy of the order of knighthood.'

Robert was astonished. A knighthood. With such a social rank his captaincy would never be questioned or challenged, and on merit alone he would truly be able to make his way in the world. He felt a pang of conscience. He would be dubbed Sir Robert Varian, not Sir Robert Young. He searched his feelings at the thought of how his real name would be negated but felt no remorse. What was Young to him but his father's name, the name of a traitor? Henceforth men would know him as Sir Robert Varian, a captain knighted by the Lord High Admiral, Sir Charles Howard in the midst of battle. Robert felt his chest swell with the force of his pride.

Howard turned to address the assembled crew. 'Step forward the honoured few – Lord Thomas Howard, Lord Sheffield,

Roger Townsend, George Beeston, Martin Frobisher, John Hawkins, and Robert Varian.'

Those called stepped out from the ranks and stood before the admiral. Robert moved slowly, as if in a trance, and took his place at the end of the file. One by one the men came forward and knelt before Howard. Robert was the last to advance. He knelt down before the admiral and bowed his head.

'By the power granted to me by rank,' Howard intoned, speaking aloud the words made sacred by tradition and ceremony. 'I dub thee, in the name of the Crown, knight of the realm.'

Robert felt the strike of Howard's clenched fist on each of his shoulders in turn. He raised his head and met the admiral's gaze.

'Arise, Sir Robert Varian, and take your place amongst your fellow knights.'

Robert stood and stepped back, coming shoulder to shoulder with the chosen few. The crew erupted in cheers. Trumpets blared from atop the fo'c'sle. Robert looked about slowly, unable to fully absorb the incredible moment. His eyes fell on Howard. The Lord High Admiral of England was staring back at him. He nodded respectfully and Robert smiled, looking up as the acclaim swept over him.

Evardo's pulse quickened in anticipation as he gazed upon the broad sweep of the coastline west of Calais. It was late afternoon and the Armada was being borne along a mile off land by a moderate westerly, a breeze that had sprung up at dawn. The previous day had been long and frustrating, with both fleets becalmed. Evardo drank in the exhilarating feeling as mile after mile fell into their wake.

The *Santa Clara* was sailing amidst the rearguard of the

Armada, a place of relative safety granted to Evardo's ship while the crew finished the last of her running repairs. Damage to the main mast had been the most serious consequence of the *Santa Clara*'s trial over forty-eight hours before. The mast had taken a side swipe from a round shot, at least a 24 pounder, a glancing blow that had gouged out a four-inch deep furrow in the forward section. The master carpenter had repaired the damage as best he could and the crew had covered the bindings with pitch to hide the weakness from the enemy. It was far from satisfactory, and Mendez had already warned that the mast would not hold if the ship was forced to run before a storm. Evardo had acknowledged the captain's counsel and as the wind freshened during the day he had found himself glancing at the mast many times.

At the thought he looked to the main once more and saw de Córdoba come up to the quarterdeck. The captain raised his eyebrows quizzically, seeking permission to approach and Evardo nodded genially.

'A fair wind, *Comandante*.'

'A fair wind indeed, *Capitán*.'

De Córdoba looked beyond Evardo over his shoulder. 'That is the port of Calais off our larboard bow?'

'It is, and beyond on the horizon is Gravelines.'

'Then his grace, the Duke of Medina Sidonia, has done it,' de Córdoba said triumphantly. 'He has brought the Armada through the Channel.'

Evardo smiled. Medina Sidonia had indeed all but fulfilled the primary goal of the campaign. The Armada was nearing the Flemish coast.

'If Parma's army is in Dunkirk and is ready to sail we could effect a rendezvous on the morrow,' de Córdoba added.

If, Evardo thought with a tinge of concern. As far as he knew not one of Medina Sidonia's dispatch ships had returned to inform the fleet and without firm contact there was no way of knowing which port Parma had chosen. It was possible he wasn't at Dunkirk at all. Maybe he was in Nieuwpoort, or Sluis, or even Antwerp.

The boom of a single cannon echoed across the fleet, interrupting Evardo's thoughts. It was a signal from the *San Martín.* Evardo waited impatiently for whatever command had been issued to disseminate across the fleet.

'Orders from the flagship,' the masthead lookout shouted down after several minutes. 'All ships to drop anchor in Calais roads.'

'Here?' de Córdoba asked. He turned to Evardo. 'Why is the duke ordering the fleet to anchor?'

For a moment Evardo did not reply although he knew the reason, or at least suspected. It now seemed probable that Medina Sidonia had yet to receive any response from Parma and was halting the Armada for fear of going to leeward of the disembarkation port, whichever one that might be. It was a disturbing development. Evardo's unease showed in his expression.

'You suspect something's wrong?' de Córdoba asked.

Evardo looked around and leaned forward. He lowered his voice, fearful that one of the crew might overhear, and explained his assessment of the situation.

'And what of Calais?' de Córdoba asked. 'Maybe Medina Sidonia has received news that Parma is waiting there?'

Evardo shook his head. 'Calais is controlled by French Catholics. They might be sympathetic to our cause, but they would never open their gates to the Army of Flanders, no more than a Spanish city would allow a French army to enter. No, Parma has certainly commandeered one of the ports he already holds in Flanders to embark his army.'

'Then we will soon know which one,' de Córdoba said with confidence.

Evardo nodded, although he did not share his captain's certainty. He turned his attention to the lie of his ship and Mendez's commands as the sailing captain brought the *Santa Clara* in closer to the shore.

While still a half mile from the port Mendez called for the sails to be furled and, soon after, for the bow anchor to be released. The bow of the *Santa Clara* swung around on the anchor cable as the flukes took hold in the sandy bottom. As the prow came up to the wind Mendez called for a smaller stern anchor to be released, securing the galleon amidst her sister warships in the rearguard. Evardo immediately looked to the four points of his galleon and the surrounding seascape.

Calais was situated on a near featureless coastline, with neither a headland or sea stack to mitigate the strong cross currents fed by the local tidal streams. The Armada had halted in a very exposed anchorage and the deck of the *Santa Clara* heaved aggressively as the wind clawed at her fore and aft castles.

Evardo turned his attention to the English who were still in formation three miles to windward. Given their position, and the disadvantageous conditions, Calais roads was one of the worst possible anchorages for the Armada, but there was no better anchorage further east, certainly none that could accommodate the larger ships. Also along the coast, beginning not a mile off shore, were the dreaded Banks of Flanders, a hazard that had claimed innumerable ships over the centuries. Medina Sidonia had to communicate with Parma before proceeding. There was no other option but to wait.

Perhaps it was true that the English fleet could not be defeated in battle, not when their more nimble ships had the advantage of the weather gauge and they were intent on using only their cannon to fight. It mattered little. The Armada had weathered every attack and while the crew of the *Santa Clara* and many other vessels had endured severe casualties, not one ship had been lost to enemy fire. The Armada had reached the Flemish coast intact. They had fulfilled the divine orders of the King.

Contact with Parma had yet to be made but de Córdoba was right, they would soon know which port the army had chosen. Then the anticipated rendezvous could take place and the Armada would escort the invasion fleet across the Channel. Parma's troop ships would sail unmolested in a cocoon of warships, a defensive formation that the enemy could not break. The Army of Flanders would land in England and the heretic Queen would be cast down to Hell.

Here, now, in the waters off Calais, God's will was being done and Evardo lifted his eyes to the heavens as he uttered a prayer of contrition for ever having doubted the success of His enterprise. On this day there could be no doubt. After years of planning, months of preparation, weeks of sailing and days of battle, victory was indeed within the grasp of the Spanish Armada.

CHAPTER 19

5 p.m. 7th August 1588. Calais, France.

'Six days,' one of the *comandantes* repeated with horror, his words hanging in the silence that engulfed the spacious aft-cabin of *La Rata Encoronada.* Evardo stood amongst the group of two dozen men, his mind reeling from the news just delivered by Don Alonso de Leiva and the inevitable dire consequences such a delay would precipitate.

'Yes,' de Leiva repeated. 'The Army of Flanders will not be ready to sally out for another six days. The Duke of Parma has already begun the process of loading the men and equipment onto their transports in Dunkirk but before now he had been waiting for news of our arrival.'

'But what of the pataches sent to warn him?' someone asked.

De Leiva waved the question away irritably. 'He claims they only reached him yesterday. Right now that is not our concern – the next six days are. The English have anchored to windward but it is unlikely they will leave us unmolested while we wait for Parma. We must prepare ourselves for an attack. If we can hold them off for six days, by the seventh day the Army of Flanders will be marching on London.'

Murmured conversations began at de Leiva's words, with

some voices raised in anger. Evardo remained silent. *Six days*, he repeated to himself. It was a lifetime for a fleet so precariously positioned as the Armada. When he had been summoned to *La Rata Encoronada* thirty minutes ago he had presumed it was to discuss the logistics of supporting Parma's imminent arrival. He had never suspected that such devastating news awaited them all.

What was equally serious was the fact that Parma was requesting an escort from the harbour of Dunkirk itself. The Dutch were blockading the port with armed flyboats. Parma had only a handful of small warships to oppose them and he feared his slow moving, flat-bottomed troop transports would be easy prey for the Dutch. The Flemish shoals that guarded the approaches to Dunkirk could only be traversed during high tide, and even then only by ships with a very shallow draught. The Armada possessed such vessels, chief amongst them the galleasses, but with the English fleet threatening them to windward Medina Sidonia was unlikely to divide his forces. King Philip's meticulous plan was rapidly unravelling and Evardo felt the palpable anxiety of his fellow *comandante*s in the crowded space, an infectious dread that sapped his previous confidence.

'Enough,' de Leiva shouted, returning the cabin to silence once more. 'We have confirmed reports that a second fleet has joined the English from Dover. The enemy now outnumber us in sail, but the Duke of Medina Sidonia is confident, and his advisors and I concur, that the English cannot hope to defeat us while we hold our formation.'

There was a murmur of agreement from the room. 'The *cobarde*s are afraid to approach us and fight like men,' one man shouted and the tone of agreement rose.

'The English must know that breaking our formation is vital to their success,' de Leiva continued, his voice overriding the cacophony. 'Given our exposed anchorage, the swiftness of the incoming tide, and the prevailing westerly winds it is believed the English might try a fire-ship attack to break up our defence and drive us onto the Banks of Flanders.'

De Leiva maintained the silence with a raised hand.

'We have one other reason to suspect the English will use this stratagem,' he said. 'The arch-fiend Frederigo Giambelli is known to be in England.'

The name elicited an audible gasp from every man in the cabin.

'Merciful Jesus. Hellburners,' one of them said. The cabin erupted.

Evardo felt a prickle of fear at the back of his neck at the mention of hellburners. The infernal devices were not merely fire-ships, they were floating bombs, designed by the Italian Giambelli to explode on impact with their prey or with a delayed fuse that would ignite the charges without warning.

Three years before in the war against the Dutch Republics, Parma had built an 800 yard pontoon bridge across the Scheldt River, cutting off Antwerp from the sea in a bid to force the city to surrender to his forces. It had taken over six months to build the massive structure and, armed with over two hundred gun emplacements, it was further protected both up and down stream by booms. Against this impregnable barrier the Dutch had sent Giambelli's hellburners.

The Spanish soldiers manning the bridge had been prepared for a fire-ship attack, but no one had before devised such a weapon as the hellburners. The first ship, with a delayed fuse, exploded almost harmlessly in the middle of the river, creating a sight that actually drew more soldiers to the bridge. The second ship exploded on impact, instantly killing over eight hundred men on the bridge and injuring countless others. It was a devastating attack and Evardo could only imagine with horror the impact such devices would have on the massed ships of the Armada. As the noise in the cabin began to ebb, all eyes turned once more to de Leiva.

'In preparation for this attack your crews must be ready to slip and buoy their anchor cables at a moment's notice. Every *comandante* is given leave to lay off as they see fit, but let me be clear – the Duke of Medina Sidonia expects every ship to regain their anchors and their position once the threat has passed.'

De Leiva's eyes ranged across the cabin. Every man nodded his assent.

'Now, to enhance our defence, the duke has also decided to place a screen of pataches before the fleet. Their task will be to grapple and haul any fire-ships away. I need war-captains to command these boats, not the current traders who might turn and run at the first sight of fire. Who among you will volunteer?'

'Don de Leiva,' Evardo said at once. 'I request the honour of commanding one of the pataches.'

'And I,' another *comandante* shouted, close at hand.

'And I.'

'And I.'

Robert gazed out over the fore rail of the fo'c'sle at the anchored enemy fleet. The Spaniards had done it. The Flemish coast was within their reach. Right now Parma's army was undoubtedly readying itself to embark. If he was sallying out from Dunkirk he was less than twenty-five miles away. How many thousands of soldiers were already on the Armada? How many more would Parma add? The Army of Flanders was the greatest in Europe and once ashore in England they would sweep aside any obstacle. Only the English fleet stood in the way of that terrible fate. But how could they stop the Armada?

The Spanish ships were unsinkable, their formation unbreakable, and once the Armada set course for the English coast, with Parma's men amongst them, their victory would be assured.

'Beg to report, Captain,' Robert heard and he turned to find Seeley standing behind him.

'The tide is about to turn. I've manned the capstan in case the anchor shifts.'

'Very good, Mister Seeley,' Robert replied. He indicated to the Armada off the bow. 'What's your assessment?'

'It's a piss-poor anchorage for such a large fleet,' Seeley replied and Robert raised an eyebrow at Seeley's uncharacteristic profanity. 'If this wind holds we should try to dislodge them and push them onto the Flemish shoals.'

Robert nodded. It was an obvious conclusion but how would they achieve such a feat?

'I suspect the admiral will launch some type of attack on the morrow,' Robert said, thinking aloud. 'Especially now that Lord Seymour and his squadron have joined the fleet.'

Seeley nodded and took a moment to study the captain. Sir Robert Varian. The title filled Seeley with immense pride. It was a great honour, not only for the captain, but for the *Retribution* and all who sailed on her. A faint smile crept onto his face as he recalled how he had once suspected the captain of being a traitorous Roman Catholic. He had reached an absurd conclusion and he thanked God that he had never confronted Robert.

'Put extra lookouts fore and aft, Thomas. Report again after the tide has turned.'

'Aye, Captain.'

'Pinnace approaching off the larboard quarter!'

It was bearing Hawkins's colours and Robert went to the main deck in time to see Seeley grant the commander leave to come aboard. Robert led the way to his cabin. Once the door was closed, Hawkins began to speak.

'We're going to attack the Armada with fire-ships, tonight. The vessels have already been chosen and are being prepared out of sight of the enemy in the middle of the fleet.'

Of course, Robert thought, fire-ships. His own lack of military experience had hidden this obvious solution from him. The wind was abaft of the fleet and the tide was about to turn in-shore. It was a perfect stratagem.

'We probably won't damage many ships, much less destroy any,' Hawkins continued. 'Our goal is to create confusion and shatter their formation. With luck, and God's favour, dawn should see the Spaniards driven back out into the Channel, or better yet, into the North Sea.'

Robert nodded. 'What ships have been chosen?'

Hawkins listed them. There were eight in total including one of Hawkins's own ships, a 200 ton barque, the *Hope.*

'The *Hope* is commanded by Mathias Purdon,' Hawkins said. 'He's a good man, but he's a merchant, not a soldier. I want someone I can trust at the helm to carry this through.'

'Then I volunteer,' Robert said without hesitation.

Hawkins smiled wryly. 'I thought you might. The ship will be fully rigged; you'll just need to hold her course until the flames have taken hold. How many men will you need?'

'Just one,' Robert replied, again without pause. 'If he's willing, I'm going to take my sailing master, Thomas Seeley.'

The wind and tide driven waves slapped against the hull of the *Águila,* her cutwater slicing through the rising surf as the patache tacked across the breadth of the Armada. The sun had set over two hours before and Evardo stood quietly in the bow of the 120 ton vessel, his hand clasping a line of running rigging to keep his balance on the heaving deck. The running lights of the English fleet covered the line of the western horizon. It was difficult to judge their distance. They looked closer than the four miles that separated the fleets, and Evardo glanced over his shoulder to the lights of the Armada, the multitude that was under his care.

Fifteen pataches had been assigned to the screen, nearly the entire complement of such craft sailing with the Armada. Under the feeble light of the half-moon Evardo checked the position of the *Águila* with the boats on his flanks. He had taken over his new command at dusk. Prior to that and throughout the entire day, the pataches had been ferrying victuals from the port of Calais to the Armada. The French governor of the city had not only proved sympathetic to the Spanish cause, he had allowed the local merchants to trade with the fleet. Every ship had received fresh supplies of water and food.

Satisfied, Evardo turned and went aft, staggering along the length of the heaving deck until he reached the tiller. The helmsman was standing with his feet widely spaced for balance, his calloused hand firmly on the tiller. Evardo nodded curtly to the helmsman. From a *comandante* it was an extraordinary gesture of familiarity to a common sailor and the crewman was momentarily taken aback before he returned the gesture.

'Come up another point to the wind.'

'*Si, Comandante.*' The helmsman deftly pushed the tiller a fraction to larboard.

Forward of the tiller Nathaniel Young stood in the lee of the mainmast. Evardo had ordered the Englishman to accompany him, along with ten of his arquebusiers to defend the *Águila* against any attack. Young looked ill at ease but Evardo was confident he was suitable for the task. In any case, if for any reason they did not make it back to the *Santa Clara*

Evardo wanted the more experienced *Capitán* de Córdoba in command of the soldiers there. The other ten crewmen of the *Águila* were sailors, hand-picked by Mendez from the men who had volunteered.

'Ahoy, *Águila*!'

Evardo turned at the sudden call, peering into the darkness off the starboard quarter from whence it came. The voice sounded familiar. While Evardo tried to place it, it rang out again.

'Ahoy, *Águila, Comandante* Morales!'

A skiff came into view. It was skimming over the tops of the waves under the press of a lateen sail. A man was standing in the bow but in the darkness it was impossible to see who it was.

'Heave to.' The helmsman adjusted his course as the sailors took to the sheets.

The *Águila* lost headway and began to buck wildly in the swell. The skiff came rapidly alongside.

'Permission to come aboard, *Comandante* Morales,' the man called from the bow.

Evardo could finally see who it was. He could scarcely believe his eyes.

'Of course, Abrahan.'

The older man leapt across onto the deck of the *Águila*. He called over his shoulder for the skiff to bear away and strode over to Evardo.

'Can we talk, *Comandante*?'

Evardo nodded. He ordered the helmsman to get underway and then led his mentor to the privacy of the bow.

'Evardo,' Abrahan began. In the half-light Evardo could see his face was twisted in anguish. 'I was wrong. I was terribly wrong. You have proven over the past week that you are indeed a man of true courage, your father's son. Everyone in the fleet speaks of it. I have come here to ask for your forgiveness and to serve with you once more.'

From the terrible moment of his capitulation on the *Halcón*, Abrahan's forgiveness and acceptance was all that Evardo had wanted. Now Abrahan was asking the same of him. He felt his heart twist at the sight of his mentor supplicating himself.

'There is nothing to forgive, Abrahan. I was wrong to forfeit the *Halcón* in exchange for my life.'

'It was God's will that you lived, Evardo. I see that now. He has guided your hand in this battle and made you an instrument of His war against the heretics.'

Evardo reached out and clasped Abrahan's shoulder. For the first time in over a year he felt a semblance of peace. It was as if the wounds to his honour were finally healing.

'But what of your position on the *San Juan*?'

'I told you, Evardo. Everyone in the fleet knows of your courage. When I requested leave to join you from Juan Martinez de Recalde, he did not hesitate to grant my request.'

Evardo smiled and tightened his grip on Abrahan's shoulder.

'Then it's to your station, old friend,' he said. Abrahan nodded in thanks before moving off to take command of the helm.

Evardo felt the peace within him become stronger. He had proved his bravery. For his comrades and his mentor, the stain of Cadiz had not only been erased, it had never existed.

But for Evardo part of it still endured. He would not be free of the past until one final part of his honour was satisfied, a part that could only be sated through blood – he must have his revenge. His disgrace at Cadiz would always exist while Robert Varian lived. Only when that cursed enemy was dead would Evardo finally achieve the full restoration of his honour.

* * *

Robert twisted the cord of slow-match in his hand, the lighted taper spinning slowly in the darkness, its flame feeding off the cool wind. Seeley stood beside him, his hand on the tiller as he wove the *Hope* through the outer ships in the lee of the fleet. She was a two masted barque, with a square main sail and a lateen mizzen and had been fully rigged by her crew before departure. The westerly wind eagerly drove her on, with Seeley balancing her course with the broad rudder, the deck heeled over to larboard under the press of sail. Robert was glad the sailing master had agreed to accompany him. Seeley had a steady hand and could be relied upon if anything went awry.

The *Hope* breeched the outer fleet just as her sister ships did the same and the eight craft sailed onwards abreast, setting out across the clear stretch of water that led to the enemy. The *Hope* had been packed with every combustible material available. The decks were strewn with old sails, barrels of pitch and heavy coils of frayed hemp rope. In addition the six 3 pound *minions* and five *falconetes* had all been double-shotted, with two round shot loaded back to back. Primed and ready the guns would explode when the flames of the pyre reached them, their barrels splitting asunder, adding to the terror and confusion it was hoped these devil ships would create.

Robert estimated they were already well over half-way between the two fleets. It would soon be time to light the deck. He checked that the tow line leading back to the skiff being dragged behind the *Hope* was still attached. The skiff was their only means of escape. Once the fire had been lit they would have only minutes to lash the tiller, scurry down the rope and cut the skiff loose from its damned escort. It was no fate for a proud ship.

'I make us just over a mile out,' he said to Seeley.

'When will we fire the decks?' Seeley asked out of the corner of his mouth, never averting his gaze from the lie of the ship.

'Our orders were a half-mile from the enemy.'

Seeley nodded, and this time his eyes darted to the lighted taper in Robert's hand. His heart was pounding in his chest and he closed his mind to the fear that every sailor possessed. Once loose, a fire was the damnation of all on board a ship and as a sailor Seeley had always regarded it as a necessary evil, never an ally. To purposely fire a ship seemed an unnatural, almost unholy, deed and Seeley tried to focus on the prize for such a treacherous act against the *Hope*.

All of a sudden Seeley saw a flame in the distance. He spun around, watching in horror as one of the fire-ships burst into a ball of flame.

'It's the *Bark Talbot*,' Robert ran to the larboard gunwale. 'They've set her alight. Damn them, it's too soon.'

A moment later a second ship ignited, the *Bear Yonge*, and within seconds the flames towered above the height of her main mast. The light from the two ships illuminated the seascape, creating dancing shadows and shapes across the black surface of the water. Robert looked to the Armada. They were still nearly a mile from the windermost ships and any vessels in the path of the *Bark Talbot* and *Bear Yonge* would have plenty of time to slip their anchors and escape. Then Robert spotted smaller ships before the towering hulls of the warships. Until now they had been hidden in the darkness, their running lights too insignificant to single them out, but in the illumination of the fires their purpose was clear.

'The bastards were waiting for us,' Robert whispered as he spun around to Seeley. 'Thomas, two points to larboard. The Spaniards have deployed a screen of small ships across their front. We need to try and outmanoeuvre them.'

Robert counted seven ships within the light of the fires, and there were surely others. He glanced at the taper in his hand. They had agreed a half-mile out, but at that distance, with the enemy screen already prepared, the Spaniards would have more time to grapple the fire-ships and divert them away. He would have to wait until they got closer. But how close? Too soon and the enemy would be handed the chance to divert the *Hope*'s course, too late and they risked being captured when they finally abandoned ship. Given their task, they could expect no mercy from the Spanish. Death would be certain, but it would not be swift.

The wind and tide bore the *Hope* on without pause. Robert called for a further course change. Without crew to man the rigging the scope of that change was limited but Seeley pushed the balance between sail and rudder to the limit. The *Hope* steadied. The half-mile mark slipped beneath her hull. Robert looked to the other fire-ships. They too had seen the danger and were delaying the firing of their decks. Inside this range every captain was his own master and Robert refocused his concentration on the sea ahead. Bringing the taper up to his mouth, he blew on the smouldering flame. It flared into an angry orange light. He needed to act, soon. The fate of the *Hope* had been written, the barque committed. Only the fate of her two-man crew remained in the balance.

'Fire! Off the larboard bow!'

Every man on board the *Águila* turned at the shouted call.

'Bastardos,' Abrahan cursed. 'The duke was right. Fire-ships.'

'No more than a mile out,' Evardo replied, taking his bearings from the course of the wind. 'We should—*Sancta Maria. . .*' he breathed. In the blink of an eye the solitary flame ignited into an inferno, illuminating the stark outline of the fire-ship for an instant before it was consumed by the breadth of the conflagration. It was a terrifying sight, the pyre reaching fifty feet into the air, the ship continuing on its hell-bound course as the wind-fed flames, like clawing fingers, reached outwards in the direction of the Armada.

'Christ Jesus, there's another one,' the lookout called, his terror evident in every word.

The second fire-ship ignited more quickly, her canvas sails exploding in a ball of flame that once more transfixed the crew of the *Águila.* In the glow of the fire Evardo spotted the other enemy ships, their decks yet to be fired. One was dead ahead. He checked his bearings again. The *Águila* was sailing close hauled against the wind. If they could come up another half-point then the ship in front of them would be within their grasp. He called for the minor course change, alerting all on board to his intended target.

The cutwater of the *Águila* crashed through the tide-driven waves, her deck heeling hard over under taut sails. Abrahan had command of the helm, his deft touch assuring their best possible speed as he balanced the hull on the precipice of putting the boat in irons before the wind.

'Young,' Evardo called. 'Bring five of your men to the bow.'

In the distance another fire-ship ignited, followed by another, then another. The screen of pataches had scattered, each crew deciding their own course. The *Águila* was the only boat converging on its chosen ship.

Nathaniel staggered forward with his men. In the light of the fires he could see their faces. They were determined, aggressive, the faces of veteran soldiers who were feeding off the battle lust created by the proximity of combat. Nathaniel felt a hollow in the pit of his stomach. The fire-ships were the English navy's best chance of shattering the Armada's formation. Yet he was amongst those resolved to stop them, forced to fight for a cause he no longer believed in.

There was nothing he could do. He was trapped, surrounded

by men who had become his enemies without their knowledge. If he revealed himself he would certainly be killed. But if he continued to fight for the Spanish he would be complicit in the defeat of his own country. The accusation his son had hurled at him on the motte resounded in his mind — coward. He tried to silence the voice by raising his own as he arrayed his men along the gunwale.

Without warning an explosion ripped out the forward section of a distant fire-ship followed a heartbeat later by two more, the thunderous blasts sweeping over the *Águila.*

'Hellburners!' one of the soldiers shouted.

'We hold our course,' Evardo shouted back, steel in his voice, his will dominating the fear he felt clawing at him.

The gap fell to a hundred yards.

'Helm, prepare to come about.'

'Aye, *Comandante.*'

The *Águila* raced across the bow of their chosen fire-ship. Her decks had still not been fired and Evardo called to Abrahan. The patache spun through the eye of the wind and came swiftly around to sail parallel to the fire-ship, thirty yards off her beam. Abrahan matched her course and speed as the two ships sped together towards the Armada, less than a quarter of a mile away. Evardo swept her with his gaze. The deck of the English ship was higher than his own patache. He couldn't see the enemy crew but he knew they were there.

'Bring us alongside the bowsprit!'

Abrahan slowly narrowed the gap between the ships.

'Come on you motherless Spaniards,' Robert spat, keeping his head low, his eyes locked on the enemy patache closing in on the bow. He had spotted the boat minutes before and although the *Hope* had the weather gauge, without a crew to work the rigging the advantage had all but been negated. The smaller, more nimble enemy patache had outwitted Seeley's every effort to avoid her.

The running lights of the Armada filled the seascape before the bow and Robert let the sight fill his heart, steeling his nerve. He had delayed firing the decks, although they were well within range. Once the inferno took hold they would have to abandon ship, leaving the *Hope* in the clutches of the patache and Robert was determined that his ship would break through the screen.

'Hold your course, Thomas,' he said. 'Wait for my signal.'

'Aye, Captain. God speed.'

'To us both.'

Robert picked up a boarding axe and stooped over he ran to the bow.

'Ready the grappling hooks,' Evardo shouted. Three sailors in the bow spread out to give themselves room. They played out their ropes and began to swing the four-pronged hooks, building momentum until they were a blur of speed. Evardo waited, watching the fall and rise of the hull of the fire-ship, knowing they had to be exact.

'Loose!'

The grappling hooks soared across the gap, falling on the gunwale of the bow, and the crewmen pulled them fast. They held.

'Secure the lines!' Evardo ordered. 'Abrahan, bear away!'

The *Águila* began turning her bow away from the fire-ship. The lines tightened, taking the strain. Suddenly a man appeared at the gunwale, an axe in his hand. He severed the first line. It whipped back, striking down one of the sailors with a lash.

'Arquebusiers, fire!' Evardo roared. 'Cut him down!'

The air erupted with the crack of gunfire. Accurate aiming

was impossible on the heaving deck of the small ship but Evardo saw the Englishman go down. The *Águila* continued her turn, the heavier English ship resisting the pull on her bow. The Englishman reappeared. He raised his axe, ready to cut the other line, but in that instant Abrahan played off the rudder, fouling the tension on the lines, causing the English ship to roll. The Englishman lost his balance and his axe struck the gunwale. He fought to free his blade. The faster loading arquebusiers fired a second volley, the bullets striking the hull below him. He looked up and in the light of distant fires Evardo saw his face.

'Varian!'

Robert froze at the call of his name. He looked to the bow of the Spanish patache. Morales. Anger surged through him like a hot flame. With a ferocity born from hatred of the Spanish aggressors he pulled the blade of the axe from the weathered timber and severed the second tow line. Bullets whipped past him, tearing at the loose folds of his clothes. He stepped up to the last line and struck down with all the fury in his heart. The rope parted with a whip crack.

Robert spun around and started to run aft. The *Hope* was free but it would not remain so. Morales was bound to throw more lines. They had to cripple the patache.

'Now, Thomas,' he roared. 'Fall off! Hard over!'

Seeley eased the pressure on the tiller and the *Hope* shifted her course, the bow swinging to starboard, right into the course of the patache. Robert bent down and picked up the burning slow match. He darted forward to the nearest mound of sails. They had been soaked in pitch and Robert blew on the slow match before throwing the tiny flame onto the pile. The fire quickly took hold. Within seconds the entire mound of sails was burning fiercely.

* * *

'Jesus save us! All hands, brace for impact!'

The crew of the *Águila* fell to the deck. All except for Nathaniel. He couldn't move. Robert was on that ship. His son was in the vanguard of England's attack.

Without warning the deck beneath him heeled hard over and he fell. With incredible reflexes Abrahan was veering away from the sudden course change of the English barque, negating the power of the larger vessel as the hulls struck each other. The ships rebounded, opening a gap of five yards between them.

'Fire! The English have fired their deck.'

'We must withdraw!'

'No!' Evardo roared. 'We stand fast. Abrahan, lay aboard! We're too close to the fleet to risk more grappling hooks. We need to board and turn her course.'

Abrahan leaned in against the tiller and brought the *Águila* hard up against the taller side of the barque. The hulls hammered against each other and then parted, opening a gap of two feet, the moving surface of the waves making it impossible to keep them firmly together. The gap closed again.

'Men of the *Águila*, with me!' Evardo shouted and he leapt up to grab hold of the gunwale of the barque. He clambered up. Three other men jumped with him while others stood hesitatingly, poised to jump but wary of the fluctuating gap between the hulls. One of the men with Evardo lost his grip as he climbed over the gunwale and he fell between the hulls. A wave slammed the patache against the barque, crushing the soldier, his scream of terror cut short, the sight causing more of the men to hesitate.

'Thomas, get to the skiff.'

Seeley nodded and ran aft. Robert quickly tied a rope around the tiller, holding it firmly in place, locking the *Hope* on course. He could no longer see the patache but he had heard the strike of the hulls and he prayed they had caused enough damage to foul any further attempt to divert the barque.

The flames were spreading across the deck, devouring everything they touched. Robert shielded his face against the growing heat, stepping backwards towards the stern. Suddenly he saw Morales climb over the gunwale in the waist of the ship. Two men immediately followed.

Robert rushed forward, his sword sweeping from his scabbard. One of the Spanish soldiers saw him and grabbed the arquebus slung over his back, swiftly bringing the weapon up to bear. Robert drew the wheellock pistol from his belt, whipping it up, pulling the trigger on instinct as he took a snap shot at the Spaniard. The bullet hit the soldier in the face and he somersaulted back over the gunwale, his arquebus firing into the air.

Robert dropped the pistol and charged Morales. Evardo held his ground and they slammed into each other, their blades clashing with a force that jarred the muscles in Robert's arm.

'I should have killed you, Spaniard,' he hissed in Latin.

'My life is not yours to take, Englishman.'

Robert leapt back, sweeping up the tip of his sword, his strike parried by Morales. He stared into the Spaniard's eyes, trying to predict his next move. They were alive with the reflection of the fire and Robert felt the battle rage within him concentrate in the strength of his sword arm.

He attacked again, swinging his blade through a sequence of strokes, forcing Morales to back away. He drew blood on the Spaniard's upper arm, gaining half a step. In the corner of his eye he saw the other Spanish soldier raise his gun to shoot him. His mind screamed at him to duck, to somehow shield himself, but his fighter's instinct held him fast, knowing he could not lower his guard. From behind him he heard a visceral war cry. The soldier's aim shifted to another target. Seeley! A cold smile crept onto Robert's face and he pressed home his attack.

'*Capitán*!' Nathaniel heard above the roar of the fire. He looked aft. The old helmsman was calling to him, his face mottled with rage, his finger pointed at Morales on the English deck above. 'Order your men to follow the *comandante*!'

Nathaniel looked up at the barque. The heat was building, a physical barrier that surrounded the fire-ship. The air was filled with sparks, countless shards of the inferno rained down on the *Águila*, threatening to ignite the sail. An explosion erupted on the far side of the barque, sending flames towering into the sky.

There was the sharp retort of a pistol shot and a Spanish soldier fell overboard, his body landing on the deck of the patache. Nathaniel saw Robert attack Morales. The other Spanish soldier raised his arquebus to shoot his son but then turned in the direction of another shout and a man charged forward from the stern. The soldier fired, missing his target and he drew his sword as the Englishman reached him.

Nathaniel was possessed with an overriding urge to call out to Robert but he could not, knowing the distraction might cost his son his life. He moved to the gunwale, judging the shifting gap between the two ships, waiting for the hulls to kiss. He had to get across, to help his son. He readied himself for the jump, not noticing that others were following him, waiting for their *capitán* to lead the way.

Evardo allowed Varian to come on, holding back on his counter attack, giving ground with every strike. The

Englishman had beaten him once and Evardo wanted Varian to think he would do so again. He saw him smile and he readily gave another pace.

Above them the main sail burst into flames, the canvas streaming down in blazing strips. The fire scorched the air, making it hard to breathe. Another deck gun exploded on the larboard side, blasting shards of searing metal across the deck.

Evardo sensed the moment to attack, the heart in his chest aching at the thought of sending the Englishman to his Protestant hell, of finally healing the wound to his pride that Varian had opened at Cadiz. He parried another strike, the blades rasping against each other. Evardo recovered and he lunged forward, leading with the tip of his sword. Varian sidestepped and struck down, turned his blade inside but Evardo was ready for the counter stroke and he whipped back his sword to reverse his attack, inflicting a shallow flesh wound on Varian's thigh. The Englishman gave ground. They circled and Evardo attacked again, pushing the fight towards the bow.

The flames consumed the mainmast, racing up to the tops, creating a vortex of warm air that rushed across the deck. Robert held his breath and focused all his strength on defending himself against the blur of steel that had suddenly become the Spaniard's sword. His eyes burned from the heat and he felt desperation creep into his reactions as Morales pressed forward relentlessly, his attack never faltering, never abating.

Around them everything was alive with flame, as if they were fighting on the deck of the devil's own ship and Robert took heart. The *Hope* was still on course, he had done his duty. He centred his balance. As Morales lunged he riposted, side swiping his blade, forcing the Spaniard to break off.

They circled again, breathing heavily, blood running from their flesh wounds. The hesitation that had caused Robert to stay his killing blow at Cadiz, to show mercy to a fellow Catholic, was gone. It had been cauterized out of him by a war between nations, a struggle that demanded every ounce of his loyalty if England was to survive.

For Evardo, Varian was nothing more than a cursed foe. England was the enemy of Spain and a plague upon Christendom. The English navy had to be defeated and the heretic Queen had to fall. It had been ordained by God and Evardo was willing to spill every last drop of his blood to achieve the will of the divine.

They rushed forward as one, their war cries intertwining, each one calling to God. They were enemies, and on the flame strewn decks of the fire-ship they would fight to the death.

Nathaniel jumped, clawing at the gunwale until his grip held and he heaved himself up. Two more Spanish soldiers jumped with him and they clambered over onto the deck together. Nathaniel ignored them. He took in the entire deck with a single glance. The other Englishman was aft, a Spanish soldier dead at his feet. The Englishman saw them and shouted defiantly, goading them on. The soldiers with Nathaniel did not hesitate and they began to run aft.

Robert and Morales were in the bow. They were locked chest to chest, their blades trapped between them. Nathaniel ran towards them, his sword singing from his scabbard. There was a mighty crack over his shoulder. The lifting yard of the mainmast gave way. It plummeted to the deck, dragging with it the flaming remnants of the main sail onto the two Spanish soldiers. They screamed as the pyre consumed them, the waist of the ship exploding in flames.

A blast of searing heat washed over Robert and Evardo, knocking them both off balance. Their blades separated and

Evardo hooked up the hilt of his sword, smashing the pommel into the side of Robert's head. He fell to the deck and Evardo was immediately upon him, bringing the tip of his sword to his chest.

'Now it ends,' he whispered.

'No!'

Evardo spun around. Young was rushing towards him, his sword charged. Evardo brought up his blade just in time to stop a killing strike and he stumbled backwards. Young came at him again, his expression maniacal, shouting words in English that Evardo could not understand.

Nathaniel hammered his blade down on Evardo's as if he were wielding an axe, his fury knowing no bounds. Evardo backed away, too stunned to counter attack. He circled around, his feet guiding him to the starboard side where he had boarded. Nathaniel pushed him across the width of the deck, his blows never ceasing. The fire from the burning mainmast clawed at them. They reached the bulwark and with a final effort Nathaniel pounded down on Evardo's upturned blade until the Spaniard lost his footing and fell over the side.

Seeley ran to the stern. He wavered, his hand on the rope tethered to the skiff. The fallen yard had effectively cut the deck in two. He couldn't reach the captain. His only chance was to cast off, to lay to in the skiff and hope that the captain would jump overboard in time. With the wind abaft the flames would quickly engulf everything forward of the main mast. The mizzen sail above the tiller was still untouched but its lower rigging was already aflame. Within a minute the canvas would be alight.

Another explosion in the mid section rocked the deck beneath his feet. Seeley took a firm grip on the rope and climbed out over the aft gunwale. He quickly sidled down the rope into the cool sea and swam to the skiff, climbing in as further blasts erupted on the deck above.

An explosion ripped across the waist, hurling debris into the air. A flaming shard fell onto Nathaniel's head. He swept it away. The heat was unbearable. The air was being sucked from his lungs and he coughed violently as he staggered across the deck to the prone figure of his son. He knelt down beside him and took him by the shoulders. The side of his face was covered in blood. He was badly dazed.

'Robert.'

For a moment his eyes cleared.

'Father?'

Nathaniel lifted his son to his feet and took his weight around his shoulder. They staggered forward together towards the larboard side. A falling block struck Nathaniel a glancing blow on the head, knocking them both to the deck. Nathaniel's vision swam, but his instinct to save his son drove him to his knees. He tried to stand, his head spinning, the heat of the fire clawing at his skin, searing his flesh and singeing the hair on his arms. He didn't know which way to go. The flames seemed to be on all sides. Above him the sky was ablaze.

He heaved Robert up and staggered to his feet. His hands were scratched and blistered. Every sense screamed at him to move. He lurched forward. Above the roar of the fire, he could hear the tortured sound of the mizzen mast failing under the onslaught of the fire, the whip cracks as rigging snapped. He stumbled on, dragging Robert with him. The larboard bulwark was ahead and with the last of his reserves he hoisted Robert over the side into the sea.

He fell against the gunwale. He couldn't breathe. There was no air, the fire had consumed it all. He stood up to jump overboard. A minion exploded nearby, its double shot gouging out the barrel, spewing forth blazing iron fragments that pierced Nathaniel's flesh, the force of the explosion knocking him overboard.

Evardo struck out for the patache. As he reached the side he was lifted clear out of the water by the crew. The English barque was fifteen yards off the beam, every inch of her deck aflame. Evardo watched it burn. He couldn't comprehend what had just happened. What had possessed Young? Did the duke attack him just to defend some anonymous Englishman? It was an act of sheer madness. Young had no loyalty to his countrymen. He believed in Spain's cause, so much so that he rallied Alvarado's men in the battle off Portland Bill and took command of them at Evardo's request. It didn't make sense.

'*Comandante.*'

Abrahan indicated over the bow of the *Águila.*

The windermost ships of the Armada were less than three hundred yards away and as Evardo looked to them in the outer glow of the fires all thoughts of Young fled from his mind. The larger ships of the Armada had already slipped and buoyed their anchors and were moving off to the east. Evardo spun around and looked across the breadth of the anchorage. Eight fire-ships were alight, but only two of these had been intercepted and grappled. The others were bearing down on the fleet. The sound of distant explosions rippled across the waters, each one causing more ships to slip their anchors and surrender their position, the fear of hellburners magnified many times on the larger, less manoeuvrable ships in the tightly packed formation. The sight filled Evardo with despair.

Robert surfaced, the cool water stunning his body but clearing his mind. The stern of the *Hope* was sailing past him. He tried to swim after it but the wind driven barque was too fast and in desperation he stopped.

'Father!'

He looked around him. The sea was lit up by flames. A man was floating in the water nearby and Robert kicked out towards him.

'Captain!'

'Thomas, over here!'

Seeley rowed out of the darkness. Robert pulled Nathaniel towards the skiff.

'Quickly, Thomas, help me get him into the boat.'

'Who is he?'

'My father.'

'Your father . . .' Stunned, Seeley pulled Nathaniel into the skiff. Robert hauled himself onboard and carried his father to the stern.

'Thomas, get us back to the *Retribution*.'

Seeley rowed the skiff around and pulled through the wind towards the English fleet. He stared at the prone figure.

Robert sat down beside Nathaniel and unbuttoned his jerkin. The white doublet underneath was drenched with blood and Robert's heart plummeted. He had thought that his father was his enemy. But he was not. He had saved him from Morales' sword and driven the Spaniard from the deck of the *Hope*, ensuring that the fire-ship would remain on course. His father's eyes were closed. Robert took his face in his hand.

'Father.'

Nathaniel looked up at him. He smiled. 'My son.'

'I don't understand. Why did you . . .? You saved me.'

'I had to, Robert.' He coughed violently. Blood flecked his lips. 'I had to . . . so you can fight on.'

He took Robert's hand in his own and held it tightly.

'You were right, Robert. I see that now . . . and I am proud you have become the Englishman you are.'

Robert placed his other hand around his father's, encasing it.

'I am my father's son,' he avowed, his heart filling with fear as he felt the cold in his father's hand and he silently pleaded for his father not to go, not this time.

'Robert,' Nathaniel said fiercely, summoning the last of his strength. 'I know you live under a false name.' His breathing became shallow. 'But please don't forsake your past. Don't forget the name . . . Young.'

Nathaniel went still, his hand still enfolded in Robert's.

'Young.'

Robert turned around at the sound of his name.

'It was you,' Seeley uttered. 'You're Young.' He stopped rowing. The skiff began to rock violently in the swell. Seeley's hand moved slowly to the hilt of his dagger.

Robert nodded, grief clouding his mind.

'Your father was in league with the Spanish?'

Robert remained silent.

'Captain!'

'He was a . . .' the word traitor came to Robert's lips but he could not say it. 'He was an exile, from the Northern Rebellion.'

'A Roman Catholic traitor,' Seeley hissed.

Robert's face darkened and he leaned forward. Seeley whipped out his knife.

'Don't move, Captain. Not another inch.'

'You would kill me?'

For a moment Seeley couldn't answer. The captain was not the man he had always claimed to be, in name or faith. He was not Robert Varian. He was another, a Roman Catholic and therefore the enemy.

'I vowed to find the traitor on board, not kill him,' Seeley said. 'Your fate lies in the hands of the authorities.'

'So you would turn me over to be tortured and executed at the stake?' Robert said angrily.

'I have to.' For a moment an image flashed in front of Seeley; of the captain stretched on the rack like the Catholic clerk, Bailey. He blenched from the sight.

'Tomorrow we go into battle, Thomas. Do you truly believe that the *Retribution*, that England's cause, will be better served if I am locked in irons?'

'You cannot expect to command the *Retribution* now that I know who you are?' Seeley said, realizing he was the only one who knew the captain's real identity. Keeping his dagger charged he got up from the thwart and moved to the bow.

'Take the oars,' he said.

Robert complied, his face inscrutable in the dark. 'Nothing has changed, Thomas. I am still the man I was and my loyalty has always been to Elizabeth.'

'You cannot be loyal to her, you're Roman Catholic.'

'I am loyal, because I am an Englishman, and she is my Queen.'

Seeley was silenced by Robert's reply. He thought of all the captain had achieved since taking command of the *Retribution*. He had proved himself over and over again to be loyal to England and the Crown. He had come to the attention of the Lord High Admiral himself and had been recognized for his bravery with a knighthood. He was Roman Catholic and yet loyal to a Protestant Queen. The two seemed irreconcilable.

Beyond the stern of the skiff the wind and tide were bearing the *Hope* onwards, her flames driving all before her. The ships of the Armada were abandoning their anchorage. Their defensive formation was no more and under the press of the prevailing wind the enemy fleet was being scattered eastwards.

Dawn was still hours away. Eventually the sun would rise and with it the English fleet would weigh anchor and engage the enemy once more.

Perhaps the captain was right, Seeley thought, his mind in turmoil. The *Retribution* needed its captain now more than ever. Seeley knew he was not ready to take command, and the best available commanders were already in charge of other galleons. But the Spaniards were Roman Catholic. Their cause was blessed by the Pope. Could the captain's loyalty to the Queen of England be such that he would continue to fight against his own kind, against a cause that his father had fought for?

The lines of loyalty that had always been so clear in Seeley's mind began to blur. Men went to war for different reasons, he had long realized that. For some plunder was more important than faith, but he had always presumed that the men he fought with were all Protestant. Even when he had suspected the captain might be Roman Catholic he had dismissed it because of the bravery and loyalty he himself had witnessed. The captain claimed he was loyal to the Crown because he was an Englishman. Seeley's faith was at the heart of his fealty but perhaps not every man needed that bond. Maybe for the captain it was enough that Spain was the enemy of England.

Seeley had to turn the captain over to the authorities. It was his duty, but as they neared the *Retribution* he decided he would defer that moment until the battle had been won. Silently he slipped his dagger back into its sheath. Nothing was written, the ultimate battle had yet to be fought. But if by dawn the enemy had failed to re-establish their formation, the English fleet would finally have a chance to slay the Spanish Armada. If they were to succeed then the best men needed to be in command of the most powerful warships. The *Retribution* was amongst that elite, and so was her captain.

CHAPTER 20

8th August 1588. The Battle of Gravelines.

The day dawned under a grey and swollen sky, the wind gusting from the south-south-west, stirring up the sea into angry swells that lashed against the hull of the *Santa Clara* as she tacked eastwards, her decks heeled hard over. Evardo had regained his command an hour after the fire-ship attack, the more nimble patache quickly overhauling the *Santa Clara*. He had re-boarded his ship before the patache bore Abrahan back to the *San Juan*. They had parted with only a handshake, a simple gesture that spoke of their renewed bond.

Throughout the night Evardo had stayed on deck, watching with ever mounting frustration as Mendez struggled in vain to return the *Santa Clara* to her anchorage in Calais roads. The hours of darkness had been filled with despair but only with the arrival of dawn did Evardo fully realize the scale of the disaster that had befallen the Armada. Despite the massive breadth of the open anchorage off Calais and the preparations made by Medina Sidonia, the fire-ship attack had completely annihilated the fleet's cohesion, scattering it along the length of the Flemish coast.

The English had the devil's own luck. Their fire-ship attack should never have succeeded to such an extent. They had not been true hellburners as was first believed and not one single Spanish ship had been struck or destroyed. The fire-ships had sailed harmlessly onto the shore, but a combination of strong currents and the increasing force of the south-westerly wind had prevented the Armada from regaining its anchorage. The *Santa Clara* had struggled in vain for hours. The more cumbersome hulks and urcas that made up the majority of the fleet had fared much worse and had been driven further east.

Only the *San Martín* and four other ships had managed to regain their original anchorage. They were now over a mile to the west of the *Santa Clara*, heavily engaged with an overwhelming force of enemy warships. The duke had sent out dispatch boats to rally the fleet to his position. The *Santa Clara* had been one of those to respond, yet they could scarcely make headway against the strengthening wind. Evardo glanced at the other warships nearby that were similarly engaged in a bitter struggle with the prevailing conditions. Of equal concern was that Mendez had slipped and buoyed the *Santa Clara*'s two anchors in Calais roads. Without them the galleon would be unable to await Parma's army or even approach a coastline with safety. Evardo suspected that every ship in the fleet had suffered a similar loss.

Evardo had thought of Nathaniel Young many times during the night. He still could not fathom his behaviour. Had he felt some loyalty to his fellow countryman? Was that why the duke had attacked him? It seemed implausible, given what he had known of Young, but he could think of no other explanation. The duke had denied Evardo the satisfaction of killing Varian, but it mattered little. He had bested the English captain, and it was likely that both Young and Varian had been consumed by the inferno.

He turned his face away from the wind. For the moment the English were concentrating on the *San Martín* and her coterie of escorts but that situation would not last – they would undoubtedly range beyond Calais. From before dawn the crew of the *Santa Clara* had readied the ship for battle. Despite the heavy weather, every gun had been loaded, and soldiers were positioned in the fighting tops and castles, their muskets and arquebusiers primed and ready. As the sun rose Padre Garza had given absolution to a large number of the crew on the main deck.

Evardo took hope as he watched his men make their final preparations. The enemy had the weather gauge, they would not engage at close quarters. The warships of the Armada would be forced to fight a defensive action once more, but if they could somehow reform, and hold their position off the Flemish coast, they might yet carry the day. Everything depended on the weather and their ability to hold the English at bay. One element was in the hands of God, the other was in their own. Evardo turned back to the unfolding battle beyond his reach, praying that God would grant them the chance to fulfil His calling and retake possession of the seas off Calais.

The bow of the *Retribution* soared over the swell, her chasers erupting with fire at the zenith. White gunpowder smoke fled before the galleon on the wind, sweeping over the tightly packed cluster of Spanish galleons, following the round shot that had smashed into their heart. The *Retribution* came hard about, heeling over under the press of the wind, her rigging creaking and groaning as the waves slammed broadside into the hull. Another English galleon was hard on her heels, letting fly with their own chasers as they swept into position.

On the quarterdeck Robert looked to the heavens. He felt

numb. So much had happened in the past twelve hours. He had been so sure of who his father was; a traitor, a Judas who had turned against his own countrymen. But then, in the final moments of his life, Nathaniel Young had taken up the sword for England, shattering all of Robert's conceptions. It was a transformation that brought him little comfort, he would never have a chance to know the man who had saved his life.

In the darkest hours before dawn, as the crew of the *Retribution* readied the ship for action, Robert had bathed his father's body, cleaning away the blood from his terrible wounds before binding him in a simple cloth shroud. For the second time in his life he had felt completely lost and alone. He had blown out the solitary candle in the cabin and in his mind's eye he had pictured his father as he had remembered him when he was a boy, a tall solemn man who had disappeared so suddenly one night from his life.

In the darkness Robert had sat down to wait. When they had returned to the *Retribution* Seeley had walked away from him without a word. Robert had not seen him again and as the hours passed he had surmised that Seeley had gone to the commander's flagship to report what he had discovered. Robert had the patience of a career sailor, built over a lifetime of long hours on watch, but every minute spent waiting for the authorities to storm into his cabin had felt like an eternity. He had been consumed by hopelessness. If he could not convince Thomas of his loyalty, a man whom he had fought with side by side, then he had no hope of persuading others. At dawn one of the crew had knocked on the cabin door.

'Message from the sailing master, Captain. Enemy in sight.'

Robert had been stunned by the message and had gone aloft to find Seeley on the quarterdeck. As before not a word was exchanged and Robert had taken up his duties as if nothing had happened.

From the corner of his eye Seeley surreptitiously watched the captain. He didn't know how he should feel about him. Seeley's admiration for Robert had grown over the year since the captain had come on board. Now he felt like a fool. The captain's deception had left him with a deep sense of betrayal, and yet the respect he had had for the captain was based on what he himself had witnessed, the bravery and determination Robert had shown in every encounter with the Spanish.

He was plagued with doubts, uncertain as to whether he had made the right decision in deferring the captain's arrest. The Armada's defensive formation had been broken. The enemy were vulnerable. If the English navy struck with sufficient speed and depth then the battle could finally be won. There could be no half measures and Seeley feared that at a crucial moment the captain might show mercy to his fellow Roman Catholics. Seeley resolved to watch him closely. He would ensure that the captain was taking the fight to the Spanish at every turn. Then, after victory had been secured, he would fulfil his duty and hand the captain over to the authorities.

The call of a yeoman caught Seeley's attention and he shouted the order to bring the *Retribution* full about with the wind abaft. Despite the conditions a small group of Spanish warships had gathered in a loose formation to leeward. The Spanish flagship and her escorts, the ships that had taken the initial brunt of the English attack, had already weighed anchor and were sailing west to join the centre of a reforming Armada.

Robert cursed their fortune. Two hours before, at dawn, the English fleet had swooped down on the small group of Spanish warships that had somehow managed to regain their anchor points. They had quickly engaged them from three sides, punishing the Spaniards for their tenacity, but before any real damage could be inflicted Howard had suddenly broken off the engagement, leading his ships in pursuit of another prize, a galleass that had run aground off Calais. That the prize was significant was not in doubt, nor was the danger of leaving such a powerful ship to their rear, but Howard's diversion had given the Spanish flagship and the rest of the scattered Armada a respite, one they were now taking advantage of.

The *Retribution* and a dozen other warships had stayed on station, keeping the flagship under sporadic fire, but the shape of the battle was rapidly changing. A running battle was about to begin along the coast off Gravelines. Robert called for the *Retribution* to bear away as the English fleet began to gather anew to windward. The weather was changing. Squalls of rain swept across the distant seascape, obscuring the far reaches to the horizon. Seeley called for shortened sails, straightening the trim of the hull as the fleet began to pursue the enemy.

The Spaniards swiftly formed a rough crescent, similar to the defensive formation that had seen them through the Channel. But now that formation consisted only of warships, a fighting rearguard to protect the scattered transport ships to leeward. The English fleet closed in, passing four hundred yards, their guns remaining silent, the experiences of the past week and the dwindling supplies of ammunition causing every master gunner to hold his fire. At three hundred yards the English fleet began to dissipate, their already loose formation breaking up as individual ships sought targets amongst the weathermost ships of the trailing horns.

On the quarterdeck Robert marked his target and Seeley brought the *Retribution* to bear, the crew swarming over the rigging. The galleon plunged through the trough of a roller, sea spray blasting over the bowsprit.

'Stand ready, men!' Robert roared. 'For God, Elizabeth and England!'

The crew cheered at the call, their war cries interspersed with the continued orders of the yeomen and officers. The warship surged through another swell, shaking off the sheet of seawater that washed over the fo'c'sle.

'Tops'ls and sprit ho!'

One hundred yards. The *Retribution* raced onwards, her cutwater slicing through the crests. Seeley called for another change to the sheets, determined to steady the hull and give Larkin's gunners every advantage. Robert stood beside the master on the quarterdeck, his eyes on the target. The Spanish warship was dead ahead, eighty yards, the bow of the *Retribution* pointing amidships of her starboard side.

'Steady, Thomas,' Robert said, loud enough that only Seeley could hear.

Seventy yards. The Spanish cannons erupted in defiance, the round shot searing towards the *Retribution*, raking the fo'c'sle with fire. A falcon took a direct hit, the burning fragments of its mounting cutting down two of the crew, their cries sending men running to their aid.

Sixty yards. The Spanish ship filled Robert's vision, its towering castles bristling with soldiers, their musket fire a rising crackle of deadly shot that punctured the air, cutting down another man, and another, and another.

'Steady, steady —.'

Fifty yards.

The thunderous boom of the bow chasers fractured the air.

'Hard a larboard,' Robert shouted in the same instant.

'Hard a larboard,' Seeley roared. 'Mizzen ho! Veer sheets to the main course! Prepare to lay aboard!'

Like a scythe the *Retribution* cut through the turn, sweeping parallel to the Spanish warship. The broadside guns fired in sequence, each retort fuelling the growing din and smoke of battle. Across the narrow gap Robert witnessed the hammer blow of each round shot, the appalling devastation wrought by the close quarter salvo. On all sides the soldiers in his crew were firing their muskets and arquebuses. Seeley bore away, the galleon beginning the turn that would present the second broadside. Robert stood transfixed, his gaze locked on the Spanish warship and the gaping wounds in her hull. Larkin was right, at such a close range nothing could withstand the firepower of an English galleon.

The solid ball of forged iron blasted through the heavy oak timbers, the wood disintegrating into a hail of lethal splinters in a span of time no eye could observe, cutting men down before they could scream their last. The round shot smashed into the barrel of a *media culebrina*, tossing the 2,500 pound gun from its mounting, the force of the blow throwing men across the deck like chaff before the wind. Another round exploded across the gun deck of the *Santa Clara*, slaying all in its path before punching out through the hull, leaving only destruction in its wake.

On the deck above Evardo felt the vibrations of the strikes ripple through his body. He roared in anger at the English galleon sweeping past his ship, her cannon inflicting deep and terrible wounds on the *Santa Clara*. The enemy were engaging at an incredibly close range, never more than a hundred yards. At the outset of the battle, for the briefest of moments, Evardo had thought the English galleons were finally closing to board. De Córdoba's men had massed expectantly at the gunwales, urging the English on, willing them to fight hand-to-hand, but the enemy had pursued their previous tactics, the wind giving them every advantage as their nimble galleons swooped in like birds of prey, each attack drawing more and more Spanish blood.

The crew of the *Santa Clara* stood their ground at the

gunwales, the proximity of the English galleons finally allowing the soldiers a change to effectively fire their small arms. The air was thick with the harsh crackle of gunfire. The man-killing *falconetes* and *falcon pedreros* were being fired almost continually, their barrels blistering to the touch, but for every Englishman that fell on the opposing galleon, many more were being lost among Evardo's crew.

The English were firing their main cannon at an unbelievable rate and already the decks of the *Santa Clara* were awash with blood from the injured and dying. The air was rank with the smells of battle, of blood and viscera, voided bowels, gun smoke and fire, a fetid miasma that clung to the back of Evardo's throat. All around him he saw men being obliterated by the withering enemy fire. Shot after shot struck the fore and aft castles, turning them into bloody shambles. No protection could be sought behind the weathered hull and through the gaping holes Evardo could see the vulnerable innards of his galleon, the stanchions and deck beams torn asunder by iron.

His galleon and his men were paying a terrible price for their fortitude. Evardo called on every ounce of his determination, compelling himself to stand firm. He looked about the quarterdeck. Mendez stood near at hand, his voice raised as he relayed his orders, his focus entirely on the position of the *Santa Clara*. He was seemingly oblivious to the English, as if their attack was no more than a storm, the incoming fire merely a driving rain that could be ignored.

Not two hundred yards away the Portuguese galleon *San Felipe* was taking fire from nearly a score of English ships. Her foremast, the guns on her poop deck, and much of her rigging had already been blown away. Blood ran freely from the scuppers but amidst the smoke Evardo spied the *comandante* Don Francisco de Toledo on the quarterdeck, calling on the nearest enemy galleon to come to close quarters. His entreaty was answered by an Englishman in the opposing maintop, shouting what seemed to be a call for de Toledo to surrender his ship. In sight of all the Englishman was promptly shot down and a defiant blaze of musket fire followed the enemy galleon as it turned away from the *San Felipe.*

The sight further steeled Evardo's will, filling his belly with fire. Many of the English galleons were dashing forward, trying to drive a wedge into the formation in an effort to create a breech. Their aggression had already resulted in collisions amongst the Spanish ships but the crescent formation was holding firm, maintaining the protective screen that kept the English jackals from the transport ships to leeward. With the wind rising and the English committing more and more ships to the battle Evardo knew it would take more than determination to hold the line. The main guns of the *Santa Clara* were silent, their preloaded shot long since fired. But while his crew could still draw breath, and his galleon could bear more punishment, Evardo vowed to keep them in the fight.

The *Retribution* surged forth from the clouds of smoke from her own guns, her bow lunging over the swells, her swollen sails stretched taut, bearing on the 450 ton galleon as her cannon roared anew, spewing out round shot that whistled through the air, carrying all before them as they struck home. Robert shouted a change in course, his order echoed by Seeley, the crew taking doggedly to their task, hauling in the sheets as others scaled the heights of the rigging.

The battle was eight hours old, a seemingly endless fight where round followed round. Robert wiped the sea spray from his wind-lashed face as he sought out another target for Larkin's guns. The English fleet had held the advantage throughout the day and had mercilessly battered the Spanish formation from every quarter. The enemy had held firm, making the English fight for every league as the wind drove all eastwards. The *Retribution* had made countless attack runs, striving each time to isolate one of the Spanish host, separating the weathermost ships from the formation so they could be overwhelmed and battered by many times their number.

Still the Armada sailed on, its formation ever increasing in size as it gathered up the slower moving transport ships to leeward. But the wind had shifted to the north-west. If it held, the Spanish would be blown onto the Banks of Flanders. Without command every English captain knew their duty was to continue to press home the attack, allowing the Spaniards no respite as forces beyond the control of all began to dictate the shape of the battle.

Robert leaned into the turn as the deck tilted beneath him. Battle lust had ebbed and flowed within him over the hours and every muscle in his body ached from the tension of combat. His every sense was on edge. The weather was rapidly deteriorating and Robert could see nothing beyond the immediate battle. His eyes moved from one enemy warship to another. Those he could see had been damaged beyond what he had previously believed any ship could endure. He spotted one coming about on the windermost flank, her manoeuvre hampered by damaged rigging. It quickly became apparent that she was having difficulty maintaining her position in the enemy formation. Robert pointed her out to Seeley and the master called for the new heading.

The *Retribution* swiftly bore down on her prey. On the main deck Robert saw the gunner's mate command his men to run out the demi-culverins. The men responded with alacrity, their faces contorted in exertion as they hauled the 3,400 pound guns into position. After hours of near continuous labour their efforts spoke of an almost inhuman strength, but

Robert knew that soon they would have to cease. The ammunition stocks on board were desperately low. Already the 24 pound shot had been expended. As the range closed on the Spanish warship ahead the bow chasers remained silent. Despite the need for a sustained attack on the Armada, Robert realized his galleon would soon have to withdraw from the fight.

Seeley brought the *Retribution* hard about at fifty yards and smoke engulfed the ship once more as the heavy guns on the broadside erupted with fire. The *Retribution* bore away to give the gunners time to reload. Nearby other English warships had seen the *Retribution*'s attack and were following suit, converging quickly on the isolated Spaniard. Beyond, the battle was becoming more chaotic. Visibility had fallen further and the growing anger of the sea was making it harder for ships to engage.

Suddenly Robert's heart lurched in his chest. The *Santa Clara* was three hundred yards off the larboard bow, sailing on the flank of the trailing wing. She looked to be heavily damaged. Her courses were shot through, her rigging hung like vines from the stays but atop her masts, her banners flew defiantly on the wind.

'Hard a starboard!'

Seeley immediately repeated the command, the *Retribution* heeling hard over.

'Where away, Captain?' Seeley called.

'Four points off the larboard bow, Thomas. It's the *Santa Clara*.'

Seeley's expression hardened at the name and he nodded curtly as he spied the Spanish galleon. He called for a slight change to the helm, matching the approach of the *Retribution* with the course of the *Santa Clara*, ensuring that their first attack run would have the maximum effect. The wind gusted and swelled the sails, the waves slamming laterally into the hull, booming punches that reverberated throughout the ship as the ruptured water smashed over the bow. The rhythm steadied, the crew toiling at their stations. Yard by yard the *Retribution* hurtled towards her nemesis.

Evardo strode across the quarterdeck, shouting commands to all within earshot, his focus continually shifting from one point to another. The crew rushed about him, taking advantage of the brief respite to bring order to the decks. It had been fifteen minutes since an English galleon had attacked and the men worked frantically to gather up what wounded they could and bring them below to the already overcrowded surgery. Others loaded what deck guns remained, bringing up the last of the powder and shot for the small calibre pieces.

Evardo's head was spinning and he drew a deep breath down his parched throat, blinking away the stars that exploded in his vision. He was assailed by terrible grief and anger. So many of his men were dead or injured. Down on the main deck the rising sea was crashing waves against the bulwarks, forcing clear water through the scuppers that quickly turned bloodstained as it ran across the deck.

The *Santa Clara* bore terrible injuries. Heeled hard over under the press of the wind, her hull had been exposed to enemy fire below the waterline. She had been struck there twice and although the shot had not penetrated, the seams had been split. The pumps had been unable to keep pace with the seawater rushing into the lower hold and Evardo had been compelled to order one of the divers overboard. In the midst of battle the man had jumped naked into the sea. He had patched the hull with oakum and pitch, a temporary measure that had slowed the intake of water and given the pumps the upper hand.

The *Santa Clara* had been lucky. The *Maria Juan* had gone down only an hour before. In a moment of ill fortune she had become isolated from the formation and had come under immediate attack from a pack of English galleons. They had pounded her from all sides, meting out a slow and horrific fate, her crew fighting desperately against overwhelming odds, while the closest ships in the Armada remained trapped by the wind to leeward, unable to go to her assistance. She had finally gone down by the bow, slipping quickly beneath the waves, taking with her all but a single boatload of the three hundred men on board.

The *María Juan* had been the first ship to be lost in battle to English cannon fire, but she would not be the last. Earlier the valiant *San Felipe* had fallen behind and was now lost from sight amongst the English warships, her fate unknown, while her sister ship, the *San Mateo*, was already a half-mile adrift of the fleet, hopelessly trying to regain her position, her rudder and masts damaged beyond purpose.

Evardo turned his back on the stricken Portuguese galleon and looked to his own ship. Despite almost constant attacks the *Santa Clara* had held her position. She was a fine ship, Evardo thought forlornly as he straightened his shoulders and shrugged off his exhaustion. For six hours his galleon and crew had taken everything the English had thrown at them. Although hopelessly outgunned, not a single man had left his station. They were undefeated but Evardo wondered how long they could remain so.

A second foe had joined the battle on the side of the English, an enemy that was pushing them relentlessly towards annihilation. If the north-westerly wind held, the Armada would be on the Banks of Flanders by noon the next day. The larger ships of the fleet would almost certainly run aground and once they did they would be dashed to pieces by the endless wind-driven waves. The smaller ships would be easy prey for the Dutch. It was a fate that had not yet been written. The wind might yet change.

'Enemy ship on attack run off the starboard bow!'

Evardo rushed to the gunwale at the call, the crew taking to their stations, the tempo of battle making orders unnecessary.

'The *Retribution*,' he whispered. The deck shifted beneath him, Mendez manoeuvring the *Santa Clara* in an attempt to foul the English warship's advance. It was a forlorn endeavour, born from the will to fight on against the odds. With every English attack run and every gust of the north-westerly wind the chance of ultimate victory was slipping further and further from the Armada. But no Spaniard had turned his back and Evardo lent his voice to the cacophony of war cries from the men of the *Santa Clara* as they waited to receive the incoming fire of the enemy.

The *Retribution* came swiftly on under shortened sail, sweeping past other ships of the English fleet, their courses intertwined as each ship forged its own path through the battle. On the gun deck Larkin called for the last of the culverins and demi-culverins to be run out, using the roll of the deck to assist the gun crews. They were primed and ready, with the remaining supplies of ordnance for each gun close at hand. In the worsening weather they might not get another chance to fire upon the cursed Spanish galleon that had sought them out in battle and Larkin steadied his men as he walked the length of the deck.

With two hundred yards to go an expectant hush descended upon the entire crew. In the rigging and on deck all eyes were on the *Santa Clara*. Robert felt the killing urge slowly rise within him. Here was the enemy. The Armada was an inhuman beast, devoid of a heart that could be pierced, but the men of the *Santa Clara* were flesh and bone and Robert would make them pay the price of Spain's belligerence in blood.

The relentless wind closed the gap. Spanish musketeers fired from the fighting tops and castles of the *Santa Clara*. A soldier on the poop deck fell injured, his cry fuelling Robert's determination, his battle lust suppressing any fear as the small arms fire from the Spanish ship intensified.

'*Sumus omnes . . .*' he said.

'In God's hand,' Seeley said beside him and Robert glanced over his shoulder at the sailing master, their eyes meeting for a second.

The bow of the *Retribution* closed to within fifty yards of the *Santa Clara*, poised to run past her on the starboard broadside. Robert swept the decks of the Spanish galleon, looking for Morales. The broadside guns of the *Retribution* fired, smothering the fifty yards between the ships in smoke and noise. Musket fire filled the air, the soldiers of the *Santa Clara* firing blindly at close range, their hail of lead cutting down English sailors from the lower rigging.

'Hard a starboard! Come about!'

The helmsman responded to Robert's command and the *Retribution* turned swiftly in the waters behind the *Santa Clara*.

'Bring her up on the larboard broadside!'

'Helm, two points to larboard! Prepare to lay close! Yeoman of the jeers, fore course and mizzen, ho!'

The *Retribution* bore swiftly down on the *Santa Clara*, this time on the opposing broadside, the larboard battery firing at a range of forty yards.

Countless muzzle flashes marked the exchange of fire through the haze of gun smoke as the ships passed each other. Evardo stumbled behind the line of soldiers at the gunwale, his hands stained in blood as he pulled at each fallen man, calling for help for the injured, leaving the dead where they lay, the chaos and noise numbing his senses.

A round shot blasted through the bulwark, cutting a bloody swathe through the soldiers. Evardo was blown from his feet and he hit the deck hard. The screams of the dying were all around him. He got up, his vision swimming before him. The deck was strewn with broken bodies. He tasted blood and he vomited up the bile in his throat.

He looked to his sword. The blade had been snapped off half-way along its length and he let it fall from his hand. He picked up a discarded arquebus and checked the priming. It was loaded and he took the place of a fallen soldier in the front line. He raised the weapon and pointed it at the *Retribution.* The heaving deck and choking smoke made accuracy impossible and he lowered his head against the flash as he pulled the trigger. The arquebus bucked against the middle of his chest, a solid punch and Evardo roared a guttural curse at the English warship as he tossed the weapon aside.

The rate of fire fell away as the *Retribution* sailed beyond the starboard bow. Evardo spat the last of the bile from his mouth and stepped back from the gunwale. The roar of battle gave way to the wailing of the injured. Men were shouting on all sides, rushing to bring more ammunition aloft and take the wounded below. The lines reformed at the gunwales while the last of the 2 and 3 pound shot were loaded into the *falcon pedreros* and *falconetes.*

Mendez called for the sails to be shortened further. He was bleeding heavily from a shoulder wound, the blood dripping from his limp arm, staining the side of his breeches. Evardo stood beside him and watched as the sailors followed the captain's command, their task made almost impossible by the damaged sheets. They had little time. Beyond the bow the *Retribution* was making ready to attack again.

'Bear away. Prepare to come about on Larkin's command!' Robert ordered.

The *Retribution* turned neatly through the wind, bearing away to gain sea room. On all sides the battle raged, the Armada struggling desperately against wind and fire, the English sustaining the pressure, giving no quarter, England to their backs and the fate of the realm in their hands.

The *Retribution* came full about with the *Santa Clara* four hundred yards off her larboard bow. The carriages trundled across the deck, the gunners hauling on the loaded guns, the black barrels thrusting out through the ports beyond the muzzle rings. Seeley steadied the helm and the wind stretched the canvas to its limits. The galleon shot forward. Seeley struggled to hold their course, the rising sea battering the hull and rudder, constantly threatening to turn their keel off true.

The *Retribution* came broadside to the *Santa Clara*, thirty yards off her beam. The four guns of the larboard battery fired almost as one, their shot flying over the main deck of the Spanish ship as it dipped into the trough of a massive swell. The smoke of small arms erupted and was whipped away by the breeze. Men shouted war cries from both sides, their voices hollowed by the wind, their battle lust waning, leaving only hatred for an enemy they could not defeat.

Robert saw the Spanish commander on the opposing quarterdeck.

'Morales!'

His voice carried clearly above the dwindling noise of battle and Evardo spun around. They stared at each other across thirty yards of angry sea as their galleons raced onwards. They didn't speak. There was nothing to say. Neither one of them had been victorious. Both lived in defiance of the other and bound by an unbreakable connection, forged by war, they would be enemies forever.

A call rang out from the mast head of the *Retribution.* Robert turned. A massive Spanish galleon was approaching off the bow and Seeley quickly bore away, widening the gap between the two ships. Robert looked back to Morales but the change in course had obscured his view and the Spaniard was lost from sight. The *Retribution* came back to windward. The larger Spanish galleon sailed in to lay aboard of the *Santa Clara*, shielding her from further attacks. With grim resignation Robert ordered Seeley to heave to.

Heavy squalls rolled in from the north-west and across the width of the Armada the English fleet began to disengage and draw away. The shot lockers of almost every fighting ship were empty. There was nothing more the English fleet could do. Although they continued to shadow the Spaniards they soon lost sight of the Armada in the squalls. They had fought to their last round. Now the outcome was in the hands of the Almighty. The north-westerly picked up even greater strength, forcing the Armada ever onwards towards the Bank of Flanders. For the Spaniards the day had not yet ended, but for the English, the Battle of Gravelines was over.

CHAPTER 21

9 a.m. 9th August 1588. The Banks of Flanders.

All around Evardo men fell to their knees, praising God on high. Padre Garza led them in prayer, intoning a benediction, and they responded fervently, their hands clasped tightly, their smiling faces lifted to the grey heavens.

The night just past had been a terrible time, with men pleading in the dark for deliverance as the north-westerly drove them onwards over the black seascape towards the shoals of Flanders. Dawn had followed, but the feeble rays of the sun had brought little succour to the men. All eyes had gone to the approaching coastline, clearly visible off the larboard bow. Daylight also revealed the other ships of the Armada. The dark of night and strong winds had scattered them eastwards, splintering their defensive formation, but the loss of cohesion had been of little consequence. The crescent would give them no protection against the elements and the men had begged the padre for final absolution as the *Santa Clara* sped towards her fate.

Then, inexplicably, the wind had changed, swinging around south-south-west. For a long moment Evardo and the rest of the crew had stared disbelievingly at the masthead banners before their wits returned and Mendez brought the *Santa Clara* hard over, bearing her away from the coastline and back to the deep.

Evardo studied the soldiers who remained kneeling around him, at their exhausted, almost delirious expressions. Padre Garza was walking amongst them, touching each on the head in blessing and they rose one by one, walking away aimlessly.

'*Es un milagro*, *Comandante*,' the priest said as he passed.

Evardo nodded solemnly in reply, but inside he felt nothing but disdain. A miracle. If this was God's work then He indeed moved in mysterious ways. Evardo looked to the flotsam that was the Armada.

Like a hammer blow the full scale of the previous day's defeat struck him. He knew of only three ships that had been lost, but amongst those still afloat not one of them was fit for another full scale battle. The crews of every fighting ship had been decimated by enemy artillery. Evardo hadn't the heart to go below to the surgery to discover the extent of his own casualties but he estimated at least two score of his men had been killed in the day's fighting.

The *Santa Clara* steadied on her new course, slightly abeam of the tide and the waves pounded off the damaged hull, an echo of the English cannon fire that would forever haunt Evardo's memories. He could hear Mendez shouting at the sailing crew, directing them in their task. The men moved like drudges, weighed down by fatigue and loss. Their morale was completely shattered. Evardo wondered how he would rouse the men to greater sacrifice. He too had lost his stomach for the fight.

In the distance, three cannon shots sounded in succession. It was the *San Martín*, calling the fleet to form on the flagship. She was in the rear, closest to the English fleet far to the south-west. Evardo confirmed the order to Mendez and while the *Santa Clara* turned her bow to luff close and await the flagship to come up, Evardo noticed that not every ship was responding. The fighting spirit that had carried the Armada through the Channel was gone, blown apart by countless English guns.

Off the starboard flank Evardo spied the *San Juan*, Abrahan's ship that had come to the aid of the *Santa Clara* at the close of battle the day before. Evardo searched the distant quarterdeck of the Portuguese galleon, hoping to catch a glimpse of his friend, to somehow gain strength from seeing his former mentor. The conditions defied him however and with heavy heart Evardo tried to focus his attention on his own ship.

The *San Martín* would reach them within the hour. But what then, Evardo wondered. The south-westerly was blowing them ever further away from the Flemish coast and Parma's army. They could not hope to push through the prevailing wind and the English fleet to effect a rendezvous. It was a forlorn hope, but the alternative, to run before the wind, was unthinkable. Ahead of them lay the wilds of the North Sea. The King's plans ended with the Armada and Parma 'joining hands'. There was no contingency for failure, no strategy that could overcome what God had now clearly ordained.

The enterprise was over. The Armada could not achieve the impossible. The English could not be defeated in battle and Parma remained beyond their reach. Evardo turned away from the approaching flagship and faced northwards to the expanse of the North Sea. Desolation emptied his heart. They had fought so hard, forfeited so much. All that remained was the voyage home and with the Channel closed behind them they would be forced to sail the long route back around Scotland and Ireland. It was a godforsaken prospect, a voyage that would surely condemn the most damaged ships in the fleet.

Evardo was filled with bitterness. Truly, God had finally forsworn their cause and turned His back on the Spanish Armada.

From the fo'c'sle Robert stared at the distant sails of the Armada. They seemed to be slowly converging but from so far away it was almost impossible to discern their purpose. The change in wind had saved the Spaniards from the Banks of Flanders. Now they were reforming and Robert felt anxiety gnaw on his every sense. Whatever the enemy decided to do next, the English fleet was powerless to stop them. They had no ammunition. At dawn, Robert had lent his voice to the desperate calls from every ship for supplies of powder and round shot.

They still had the weather gauge. It was their only remaining advantage. Robert glanced behind to the quarterdeck. Seeley was there, in firm command of the helm. Robert felt his anxiety descend into panic. For some reason Seeley had remained silent but Robert feared it was only a matter of time before he exposed him. In the eyes of all Englishmen Robert would be an ally of the Spanish. He would be executed as a traitor and the injustice of this sentence washed over him in a wave of anger.

'Pinnace closing off the starboard beam!'

From the quarterdeck Seeley watched the small boat. She bore no markings. He called out a slight course change to aid her approach and then checked the trim of the *Retribution*. He saw the captain descend from the fo'c'sle and move towards the main deck. At the beginning of the battle off Gravelines Seeley had scrutinized every order of the captain's, ready to countermand them. But never once had the captain shirked from the fight and as the day wore on Seeley had found himself following the captain's orders without hesitation. Every command had cost the Spanish dearly. The captain had fought like a lion and Seeley wondered if more could have been asked of any Englishman.

Robert waited on the main deck as the pinnace came alongside the *Retribution*. From over the bulwark he heard a call for permission to board. Robert nodded at the crewmen as they quickly lashed on the smaller boat. A man appeared over the gunwale and spoke briefly with a crewman who indicated to Robert. The man stepped forward quickly.

'Sir Robert, my name is John Cross. I am an agent of the Crown. I wish to speak with one of your officers, Thomas Seeley.'

Robert's stomach lurched at the request.

'Why do you need to speak to him?' Robert asked, concentrating on keeping his voice steady.

'He has information I seek, about a traitor I am hunting. A man named Robert Young.'

Robert felt the blood drain from his face. With an enormous effort of will he indicated Seeley on the quarterdeck. Cross turned away and Robert looked desperately towards the pinnace as he searched for a way to escape. It was impossible, he was trapped. As Cross started to walk towards the quarterdeck Robert followed him, his hand unwittingly falling to the hilt of his sword.

'Thomas Seeley?' Cross reached the quarterdeck.

Seeley nodded and stepped forward.

'Clear the deck,' Robert ordered and all but the three men went below to the main. Robert stood slightly apart, his hand still on his sword. He glanced over his shoulder, ensuring that the rest of the crew were out of earshot. Cross introduced himself to Seeley.

'It would seem, Master Seeley, that you and I are searching for the same man. A traitor named Robert Young.'

Seeley's eyes darted to the captain before returning to Cross. 'How do you know of this?'

Cross briefly explained about his meeting in the tavern and the ambush on a motte outside Plymouth where Robert Young and his father had escaped him.

'I followed the fleet from Plymouth,' he continued, 'and had you not crossed over to Calais and engaged the Spanish there I would have reached you sooner. But I pray that is of no matter. Tell me, Master Seeley, have you found Robert Young?'

Seeley hesitated. This time he did not look at Robert.

'I found him,' he replied.

'Where is he?'

'He's dead.'

Cross's face froze. 'Dead—are you sure?'

'Yes. We found this icon in the surgery.' Seeley reached into his pocket and pulled out the small inscribed crucifix. 'This prompted our investigation and although we searched the ship, and I personally questioned all the crew, we were unable to reveal his true identity. It was only when one of the men killed on the first day of battle was being prepared for burial that we discovered this in a concealed seam of his clothes.'

Again Seeley reached into his pocket. This time he withdrew the statuette of the Blessed Virgin Mary, turning it over to reveal the name underneath. Cross took the icon in his hand and examined it before handing it back.

'Who was he?'

'A mate,' Seeley spat with false anger. 'One of the junior officers – may he burn in hell. We threw his body over the side. Isn't that right, Captain Varian?'

Robert couldn't believe what he was hearing. He had barely recovered his composure before Cross turned to look at him for confirmation. He nodded, not trusting his voice, and Cross looked back to Seeley once more. The agent uttered a dejected note of thanks, cursing his ill fortune for having lost the chance to take Young alive. Seeley echoed Cross's lament before leading him from the quarterdeck.

Robert watched them walk away, unable to take in that he had been granted a reprieve. Seeley turned his head to look back. Robert stared at him, trying to read his intent. Seeley nodded, just once, and Robert understood. For Seeley there was no lie. Robert Young was dead, and in his place a true and loyal Englishman commanded the *Retribution*.

EPILOGUE

21st September 1588. Santander, Northern Spain.

The eight ships slowly rounded the western headland of Santander Bay. Lashed by shot and tempest, under tattered sails they resembled ghost ships soundlessly approaching the ancient port of Santander. The bells of the town church rang out as people rushed to the shoreline, staring in awe and despair at the flotilla of Spanish ships.

Evardo leaned heavily against the mizzen mast, his eyes closed as he listened to the peal of bells. They were the sound of home. Tears of relief welled up inside him. He pushed himself upright, swaying slightly with the fall of the deck and the fatigue that reached to the very depths of his soul. The last of their water had run out two days before and he wiped away the scum at the corners of his mouth, smacking his lips in an attempt to wet them before ordering the crew to prepare to drop anchor.

Mendez was dead, along with more than half the crew. The remaining men moved slowly about the ship, stepping over those who could not rise as they summoned the last of their strength to follow the *comandante*'s orders. The voyage from the head of the English Channel had taken six weeks. From the outset Evardo had reduced the crew to half-rations, knowing the journey ahead would be long, but as the weeks passed he had been forced to reduce them again and again, until the men began to starve.

Pestilence and death had followed in the wake of the *Santa Clara*, waiting patiently for the weakest to succumb. The wounded were the first to die. Too weak to fight infection they were easy prey. Disease became rampant, taking the ship's boys and the oldest crewmen in the first week. Within a fortnight three to four men were dying each day. Padre Garza had presided over each funeral, his rites echoing across the decks until he too fell.

The weather had been cruel and savage, much worse than any could have imagined, and summer storms had driven the ships of the Armada onto the wild, uncharted west coast of Ireland. Evardo had no idea how many ships had been lost there. Each dawn had revealed more losses with ships disappearing in the darkness of night or in the midst of terrible squalls, their fate known only to God and the damned who sailed in them.

The *Santa Clara* had managed to stay in contact with a small flotilla and led by the *San Martín* they had finally reached the Bay of Biscay a week before. Crossing the bay, they had sighted other small groups of sail on the far horizons. The sight had given Evardo some comfort. They were not alone. Many others had been spared and would soon reach home.

With a splash that brought a handful of hollow cheers the *Santa Clara* anchored in the lee of the port. A host of fishing boats began to stream out from behind the rough hewn seawall that protected the inner harbour. Evardo looked up at Santander church high atop the steep promontory at the edge of the town. The bell had ceased to ring. With disdain, Evardo turned his back. God had not brought him home, the *Santa*

Clara had. Evardo reached out to touch the mizzen mast once more, running his hand down the smooth weathered spar.

She had carried him through war and storm and they had endured much together since sailing from Lisbon months before. Because of her, because of her crew and men like Mendez, Evardo had regained his name and his honour. He had found peace with Abrahan and earned the respect of all who sailed in the Armada.

During the long desperate weeks in the north Atlantic Evardo had found strength in his determination to carry the war ever onwards against the English. They had not defeated the Armada, not decisively. Their cannon had battered and subjugated many of its ships, but it was the elements that truly sealed the Armada's fate – the winds and tides of the Channel that had robbed the Spanish of the opportunity to employ their own tactics in battle.

The war was not over. It had taken the Spanish centuries to re-conquer their peninsula from the Moors, but against overwhelming odds they had eventually triumphed, and from out of that victory the greatest empire of the age had been forged. Over the previous hundred years the Spanish had swept all before them. The English were no fiercer a foe, no more determined than any other. Like so many enemies before them they too would be defeated in time.

Soon a new Armada would set sail from the shores of Spain, and Evardo would be one its *comandante*s. As the locals began to board the *Santa Clara* he straightened his shoulders and adjusted his torn and salt-stained clothes. The gesture reminded him of another moment over a year before. From the depths of an English prison he had risen to command a galleon of the Armada and regained all that he had lost. He could make that journey again. His body and spirit may be weak but his will remained strong and suddenly he was filled with an eagerness to begin anew, to take the fight back to the English, for God, his King and Spain.

Robert dismounted and began to climb the slope of the motte. The sun was on his back and he paused at the rim as he had done many times in the past, looking back at the ancient church of Saint Michael's. He was breathing hard but for the first time in weeks he felt strong. He held his face up to the late summer sun, drinking in its warmth as he inhaled the scents of the English countryside.

For days after Gravelines the English fleet had shadowed the Armada as it sailed towards Scotland. Seymour had taken his squadron back to the Flemish coast, fearing an opportunistic attempt by Parma to cross the Channel, but the other four had continued on, finally abandoning their pursuit when the Spaniards cleared the Firth of Forth.

Still uncertain, they had returned to the Channel. No one knew the enemy's intentions. If conditions changed in their favour, there was every chance the Armada would return southwards to try to link up with Parma again, or they might refit and restock in a Scandinavian or Scottish port. Their fate and course was unknown. Howard had been forced to keep the fleet on alert in the waters off Dover.

The first cases of pestilence surfaced within days. Crowded together, with shortened rations, the flux had spread rapidly throughout the fleet. On the *Retribution* alone nearly half the crew were struck down by the terrible disease. Few had survived. As one of the more heavily engaged ships in the battles against the Armada, the *Retribution* had suffered twelve killed in combat. The flux took more than six times that number, nearly a third of the crew. Little or nothing had been done to relieve their plight and every entreaty from the fleet commanders to the Privy Council had been all but ignored.

After four weeks the fleet was finally given leave to stand down, but by then it was too late for many. Through eyes closed against the sun Robert pictured the faces of those who had died – his old comrade and master's mate Miller, the boatswain Shaw, the master gunner Larkin, and dozens more who would remain with him forever.

He turned and began to pick his way through the ruins, looking for signs of where the ground had been disturbed. He thought of Thomas Seeley and their parting earlier that morning.

'Home to recuperate,' Seeley had answered when asked by Robert what he would do next.

They had been standing on the main deck of the *Retribution*, at the head of the gangplank onto Plymouth docks.

'And what then, Thomas? We sail in two weeks to Dover for refit, and the *Retribution* needs a Master.'

Seeley had nodded, looking past Robert to the range over the galleon. He had turned to leave but Robert had stopped him, offering his hand.

'Thank you, Thomas. For everything. I hope I'll see you again.'

For a heartbeat Seeley had hesitated, a shadow passing over his face. He had taken Robert's hand, but only briefly. 'You will, Captain.'

Seeley had then taken a small cloth parcel from his pocket and handed it to Robert before walking down the gangplank and away along the docks without a backward glance.

Robert stopped as he spotted a mound in the centre of a small clearing in the ruins. It was covered by dense undergrowth, a sign that the earth had been recently turned over and richer soil had been uncovered. He walked over to it and looked down at the grave, his thoughts returning to the night Father Blackthorne had died, and of his father and how they had fought, sword against sword in the darkness.

Robert knelt down. He reached into his pocket and took out the cloth parcel Seeley had given him, opened it and took out the silver crucifix and marble statuette of the Blessed Virgin Mary. They felt light in his hand. They were all that remained of his father. His body had been cast into the sea, along with the other Englishmen who had died in battle.

He pulled out a clump of weeds from the mound and dug a small hole in the loose soil, placing the crucifix within it. He closed his eyes and prayed, for Father Blackthorne and for Nathaniel Young. He buried the icon, hoping that its presence would sanctify the ground that held the body of his confessor. He stood up and examined the statuette in his hand. He looked at its base, his finger tracing the inscription, *Young.* It was the only physical link that remained to his real name and he slipped the statuette into his pocket.

Robert returned to where his horse was tethered. He mounted and looked up one last time at the summit of the motte, wondering if another Catholic priest would one day take responsibility for Father Blackthorne's flock and recite mass amidst the ruins. Robert would never know. Although his faith remained strong, he would never again return to the motte. That part of his life was behind him, not forgotten but gone forever. He kicked his horse into a canter. He was Sir Robert Varian, knight of the realm, a loyal recusant and captain of the *Retribution.* As he passed Saint Michael's, he turned his mount towards Brixham, and home.

HISTORICAL NOTE

As the Armada sailed north from the Banks of Flanders on the 9th August 1588 few considered the battle to be over. The Spanish fleet had reformed into their defensive formation and in a council of war held on board the *San Martín* the senior commanders voted unanimously to turn around, if conditions allowed, and make a second attempt to link up with Parma. But in many ways it was a hollow resolution. They had been badly mauled. Many ships were struggling to keep up with the fleet and few believed they could force their way through an enemy fleet that had already defeated them in pitched battle.

What they did not know however was that the English pursuing them to windward were no longer capable of continuing the fight. They were sailing in good order. Their warships had sustained only minimal damage and they now knew that the key to victory was to close to within arquebus shot before discharging their heavy guns. But at that moment such knowledge was worthless for their shot lockers were empty and they were desperately short of victuals.

The English commanders were equally concerned as to what the enemy might attempt next. They had sunk one Spanish warship and driven two more onto the shoals but against such a large fleet these were mere scratches and the Armada as a whole remained intact. The enemy seemed far from beaten. Ahead of them lay Scottish and Scandinavian ports where they could regroup before returning south to renew their campaign. To the rear of the English fleet Parma was continuing to embark his invasion army.

In the end, however, Gravelines proved to be the last encounter of the campaign. On the 10th August Medina Sidonia ordered the fleet to return to Spain via a route around Scotland and Ireland and into the north Atlantic. The English fleet, as Howard described, 'put on a brag countenance and gave chase,' shadowing the Armada until the Firth of Forth while Seymour returned to the Channel with his squadron to guard against a crossing by Parma. Over a week later the Privy Council deemed it safe enough for Elizabeth to travel to her army massed at Tilbury where she delivered her famous speech.

From the moment of its conception, few in Spain doubted the enormity of the challenges facing any attempt to invade the shores of England. Many strategies were advanced by senior advisors and commanders but ultimately King Philip chose a plan that would require two forces, a naval Armada and the Duke of Parma's Army of Flanders, to link up and bridge the English Channel. From the beginning Philip was deeply involved with every aspect of the campaign and communication between Santa Cruz in Lisbon and Parma in Holland was channelled through the King's office, ensuring that Philip was privy to every decision.

The seafarers of the Spanish Empire were masters of their craft but the more experienced naval officers of the Armada knew the English navy would be difficult to defeat. The speed and nimbleness of the English ships was already renowned, as was their superior prowess in gunnery, and Spanish concerns were reinforced by the panic and delays caused by Drake's attack on Cadiz in 1587.

Despite these reservations King Philip contended that the English would either have to engage in ship-to-ship combat or flee before the Armada. For a time it seemed his words were prophetic. Spanish military discipline was second to none and apart from one incident on the first day of battle, when ships of de Recalde's wing retreated, the Armada remained in strict formation while under English guns, allowing it to sail the entire length of the English Channel without the loss of a single ship to enemy fire.

Faith also played a large part in the planning of the Armada enterprise and its power should not be underestimated. Philip was a devout Catholic and any shortcomings that were recognized were confidently excused in the knowledge that God would assist their every endeavour. This depth of faith was prevalent on both sides and is evident in much of the correspondence between commanders and their superiors.

Don Alonso Pérez de Guzmán ('el Bueno'), Duke of Medina Sidonia, was one of the most senior nobles in Spain and his administrative skills made him an ideal choice to replace Santa Cruz who, though a highly experienced military commander, had few. Medina Sidonia was faced with a mammoth task when he arrived in Lisbon to take charge in February 1588. His reluctance to accept the post is well documented but his subsequent actions bear witness to his determination once his position was confirmed and he swiftly brought order to anarchy in Lisbon.

Many historians have directed a large portion of the blame for the Armada's ultimate failure at Medina Sidonia, citing his limited naval combat experience and his lack of initiative. The duke however knew his limits and he continually sought and followed the guidance of his highly competent military advisors. The Armada might have fared better if Medina Sidonia had showed greater resourcefulness but it must be realized that at all times his options were limited by Philip's inflexible orders. His courage was beyond doubt and the *San Martín* was at the heart of nearly every action in the campaign.

What proved to be one of the greatest weaknesses in the Spanish plan was the inability of Medina Sidonia and Parma to communicate effectively. At every stage in his advance Medina Sidonia dispatched updates to Parma to inform him of his progress. He never once received a reply or even an acknowledgement that his letters had been delivered. Crucially Medina Sidonia seemed to believe that Parma would sally out to meet him and they would rendezvous at sea, while Parma was firmly of the mind that any such sortie would result in annihilation of his transport fleet by the Dutch flyboats and so the Armada would have to come to him. The King's command was simply that they 'join hands'. No precise instructions had been given for how this would be achieved and with no deep water port in Spanish possession, the main purpose of the Armada remained shrouded in confusion until it reached Calais.

At the time of the Armada Lord High Admiral Charles Howard, Earl of Nottingham, was at the pinnacle of his long career. He was fifty-two years old and came from a distinguished line of naval officers. But despite his naval background he, like Medina Sidonia, had never experienced war at sea and relied heavily on his subordinates. Chief amongst those was Sir Francis Drake. A daring privateer, Drake's raid on Cadiz in 1587 delayed the sailing of the Armada. He successfully predicted that the Spanish plan would involve a link up between Parma and the Armada and therefore advocated stationing the bulk of the English fleet at Plymouth, as far to windward of the narrow seas around Dover as possible. He contended that, 'the advantage of time and place in all martial actions is half a victory,' and his plan successfully ensured that the English fleet had the weather gauge when the Armada entered the Channel.

At the core of the English fleet were 'race built' galleons, a new breed of ship that saw accelerated development during the Tudor reign. Fast and nimble they carried a high proportion of armament in relation to their overall tonnage, upwards of ten per cent which was more than double that of their Spanish counterparts. Their heaviest guns were mounted in the bows and their method of attack was as described in the book. The galleon would swoop in from windward and fire in turn their bow chasers, lee broadside, stern chasers and second broadside before tacking away to reload. The English had high expectations of the damage these guns would inflict on the Spanish ships and were forced to rapidly alter their tactics after the first encounters proved they were not as effective at longer ranges.

The 'race built' galleons were warships designed for a primary purpose, to defend the coast of England, and so had little need of the massive holds of the Spanish galleons which were required for transoceanic trading. This gave them the option of carrying heavier guns closer to the water-line, a factor which had a significant impact in the Battle of Gravelines. The main weakness of these new English galleons was their scarcity and the vast majority of the remaining ships in the English fleet were of little value in heavy fighting.

The *Retribution* and *Santa Clara* are fictional galleons but both are based on typical ships of their class. The *Retribution* would have been one of the premier ships of the English fleet, while the *Santa Clara* would have been second to the larger galleons of the squadron of Portugal. The lead ships of the other Spanish squadrons, in the most part heavily armed merchantmen, and the Neapolitan galleasses, made up the rest of the 'troubleshooting' warships of the Armada.

There are a multitude of books written on the Spanish Armada, with many and various contradictory conclusions as to why the English triumphed over it. The source documents for more recent books are mostly contemporary, particularly on the Spanish side, where volumes exist on the meticulous preparations for the campaign. These, along with more recent findings, in particular the discovery and exploration of Spanish wrecks along the coastline of Ireland from the 1960s onwards, have led to many challenges to the assertions of earlier historians who laboured under misconceptions regarding the size of Spanish ships versus English, and the ordnance carried by both sides.

The Spanish had four times as many ships over 500 tons as the English, but the majority of these were armed merchantmen, while all the English ships of this size were galleon warships. The Spanish merchantmen in the main did not take part in the battle, but rather sailed in the centre of the Armada's formation. Where ships of comparable size did clash, the Spanish galleons or merchantmen flagships were no match for their English counterparts.

Many of the ships in the Spanish Armada were heavily armed, with some carrying upwards of fifty guns. But most of these weapons were of smaller calibre and some of the largest guns listed on the manifest for the fleet were actually siege pieces that had been stowed below decks for the voyage to England. The latest research claims that the Spanish had 138 guns of 16 pound calibre or above while the English had 251 such pieces.

The English were far superior to the Spanish in artillery

skills. Estimates of their rate of fire are between one and three rounds-per-gun-per-hour. On the Spanish side it is closer to one round-per-gun-per-*day*. Also much of the Spanish fire came from their lighter, more easily serviced guns. When Medina Sidonia sent a dispatch to Parma requesting supplies he asked for 4, 5 and 10 pound shot only. The larger guns were barely fired at all and both the manifests of the ships that returned to Spain, and that wrecks explored off Ireland reveal that they expended only a small fraction of their heavier shot in battle.

Ultimately, the Spanish were defeated by a number of factors. Their plan of campaign as imposed by Philip was fatally flawed, they were out-sailed and out-gunned by the English and the weather conditions were rarely in their favour. Neither side lacked bravery and conviction. It is possible that had the Armada reached home safely and in good order they might have restocked and made a second attempt to link up with Parma. The casualties suffered on the Irish coast however turned defeat into disaster. At least forty ships were lost and those that did return were badly battered by the unseasonably harsh weather.

The English fleet too suffered their greatest casualties after the battle. Disease quickly spread amongst the crews and in some ships over fifty per cent of the men were lost. Elizabeth and her Privy Council did little to help with Burghley hoping that, 'by death, by discharging of sick men, and such like . . . there may be spared something in the general pay.' Howard remarked that it 'would grieve any man's heart to see them that have served so valiantly die so miserably.'

The English triumphed over the Spanish Armada and although victory was achieved by a very narrow margin, it was enough to embolden both the English and the Dutch to continue their wars against the dominant empire in Europe. Further campaigns were launched by both sides in subsequent years. The English, hoping to build on their victory of 1588, sent a fleet into Spanish waters in 1589. Led by Drake the venture ended in disaster and irreparably damaged his reputation. The Spanish dispatched two more Armadas, in 1596 and 1597, only to have both driven back by storms. A peace was finally concluded in 1604, after the deaths of Elizabeth I and Philip II.

Note: The dates referred to throughout the book are based on the Gregorian calender.

ACKNOWLEDGEMENTS

Thanks to my agent, Bill Hamilton, for his unswerving support and advice, and all the team at AM Heath, in particular Jennifer Custer, Kate Rizzo Munson, Vickie Dillon and Charlie Brotherstone.

Thanks to HarperCollins*Publishers*; my editor Katie Espiner, who seeks the heart of every chapter and the soul of every character, and to Louise Swannell, Kiera Godfrey and Louisa Joyner.

Thanks to all who support me in Cork; Ann Luttrell, Ben Cuddihy, Tony Sheehan of the Triskel Arts Centre, Joe McNamee, Martin MacAree, and I greatly acknowledge the support of Cork County Council in the writing of this book.

Thanks to my Mum and Dad, Gerard and Catherine, whose unfailing support I hope I never take for granted, and to my Mum- and Dad-in-law; John and Frances Moran, for their endless generosity.

A special thanks to Pam Moran, who watches over our children and ensures they have all their hearts' desire, and to my brother, Colm, who has given me both time and space to write this book. Thanks to all in my family; Karen, Pam, Paul, Fiona and Doreen.

Lastly, thank you to Adrienne, for sharing this journey with me through uncharted waters, for your courage, fortitude and love, and to my children, Zoe, Andrew and Amy.